Basil's
Dream

Christine Hale

CHRISTINE HALE

LIVINGSTON PRESS

THE UNIVESITY OF WEST ALABAMA

Typesetting and page layout: Angela Brown
Proofreading: Margaret Walburn, Tricia Taylor,
Emily Mills, Asa Griggs, Jennifer Brown, Ivory Robinson,
Shelly Huth, Stephen Slimp

Cover design: Jennifer Brown
Cover Layout: Jennifer Brown
Cover photo: Christine Hale

This is a work of fiction.
Surely you know the rest: any resemblance
to persons living or dead is coincidental.

Livingston Press is part of The University of West Alabama,
and thereby has non-profit status.
Donations are tax-deductible:
brothers and sisters, we need 'em.

first edition
6 5 4 3 3 2 1

For my children

and

for the island

Basil's Dream

We are such stuff as dreams are made on, and our little
life is rounded with a sleep

— William Shakespeare
The Tempest, Act IV, Scene 1

The Map

From the air, through the plastic porthole of a descending plane, Bermuda appears improbable. The sea, clear and vibrant turquoise, stretches unconstrained all the way to the curve of the globe in every direction, yet—here is this thin tailing of land parting the waters, a nattering of limestone lace raised from the ocean floor on a solitary spindle of volcanic rock fourteen thousand feet tall. Lucy Langston tries imagining from the airline seat into which she's buckled the force of the eruption that formed the cone that created the island. She tries to account inside herself for the anomaly of chance that placed this island here and nowhere else, so completely alone, six hundred miles from the nearest land, North Carolina's Outer Banks, and a thousand miles from the Caribbean islands to the south-southwest with which she, like most Americans, would have lumped it until there arose in her life the circumstances that place her—and her husband Darrell on the aisle, and their twelve-year-old son Peyton between them—in these seats on this flight on their way to open a new chapter of their lives as expatriates in this tiny, isolated, insular British colony.

Lucy knows no one in Bermuda, and she did not want to come. Peyton has left a best friend, and a soccer team, in Darien, Connecticut; he, also, did not want to come. Darrell, whose new job brings them to the island, wanted to come:

they are his family, so here they are. The three of them, about to reach the place he is taking them. To Lucy, the island below resembles a scar—a dry, definite ridge stitching up the dead lips of an old wound—a rip in the earth's skin through which lava had once poured boiling.

The jet circles on its approach, dipping a wing, enhancing her view while the pilot narrates from the cockpit about Bermuda's famous fishhook shape and its composition: not one island but a chain of one hundred and fifty little ones, nowhere more than one mile wide, meandering twenty-two miles along the rim of that long-extinct volcano. He cracks a joke, a stale one about all that's gone missing—sailing ships, submarines, wallets, homework, even some mothers-in-law—inside the Bermuda Triangle. Peyton, whose whole attention has appeared to focus on the ancient Game Boy he works madly beneath his thumbs, hisses contempt from between his newly straightened teeth at such obvious lameness. As tourists from the off side of the plane crowd the aisle in defiance of the Fasten Seatbelts sign, craning over the Langstons' heads to see—"What?" Darrell asks them, snapping his *Wall Street Journal* in the faces of the most aggressive leaners. "You think you can see lines on the water?"—the pilot congratulates the navigator on even finding the island one more time. Then, making Peyton put the game down and laugh, and eliciting a small smile from Lucy, who's lain awake most of the night in the grips of a recently recurrent bad dream, the pilot claims even the postal system gets it wrong sometimes: mail reaches Bermuda by way of erroneous detour to Barbados or Bahamas, two more "B" islands sharing with Bermuda the social customs and political institutions common to their British heritage, but *not* latitude and *not* longitude.

Lucy, who has read cover to cover the glossy travel books Darrell's new boss sent her when Darrell told him she was the reason he hadn't yet signed on, knows Bermuda shares with those Caribbean islands one other thing, at least: a common origin for the majority of their populace—slavery—and that Bermuda's population, excluding tourists, is a small-town of 55,000 split 60/40 black and white. Because Darrell in his new job will be in charge of an insurance subsidiary of a major American corporation, Lucy knows that in the 1970s, with tourists' tastes trending toward the more exotic, Bermuda re-marketed its reputation as more quaintly British than England and more buttoned up than its Caribbean cousins to become the untaxed, unregulated offshore office of the New York and London wholesale insurance markets, hosting mega-deals off the books in participants' home countries. And Darrell, who enjoys her intelligence, who prizes her for what she knows as much as what she looks like (slender, blond and patrician) has told her, as well, that U.S. manufacturing companies are incorporating in Bermuda to legally avoid federal income taxes.

On the surface, the island's a success story. With no veldt to farm, no minerals to mine, and only other people's capital to fund its banks and build its hotels, Bermuda's not only escaped third world poverty but prospers on the fringe of the first world, adapting and readapting to the swing of the coattails of power. She has read that independence from Britain has twice been rejected by its citizens, that the old ways — the pastel manor houses, the tea and scones and garden parties, the white British governor's white plumed hat and horse-drawn landau in every parade — have been preserved.

She does not know, yet, that beneath this tourist-pleasing patina there seethes an old grudge, papered over with institutionalized reverence for stability in government, decorum in social relations, and loyalty to the colonial order of things.

Although she will have suspected the existence of some subterranean trouble from her very first days on the island, the substance of the grudge will announce itself to her via a matter-of-fact statement from the mouth of a Bermudian guest in her home. He will tell her and her family in the same tone that he's advised taking navy showers — conserving precious rainwater by turning off the tap when soaping up — that anyone on the island with any common sense, people who appear in his analysis to be mostly white like him, must and will defend themselves by any and all means from those who demonstrate a complete lack of common sense, people who appear in his analysis to be mostly black. In that same conversation she will learn that an affluent white islander has been shot in his home with his own gun by a perpetrator casually assumed to be black, and that in her guest's view full responsibility for the country's present racial troubles rests with a black man.

The real reason for the grudge, never acknowledged openly but erupting once or twice each generation for three hundred years into flames and bloodshed, is a question: What is the proper behavior of Black people? — or black people, the capitalization convention differing depending on which side of the grudge one stands on. Should people who do not want to be white have to follow the white lead? But should not everyone's behavior support the status quo since everyone's livelihood — the economy, so dependent on the American economy — depends on it? The proper answer, it appears to her, depends on whether one's ancestors were brought to the island in chains, and whether one's children have no colleges to attend and no jobs to aspire to that do not serve white tourists, the white expatriate executives of American corporations, or the newest generation of white bankers and merchants descended from the original band of British ship-wreckers once known as the Forty Thieves.

She will form this conclusion, when, several times during the days subsequent to the dinner, she goes to the island's small library to research and read. She has been a stay-at-home mom since Peyton was born; Darrell's income has meant she's not needed to work and anyway it goes better if she's home to make things run right for him. But when they met she was a graduate student in American history at Columbia and she knows how to follow a trail even when it leads her through hours and hours of bad microfiche.

As the jet's tires strike the runway, bounce once and then bite, Lucy Langston does not yet know any of this. She stares out the window, at heat shimmer rising off tarmac, white roof lines and blazing pink oleander. Her hand rests on Peyton's arm, to comfort him, she thinks. She does not notice that her touch is a squeeze, that she's leaving reddening half-moon nail marks in her son's fair and nearly hairless skin and that he stares resentfully at the offending hand but does not remove it. Darrell has his cell phone on already, checking voicemail, punching notes into his digital planner.

She leans her cheek against the window. The plastic is warm; it is mid-July and the air outside steamy. She replays her dream one more time. Rummages inside it without success for what makes such a dreary dream so profoundly troubling.

In it she runs in slick, flat shoes all wrong for the job, causing her to slip and fall hard and skin her knees, and digging blisters, and blisters on top of blisters, into her heels and the tops of her naked toes. She runs on a dirt road — red dirt rising up in gritty puffs at each footfall, sticking to her sweat — and the road is endless. She runs all alone, in the dark, very tired, exhausted really, always, always in a desperate hurry, but always too with no sense of where nor why. Hurry, hurry, where? Where? She runs and runs, thirsty, hungry, her mouth full of dust and her stomach gnawing its own lining bloody, and she never sees anyone, ever, not a soul, although she remembers now — for the first time, seated on this plane that has just taxied to a stop in front of a low white cinderblock terminal, the windows and the rooftop railing of which are lined with a sea of black faces — that the whole time she runs she hears a crowd she never sees. A crowd. Not cheering. Seething. Sometimes howling and hurling. This rising and falling of the sound of the unseen crowd is like the restless suspiration of the sea.

She stands up because everyone around her has already done so. Quickly she peers back out the window, to see if the ocean is in view. It is not. She sees tarmac and baggage and baggage carts. Thick green vegetation, palm trees and flowers, bright blue sky and houses painted pale Easter egg colors. And people, so many people, every single one of them a stranger to her.

Heart racing, feet moving, she follows her family — her son, her husband, their familiar shapes, the familiar-shaped troubles her mind makes of them—down the aisle toward the jet's wide-open doorway. The shoes she's wearing, she sees, are the ones from last night's dream. Old and nearly worn out. Royal blue with a parrot, green wing, red body, stitched large on each toe. The heel of a wingtip not Darrell's lands solidly atop one of her birds and she cries out in pain. The man, backing from his seat into the aisle with cell phone clamped to his ear is big, jowly, black, wearing a Brooks Brothers suit, a Wall Street yellow tie and suspenders, and a half-carat diamond sunk deep in one fleshy ear. Without really slowing down, shoving past her and her family who've stopped at the sound she made, he says, unctuously, "Madam, excuse me. How clumsy. Forgive me." And in the very next beat into his phone, he says curtly, "You *know* better than to call me here, this line's not secure."

Lucy watches Darrell's lips purse while his ears redden. The man, tailed by a scurrying assistant, is gone—not even noticing Darrell's intention to face him off. She puts a hand on his hand to suggest he not follow, that he let it go. Darrell turns on her, flinging her hand off and saying vehemently to her what he hadn't said to the black man. "What an asshole."

She steps back, knowing suddenly what she runs from in the dream. It is Darrell.

She follows him off the plane. Peyton has bounded ahead; she locks eyes on his blond head so as not to lose him. Now at the top of the stairs, she hears the sea. Breathing, and breaking on the shore.

1

The back of Peyton's blond, bowl-cut head and his narrow shoulders bob among faces. A collage in flux, those faces: some black, but more of them—in these downtown blocks of Hamilton—white, and most of those marked across the forehead and down the nose with a sunburned "T" for tourist. Lucy steers herself through them, keeping carefully to Peyton's wake and saying very clearly, "Pardon me," to anyone she happens to brush, feeling embarrassed and even angry at people, including her son, who don't excuse themselves when they bump others.

Peyton will not walk beside her. He refuses to walk, period. It's late August now, blisteringly bright and hot, and her son has insisted she leave the cool oasis of the Hamilton Princess Hotel, where they live, for now, with Darrell's employer, TransGlobal Reinsurance, paying the bill while they wait for their leased house on the South Shore to come open. Peyton leads her on a "reconnoitering mission" through the sweltering downtown, his choice of term for what they are doing, and his choice of route through the crowds of shoppers and the pastel arcades of Front Street, Reid Street, Queen Street. He charges forward on irritable, manic overdrive that leaves her nerves jangled and both of them bathed in sweat.

Both of them are bored to distraction by the lives they lead so far, in their first month on the island. Lucy copes, despite feeling guilty about it, by sleeping late in the soft, tight, Egyptian cotton sheets on the hotel beds, ordering sumptuous late breakfasts on a terrace with carp pools, and wallowing in afternoons of narcotic languor by the pool. But self-indulgence doesn't do it for Peyton. He's way too restless. He is, in fact, about to burst out of his skin, and she has to do what she can to help him hang on two more weeks until school begins, after Labor Day, when he will find — she hopes to God — some friends.

He is twelve. She is forty-one. Until recently, they have been very best friends all his life, a kingdom *à deux*. They were leaving that land, by way of his pre-puberty, even before they moved to this island, but being here has hastened the departure.

He has stopped, at last, in front of a candy counter in a drugstore loaded with merchandise so overwhelmingly American Lucy could not have distinguished most of it from the stock of a Revco back home. Peyton reaches tentatively for a pack of Smarties, a British-made variant of his old favorite, M&Ms.

"Do you want them?" Lucy asks, her hand already on the clasp of her purse.

"No," he says. "I don't want *candy*."

He almost said yes. She saw the word forming on his lips before he killed it.

"Peyton," she asks him in a tone she usually dissuades herself from taking, "what *do* you want?"

"I don't know," he says, anxiety evident beneath his petulance.

"Do you want to shop?" She reaches one-armed to hug his shoulders, in sympathy for the part of him she understands, but he snaps his arms tight against his ribcage and evades her.

She draws a careful breath to separate herself from her feelings. "Shall we go back to the hotel? We could swim."

"No."

"Then *what*?"

Now she is really angry at him, for drawing that tide of

misery out of her. His absolute need to *provoke* is frightening; she's never felt the like in him before.

"I'll find something to do," he says, with finality.

For the next hour they move in and out of shops selling T-shirts and souvenirs, expensive clothes and jewelry, European shoes, Japanese electronics, CDs, musical instruments, toys and high-concept health food. They walk past the Bank of Bermuda "tower" — six stories high — where Darrell is upstairs, working. Peyton declines to go up and say hi and Lucy, despite having suggested it cheerily, feels guilty relief. She tries to loiter before the windows of Bluck's and Trimingham's, opulent with British porcelain and Asian teak — she wants to just look at these beautiful things — but Peyton keeps moving and she follows dutifully, up and down the hill on which the island's single small city is perched, crossing and re-crossing their own path, and everything they pass in the twelve square blocks that is downtown Hamilton is bright, shining and pricey, like the inside of an American mall.

Peyton pauses to retie his shoe on a corner of Front Street, before a window displaying thick woolen sweaters in jewel tones and every shade of the earth, merchandise that Lucy would love to take home to Connecticut by the armload but which, since she is not going home — their house there has been sold — only makes her more conscious of the sweat running in rivulets down her bare legs underneath her loose skirt. "Peyton," she says, "we must stop. I have to sit down. I have lakes in my shoes."

He looks at her abruptly, as if he only that minute recalled her presence. She pulls off her flat, old and blue and parrot-bearing, and turns it over. Actual water drips to the pavement and Peyton's face softens. Here is the boy she knows.

"Okay," he says. "Where?"

A stream of passersby parts to surge around them. Across two lanes of traffic and a line of parked cars is the sea, sighing against its retaining wall, a deep-water harbor flush against downtown. A concrete esplanade with shade trees and benches, vendors and an early-lunch swarm of people runs along the waterfront; a cruise ship the size of several large buildings is tied the length of it.

"Over there?" Lucy suggests, her eyes on the words "Ice Cream" emblazoned on one of the vending carts.

"All right," Peyton agrees, and she steps off the curb into the space between two parked cars, reaching back for his hand. She's still enjoying having caught his fingers in hers when he yanks her back sharply and a car buzzes her from the right, beeping insult. She's glanced the wrong way before stepping into the street again, forgetting—again—that traffic keeps to the left on this island.

"Mom," Peyton tells her, "you've got to pay attention or you'll be roadkill."

He continues to hold onto her, propelling her by the arm across the street when the way is clear. He approaches the ice cream vendor first. "Chocolate," he says, "in a cone." The vendor, a wizened black man with reddish skin, a frayed shirt faded colorless, and a very old flat cap pulled low over his eyes, scoops up a generous portion for Peyton, calling him "young gentleman" and telling him this is the very best ice cream in the world, made from the milk of local cows in the island's only dairy.

Lucy peers into the man's wheeled freezer at the big round cartons of local ice cream—chocolate, vanilla and strawberry only—and the Popsicles and bars piled to the side in their standard American paper wrappers. All at once she knows just what she wants and wonders if there might possibly be one buried in there. "Lemon ice?" she asks the man, smiling at him, a girl again on an early outing to New York, Lincoln Center with its music and ballets behind her, and a paper tub of Italian ice softening between her small warm hands.

The vendor does not smile back. He looks, instead, both tired and annoyed, and without meeting her eyes, digs in the freezer, pulls up a frost-furred lemon ice and hands it to her along with the requisite wooden paddle-spoon. She pays, he makes change, and she walks away aware that she's offended him without meaning to and aware as well, as she's learning she better be on this island, that it's easy to offend people simply by being who she is, an obvious American with obvious American taste and money.

Peyton has settled himself on a shady bench, and she sits down beside him. For a while she studies the people who pass, the ambling, underdressed tourists and the briskly moving office workers on lunch hour, overdressed for the heat in coat-and-tie or suit and heels. Where are the poor people? she wonders, and her head turns on the thought back to the ice cream vendor and the other cart vendors around him, and she answers her own question: they are invisible, or the next thing to it, at least in glossy, tourist-friendly downtown. The frozen treat melts on her tongue with a satisfying sweet tartness, and she watches her son swirl his ice cream into a peak atop the cone and then bare his teeth to bite it off like the child he still is.

"Is it good?" she asks him brightly.

He doesn't answer, not even when she repeats the question. He is perversely determined not to comply, even in so small a way.

She sighs. She tries to savor the relief of being off her feet and in the shade. She wants a cigarette, intensely, but a promise she's made herself about this move is to leave the cigarettes behind. Smoking was her mother's single, fatal vice, so of course it upsets Peyton and makes Darrell tense. She lifts her hand to brush her long flyaway hair from her damp face, and smells lemon tang from the ice on her fingers.

She stirs the slush in the cup with the wooden paddle. The crystals clump and slide. Day by day, she works to keep her thoughts upbeat and moving, and if they start to hang, she pushes them on. But sometimes she can't. Sometimes some detail from the past snags her and she obsesses. Her father's voice traps her this time, his anxiety for her flattening the question he is asking her into a non-question: *You and Darrell are planning to divorce.*

When he'd said that, she stood beside him, the two of them next to their parked cars in his driveway in Darien. February, three years ago. A light rain fell, the temperature just short of freezing. She'd been away six weeks by herself, in her father's log house in the Berkshires, the home he'd built to retire in with her mother, persisting with the construction in stubborn optimism or denial even when they all knew the cancer was killing her and she'd never see it finished. Lucy had been the first family member to use it for more than a long weekend. The day she returned, she and her father, holding their respective driver's side doors, talked quietly and too long, standing in cold rain, their hair sticking to their chilled scalps.

He missed his train to Philadelphia, where he was involved as ACLU counsel in the latest appeal for new trial on behalf of Mumia Abu-Jamal, a black journalist and political activist on death row for the murder of a white policeman. He asked Lucy all the same questions he'd asked on the phone while she holed up in the cabin. He turned aside an anguished cell phone summons from her sister Cyn, his law partner — Lucy could hear her hissing from the courthouse foyer into their father's ear, *What's little sister's problem now?* — as he asked Lucy patiently, again, why did she leave her husband and her son? What was wrong? Could he help? What was it she was *doing* up there all by herself?

She did not know the answer to any of these questions, and she told him so. That provoked him to repeat the non-question, and, getting in the car, preparing to drive herself home, to Darrell and Peyton, she answered, "We haven't talked about it."

But they had, twice, in the month before she left. Both before and after Christmas. They hadn't come to any conclusions. Lucy could not justify a divorce. Nothing that anyone could see was wrong with the marriage itself. Darrell did not drink, cheat, gamble or beat her. He made plenty of money and spent it on her liberally. What *was* wrong, he thought, was wrong with her, but to Darrell, divorce was disaster, a catastrophe he and his mother had endured when he was younger than Peyton was then. She understood his reluctance — his determination — not to visit this upon Peyton, who was then nine.

So she went home. She'd found herself better able to breathe after taking that break, and the inability to draw breath — the persistent sensation of a brick crushing her chest—had been the cause of her departure, although she'd not said so to anyone, since it seemed an inadequate, nearly hysterical excuse for leaving a husband and son. Darrell said very little to her about her absence except to ask her, as she came through the front door with her suitcase in hand, "Did you find yourself?"

She had not answered him. She'd put the suitcase down in the hall and begun cleaning up the kitchen, where unwashed glasses and discarded take-out containers obscured every counter surface. For nearly two years thereafter, the curt question lay dormant, never voiced, not examined. They made their way, the three of them, through their lives, playing their familiar roles: Darrell working, Lucy looking after Peyton and the house, and Peyton serving as the center of his own life and hers. Then Darrell, stressed and unhappy as a middle management cog in a multinational corporate machine, received the offer to run the subsidiary in Bermuda. They both knew he wanted badly to accept it, and she knew from the moment he described it that she didn't want to go but would have to.

He asked her as they unpacked from a frantically rushed thirty-six-hour visit to the island to check it out—at company expense, between Christmas and the New Year—"What do you think, Lucy? Will you do it?"

She paused, the cosmetics bag in her hands very heavy. Bermuda had been cold, damp, desolate, ravaged with waves and wind. They'd been put up in a shabby studio apartment with molding walls and no heat. The company representative who'd shown them around, with a chilly politeness not disguising the imposition they made on her holiday season, explained to Lucy succinctly and privately the social challenges that would face her as the wife of an expat executive. Darrell would have his position in the company to assure he'd be treated with professional courtesy when it came to social events. But Lucy would be on her own. Proper Bermudians' view on expatriates, especially American ones— privileged by passport and employer to live better than the best of their hosts—might be summarized thus, the woman said: "You may step into the garden, but please don't come to tea." She'd followed this zinger with a tight, malicious smile. And Lucy had felt her gut pitch. Darrell, when she repeated it to him that evening, had laughed heartily, a rattle-y sound in the wet, drafty silence of the comfortless room. Now his high-beam gaze, when she lifted her eyes to his, paralyzed her. He needed her not only to say Yes, but say it with enthusiasm. And she could not get her mouth to work.

He read her silence perfectly. He reacted as she knew he would, inevitably, like dominoes falling.

"Don't do this, Lucy," he said. His lips pursed, then set into an almost-white straight line. "Don't sabotage it. We've got a chance. We need to take it."

"All right," she said, turning to tuck lingerie into a drawer and break the hold of his glare.

"All right?" Darrell said. "Is that the best you can muster?" He'd stepped up close behind her and her shoulders tensed.

"I'll do it, Darrell," she said. "I will." She could not make herself turn around. The tears in her eyes would incite him.

"You'll do it," he mimicked her, with exaggerated resignation and mournfulness. "You'll do it, crying and dragging your ass, making me miserable, making Peyton miserable...."

"I will do it, Darrell. I'll do my best. And I don't cry, that's not true," —because she didn't, not in his presence, not anymore.

"Your best, Lucy, is pretty fucking half-ass, at best."

She felt, in the shiver that shook her, the possibility, ever present, never yet quite realized, that he'd strike her. She didn't turn around. She couldn't look him in the eye.

He did not touch her. He stepped away, dumped the contents of her suitcase on the floor for her to pick up, and told her coldly, "I honestly don't care if you come or not. If you want to stay here, run home to daddy, go ahead. But Peyton is coming with me. I'll not let you ruin my son."

"Do you think they would let us aboard that ship?" Peyton

inquires, and Lucy jumps, snatched back from deep water. When she'd come home from the Berkshires, Peyton asked her no questions at all and evaded her confused attempts at explanation. Since then, she'd kept her troubles to herself.

"Maybe so," she answers him, smiling and hopping up, directing herself to be energetic. "We can surely ask."

But they are not allowed on board. A uniformed man at the top of the gangplank turns them away when they admit they are not passengers. "Security," he says firmly, as if that explains everything.

At the foot of the aluminum plank, Peyton again takes her hand. "Let's go see if Dad is in," he says. "Let's find out if he's working late tonight."

Mutely Lucy nods and follows. Peyton's change of heart about visiting his father's office is probably a good thing. Darrell is busy in this new job — chief operating officer of TransGlobal's brand new Bermuda subsidiary — but very happy, too, high on the demands and prestige of a position many levels above any job he'd held before. For most of the last month, she and Peyton have seen him only during or after dinner except on Sunday afternoons, when he takes them on sightseeing drives around the island. Often Peyton appears completely disinterested in his father's attempts to entertain him, which makes Darrell angry at her.

They make their way back uphill to Reid Street and the Bank of Bermuda tower-ette, as Peyton dubs it. They find the sidewalks far less crowded now that lunch hour is over for office workers, and the afternoon's most intense heat has sent the tourists back to the pools or the beaches or their air-conditioned hotel rooms. The bank building has a newly remodeled façade of white Italian marble faux-flecked with gold — Darrell's employer has leased premium office space to establish the new company's image — and the very thick glass double doors have polished brass handles so massive Lucy cannot comfortably fit one hand around the one she needs to pull and so must use both hands. How incredibly inconvenient for the employees' coming and going, she thinks, noting as well that one of the cylindrical marble planters on either side of the huge doors has sprouted a hot dog wrapper, oozing, like excrement, mustard and chili.

Darrell greets them at the open door of his top-floor corner office, wraparound windows offering a view, from this height, of the harbor and the cruise ship from which Lucy and Peyton have just been turned away, and, slightly to the west, the docks where container ships tie up to unload every luxury and necessity—from food to automobiles to medical equipment—not created on the island, which is, Darrell points out to Peyton as they take in the view, absolutely everything anybody uses, with the minor exceptions of what comes in by air cargo, and some locally produced root vegetables and milk.

Nearly at the height of the building from which they watch, the spindly arm of a crane slowly lifts one box-car-sized, brick-red container at a time from the many dozens stacked on the ship's deck, then even more slowly, by inches, lowers it to the concrete wharf to a clearing amid many more such containers, where, like ants in slow motion, several dark men grapple the boxcar's corners with hooks and guide it onto the two-pronged metal tongue of a forklift, which begins to back up, and then stops, while the crane also stops, and the men get down off their machines and confer in a group. The docks, Darrell tells Peyton, are not just an economic bottleneck but a political flashpoint: their operation is controlled by the island's single militant labor union—"neo-Marxist, anti-British and anti-American, completely irresponsible," he says over his shoulder, to Lucy, arching his brows to jibe at what he knows are the liberal politics she incubated at her father's table. "They've got their collective finger on this island's jugular," he adds, whether to Peyton, her, or himself, she's not sure.

Still, this is a good moment, one she can remind Darrell of later: Peyton listening to him, standing close under his arm. She glances down at the island's newspaper, the *Royal Gazette*, lying open on one end of Darrell's enormous glass desk—a small town paper with big photos and extended captions, and (she knows this from lazy reading by the hotel pool) plenty of gossip, under the by-lines as well as in letters to the editor, compensating for lack of much real news. She's lifting her eyes to answer Darrell's query about maybe breaking for late lunch when she recognizes, in one of the oversized photos, someone she's seen.

Darrell's index finger lands on the newsprint replica of the jowly face of the big black man who'd trod so heavily on her foot the day they arrived on the island. "Yeah, Lucy, I was saving that to show you. Mr. Bigfoot-Big Attitude from the plane, he's the Justice Minister on the island. And I tell you what, maybe he needs that attitude. He's got himself one heck of a set of problems to work with."

He tells her then that what's happening on the docks is a "go-slow," the local term for what's known in the States as work-to-rule, a union pressure tactic just short of, and usually preparatory to, a strike.

"What would they strike about?" Lucy asks.

"Anything, apparently," he says, rolling his eyes. "Labor trouble's endemic, really it's just the standard expression of anti-capitalism here. Look." He points again at the newspaper article, this time planting his finger on the text. "Labor says the go-slow's for reasons well known to management and its friends in Government. Management says there is no go-slow. Government claims the real problem on the docks is agitation by radicals in Parliament, particularly their leader Passjohn, 'defender of anarchists and terrorists.' That guy is quoted right here saying a labor action is the proletariat's rightful response to government oppression, and the premier, who's supposed to be in charge since he's the head of the majority party, isn't quoted. He's on vacation."

Peyton says, "Dad, the crane is moving again."

Darrell, turning back toward his son, says, "That's good." To Lucy, very quietly, intending it to be inaudible to Peyton, he adds, "Be careful where you go. The radical, violent element is everywhere among the black people, apparently, especially the poorer ones. Every so often—they try to keep it out of the papers—white people get attacked."

Peyton, whose face says he's heard everything Darrell said and finds it intriguing, says, "Dad, I want to go down to the docks."

Darrell, for a moment, doesn't say a thing. He stands staring at his son, then looks back at Lucy, quizzical. Irritable. It's not me, she almost says. She bites her lip, literally, to keep from saying in her own defense, I can't make him do things or say things.

Darrell says to Peyton, "We'll go. Sometime, we will." And then the phone rings, and he answers it, and soon it's clear the call will take some time. He covers the mouthpiece with his hand and tells them he can't go to lunch, after all. He's sorry. He'll see them for dinner, he won't be late today, for sure, and in the meantime they are to go have a good time. "Go spend some of this money I'm making," he orders them jovially, his attention returning to the phone.

Neither one of them speaks in the elevator. When they step through those big glass doors to the street, the heat and humidity—and the smell of fresh urine—strike Lucy. She looks up and gasps—she can't help it, it's happened before she has time to censor herself—at the sight of a rag-thin man well over six feet tall, a lion's mane of dreadlocks reaching his waist, tucking himself back into his unwashed pants. She stops, and automatically, as if Peyton sat in a car seat beside her, her hand rises to stop him, too. A small stream of urine runs downhill just in front of her toes from a puddle at the base of the door formed by the drips from a splash mark waist-height on the glass. The man, who smells as unwashed as his pants, whose teeth are broken and eyes jaundiced, laughs at her.

Lucy stares at his very black face. She simply stares, immobilized, one hand on Peyton who is, her touch tells her, not moving either. Surely he'll not confront her, she's done nothing to deserve it, but she's just as sure of the imbalance between their circumstances and the precipitous possibility he could choose violence to right it. She experiences a sort of miracle—welcome but absurd—when a white policeman, a stick-wielding, dome-hatted bobby of the sort she's occasionally noticed patrolling in downtown Hamilton materializes at precisely that moment to crack the man on the back of the legs with his baton. Before he falls from a second blow to the shoulder, glancing against his skull, he spits, copiously, and the wad lands with stunning or serendipitous accuracy atop the red parrot on her old blue shoe.

Peyton cries out.

She slumps against the door, remembering to locate and avoid the urine stain. The man—"a Rastafarian," Peyton tells her; she knew that but how does he know, she wonders, and why does he think she doesn't?—is bundled away in handcuffs, limping. Another officer has materialized now, asking her for her name, which she gives, and permission to press charges in her name, which, rallying suddenly, she denies. "It wasn't personal," she tells him, knowing from his expression he thinks her irrational. "He was angry, but not at me."

She takes from her purse a packaged antiseptic wipe with which she hastily cleans the shoe. Then, as quickly as she can, before he wants her to, she hurries away, pulling Peyton with her, aimed downhill and away but having no real sense where she's headed.

At the foot of the hill, at the end of the esplanade, they come upon a railing and an empty stretch of deep, oily-smelling water separating them from the dock alongside the cargo ship *Oleander*. On its flat deck, the size of a football field, sea containers are stacked and chained in a double layer, the red and brown metal boxes, rusted, battered and stenciled with numbers. The contents of the Langston home in Darien had been packed into containers just like these, and drawn away by two dirty, belching diesel trucks, their presence incongruous in a neighborhood of spacious lawns and carefully understated affluence.

In prolonged slow motion, the crane plucks a container from the ship onto the crowded dock where containers are already stacked three high, and a team of five men grapples it to its place in rows divided by aisles barely the width of one man.

"I wonder," Lucy says quietly, "if any of those containers are ours."

"Maybe," Peyton replies. She hears his restless energy rising, barely contained, seeking something to hook to.

He isn't looking at her. He's watching the street, and she becomes aware of what draws him—a steady buzz, a sound like the seething of disturbed bees. She locates it in a pack of approaching motor scooters.

"Probably our things are here by now, just not unloaded yet, on account of the go-slow," she says. She knows Peyton's not listening; *she's* not listening to what she's saying, not really. The scooter riders are boys, black boys, in dark, non-descript clothing at odds with the cheery pinks, blues, and lime greens of the storefronts they pass.

"On the other hand," Lucy tells the back of Peyton's head, "it really hasn't been that long. Our containers might still be in Secaucus, or rolling along on the high seas."

"Could be anywhere," he agrees absently.

His eyes follow the crowd of boys. Most of them ride with one hand shoved deep in a pocket of baggy jeans, and every one of them has a foot dangling, a heavy sneaker flashing silver, barely skimming the pavement. They are reckless. They are *cool*. She can clearly feel Peyton making that translation in terms.

As the riders approach, Lucy takes in their nonchalant young faces, beardless but militantly square-framed by their helmets. She begins to feel fear for all that's uncertain, and dead ahead. They are silent, but their machines hum, the pitch of the drone Dopplering past her, enveloping her like a breaking wave.

2

Marcus Passjohn, for ten years the leader of the Opposition party, the eleven-seats-out-of-forty, voice-of-what-they-don't-want-to-hear party, will deliver yet another speech he expects no one to listen to shortly after eight this evening in the island's National Stadium. Now, a few minutes past six o'clock, he sits at his desk on the stuffy third floor of Bermuda's Parliament House, notes for the speech before him along with a draft of his latest attempt to legislate some relief for the island's housing shortage. In his right hand, claiming his attention, a newspaper photo of his oldest friend on the island, Lemuel Trott, an old man with both legs gone at the knee, parked in his wheelchair in the dust just behind the curb in Warwick Parish, waving traffic along, and smiling. That smile is beatific—the photo caption uses that term, but Marcus and two generations of passersby already attach it to Lemuel, a man so lit with inner joy that his white hair and his beard and even his teeth seem genuinely to glow.

It's that weird luminosity, and the tranquility he knows to be its source, that keep Marcus puzzling over the picture until his wristwatch alarm sounds and he jumps up to leave, tucking the clipping back into his shirt pocket with the letter that accompanied it to his desk this morning, taking the draft bill with him to read at home in bed, and abandoning the notes that have failed to gel into a speech. Lemuel has sat legless by the road for nearly three decades; his sister Althea's letter is just the latest in a series of pleas for legislation on behalf of the indigent handicapped that Marcus pushes but usually cannot deliver. Affordable housing has been an issue on the island for longer than Lemuel's been crippled, and Marcus has introduced or co-sponsored seven bills addressing it in the sixteen years he's sat in Parliament. Some passed, and two were funded, but none of the housing projects is more than partially complete: the result of political cross-currents, incompetence and corruption, hurricanes, or plain bad luck. Hurrying down the building's back steps, Marcus cannot imagine what he might say now, in one more speech, impassioned or not, that would do anything to address either of these problems, small symptoms of intractable, festering social injustice.

Lemuel had been middle-aged and in possession of two working legs, and Marcus reading the law in London on scholarship and a busboy's wages, the last time the suppressed rage exploded, in 1973, in the form of three bullets. The British governor, his aide-de-camp and the governor's dog were assassinated only six months after a bullet took out the Commissioner of Police. All the dead men were white. The dog was a Great Dane. Government declared a state of emergency, houses were searched, all eight hundred of the island's licensed guns called in for ballistics tests, fifty people questioned, and six, associated with a militant black movement, detained. No evidence linking anyone directly to the crime could be found.

But three years later, Erskine Burrows, a black man with a criminal record, was under death sentence for all three murders, largely due to testimony from informants granted immunity. His behavior under prosecution struck observers as odd. He denied the charges and grinned, refused counsel and offered no defense, clutched a Bible. One day, abruptly, he confessed, in a long letter full of lyrical references to Jesus Christ as his Lord and master and savior forever, "...a supreme authority we can appeal to and pray to, to free us from suppression, sin and any evil domination we might be under." Burrows called himself "former commander in chief of anti-colonialist forces in the island of Bermuda," implicated unnamed accomplices, and explained that while he did not forget that "killing is wrong and sinful," the Governor had been assassinated to expose the evils of the colonialist system, because it "encourages black people to hate and fight each other while those who are putting this evil strategy into effect laugh and...say, 'We have got them conquered.'"

In the year that followed, Burrows' defense exhausted all avenues of appeal in Bermuda and Britain, including a petition for clemency directed to the Queen and signed by 6,000 Bermudians. The new Governor, consulting with the Premier, the leader of the Parliament's majority party, and his ministers, considered a stay of the execution for fear of civil unrest, but the Governor reported himself convinced that "racial harmony, respect for the law and order, and the security situation would suffer more if a stay were granted."

When Burrows was hanged on December 2, 1977, along with Ladry Tacklyn, an alleged accomplice, Marcus read about it in the London newspapers. The executions were the first on the island in thirty years, and protestors filled the streets claiming these black murderers died only because their victims were white. Demonstrations turned to riots, buildings and cars went up in flames, three people died, and gangs of youths attacked white motorists while the police fired tear gas and were answered with home-made fire bombs. Three hundred British soldiers, fifteen days of martial law, a week of heavy rain, and a desperate appeal for common sense from the black leaders of the Opposition party finally wore down the violence. But the damage to the economy lingered for years as American tourists took their business elsewhere. And only gradually, much of this during Marcus's dogged tenure in the parliamentary opposition, has government-sanctioned amnesia erased the blot of these events from the island's money-making reputation for stability and order.

Cutting across the nearly empty parking lot, thumbing the pages of his bill and examining yet again Lemuel's remarkable lack of rancor, Marcus puts his foot in a pothole and trips.

He's cursing the torn knee of what is no longer the best of the three suits he owns, and gathering the scattered papers off the gritty pavement, when he glances up to see two men in white coveralls standing near the dumpster in the shadow of the backside of the Bank of Bermuda building next door. A short distance down Court Street, deserted since the business day is over, an ambulance is parked at the curb. Its lights are not flashing, and Marcus senses no urgency in the posture of the two paramedics, talking to each other, but he jogs anyway. It's a reflex: someone is down.

Could be an elderly person collapsed from heat; the day's been quite warm for early November, or could be a tourist, the typical mishap with a rented scooter, except the tourist season ended abruptly and two months too early, on America's 9/11. He opens his mouth to say, "Can I help...," but a police officer steps from behind a spindly tree to block his view into the dumpster, open on the street side by way of the small door that might be used for cleaning it. The bobby is known to Marcus; his name is Eugene Outerbridge and they grew up on the same seedy street in the back of town, their mothers both very young and unwed in the late 50s. Eugene is clearly embarrassed at having to be peremptory with Marcus, champion of the poor and all black people, the lion they can turn to, he always tells them this, when the law turns on them, even if they happen to be police officers. Marcus's speeches for the rights of the little people and the self-worth of dispossessed black people have been compared by his supporters, albeit not recently, to the passionate incantations of the late American Dr. King, and even his opponents in Government occasionally claim he moves them to tears, right before they disregard everything he says and do precisely what their foreign masters, the ones holding the island's purse strings, require them to do.

"Eugene," Marcus says gently, "slide your black butt over. You know it's too narrow to keep me from finding out what's behind it."

Eugene's thin face is pinched uncomfortably between a tight chin strap and the hard blue plastic visor of his bobby's hat. He shakes his head no, but moves anyway, and Marcus peers through the dumpster's open door. Inside he sees two swollen bodies, wrapped like cigars in thin sheets of white plastic packing foam that would have shrouded them completely but that have burst down their perforated seams as the day's heat built up inside the dumpster.

A stench of decomposition is noticeable but not overwhelming. The two black men have not been there a long time. Still, green flies are thick on their faces, and the moist whites of their eyes, in particular, seem to appeal to the insects.

Marcus steps backwards. He's explaining to himself how amazing it is he can behold such a sight and not be undone, and then what's before his eyes are the clouds that veil the darkening sky and he realizes he is reeling. He stumbles to regain his balance, Eugene says abjectly, "I'm sorry, I tried to stop you," and one of the paramedics tells the other, "We got to go on and pick them out of there." Both paramedics are black.

Marcus almost asks, "Wait a minute, what about the police?" Looking Eugene, a beat cop, in the eye, he says, "Are you doing the paper on this? Where's the detective?"

"No detective." Eugene's shaking his head again. "Paper's filed already. Two dead vagrants, that's all."

Marcus blinks. Crimes of passion happen here occasionally, but not murder; British probity forbids the mess. More commonly, there's retribution in the back of town for a drug deal gone wrong. This year, a lean one economically even before 9/11, a virus of arsons, vandalism and racial incidents has spread across the island, disturbing white neighborhoods as well as black. Trouble in the traditional form is brewing, but to Marcus's knowledge it's produced no bodies, not this time, until now. "Someone killed these men," he states.

Eugene, looking at the pavement beneath his spit-polished, department-issue shoes, says doggedly, "Two vagrants, climbed in the dumpster for shelter, drank themselves to death."

A dumpster is no shelter from heat, and no liquor bottles are in proximity to the dead men.

"That's the line from upstairs, is it?" Marcus says. He's still clutching the draft of the housing bill, the pages rolled in his hand like a small baton. A paper billy club. How he wishes he had a real one and the authority to use it to knock the truth out of somebody. "No autopsy? No investigation?"

He approaches the bodies being belted to stretchers. The paramedics' faces are averted. They are holding their breath. There's blood, Marcus is nearly certain of it, congealed on the inside of the packing foam sheaths. He seizes the material in both hands and rips, exposing the two faces and chests.

The men have been beaten: bruises, lacerations, missing teeth, shards of bone embedded in torn flesh. One of them, despite the disfigurement and bloating, Marcus recognizes. A relative, some degree of cousin, to Althea and Lemuel Trott. A kid, really, maybe nineteen, but the gone-wrong kind with a taste for violence and money and the people who traffic in both.

"Someone killed these men," Marcus insists.

"Vagrants," Eugene repeats. "Drunks."

Marcus feels how Eugene wants to run. He feels how the paramedics are sickened. *He* wants to run. *He* feels sick. These bodies who were men have been disposed of as trash, the way Lemuel, a black man, too, is trash.

"You are killing *yourselves* when you do this," Marcus shouts at the three living black men in front of him. "You're complicit in your own oppression."

He's ashamed of the bitterness boiling through him but he can't stop it from coming out. He turns on his heel and strides back to his car. Tears burn his eyes but do not fall. His responsibility to himself and to the island is to make an issue of this. He should demand in tonight's speech and tomorrow's newspaper that these two men's deaths be treated with respect. He should endeavor one more time to pound home the moral point that predation against any human being, or any group of human beings, is predation against all humankind. He could insist, as he has on innumerable occasions in the courtroom and from the political stump, on a pragmatic truth: the deaths and misfortunes of the underclass are the responsibility of educated and privileged people, since only they are in the economic position to address social ills. And if they don't, they will pay for them, one way or another.

The French revolutionaries wrote the first point in blood with their "Declaration of the Rights of Man." Karl Marx carved the second into the pages of *Das Kapital*. Governments and ideologies have risen and fallen for centuries on the forces behind these truths. But Marcus at forty-eight is too exhausted to believe he can restate them in a way his people and their present masters will finally hear.

He wipes sweat from his high forehead with the sheaf of papers he still holds. He hears the ambulance pull away as he unlocks his car but does not look back. On the back of his right hand he sees a dirty smear of congealed blood from the chest of Althea's cousin. He can imagine what he looks like: perspiring heavily, trembling from the adrenaline that just raged through him, a tear in his pants knee, but he doesn't want to imagine what he might say when he finally gets to the podium later tonight. Humming in his brain is a credo he read years ago in some stage of researching his endless defense of the island's small band of endlessly persecuted black separatists. *You cannot kill a problem, it beggars your solution.*

He remembers how the line stopped him cold. How he turned it in his head as if he held it in his hand, parsing the facets of the verb "beggars." Admiring the brilliance and hardness of paradox. If a problem will not die when you kill it, if the problem gains new and tenacious life precisely because of the killing, then the supposed solution goes begging for what it cannot ever deliver.

Once inside his car, a battered Bentley handed down to him ten years ago by his predecessor at the Opposition helm, Marcus uses a crumpled tissue from the floor to scrub the sticky blood from his hand. It falls to the floor as he digs in the glove box and under the seats and finally roots in the chaos of the backseat foot well for a small black plastic snap purse. When he finds it, he extracts a needle and a tiny ball of dark thread. His mother taught him to sew on buttons and to darn, before she died from a bad choice of men when he was six. She learned how to sew from her granny, her mother having also passed on young. Marcus threads the needle in two tries, and seated in the car with his feet on the crumbling pavement, leans over to whip together the raw edges of cloth skimming his kneecap. He bites off the thread close to the knot. His stitches are uneven; his mother would have done better and his housekeeper, tomorrow, will certainly best his effort. For tonight, however, for the duration of his appearance at the Guy Fawkes Night rally, his own crude repair will have to see him through.

He jams the sewing kit under the driver's seat, turns the key in the ignition and points the Bentley toward home to pick up Zef. His son asked to come along tonight, and at the moment that happened, Marcus was awash with pleasure and hope that Zef was showing an interest in him and his work. Now, he feels guilty, and the weight of that feeling is familiar. A sticky note lettered Z-E-F—which he put on the gear shift lever this morning so he wouldn't forget to swing by home—has just served to remind him that he does, indeed, have a boy as well as a country to tend.

3

Bermuda's youth, liberated via scooter licenses at sixteen, and finding the island very quiet, bore out the cylinders of their machines to increase their power, and then they race them—at night, on dark roads tourists never see. In particular, Palmetto Road, a spur running from the North Shore to Marsh Folly with a single sharp bend at Frog Lane, passing through the shadow of the dump (fifty feet high), sweeping through the unlit tunnel at Black Watch Pass into the back of town where the houses are cubes of cinderblock and tin and no property lines divide the dirt where the chickens scratch their living— Palmetto Road is a racetrack. Every year, some boy dies there, brained on a wall or on the nose of an oncoming van.

The North Shore Road runs close to the open sea from the bridge at Flatts Inlet to the roundabout at Palmetto Park, and on a blowy day, the sound of waves beating the rocks drowns out everything else. But today, still and hot like summer although it is early November, the combustive buzz of a two-stroke engine is the sound of a single, angry hornet. The scooter's rider is to any local obviously both underage and mixed race—"high yellow" in the parlance of proper white Bermudians and simply "bright" in the eyes of any black Bermudian, but in any case belonging not fully to either of their worlds. He takes the full three-sixty of the roundabout, testing the laws of gravity and centrifugal force, leaning the scooter low until the inside handlebar threatens to brush the ground, cantilevering with his outside foot. Then he straightens the scooter and rides down the raceway at precisely the speed limit, ignoring the older boys already gathered in the shadowy brakes of oleander, awaiting darkness and the thrill of speed. When he exits the tunnel, the road narrows, shabby houses crowd the shoulders, and the air grows thick with smoke and talk. A billy goat, tethered to a stake, watches the boy from the flat concrete cover of a backyard water catchment. From the house nearest the cistern, which has a blanket hanging where its door should be, a tall rag-thin Rasta man in a bulging crochet cap lifts his arm in salute.

"Bredda Zef," he calls out to the boy.

Zef Passjohn lifts his own arm in response. The scooter, a rebuilt one cobbled together by the Rasta from the least-worn parts of four junked ones, slows, wobbles, begins to curve from the road toward the raked-dirt yard. The Rasta, Ramo Wylie, waves the boy on, shouts, "Stop here tomorrow, early in de day."

He is a good boy, Zef, a willing pupil. He calls Ramo Father, sometimes shyly with downcast eyes and other times defiantly, the cords in his neck taut with fervor. But tonight, Ramo thinks, the boy should not be late for his appointment with the man who sired him, Marcus Passjohn, whose own appointment tonight at the National Stadium is a date with his destiny: the *politricks* of the island's ruling class.

Ramo does not yet know about the murdered black men Marcus has just discovered in the dumpster in town, but when the news reaches him—as it will in less than an hour, word spreading now like foul scent from the scene—he will not be surprised. Angry, yes, but not surprised. And he will feel the burden of his own destiny grow weightier.

Ramo is a black man resolved to be truly black, to see with a black man's eyes. He tells Zef, and Marcus when he has the chance, and all black people, and white people, too, even though they cannot hear him, that the eyes of black people have been made to see white only. The white way of seeing is all his black brethren know, all they have been shown, all they have been allowed—how could they see more than they have been shown? Such is the legacy of slavery: *sickxploitation*.

He squats on the stone stoop of his block and tin house, the painful ossified bumps that misshape his battered vertebrae grating against the newel of his porch rail, his bony fingers palpating the sore lump on his clavicle where a bobby's nightstick cracked the bone two months ago downtown on Reid Street. His eyes, perpetually yellowed from the jaundice of untreated gallstones, fix on the short broad back of his legless old friend Lemuel Trott in his wheelchair parked facing the road. He recalls the long ago days when Lemuel had two legs and a sharp mind and held Marcus on his knee. Little Marcus Passjohn, an orphan with ashy knees and his thumb jammed to the second knuckle into his mouth at ten years old when Ramo, at fourteen, already ran the streets, heaving bottles, slashing tires, feeding the fire of his anger but seeing no more than what he'd been shown.

He could not have known then what he's been shown since, in the white man's courts, in the white man's prison. His fingers parse the marks that have supplied his motivation: the blows of *downpression* on his back and on his skull. In the riots after Burrows and Tacklyn hanged, and in Casemates Prison for two years thereafter, and a second time for another eight years when someone firebombed the Governor's landau and he was the suspect at hand—ten years, altogether, he's passed in that cold stone fortress where he's been tutored by boots and bottles and billy clubs, and where he found Jah, felt Jah, heard Jah, took Jah into his heart.

Jah Rastafari is black and Jah Rastafari is God, and Jah has given Ramo eyes that see, resolutely, black.

The black man's eyes—he has told Marcus since, and told Zef, and the court, and arresting officers and onlookers too many times to count over thirty years of witnessing his truth to those who cannot see it—are different from the white man's eyes. Watching Marcus for twenty years try with white law to defend black men from the White Lie that their truth is the only truth, he has told Marcus, who does not listen: the black man sees deeper, and from the other side.

Ramo hauls himself up by means of the porch rail, arthritis singeing his joints, and gall bladder pain, his near-constant companion, firing in his chest. He steps inside his house, takes up his broom and sweeps his floor. Pushes dirt across the dirt out the door into the dirt.

He's been called. Called to speak in Jah's tongue to Jah's lost people, the forgotten dark Israelites enslaved in white Babylon. If nobody understands him, so be it. He sweeps. If he must be beaten and bleed, or die to be heard, so be it. In prison, he has heard the Bible read at length and often. He has memorized — he cannot read — great fiery passages of it and he knows — he knows! — such is the way, sometimes, of Jah.

Marcus Passjohn is one of Jah's lost. When he defended Ramo from white law the first time, after the Governor's landau burned but the Governor did not, Marcus lost the case and blamed Ramo. Placed on the stand, Ramo told the court, "Jah's tongue speak in fire." The judge, a white man black-robed and white-wigged, called out, "This Rastaman has confessed!" To Marcus, Ramo explained, "Ignorant man hear what he thinking, not what *I-an-I* say: if the Governor's carriage burnin', then Jah judge the carriage need burnin'." And while they fastened his shackles to take him away, Ramo spoke again to the court in Jah's tongue: "Jah is God and Jah is black and for the white people this turn the worl' upside down, therefore when *I-an-I* speakin' the truth you think: Rastaman, he ravin'."

Marcus shook his head, shut his briefcase, and went home to his English wife, white as the Governor's plumed hat. The first day Ramo saw her he saw trouble, Marcus come home to the island from eight years in London, and she walking in front with Marcus behind, dog sniffing a bitch. When Ramo said so, Marcus turned icy cold. It was the woman's hot politics he followed, he said, "the words of our brother Karl Marx, whose principles shall set us all free." As they hauled him from the courtroom, Ramo called out to Marcus's stiff departing back, "You black, Marcus, or you black-in-white?"

He is yet among the lost but might any day become among the found. Already young Zef begins to see. Already

Zef listens, sometimes, for Jah. First the son, then the father. Maybe. Ramo will show them what they do not yet see. He will lift black truth high. Spin lies into truth, if that's what it takes.

In the dream he lives by, Erskine Burrows addressed him. His head in the noose, neck stretched and twisted like a chicken's for the knife, tongue purpled and thick as a shoe, he called out thus: "Ramo! Ramo Wylie! Reveal my people to themselves."

He offered to Ramo in bare hands that steamed as the flesh seared beneath it a hot glowing coal. A violent orange grudge. In the dream, Ramo accepted it. His own flesh burned, his palms blackened, the feet of ten thousand black men stamped in fervent religious *livity* as they drummed, and the coal became a crow and flew away, its glossy, iridescent wings brushing Ramo's face with rainbow sparks, each one a pinpoint of fire.

Jah spoke to him then, very tenderly. He said, *Our grudge is our truth. You tend it.*

And he does. But he tends as well Marcus Passjohn, the man who so grudgingly tends him in his troubles with the law, and he tends especially well Marcus's son Zef, who is, he feels, his son in spirit and who bears his own grudge wrapped in a fist shoved deep in a pants pocket. Smaller, cooler, formed of die-stamped orange plastic, a round button from a woman's duster, memento of the mother who abandoned him.

Zef was an innocent then, a baby, two years old, left in the uncertain care of a father obsessed with an idealistic appeal of Ramo's conviction, persisting for a dogged six years before succeeding, many months of those years spent sweaty, unwashed, confused, inefficient, and occasionally drunk, hemorrhaging black blood for the white woman who left him.

4

Union men prepare the Guy Fawkes Night bonfire in Bermuda's National Stadium. It's built to torch in effigy the traitor who would have, could he and his co-conspirators have gotten away with it, blown up the British Parliament along with King James I in 1605, igniting barrels of gunpowder stashed beneath the House of Lords. Fawkes was not the ringleader of that cell of militant and devout Catholic terrorists; he was an accomplice assigned to light the fuse. But the plot was betrayed and Fawkes caught in the act, and the date he was taken, November 5, has remained ever since a rowdy holiday all over the old British Empire.

Its observance on the island has been advertised for months this year by an eager Ministry of Tourism, but with the economic slump in the States breeding a deeper slump here, the crowd tonight will be largely local: the partiers, who will turn out for anything promising a night's escape from their troubles, and the patriotic, answering the call by Government (facing re-election in less than a year) to school children and civic groups for a show of spirit in the face of adversity. In the National Stadium, usually the site of hard-fought soccer matches against Caribbean opponents, a temporary speakers' stage is set up at the north end, and a place for the bonfire marked out midfield.

Throughout the day, union dockworkers unload two

trucks full of combustible material donated by their employer the Docks Corporation. With a forklift they pile the broken crates and shipping pallets and flattened sheets of pasteboard container into a flat-topped cone ten feet high, twenty feet wide at its base and surrounded at another twenty-foot radius with yellow plastic tape. Despite the go-slow, now turned *de facto* strike, that has choked the docks for many weeks, the men labor diligently and according to specifications supplied by the Minister of Tourism. Just before the second truck leaves in the twilight at seven o'clock, the driver, known as "the Gimp" from the crane accident that crushed his hip a decade ago, pulls from beneath a tarp in the truck bed a large can of gasoline and gives the base of the bonfire a liberal soaking. He explains his action to his mates — when the youngest one, the only white one, questions him — by first looking up at the cloud-slung sky that threatens an end to the recent streak of fair weather, and then rubbing between his thumb and a hammered, swollen forefinger a limp wing of cardboard protruding from the pile.

"Damp tonight," he says. "Be shame, the t'ing not go."

When the group of them traipses off to have a whizz in the weeds beside the gate, the Gimp stays behind. From the pockets of his faded blue work pants he pulls three cherry bombs half the size of his fist, and a three-foot length, coiled small, of artillery poppers. Harmless, noisy, and illegal on this island, like all fireworks and all firearms since the riots in '77 when Burrows and Tacklyn were hanged. Limping and huffing, he circles the bonfire pile and plants his surprises deep inside it: some waist-high, some shoulder-high, the poppers as high as he can reach.

Cash to buy the gasoline and brief instructions for its use appeared in his lunch bucket several days ago as if by magic, but such apparitions are not unusual. Cisco Suggs, former union enforcer turned freelance provocateur, has explained to him this is important work. Keeps Government, operated by brown-nosing idiots, on their toes, and Opposition — the crazies and radicals who deserve the blame they usually get — on the run. Suggs has told him he's to take orders as they come and play dumb as necessary. And he does. He and others have carried out quite a few instructions involving fire, spray paint and the wielding of lead pipe since last spring. He and others serve a variety of paying clients, but they exercise initiative, too, as he's doing now.

He shakes the last drops of gasoline from the can and wipes away his prints with a rag. From his shirt pocket he pulls a small card the length of his thumb: a Rasta's face and dreads in black ink, along with the slogan, *One God, one Aim, One Destiny: All Black men are brothers.*

He shoves the card—pinched from the dresser of his no-good son who lies in bed all day reeking of ganja, rocking to reggae and refusing to look for work—partway down the gas can's spout, curses when the banged knuckle on his forefinger breaks open again against the metal lip, then drops the can in the weeds outside the stadium's south gate before he loads his mates in the truck and drives away, towing the forklift. *Fucking fire-breathing black-assed freeloading Jamaican bastards,* he tells himself. *Dragging the black race down by association while working men are slaves to get less than they're due.* He squeezes the wheel and presses the accelerator hard.

When Marcus and Zef arrive at the National Stadium shortly before 8 p.m., the sandy field that serves as parking lot is more than half-filled with vehicles, tailgates standing open for the unloading of chairs and coolers and boom boxes and other party gear. Zef gazes avidly at the row of SUVs, Japanese versions of the American item engineered for the local market with a shorter wheel-base and right-side drive, but as tall and wide as the law will allow, all loaded with chrome and some armored with grills of roll-cage bar. After import duty, vehicles like this cost as much as a good house, and their owners are the upwardly mobile black middle class—families of the boys Zef's grown up with, gone to school with and been ostracized by. Beside them, Marcus's Bentley is odd and decrepit: once a sophisticated cream color, it's now sun-leached of all pigment and spider-veined with rust, the side view mirror held on with an inexpert local weld reinforced with a twist of baling wire. Climbing out of it, Zef addresses Marcus without looking at him. "You want to know why nobody listens to you, take a look at what you drive." He slams the door, which never closes properly, and glares at his father across the Bentley's long hood.

"We are *not* other people," Marcus snaps. He's already around the car, lifting the door and shoving the maimed latch shut. "We are not defined by what we drive —" He stops because he realizes he's lying, and already Zef's face is set into its familiar freeze frame of extravagant boredom. What can he possibly say, one sentence or two hundred, that will make his son care about the path and the principles by which he's come to stand in this weedy field with the keys to this shoddy car in his hand?

"Okay," is what he says. "I know I embarrass you. I'm sorry. But if I know what I'm doing is hopeless, and I choose to do it, does that make me a fool? Do I deserve your contempt simply for being who I am?" Zef's expression unfreezes, long enough to shift to one Marcus does not recognize, and oddly suggestive of the moment just before tears flow. "Look," Marcus says, "since you're here, come with me to the speakers' stage, I'll ask Harry if you can help throw the guy on the fire —" He doesn't know if Harry, the tourism minister, would go for this, but he's willing to ask, and he's veered into the pleasurable picture of his son's participation in it all when Zef says, "You think Harry would give me a lolly, too? Fucking get real, Marcus."

With that, he's gone, merged from sight among the people and their vehicles dressed to kill. For a moment Marcus stands looking at the lightly littered sand and flattened grass beneath his scuffed shoes, breathing slowly and deeply. He has to make a speech; he cannot afford the time nor the hemorrhage of energy that self-pity would cost him. He points his feet toward the stadium gate. Zef, who despises him, is his whole family. His father never known to him, his mother a frayed folder of snapshots, and the various aunties who raised him, related by blood or not, constituents now, seeking favors on behalf of their real sons and nephews. Zef is what he's got: a responsibility and a problem, legacy of the mistake that keeps on giving, the failed marriage to Lydia. She was the first person to anoint Marcus a radical—her hand on his thigh in political theory seminar—and then, when he borrowed against his scholarship stipend to buy her an engagement ring, the first to predict his capacity for bourgeois compromise.

He shoves his keys deep in his pants pocket and picks up his pace through the crowd. Lydia considered him a fool. When she said she'd go bonkers if she couldn't get off this effing island, he briefly and naively envisioned their brave new life together in London, some cheap flat, *some* kind of job, and he flung himself at hope and possibility. But she left anyway, by herself and secretly, while he sat in a session of Parliament. He came home hungry and hassled to baby Zef screaming in the stolid arms of the Portuguese woman who would become their housekeeper, and to Lydia's side of the closet cleared out, right down to the trash off the floor. She left him no note but the last words she spit have never left him. He pleaded, "I'll come with you," and she answered, "Sure, you might as well quit Parliament. You'll never accomplish half what you think you're destined to."

He nods at the SUV owners who glance his way. Some nod back. He is a brother, yes, but a maverick one they distrust. The white people he passes smile politely and continue their business of unloading neat picnic parcels and folding stools from their British-made Fords or sensible Toyota hatchbacks. They are always polite and as well-meaning on the surface as their practical clothes, especially when they are holding most intractably to what they are sure is theirs. His very existence makes them nervous. Born in the part of town they pretend does not exist, he went to England on scholarships they funded to assuage their guilt, and returned a barrister as well or better educated than they and armed with a dangerous appreciation of the right to dissent and the capacity of their laws to uphold it.

From the next group of whites, he hears the flat, broad intonation of Americans, overpaid expatriates banded together like pigeons to sample this latest sprinkling of local color. Nearing the gate, he comes upon the Rastas, with Ramo, six-foot-six, his mass of dreadlocks bundled into a crochet cap adding another six inches to his height, towering over his ragged brethren. Marcus doesn't see Zef orbiting Ramo and he's surprised by that.

Ramo flashes teeth as Marcus hurries past. His fist rises laconically as if, would Marcus only permit it, they'd tap knuckles, a real brothers' greeting. Marcus veers away, fists clenched against his thighs. Arrogance is too easy for Ramo. Without his own considerable help, his years of *pro bono* striving, Ramo'd still be locked in prison, or dead, but instead he accepts both Marcus's help and Zef's admiration as his due, just because he is who he is, the outcast black man Marcus's job and his ideals script him to defend.

At the stadium gate, banks of halogen lights atop tall concrete poles throw down light witheringly white and unnatural. Just inside the fence, the Somerset marching band tunes, brass and bagpipes and fifes competing. Partially blocking the front gate are several vans from the African Pentecostal churches, each vehicle stuffed past lawful capacity with school children with no other way to get here, since their working class parents have no cars, and the public buses, due to budget cuts and union pressures, no longer run in the evenings. The children filing out of the vans are a solemn line of black and brown and creamy tan faces above neatly knotted neckties and navy or burgundy or gray school blazers. The church women who've driven them touch their shoulders as they go by, counting them and admonishing good behavior. Foremost among the women is Althea Trott, her eye upon Marcus as the children pass beneath her broad palms.

He greets her, raising his own palm and evading eye contact. She does not yet know, surely, that her young cousin is dead, and he cannot tell her now, not rushing past her on his way to a speech. She has known him his whole life. She tattled on him at school, and since he entered politics she's made it her business to call him, publicly, on every mistake, every backpedal, each compromise. Already, she does not forgive him for what he's not done for her brother. When he failed to get restitution for the loss of Lemuel's legs, he got instead — as a freshman MP, no small feat — a disability benefits rider on the Pension Act. Three times he's re-secured funding for in-home help for the handicapped, and he's not given up on getting transport subsidies for seniors' healthcare appointments, but it will never be enough for her nor for the rest of the working poor, and how much more will she, and the rest of them, expect when the cousin's death and the other man's death are added to the decades-long list of woes? Hasn't he promised them already, in sixteen years of stump speeches, what no one can deliver?

A worker in a Government sash offers candy in a bucket to the boy directly beneath Althea's nose. She slaps the child's hand off the rim, then relents and lets him dig in, but pries his fist open afterwards to see how much he's taken, and makes him put half of it back. The woman with the bucket skedaddles, the children on both sides of the chastened boy look daggers at him and Althea's wide back, and she, eyes flashing and big gold earhoops swinging, points her formidable finger at Marcus.

"This fine fête costin' more than it take to run the Warwick Youth Center next year, but it closin', funding cut. Why you let these things happen, Marcus? What you doin' all day in the Parliament?"

He's escaping her, almost running through the gate, when he feels a tug at his trouser leg and looks down at a small girl in a pink dress stiff with old-fashioned crinoline, her hair in a dozen knobby braids bearing two yellow bows each. She might be three years old. Shoving her chubby fist up at him, she offers him a little flag. He kneels to take it from her, placing his hand below hers where it's choked up high on the stick, right under the red field with the British Union Jack in the corner and the island's seal rampant in the center: the lion of the Empire, a storm-tossed ship, and the motto: *Quo Fata Ferunt*. Whither fate leads us. He puts his free arm around the child to hug her, and her mother or big sister or auntie, a slinky young woman in clinging jeans and a cropped top that bares her pierced navel, appears in front of him. When he jerks his gaze from the navel to her face, he finds lovely eyes and a gleaming marceled wave drooped across one of them, and a slender hand stuck out for him to shake. He takes it, slightly leery; she is young enough to be his daughter but his body needs his mind to remind him of that.

She bends to kiss his cheek. While he's getting up with the child in his arms to shield his insides from more of this woman's affection, she says, still sheathing his hand in hers, "All my family admire so much what you standing for, Mr. Passjohn. You all the time standing up, telling people what they need to hear."

Somebody bumps him hard from behind. He and the young woman and the baby he's holding are obstructing the crowd's passage through the gate. A voice says, "Goddamn politician," but he can't tell who. Althea's voice, however, carries like God's across the surging crowd. "Girl," she says, "Marcus Passjohn not doin' one damn thing for you that costin' him more than those words he so full of."

He sets the child and her flag at the feet of the attractive mother or sister or auntie and flees. Is he not just an obvious fool but a well-known coward? Althea's known him so long she might as well be family, and earlier this evening he walked away from a dead member of her family, and he's without the courage now to tell her so.

He reaches the speakers' platform and climbs the shaky metal stair. He seats himself on a folding chair slick with humidity, in a row of three such chairs. Shifting uncomfortably at the cold damp seeping through the worn fabric of the seat of his suit pants, his palm cupped self-consciously over the tear at the knee he patched earlier in the car, Marcus surveys the crowd he's about to address. On the grass around the bonfire or on the bleachers against the fence, people have established neighborhoods, their music and party supplies or lack thereof broadcasting their allegiances and affinities. In every neighborhood the people are enjoying their suppers and preparing to endure the speeches, waiting for the fire to be lit and the fun to begin. Marcus bows his head, Althea's words ringing inside it in chorus with Lydia's, Zef's, Ramo's. All of them doubt him deeply, and if he does not act bravely tonight when it's his turn to speak, he'll have given everyone the more reason to do so.

Underneath the east side bleachers, Peyton Langston is waiting exactly where Zef instructed him to.

Overhead, people shout and gab and sing, boom boxes blare hip-hop and salsa and pop rock, all of it loud, and the aluminum planks clatter like doors slamming as feet stomp up and down. The garbage people toss and spit falls like nasty human rain on Peyton's white blond hair and the tight square of bright red blanket on which he crouches. Briefly Zef feels sorry for this kid, who's a baby, really, clueless and scared as a stray kitten he might be about to torture—except Zef has never done a thing like that, never even wanted to. He does, however, want to hurt Peyton Langston, even though he's not really sure why.

He offers Peyton the brother's greeting he's tried to teach him at Somers Academy for Boys, where they met in September. Fists tap, fingers hook, separate then snap. Right hands, always, never left. But Peyton screws it up, mixes up the motions, like usual. Zef grabs him by the shoulder and—his own left hand in his pocket, thumb callus circling its complement, the button's bevel, as it does a hundred times at least in any day—pulls him deeper into the weedy dark behind the bleachers, Peyton clutching the red blanket like a life preserver.

"Where the hell'd that come from?" Zef asks.

"My bed." Peyton's chewing his upper lip. "I brought it for me and my parents to sit on, so I could find them. But my mother said not to put it on the ground."

"You brought your parents? I told you to come alone."

"How else could I get here?" Peyton's voice rises and cracks, and even in the near darkness Zef can see him redden with shame. "They didn't want to come. My dad was tired from work and my mom was sad. I had to lie. I told them I had to come, for a grade, in school."

"That's a start," Zef tells him. "Lying is good when it gets you what you want. You notice that about parents and teachers, right? They want the truth out of you, but lies are fine for them, any time it helps them out. So learn to lie, boy. It's all part of it."

He's undertaken Peyton as a project; that's how he's explained it to himself, to date, what he's doing messing with this wimpy white boy. Skinny, sissy American white boy. At Somers Peyton was practically dead meat, even the geeks and morons picked on him. But Zef has put a stop to that. He enjoys kicking ass when he knows he can win. And for that service, he's acquired Peyton's loyalty...for whatever that will turn out to be worth.

"So, whatcha you bring me?" Zef asks.

Peyton empties his pockets. He's brought candy from home, leftover Halloween candy, he explains. His mother didn't know Halloween doesn't really happen on the island, except among Americans.

Zef says, "Did you steal it?" Peyton nods, lying hesitantly. Zef divides the candy evenly after choosing the pieces he wants—all the Reese's Cups.

While they eat the loot, in the field beyond the bleachers a band is playing and some of the people sing along: *God Save the Queen*. Others sing other things, some of the lyrics dirty, or just keep talking. The Guy Fawkes Night show has started. Zef is eating the candy the way he habitually does—the reason this is his favorite kind—snapping the waxy chocolate pie in half and scooping out the greasy filling with the tip of his tongue. He knows Peyton, who isn't eating his own stash, is watching, and he takes special pleasure in tracking the boy's progression from staring to squirming.

"Why you eat them like that?" Peyton blurts finally, when the third chocolate shell hits the dirt. "Why don't you just eat plain peanut butter?"

Zef shrugs. "I like this better."

"You're wasting the chocolate."

"You want it?" Zef nudges a shell with his foot.

"No!"

"Why not?"

"I don't want what you throw down."

"You too good to eat my trash?"

"Yeah," says Peyton, then because Zef just bores a stare into him, he changes his answer. "No."

Zef laughs at him. "You too stupid to know what you think?"

Peyton says nothing. Zef is aware of his own gorge rising, the thrill of riding rage this close to fear of what he might let happen. He can feel the sharp corners of the envelope folded in his inside jacket pocket: a letter, a fucking typewritten letter from his fucking long-lost mother, gouging the flesh of his chest, and it's too much. He can't contain it.

"Fuck you!" he shouts, loud enough that the people nearest them are silenced and stare. "Fuck you, you little cunt, are you stupid or are you really really really retarded!"

Peyton stands up. He sets his teeth into a tab of skin alongside his thumbnail, and rips.

Zef stands. He's taller by half a head, and fifteen pounds heavier, all the weight muscle, gift of puberty, which he has and Peyton does not. "You're lying," he shouts, advancing on Peyton.

"I'm not."

"You are. Stop lying, you little shit."

He spits in his palms and rubs them together. Holds his two hands out, palms up, to Peyton, who obviously doesn't know what to do.

"Gimme your hands. Put them here."

Slowly Peyton places his palms on Zef's, and Zef squeezes them hard. He feels the ligaments shift and the bones separate.

"Does that hurt?"

"No. I mean, *yes.*" The answer changes and the second word's a yelp because Zef squeezes even harder.

"Don't lie," he demands.

"It hurts!"

Zef lets go. "Shake it off. Don't cry," he tells the baby. Peyton flaps his hands obediently. His eyes brim with tears; the liquid gleams in errant light from the bank of halogen bulbs atop the stadium wall twenty yards behind them. Zef presents his palms once more. "Again," he says. Peyton hesitates, then gives. Zef takes a different grip. Laces their fingers together, then twists to the outside so their wrists are on top. He pushes Peyton's palms hard with his, bending, forcing the kid's hands backward so hard he thinks he may snap the wrists. He wants to snap those wrists. The voice of his father crackles through a loud speaker, calling for people's attention.

"It hurts!" Peyton whimpers.

His father has withheld letters his mother has sent him. Returned them to sender. Her letter says so. He would have withheld this one and so she sent it by way of someone else. She would like him to visit her, in fucking Holland, to see if they can have now the relationship they could not have earlier. Zef hates them, his parents; they are each of them a major issue to themselves and nothing to him. He pushes harder, and veins stand out blue in Peyton Langston's pale wrists.

"It hurts! Let go. Please," he begs.

This game is called Mercy. Boys play it at school, and the one that cries give-up is a coward.

"What do you want?" Peyton cries at Zef over the noise of music and talking and his father's voice pouring out of loud speakers.

"I want you to mind me," Zef shouts, as close as he can get to the white boy's face.

The boy rips his coward's hands free and runs off. Out from behind the bleachers and into the crowd filling the center of the stadium, clutching the blanket he pretended he thought would protect him. Zef shakes his head, spits on the ground, tells himself his mother's a liar and a whore and his father a fucking loser who married and lost a liar and a whore. He spits again, and gives chase.

Marcus Passjohn suffers an attack of severe indigestion the

moment it is his turn, third and last, to speak. Acid boils up his esophagus, threatening to spill into his mouth. His belly gurgles and pain radiates through his bowels. But he grips the podium with both hands and thrusts his face toward the glaring lights. He fills his lungs and booms an orator's voice through the P.A. system. He will make them listen, he is resolved to do so.

When Harry Pitkin, the tourism minister, kicked things off, he praised the Queen and the tradition of parliamentary rule, and some people pretended to listen. They like Harry well enough; he knows to keep it brief and bland. When the Minister of Justice Isaiah Barnes took the podium, the crowd ignored him, and Isaiah, former linebacker for a black college in the American South, ignored them right back. Sweating beneath his weight of flesh, subbing for the Premier who has better parties to attend that night, Isaiah belted out Government's party line: Prosperity Earned with Hard Work and Cooperation. He added a few cheers of his own: Market forces call the plays when global commerce is the field. Hard times require hard choices. And so on. When he finished, he glanced at Marcus, then cribbed, in conclusion, the American hard line: Those who stand not with us stand against us. But now Marcus has his back to Isaiah's sly smile and Harry's fretful one.

We have got some problems, and they are getting worse, he begins.

The volume of the crowd's inattention drops suddenly and sharply. He's surprised them. For a minute or two, they'll be his.

He invokes Guy Fawkes. Quick, before he loses their brief attention, he tells the real story of the real man. His zealot's stake in the rights of his persecuted people. His death — called by the Crown a service to God — as state's example to dangerous, conniving Papists. Fawkes was tortured, hanged, cut down alive and disemboweled: genitals, bowels and beating heart cut out and held up to a cheering crowd.

The real Guy's death is forgotten, but his scapegoat's guilt is a party.

Some in the crowd stand up and shout at Marcus to sit down. He does not.

He serves no platitudes and no cant. He hands his people, black and white, their history. He asks them point-blank if they remember Erskine Burrows and Ladry Tacklyn. How they died, not so long ago, only twenty-five years ago.

Two ordinary black men, hanged in Casemates Prison, for killing white men.

Someone calls out, in his orator's pause that follows, "Hey, lighten up, Marcus. You killin' de party, don' you know it?"

A mix of hissing, stamping, singing and applause fills the stadium. The crowd sounds like the sea building to a storm. He's said out loud what is never said, not publicly, and not in the presence of both races. Behind him on the platform, Harry Pitkin calls his name softly. Harry, a well-behaved black man who made sure Marcus was invited to speak tonight because Harry believes what he was taught in civics class fifty years ago, that the function of the loyal opposition is to voice the opposing view politely, and then sit down. He says, urgently, "Marcus, no, don't do this, please."

He turns to Harry. "Trust me," he says, knowing that Harry cannot. He glimpses Isaiah's face, some light of satisfaction playing just beneath its sweat-glossed surface, and Marcus feels forewarned. Isaiah is always dangerous, and tonight he is in some way armed.

Marcus plays the crowd. They shout at him, and he calls out to them, *Do you remember? Don't you think about it still? Why was your governor shot?* Erskine Burrows, he reminds them, wrote a letter that told everybody precisely why.

He did it to reveal the black people to themselves.

They are surprised; he reads this from the pause in the shouting. Some of them are too young to remember and others do not believe him. The confession letter, published in the paper at the time, is forgotten or suppressed, the ravings of a madman killer.

He told us that we stood in the streets and cried for a white man who did not care if we lived or died — like we would not cry for our own fathers. He told us...

Marcus pauses. He's seen his son Zef running across the field beyond the unlit bonfire. Zigzagging through the crowd in pursuit of a white boy with a shock of white-blond hair. He watches them a full three seconds until they disappear beneath the west side bleachers, then he slams a door on how deeply this disturbs him. Zef is not, at least, with the Rastas, standing silent in a group by the south gate where Ramo, so much taller than the rest, stares straight at Marcus and, when their gaze locks, lets his fist rise slowly to its full extension above his head.

Marcus fills his lungs.

Burrows told us it has ever been the colonialist's tactic to set black people against each other. To conquer us with our own division. He meant with his death to show us that division. He meant with his death to pull us together. Did he succeed?

No answer. There is stirring, sifting, resistance. But no answer.

He supplies it.

Burrows did succeed. He brought us together. Six thousand of you signed the petition for clemency that Her Majesty was advised to ignore so that executions might proceed and racial harmony be restored. And your response when Burrows and Tacklyn were hanged? You remember this. You do. A riot.

The crowd ripples. More people are standing up, neighborhoods consolidating or breaking apart as some whistle and stamp their feet and others pack their gear to leave. The police, clustered at the gates, are spreading, a dark blue stain. Marcus blocks out everything but his purpose. Lifts his hands, palms out, envisioning himself blessing this crowd. His two gold rings—a class ring from the island's one black prep school on his right hand and on his left, the parliamentary signet ring he bought himself to replace his wedding band—these tell him by what right he speaks in this way.

Two more men have died today, he confesses to them. *Two black men. It's not a riot we need in response. Not murder. Not destruction. We need truth, we need justice and we need mercy...*

From somewhere near the south gate, the crowd parts like

the Biblical waters. And up the rift a foursome of people come running toward Marcus, something elongated and lumpy, like a body, a body wrapped in rags, borne on their shoulders.

He is on the verge of raising his hands again to conclude. He is on the verge of saying: We *have* got some problems, and they *are* getting worse. Familiar, unsolved problems, our ancient, bitter grudge we now must face together —

But he's cut off by the arrival of the life-size effigy of the traitor Guy Fawkes, the scapegoat Guy Fawkes, speeding past him through the seething crowd toward the bonfire on the shoulders of those four men running. They halt, they fling the guy high. He hangs a heavy moment in the air and then snags on a broken plank to dangle there like a broke-neck corpse, and somebody lights the pyre.

The combustive roar and the wall of flame that erupt then shut everybody up. It's no bonfire, it's a conflagration. Explosions, one… two…three, punctuate the seconds it takes Marcus to grab Harry and pull him down behind the podium for cover. Gunfire follows, a rapid series of sharp pops seemingly coming out of the fire. Sliding face first into the grit coating the metal floor of the speakers' platform, Marcus has time to ask himself, *Where is Zef now?* And the stadium goes dark. All the lights, all at once.

He wonders next about bombs. About the scope of this disaster. People running, screaming. Chaos. Lying on the speakers' platform thirty yards from the fire, Marcus feels its heat coat him like paint. He'll have to get up and try to leave; they may all be burned alive. He is just shifting his thoughts toward who might be responsible for this and why, when, just as suddenly as it disintegrated, order starts to reassert itself. The lights come on. Police bullhorns announce a prank by someone who will be apprehended and punished. Slowly, Marcus and Harry get up. The bonfire is blazing, flames shooting abnormally high but contained within the drooping yellow tape that circles it.

"Firecrackers. Some fucking idiot put firecrackers in the goddamn pile." This is Isaiah, hands on hips, watching the burn and the fire hoses already trained on it.

Harry's fingers dig into Marcus's elbow. His other hand is pressed to his chest where his breath is rasping; he's asthmatic. He says, "Marcus, this your work? Your idea to bust things up, grab everybody's attention?"

"The hell, Harry, what do you mean?" Doesn't Harry know, after all these years, what he would and wouldn't do? And the guy, the blaze, the lights-out, the whole thing interrupted *him*, kept *him* from saying more when more and more of the crowd was maybe starting to lean his way. He spins to face Isaiah but finds only his back.

At the edge of the platform the Minister of Justice pumps his big arms like a drum major at the Somerset marching band, and the members who've not scattered advance into the mêlée like militia, blasting *God Save the Queen* off key. People still run and push; there will be injuries, for some have been knocked to the ground. But no bombs and no guns are in the stadium, and no terrorists either, at least not of the foreign sort.

He lets his palm land with a slap in the center of Isaiah's broad, sweaty back. "Where do you stand, Isaiah, on the issue of dead men in dumpsters?"

The man's response is a portrait of surprise and dismay, such a portrait, in fact, that Marcus feels certain it's a mask. Isaiah says, his own big palms patting the air, "Marcus, man, calm down. I got no idea what you're talking about."

"If you don't," Marcus tells him, studying the firelight reflected in the man's enlarged pupils, "people who work for you do. There's too much trouble on this island lately, and too many tidy solutions favoring your views, for me to believe your hands are clean."

Isaiah shrugs. "You see dirt everywhere, Marcus. And that's typical of you. Like Harry just pointed out, if there's any kind of trouble on the floor in Parliament or down on the docks, nobody has to look far to find your hand in it."

Marcus makes a connection, so obvious, so unexpected, it almost makes him gasp. "You're looking to pin this fiasco tonight on me, aren't you?"

Isaiah says, speaking slowly, as if thinking his own way through the connection, "Bum luck, Passjohn, mess like this going down during your speech. Folks may well associate the two, just like Harry did." Isaiah nods, agreeing with himself. "I think they may," he says, head bobbing, words coming more quickly. "And, yeah, that would be a shame. Entirely undeserved, although" — his voice trails off, then rises — "if I was asked, I'd have to say you did let loose some fire power, talking the way you did."

His head bobs again, and hitching up the bright yellow braces he wears instead of a belt, he hurries away toward the VIP gate at the back of the stadium where his brand new Isuzu SUV, with custom American-import 22-inch chrome rims, is waiting.

Marcus watches him, feeling the raw result of acid reflux in his throat and his stomach. What people will remember about tonight *is* the way it ended, with trouble and a trick, and if anyone needs help in associating his speech with fear and stress and ruined fun, the justice minister will need only a little help from his friends in the media, to take care of it.

He gazes out across the field at the subsiding chaos. It's begun raining, a fine steady drizzle, creating mud and more reason for some folks to go home. Harry and his minions are moving through the people bottlenecked at the two main gates, wielding the candy buckets among adults and children alike. A thick canvas hose spews water at the bonfire from a pump truck that Marcus now recalls as parked strategically nearby throughout the evening. The more liquored-up and excitable members of the crowd have recognized a chance to party heartier than they expected, and in the last minutes before the fire's put all the way out, whatever's handy and not tied down is going into it: bottles, trash, shirts, and some people's chairs and coolers. The police, and not just the bobbies but members of the Regiment, the local guard, demonstrate equal excitement, discouraging the chair-throwers with billy clubs, and imposing order at the exits. Someone seems to have anticipated the need for heightened security tonight, and planned ahead for arrests. The rotating blue light of a paddy wagon at the south gate tinges the faces of the officers rounding up the Rastas.

Marcus steps down from the stage and starts across the

ruined field to intervene, or try to, on behalf of Ramo and others — and to find Zef, so they can both go home. Wearily, he wonders if tonight he mixed up his heart with his mind. Let his heart seize his throat like it used to in his youth, the way he and Lydia did in the heat of their leftist passion when they were twenty, believing that just because they yearned to, they possessed the power to make things change. Call down the lightning, and watch it strike.

Lost in thought, he nearly steps on a white boy sitting in the trampled grass, head between his knees, crying, a muddy red blanket clutched to his chest.

The boy's platinum hair is familiar. Marcus can't be sure this is the same boy Zef was chasing, but that would fit, given the boy is alone now and upset. He kneels, raises the boy's face and sees that he's scared and bruised but not seriously hurt. He's grey-eyed, skinny, still a child, younger than Zef.

"What's your name?" he asks, and the boy tells him. Peyton Langston. The accent unmistakably American.

"You know my son Zef?" The boy's eyes, which had sparked with trust and relief at the first question, now shift away. He knows what not to tell, and that, too, fits with Zef. "Where is Zef?" Marcus insists, and the boy answers, "I don't know."

Marcus nods. He lifts the boy to his feet by one arm. "Lose your parents?" he asks. "You did come here with some adult?"

"My parents. Both of them."

"They'll be at the gate now. With the police," Marcus says. "That's where I'm going, so you come along."

The drizzle's turned to rain now. Marcus's suit is soaked through, and the boy, snuffing tears, following him like a puppy, is so drenched his hair drips. He steps on the back of Marcus's shoe, apologizes and hurries up alongside him, then bumps his arm and bumps it again until Marcus realizes the boy *is* like a dog, asking mutely to be taken under that arm. He obliges. He curves his arm lightly across the thin back, and the child relaxes.

At the gate, in the strobing blue light from the paddy

wagon, everything glitters because of the rain. The droplets dangling in Ramo's dreadlocks. The steel cuffs on his wrists. The question in his eyes as he looks quickly from Marcus to the white boy and back. Zef's eyes — of *course* he's with Ramo; where else would he be? — flash anger, and Marcus removes his arm from the boy's shoulders. He asks Officer Poole, a dark Bahamian who owes him a favor or two, "These Rastamen really in need of a free meal and a Government bed?" Poole averts his eyes. The captain, he mumbles, has put the order in already. They're to make arrests, tonight, of the most likely suspects. Marcus is mustering the argument that such an order is already a violation of rights and proper procedure, when he sees the white boy's parents bearing down on him.

Peyton surges toward them. The man, short and wide, shouldering his way through police and gawkers, steams, his scalp glowing pink through his thinning, sandy hair. Peyton bypasses him completely. The woman hurrying along behind him, the source of Peyton's pale hair and fine bones, has been crying hard.

Peyton's head and the dirty red blanket bang against her chest. Her arms close around the boy, her face fierce with emotion. The husband steps forward, all business, on top of things. "Darrell Langston," he says, extending his hand. Marcus shakes it, introduces himself, and notes Langston's look — the man had no doubt who he is. While the wife and son cling together, Marcus watches the American assess what he's walked into: Poole's evident discomfort, Ramo's uncowed stance on the paddy wagon's stair, and Marcus's uneasy position in between. Langston's glance lands on Zef and flicks back to Marcus, taking in, perhaps, the resemblance of their broad noses and tall brows but also Zef's far lighter complexion and green eyes. And then the man is brusque: American thanks and good-bye. Marcus nods. It's enough. He's done nothing but walk a boy across a field, but the woman doesn't get it.

"You *found* him," she insists. "*Thank* you. I can't tell you how much...." Her husband's introducing her now — "my wife, Lucy" — but she talks right through it, ignoring the fact that it's raining, everybody's wet and her husband's ready to go, his two hands on his son's shoulders, turning him. She's giddy with strain and relief. And, despite the tear trails, the reddened eyes, the wet hair, she's beautiful—in the blond and delicate white-woman way to which Marcus should not be susceptible but still sometimes is. She's as lost and lonely as her son was a few minutes ago. She's transparent right to the heart.

"It was nothing," he says politely. "I've done nothing that anyone wouldn't do."

"Oh, no," she says, her voice brimming with more of her abundant emotion. "You've been purposefully and determinedly helpful. You tried to help everyone here tonight. I heard that."

Her passion, her disheveled, spun-glass hair, the tears she can't stop, her absolute incomprehension of the complexity of his situation—Marcus can't help it. He bursts out laughing.

Tomorrow's *Royal Gazette* will give him no quarter. That he's a fool will be the best thing the editorials will say. More likely he'll be labeled a civic traitor. He will read his press and writhe at what his burst of passion has cost him. But tonight, while the American woman's smile trembles between reverence and self-doubt, he stops laughing and helps himself to a small comfort. He takes her hand, in front of everyone, and pats it with his other one.

"Thank you," he tells her warmly. He looks her in the eye, apologizing there for the amusement he's displayed at her expense. Still holding her hand, squeezing it gently between both of his, he says, "I want to believe you are right."

Her face, he notes, now holds a question. She wants to know more. She wants to understand just what he means. And he wants to tell her. But when Ramo—behind her, above them both on the paddy wagon stair—snorts with derision, he watches her go, following her husband and her son through the stadium gate into the night. When she turns back, once, to look in his direction, he raises his hand, if not to wave good-bye then in salute to her beauty and her open heart.

5

Kenrick Desmond, young lion in Bermuda's Parliament, unofficial whip to Passjohn's Opposition, enters his daily practice of aikido. He is a small handsome man with a hard body of neat angles. With rigor of purpose, intensity of focus, he raises and directs his *chi*. One curved arm rises, the hand with thumb and forefinger touching, a delicate eyelet drawing energy up and out.

It's dawn, the morning after the bonfire at Guy Fawkes was gasolined by unknown parties. The sun lifts blood red from the sea, and Kenrick breathes its fire deep into his, visualizes their fusion, and directs the result to meet the force his opponent flings at him. In the vision in which he acts he does not fear his enemy. He does not, actually, see an embodied foe.

Kenrick is his own enemy at the moment. Two days ago his lesser self seized control of his better one, breaching the discipline on which he prides himself, and in a stew of satisfaction and repugnance Kenrick placed into Zef Passjohn's hands a letter from his mother, the lily-white Achilles' heel in Marcus Passjohn's black armor. Although she is ex-wife by a dozen years, her politically embarrassing reality lives on, in Marcus's public image and Zef's too-pale visage. Her cover letter to Kenrick reached him from her knowledge of his role as "functionary" to her ex-husband; she describes herself as "minor functionary" in the World Court at The Hague. "You don't know me," Lydia wrote, "and to the extent you do, you will have heard only ill of me, but Stefan is my son as well as Marcus's, and I believe that as his mother I am entitled to the chance to find out if we can now have the relationship that so many circumstances made impossible when he was younger."

Kenrick's breathing within his practice is slow and deep. He draws breath down to the seat of power buried in the loins, then raises it up along the spine. Elemental strength rising. Lightened and clarified: this is what he should feel and what he doesn't. He feels some odd pity for Lydia, who does not even know the name her son goes by now. He feels, too, a twist of shame, for he has through secret transmission of that letter betrayed a man whose values and dedication he admires, all because…he does not like that man's son. Because…what a fucking relief it would be if that kid, a budding delinquent, would just take off. Turn into his mother's problem.

Kenrick expels breath. How is it a twelve-year-old boy can seem an adversary? Cause a grown man to act like a kid? Kenrick prides himself on adherence to aikido's strict mental and physical discipline; it has kept him away from drugs, in school, and his principles are now his path. He did not commit this treachery without devoting to the conundrum of his motivation considerable thought. He sought advice from his oldest friend and ally on the island, his impoverished mother's best friend Althea Trott. She said, about the letter, about the boy Zef, "Give it to him. He old enough to make up he own mind." Kenrick took her advice. He did so because it suited him. Her motivation, he knows, is not pure either. She dislikes Zef. She, too, has a lesser self whose appetites she conceals although, unlike him, Kenrick thinks, she is not ashamed of what convention requires she hide.

Kenrick concludes his practice, acknowledging to himself that today he failed and that the cause of the failure is his moral impurity. He showers, razors a fresh demarcation between his pencil-line beard and the unquestionably deep brown skin of his jaw. He dresses in a designer suit of taupe merino wool and a collarless silk shirt in black. He puts down food on the stoop for his cat, Sensei, and bolt-locks the door of his flat in Shelly Bay, a working class neighborhood, racially mixed. Riding his scooter into town with the rest of the morning commuters he keeps his lips closed to avoid a bug in the teeth and recalls in detail a dream he's had four times now.

Men who live in suits, boxy suits. Men without a practice, who mistake the source of true power, who think their own petty force, and plenty of it, is the way to move the world. In the dream, a massive crowd of such men extends to the horizons. Curiously, Kenrick cannot recall any faces; skin color has not registered in his memory. Clearly he recalls them surrounding an opening, black as soot, and he knows he's seen Ramo Wylie go through it, bent double. He himself is drawn toward it but does not move. He senses himself seated deep in an enveloping chair, and tilts his face down to see its thickly padded arms, luxuriously upholstered in tufted silk damask. This is good, but not-good is what curls in his lap, a thick, dark, golden-hooded snake, scales sighing as its coils shift, flesh pulling across muscular flesh.

When he leaves the office that same day, Kenrick seeks out Marcus — who's not turned up at work — in his home Rose Hill, and finds him lying in a canvas slingback chair on the veranda, a bottle of dark rum and a bucket of ice beside him. Down the hillside in front of the two men is a vista from a tourist brochure: rose beds lovingly tended by Marcus's Portuguese gardener, the broad lime-washed roofs of his prosperous white neighbors, and a bristle of masts in the Royal Yacht Club basin.

Marcus says dryly, without lifting his head from the chair's cradle, "You're willing to be seen consorting with the devil who put the island's entire populace at risk on Guy Fawkes night?"

In reply Kenrick quotes from the bad press Marcus alludes to. *"The Honorable Mr. Passjohn's reckless and incendiary tongue."* He laughs at the absurdity of it and waits for Marcus to do the same. When Marcus doesn't, Kenrick waits for him to offer a chair and a drink. This happens only after half a minute of brooding silence, after which Marcus jumps as if he's been poked, starts to get out of the chair, has difficulty, slumps back to his original position and says, "Get yourself a glass from the bar. Please." The bottle Marcus is holding out to him is one-third gone.

Thereafter, while a swollen orange sun sinks into the sea beyond the dark curve of the western parishes where Marcus once helped uncles and cousins rake and burn beach trash for part of their living, Kenrick and Marcus drink together, sharing what they know so far on the fallout from Guy Fawkes Night. The police have only an empty gas can, a dry rag and a little card they call "an item of Rastafarian propaganda." Ramo and a handful of his brethren remain locked up on the new precautionary detention policy Government recently railroaded through Parliament—despite Isaiah's flubbing his ghostwritten speech so badly members of his own party laughed behind their hands. Even with no charges filed against the 'miscreants' (that being the word that caused Isaiah's delivery to stumble, inspiring in Marcus the regrettable satisfaction of providing him, audibly from across the aisle, the correct pronunciation), the Justice Minister can reliably expect that Marcus will file as counsel of record, publicly tightening his association with a convicted arsonist and a band of suspected political terrorists.

What's still missing in Government's smear campaign is a direct accusation—something anyone can at any time leak and then nominally retract while it does its insidious work— that the Honorable Marcus Passjohn arranged for a Rasta to sabotage the rally as part of what the media has already labeled "the Opposition's call to violence and racial hatred." The groundwork for such exaggerated extrapolation has already been laid in the response of Government, the press, and the union itself to Marcus's cautious and bland statement to a reporter a few months back in support of the working man's *theoretical* right to strike; this on the occasion when Isaiah, suddenly for reasons neither man can so far fathom, undertook to break up the longstanding practice of kickback collusion between union management and customs officers. Union leaders howled for Marcus to defend them from Government oppression but he offered only that mere rote mouthing of Marxist cant two lines long. Then, in revenge or in simple appropriation of his public image, the union and the black social clubs demonstrated at the airport and the conference hotel on the day a Government-Commerce task force held its Three Worlds Conference on international business development in Bermuda, waving placards of their Lion of the Working Man's Rights, Marcus Passjohn. He not only wasn't present, but had not been informed of the action.

Marcus lifts his glass of rum to his lips and sips. An ice cube pops as dark liquid coats it, and the first tree frog of the evening chimes from the hibiscus bushes growing flush with the veranda's slate lip. "I issued a rebuttal," he says. A counterspin pointing out every misrepresentation in the Guy Fawkes story, impugning both the reporter's and the newspaper's motives.

Kenrick replies, "You've got to admire Isaiah's nerve. I mean, he's equally undeterred by the truth and by the considerable risk of destabilizing social order. What he's set off with the union—and my guess is the dead guys in the dumpster are related to that—may have blowback he ultimately can't handle, but he's giving it his linebacker all, isn't he? If he can just neutralize you, all his troubles will be over. Or so he thinks."

"Neutralize me." Marcus empties his glass and swallows. He heaves himself clear of the chair, paces the length of the veranda, rests a bony shoulder against a thin cedar column supporting its roof. Always a lean man, Marcus in recent months has headed toward gaunt. His eyes have hollowed, he's restless, and he's become prone to that bitter brooding Kenrick observed when he arrived. He stands up. He feels doubly disloyal—about the letter and about his excess of jocularity as to political attacks that clearly have come to seem very, very personal to Marcus.

Kenrick leans against the other side of the cedar post,

willing both himself and the older man into the kind of companionable moment that used to arise spontaneously. He says, "It's confusing, isn't it? Hard to know sometimes what will really help people."

For some minutes they are quiet. The tree frogs' trilling grows cacophonous, lights from the windows down the hillside flood dark lawns, and in the basin yachts sway at their moorings, steel halyards clicking rhythmically against aluminum masts. The evening breeze is unusually stiff because a late-season tropical storm is churning past, three hundred miles offshore.

"Tell me I'm a fool," Marcus says abruptly, turning to thrust his empty glass at Kenrick.

Startled, Kenrick taps the glass gently with own, half-filled. "To fools," he says, raising his free hand to rest on Marcus's shoulder. "Two of them. May our ways and our kind prosper."

When the French doors behind them swing open, Kenrick expects to see Zef and knows he will need to leave quickly. But the figure in the doorway is only Marcus's housekeeper, Mrs. Alvarra, the Portuguese gardener's widowed sister.

In her thickly accented English, she announces she is leaving for the day. Marcus bids her goodnight, but she persists in the doorway, saying, finally, "Your son does not come home yet."

Marcus, still at the edge of the veranda, answers without looking at her, "That's not unusual."

"You come inside. Your dinner is ready a long time now," she says, and Kenrick almost laughs aloud at the high-handed manner in which she issues this order.

"Mrs. Alvarra," Marcus says, his voice patient, "I am busy right now."

Kenrick follows her glance from Marcus's back to the ice bucket and the bottle of rum near it. Afterwards she stares stolidly into Kenrick's eyes, making it clear he should not be here.

"Your son is telling me this morning Ramo Wylie is again in the prison," she says to Marcus.

"Not prison," he snaps. "Ramo is in jail, in town, not at Casemates. He's not been charged nor tried."

Mrs. Alvarra replies, "I think Zef will be going there to see him. Missing more school."

The housekeeper is at least sixty and barely half Marcus's size. Yet she seems to feel no compunction about expressing her judgment of him, one Kenrick thinks takes too little account of what a natural-born pain in the ass the kid in question is.

"Your son is telling me this morning he will keep Ramo out of the prison if you do not."

"He's a child," Marcus says. "There's nothing he can do. Except make trouble."

"Yes, all the time he is making more trouble. And you do nothing to change this."

Kenrick sees the flare in Marcus's eyes. But instead of setting the old woman straight, he ushers her into the house where they will, Kenrick hopes, settle it in a way that returns to Marcus the dignity he needs and deserves.

When he first met Marcus sixteen years ago, he himself was sixteen and newly in love with the discipline of aikido he'd discovered at the Warwick Youth Center where Marcus, a liberal barrister of thirty-one, appeared at a victory reception hosted by the black and union coalition that had just elected him to Parliament for the first time. He was, in those days, a shining man. That is how Kenrick remembers him, and how he prefers to think of him still. The white wife at his side, her mouth and her spine both straight lines, her blue eyes as chilly as her porcelain complexion — she puzzled and irritated many people, but Marcus was vivid. Exuding energy and sincerity, his hand always reaching for contact, his smile ready and 100-watts, every time. Skin tone squarely in the warm brown middle, dark enough to be real, light enough not to scare the white votes he had to have. He wore a conservative British suit, but kept his hair in a modest Afro — just enough out of style, in '85, to be a statement. Folks glad-handed him like he was a preacher, but what came out of his mouth — Kenrick sensed it even then when he was an ignorant kid — was more than the right words. Behind the words was a powerful mind, a will to match it, and an inner fire that drew the right people as well as some of the wrong ones straight to him.

He had wanted to be among those at Marcus's side. At twenty-five, he finished the schooling paid for by his American father, a navy man who'd not married his mother. He returned to the island to stand for Parliament and found himself a joke. He had a glib tongue and a graduate degree in business that no one on the island seemed then to understand. He'd tried to talk his way into either party or the ministry of finance. "I got an MBA at Wharton. I interned on Wall Street, for godsake," he told them. The officials he talked to had no idea what he was offering them. Only Marcus listened. Over forty by that time, divorced from the white wife and beleaguered already by the son's behavior problems, he pushed his chair away from the dusty chaos sliding from the desk to the floor of his tiny office, rubbed an eye plagued with an infected tear duct, and wiped the back of his hand on suit pants that were ten years out of date and badly needed pressing. "Talk to me," he said. "Teach me what the capitalists taught you."

The stiff shore breeze has clocked around by ninety degrees, the air turning fresh. Sheets of rain blow across the veranda, driving Kenrick out of his reverie and into the house through the doors Marcus now holds open.

Inside, Marcus fetches him a towel. Mrs. Alvarra has left. Kenrick sees the headlights of her car swinging across the dark front yard as she reverses to leave the drive, cutting the wheel sharply, stepping hard on the gas. She's going home in a bad mood. Kenrick is patting his clothes and joking with Marcus about his sudden wetting, when the French doors again swing open.

This time it is Zef standing there, and he is not particularly wet, despite the downpour just beyond the veranda's sloping roof.

"Where have you been?" Marcus asks sharply.

"Outside," replies Zef. The boy's hand, shoved deep in his pants pocket, twitches as if he's rubbing a coin, a habit Kenrick has noticed before and which makes him wonder if what the boy really carries and caresses is a knife.

"Yes, bloody hell, I see that," Marcus says. "You were hiding — eavesdropping — by the looks of it." He steps toward Zef and points at the dry front of his windbreaker. "I want to know where have you *been*, really, before hiding under the eaves listening to what's none of your business."

"Out," says Zef.

A smile flickers behind the boy's sullen mask, and Kenrick has seen him bait his father too many times to endure a replay. He will leave them to it, he thinks. Maybe they will argue and Lydia will rise from that letter he put in Zef's hand and snatch him off the island, leaving Marcus in the clear for Kenrick to guide and influence and maybe save — but he stubs a toe against a white leather couch and very nearly falls to his knees.

He pulls himself up in front of Zef's smirk and feels his own fists form. But Marcus has seen the smirk, too, and taller than his boy by a head, he grabs Zef by the forehead, squeezing the thick waving hair up off the brow.

"You've been driving that damn scooter from Ramo's," he says. "I see the mark from the helmet. Was that white boy with you? The Langston boy?"

Kenrick, half way to the door halts. *White boy?*

Zef twists clear of his father's grip. Marcus says, "I want to know where you've been."

"Riding 'round," Zef says diffidently. "With that white boy."

"What in hell are you up to?" Marcus's voice is rising. "That kid's a baby. You're going to get him in trouble you're not big enough to handle."

"We *are* in trouble. Already. For skipping." Zef pulls from his jacket pocket a crumpled note. "Headmaster wants to see you. Says I'm causing trouble with the white boys."

He drops the paper on the couch. More bait, Kenrick thinks, and Marcus, his hand drawing back to strike his son, is rising to it. Kenrick's hand closes on the door knob. "Goodnight," he says, wondering as he does so why he's interrupted a slap that might do Zef good. Marcus stares at him, open palm suspended midair.

For a long second they regard each other. Then Marcus, hand dropping to his side, says, "Don't go. You're wet. It's raining out. I'll get you some tea." Each sentence comes out more slowly. He moves toward the kitchen, then stops. His voice thick with embarrassment, his eyes averted from Kenrick's, he says, "Mrs. Alvarra usually leaves tea in the cozy."

Kenrick feels acutely embarrassed, too. His eyes fix on Zef. Behind his father's back, he lifts from the coffee table a heavy silver cigarette lighter, monogrammed, that Marcus has received as some commemorative or obligating gift. Staring coolly at Kenrick through light green eyes and focused malice, Zef balances the lighter on his fingertips, exactly long enough to underline for Kenrick what he's doing. Then, as Marcus turns, Zef palms the lighter, his hand sliding into a deep pocket of his drooping pants.

Marcus waits humbly for Kenrick's answer about the tea. Kenrick finds it difficult to understand what response would now be helpful. He feels pity for Marcus, outrage at Zef, and confusion at his own complicity in this moment. "I'll take some tea, yes," he says finally. Zef is not his opponent; however much Kenrick would like to find within himself permission to take the kid out, he is his father's responsibility.

The ignorant, arrogant child grins at Kenrick's impotence. Then he saunters down the short hallway to his bedroom, shutting his door with a smart-ass click.

In the kitchen, standing at the counter, Marcus says, "I don't know what to do with him."

Kenrick, sipping from his cup, nods agreement. They have never before drunk tea together and the situation feels painfully womanish.

"Sometimes," Marcus says, "I've just had *enough*."

"Yeah. I can imagine." Kenrick watches raindrops strike the window glass behind Marcus's head. They avoid looking at each other.

"I don't know as I ever had a chance to rebel. At his age I was always in my books, grinding away for that Duke of Kent scholarship, and once I got it and it carried me to

London, there was nothing but school work and shit work and examinations."

It occurs to Kenrick that this is not entirely true; Marcus's marriage over there to Lydia was a clear act of rebellion with far-reaching consequences. He sets his cup on the counter. He will not bring up Lydia. He has never, not once in the six years they've worked together, mentioned it, despite its salience as political fact. They both understand, he thinks, the need to paper over with silent tact this breakdown in Marcus's blackness.

Marcus's cup comes to rest on the counter alongside Kenrick's. "What would you do, if he were your son?" he asks.

Too many moments pass before Kenrick can find words that will not breach the tact. "They grow up, don't they? Eventually? You did. I did."

Marcus is grateful he has said no more. Kenrick reads that in the out-rush of his breath and the sudden drop in his shoulders. On the doorstep Marcus rests his hand briefly, speechlessly, on Kenrick's back.

Making himself look up into Marcus's weary eyes, he says, "Get some rest. Refuel that incendiary tongue, because tomorrow there'll be more this island needs to hear."

Marcus nods obligingly, and Kenrick, stepping out into a dripping night clamorous with tree frogs celebrating rain, hurries away to his scooter before any more honesty can be called for between them.

Even after the sputter of the scooter has receded down the drive, Marcus stands on the doorstep of the manor house he bought himself seven years ago after an unexpected big win in a civil case for a white client. Rose Hill is nearly one hundred years old, built by a descendent of the Forty Thieves, its rose-colored stucco and burnished cedar framing featured in pictorial histories of the island. How he'd reveled in the purchase, a reward for what he then thought his lucky ability to play both sides — black and white, his principles and their system—and a spite to Lydia's nay-saying ghost. He was, in those days, dating, sometimes hopefully and sometimes rapaciously. Tonight, with multiple threats piled on his shoulders, all that once so pleased and empowered him about the venerable, slightly shabby house just adds to his anxiety; he's told no one that he's behind on Rose Hill's mortgage.

He steps inside, pauses by the couch to gaze at the note Zef dropped there, and sighs. He retrieves it and unfolds it slowly. A conference at Somers Academy for Boys is scheduled for Monday afternoon. Peyton Langston and Zef's influence over him are cited. A parent for each party is expected to be present.

He sits down and then lies down on the leather couch. His stomach hurts. He's not eaten since morning, and now he is overfull of rum topped with strong tea laced with milk, a wretched combination. He reaches, as antidote, for the memory of that white woman's nervous, admiring, electrifying gaze. All day he has done this, more times than he wants to admit.

He crumples the note and throws it to the floor. The parent who comes to the conference with Peyton may not be his mother. Could be his father. Or both of them. Surely what those people do is of no consequence to him. Their presence there will be incidental to the predicament of Zef, who could be expelled and who is already *persona non grata* at all but the worst government-run schools on the island. And yet, despite the trouble pending, or because of it, he feels excited by the possibility of seeing the white woman.

Lucy.

He pictures her. Blond and pretty, soft and probably silly.... His delinquent thoughts have skidded through another gate and he gasps as the old pain of Lydia punches him.

He draws his knees up toward his chest to ease the tension in his groin and his stomach and tries to talk himself down from his confusion. If she comes to the conference, he'll see what she really looks like, which may not compare well to the picure she holds in his imagination. Headmaster Cotter, an asshole, will do his best to provoke him, and that, plus the probable presence of the woman's cocky husband, will keep fantasies from rising. Still, he is amazed at the way the vapors of desire arise now, with force, and although—he has been alone a long time now—they are sexual in intent and detail, sex alone will not satisfy them. The nature of his lust is more ambiguous—and less comprehensible—than that.

In England, he and Lydia once went to the races at Ascot. They went to sneer at the money and class pretension, and to make the political point of his being there at all. He also went (he admitted this to himself even then) to see the thoroughbreds. In Bermuda, rich people, usually white Europeans avoiding the continent's high taxes, had beautiful horses. Some of them had whole stables full of high-strung, overbred show horses with temperaments so extreme they could hardly be ridden. One of the many jobs he had as a boy, to contribute a little cash to whichever auntie was housing him, was as stall picker at one of those rich stables. It was risky work. The nervous horses were not to be upset, and he was expected to slip in and fork up the shit they dropped and slip out again without causing them to kick down the walls or bite a chunk from his arm. He warmed to the work, because of the challenge and because of the heat of the horses. The danger, and the desire sparked by all that passion rippling inside expensive flesh, forbidden but exactly within his reach.

When he was growing up, people he knew kept horses sometimes, but they were cart horses for pulling the tourist carriages in town or a hand plow on somebody's odd plot of vegetables. Those horses stank, their coats were coarse, and their minds so dull that no matter how you carried on around them, the strongest reaction you'd get was a rolled eye or a swished tail.

At Ascot, with Lydia beside him in tight bellbottoms and a fine fury of offended principles, he felt himself grow weak in the knees when the thoroughbreds in racing silks pranced by, dancing on nerves, lunging for the starting gate. And now, what seems more than a lifetime later, he feels exactly the same way just remembering the American woman, Lucy.

6

It was in the headmaster's office, taking licks, that Peyton became Zef's boy. It began the first time they spoke: in September on the second day of school, in the schoolyard during recess. All the seventh and eighth form boys had been turned out into the dust and glare and heat of the yard, unshaded except for one ancient, enormous banyan tree — its pleated trunk ten feet in diameter, its limbs, buttressed with air-roots thicker than Peyton's leg, canopying another thirty feet. Peyton, dressed in the first school uniform of his life, including hideous brown lace-up shoes his mother claimed were the only kind she could find on the island in his size, stood in the middle of the shouting and scuffling, sweltering in shirt and tie beneath a white sun at its zenith, nauseous with shock from the way his second day at Somers was confirming his conclusions about the first.

Thomas Heppering, a pink, doughy bully, came at him from behind, grabbed his belt and yanked his pants high up his crack. When he spun around, shivering with rage, fists cocked but pressed to his skinny thighs, Thomas looked like a wall of flesh. Ridiculous, but threatening.

"Quack, quack!" Thomas said, pointing at Peyton's shoes. Quack, and quack again, Thomas advanced on him, backing him across the yard through the treacherous raised knees of the banyan's spreading roots toward the stone wall beneath it while the other boys, the white boys, Brits and Canadians and locals—he was the lone American—circled them, snickering and egging Thomas on. The black boys, five in the class of thirty, stood off to one side, a clique of silence and stiff backs.

Trying to watch everyone, eyes darting face to face, Peyton missed seeing Zef Passjohn take Thomas down. Zef might have dropped down from the tree to do it—he never hung out with either group—but the fat boy was simply down, on his back in the red dust of the schoolyard, feet in the air, clutching his balls in two hands, face white and astonished and enraged. Peyton raised his glance from Thomas and found Zef, who had kneed Thomas quite expertly.

"Get up, shithead," Zef said, and Thomas, sputtering that he would tell, obeyed. He and the other boys, white and black, melted from Peyton's field of vision. It was his first taste of Zef's magic. First he made you look, and then he made things happen.

"Thanks," Peyton said.

"Shut the fuck up." Zef kicked dirt at Peyton's feet. "Your shoes suck."

Heartily he agreed they did. He marveled at the stubble protruding from the point of Zef's chin. And he noticed for the first time that this light-skinned black boy's eyes were green.

"You know my name?" Zef demanded.

"Sure. It's—"

"No, you don't. Nobody in here knows my right name. It's Zef, period. You got that? You call me Zef and nothing else."

"Okay," said Peyton, taking one step backward for safety. That was his second taste of Zef: how fast his moods changed, how he had to be boss. He took in, too, how Zef dressed, better than some and different from everyone. His uniform pants sharp-creased and his shirt starched. His brown shoes, heavily scuffed but the kind of soft, expensive, low-vamped Italian loafer Peyton's father wore with dress slacks.

Zef, stepping toward him, said, "Good dog." Peyton looked up from the shoes. Zef touched his forearm, his fingers light and warm on Peyton's sweaty skin. "I'm outta here, dog," Zef said. "You coming?" His light eyes glittered with what Peyton read as promise: *We neither one fit in, so let's be outcasts together.*

The low stone wall beneath the banyan tree, dividing the schoolyard from the Middle Road and fields of vegetables beyond, looked mossy and inviting. They had almost reached it, running, and Peyton could see how the stones were alive, small lizards darting from crack to crack, when the word "Halt!" struck his ears like a blow. His feet faltered and his knees crumbled. Mr. Ratherly, their teacher, came raging down the front steps.

Zef turned, and in the slow motion of apprehended terror, Peyton watched Zef's face absorb the news the way a sponge takes in water—immediately, and leaving no trace. He raised his own chin, trying for the same hard glaze, but his face worked like a bucket of squirming worms.

"Langston," said Ratherly, "you show poor judgment in your choice of friends."

His hand closed on Peyton's shoulder. With his other hand Ratherly hooked Zef by the shirt collar. He swept them up the front steps with triumphant ease, and Peyton could hardly keep up. His feet tangled. The laces of his horrible shoes came undone. He stumbled, hit his shin on the stair and sought Zef's face as he picked himself up, both of them momentarily below Ratherly's eye level. Zef's expression did not change, but his eyes signaled. *Be cool.* Peyton bit his lip, imagined a plaster cast settling on his burning face, and let Ratherly drag him down the dim hall to the headmaster's door.

There Ratherly let them go. He wiped his hands on his pants legs and straightened his tie before knocking. When the clipped British voice on the other side of the door invited them in, he motioned for Peyton and Zef to go before him. Zef strode right in and Peyton tripped again, on the edge of the oriental carpet. The office was very poorly lit.

"Tie your shoelaces," said Headmaster Cotter. Small and thin, he had innocent round glasses and strings of gray hair draped carefully across the bald dome of his head.

Ratherly spoke eagerly, as if his tail wagged. "Passjohn, Mr. Cotter, *again*. And this time Langston with him, roughing up the other boys. Picking on Thomas Heppering, who sustained injury when they knocked him to the ground."

That was all he said. Peyton glanced at Zef. One hand hid deep in his pocket, and Peyton thought it might be shaking, but nothing showed on his face. Mr. Cotter caught Peyton looking, and seemed, without moving, to jump into his face.

"Young Langston," he said, "I suspect your misbehavior today is less than entirely your fault. You are very recently arrived on the island. I had hoped you might become one of my very best students. Your father assured me you would. I hope he is not mistaken." He blinked, releasing Peyton, whose stomach flopped as if dropped from a height.

"Mr. Ratherly, prepare notes home for these boys. I shall send them along to your classroom directly. We are almost finished with our business here."

Ratherly signaled Peyton by a quick arch of his brows that he knew what was coming and that it pleased him. Mr. Cotter drew from the drawer of his desk a long narrow wooden paddle perforated with round holes, and Zef, rolling his eyes, bent at the waist and grasped his legs just above the ankles. The headmaster stood politely waiting until Peyton copied the position.

They took their licks, two for Peyton, twice that and harder for Zef, with tight straight faces, and afterwards, on the hard bench in the hallway where they spent thirty minutes' detention in enforced silence, they glanced at each other sideways. Peyton's body quivered with pain and insult. He had never in his life been struck in punishment, and shame and outrage warred in his heart. When he thought of his parents, the trouble he was in and the note he must hand them, he almost cried, but whenever he caught Zef's look, he felt better. Sometimes Zef smirked and sometimes he made a stupid face, and finally Peyton laughed. He smothered it quickly and dropped his gaze safely to his shoes, but Zef whispered, breath warm on Peyton's ear, "You can't let the assholes get you down. You stick with me, I'll show you how to get them down."

Zef's words, slicing the silence they'd been ordered to maintain on pain of more licks, made Peyton's stomach lurch again. But those words exhilarated him, too, with possibility he'd never in his twelve years considered: he could cast off his parents, who had, without asking him, cast off a life he'd needed to hold on to.

He decided all by himself on that bench beside Zef what to do about the note Ratherly would give him. He did the same thing with each of the five notes that followed, each time he and his new friend were apprehended having skipped school or trying to skip. He resolved to be his own man. He tore the paper into pieces he scattered in the road.

Marcus arrives late for the meeting with Cotter. The white woman Lucy is already there, seated in one of four ladder-back chairs facing the headmaster's desk, with her pie-eyed son on her left and his own son on her right. Marcus drops into the remaining chair, beside Zef, foregoing whatever apologies some people might think are called for and grateful that the boy is here without his having to fetch him. Marcus was delayed on his way to this meeting by two phone calls at his office, one after the other. The first caller was Mrs. Alvarra, reporting that she'd arrived at Rose Hill at ten in the morning and found Zef still in bed. The second call was from Murcheson at the Bank of Bermuda, announcing in very poor temper that as a result of a cashier's check Marcus drew that morning to bail Ramo Wylie from jail, a second, personal, check, a late and partial mortgage payment to the Bank itself, had bounced. Murcheson's parting shot was a question: "Who will bail you, Passjohn, when you're finally picked up for whatever it is, exactly, you've done?"

Cotter also dispenses with niceties of apology or greeting. Watching Marcus take his seat, he continues a formal recitation of the boys' infractions of Somers Academy rules thus far this term. Lucy, who looked sharply at Marcus as he came in, now sits up straight as if pinned to the back of her chair. Cotter's tone indicates that better parents than those in front of him would not have required a summons to the headmaster's office in order to acquire the facts about their children's behavior.

Missed assignments, he intones. Six during the term so far, for Peyton Langston. Twenty-six for Stefan "Zef" Passjohn.

Tardiness, in the morning or after recess. Four instances for Peyton. Sixteen for Stefan.

Insubordination to a teacher, requiring a visit to the headmaster. Once for Peyton. Eleven times for Stefan.

Unexcused absences, amounting to truancy. "Twelve instances for Master Passjohn," Cotter says, "and five for Master Langston."

Zef snorts. Marcus sees, when he turns to shut him up, that the Langston boy is sick with fear, his hand curled defensively against his abdomen. His mother's hand, a wide, capable one at odds with the fine bones of her wrists, reaches for his.

"Mr. Cotter," Marcus says abruptly, distracting himself from staring at her, "just how is it you establish the fact of truancy? To my knowledge, neither of these boys has been apprehended by anyone official in any place other than school during school hours."

"If the parent does not confirm to us, in writing, that the child is absent for sickness or other cause, Mr. Passjohn, then the Academy must assume that the parent is unaware of the absence and that the child has taken into his own hands the decision to shirk his schooling."

Cotter smiles coldly at Marcus, inviting further challenge. "Do you assert that your son's truancies are absences? Shall we go over the record so you may provide explanation?"

"I'm sure your records reflect your meticulous purpose, Mr. Cotter. And no, I am not prepared to justify the moment-by-moment whereabouts of my son—my obligations are bigger than playing governess—"

"What is the point of our being here?" Peyton's mother interrupts them, her voice coarse with anxiety.

"My, you are direct, Mrs. Langston," Cotter replies. He seems on the verge of laughing at her, and she is, despite the skin color she shares with him, as out of her league in Cotter's over-decorated office as Marcus is. She is ingenuous in her casual American slacks and sandals and the absence of any makeup, while Cotter is as baroque as his furnishings—his Sarouk carpet and Sheridan chairs, the many pounds of mildew-spotted silk damask masking the tall windows.

"Mrs. Langston," Cotter says, "there is more at issue here than making up missed work, at least in your son's case." He glances not at Peyton but at Zef. "Since Master Langston is new to the island and our school and is perhaps not well-acquainted with the level of discipline and respect we take for granted here." Now he looks at Lucy, with unmasked triumph. "Your son failed to deliver home to you six notes detailing his misbehavior and requesting conferences. Such behavior is irresponsible. It is possibly pre-delinquent. It certainly makes a comment on the young man's integrity."

For a moment, she says nothing. Then, leaning forward and meeting Cotter's eyes, she says, "The notes. I got them, all six of them. But I've been busy. I've simply been unable to call or come in until today."

Marcus cannot quite suppress a gasp of surprise. He can feel Peyton's astonishment at the lie, a palpable vibration.

Cotter, after one beat of silence, says, "I see. You share with Mr. Passjohn a busy schedule that impinges on your ability to supervise your child."

He sighs and leans back with flagrantly fake sympathy. "Mrs. Langston, it is your son's well-being that concerns me. I want simply to be sure I have engaged your cooperation. And your husband's cooperation. He was not able to join us today?"

"He's off the island," Lucy says, quickly and flatly. "He travels a great deal."

Marcus can see the second lie in the tension of the muscles around her mouth and her brows, and he cannot miss Peyton's eyes, huge and stunned. Lucy has not told her husband about this meeting. Marcus smiles at her courage and her capacity for folly and comes to her rescue as best he can.

"Cotter, I don't believe we've yet determined what it is we

are going to do here. Do you have a proposal or not?"

The headmaster makes a tent of his fingertips. "For young Langston I'm ordering a three-day suspension."

"That's...that's unreasonable," Lucy bursts out. "Peyton has never been in trouble at school in his life. He is a good student. His teachers have always adored him—"

Cotter cuts her off. "Perhaps that's his problem. Perhaps he's spoiled, as well as unsupervised."

High color flames her cheeks. "He is not spoiled. And he's not unsupervised either. He's unhappy here. He's—" She looks furiously at Zef, who lolls in his straight chair as if it were a beanbag. "He's fallen under a bad influence."

"Quite so," Cotter replies. "Master Passjohn is to be expelled."

"Damn," says Marcus.

Zef says, "Cool."

It is all Marcus can do not to stand up and throw a punch at someone. They have got him. While he was watching the woman and enjoying the fantasy that he was of some assistance to her, Cotter's cashed in his well-tended grudge and Zef has shoved him harder than ever against the wall of his rebellion. Two years ago when Zef was expelled from his alma mater Berkeley Prep, Marcus made Cotter take him in with pressure from the Academy's board, some of whom owed Marcus and some of whom wanted him to owe them. Zef hated Somers from the beginning, wanting only to drift unhindered through whatever decrepit government school would enroll him. Now Cotter and Zef both have what they want. They have made Marcus pay. And there will be installments. No doubt this news will make the frigging *Gazette*.

Marcus gets up. He takes Zef by the arm, jerks open the highly polished cedar door, and shoves Zef into the hall. Closing it, he hears Cotter describing its provenance to Lucy, playing tour guide now that he's finished with her son.

"Lovely door, isn't it, Mrs. Langston? Native cedar. Slave work," he says, "like so much else on this island. Somers Academy was built by slaves—freed slaves, of course—just subsequent to the Emancipation in 1834."

Cotter segues smoothly from the lasting value of slave labor to the deleterious effect American presence has had on Bermuda's environment: when the U.S. military acquired one-tenth of the island from Winston Churchill in a horse-trade for warships, and built upon it a Cold War naval air station from which to spy on Russian submarines, the Americans brought with them not only the first cars to clog the island's scenic roadways but a blight that wiped out the local cedars, once so plentiful their aromatic scent perfumed the breezes night and day.

The sound of the door's brass tongue snapping into its groove cuts off Cotter's voice. Pushing Zef in front of him, Marcus strides down the hallway past classrooms and the murmur of recited lessons within. At the end of the hall, where the front doors hang wide open in a square of pure light, the broad, flat leaves of the banyan tree sound in the steady breeze like a thousand thin castanets.

"Are you satisfied?" Marcus demands, on the doorstep, squared off with his son. "Are you happy now?"

The tangle of creeper vine clinging to the Academy's stone portal releases a bitter familiar smell when Marcus grinds at a tendril with his shoe. Zef merely shrugs. Marcus hears footsteps, the soft slap of leather sandals on marble, coming toward them.

"Why, Zef?" He says it quietly, because she is coming and he doesn't want to look foolish, raging at his impossible son. "Why are you doing this to yourself? You *are* doing it to yourself, do you know that? It's *your* life you're ruining."

"What do you care?" Zef says, plenty loud enough for anyone to hear. "I'm not old enough to vote and I'm too tall to kiss your ass."

Marcus is paralyzed while the woman and her son walk past them. Her eyes are down, but surely not in deference to him. She's got her own troubles to contemplate.

He takes Zef by the arm and shakes him. He speaks straight into his face. "I bailed Ramo today." The rest of the Rastas had been released, but Ramo's precautionary detention was replaced with a ludicrous charge: conspiracy to incite riot.

"This has got nothing to do with you," he tells Zef. "Do you hear? Don't you go near Ramo. You stay away from him and you stay home until we get you in school again."

Zef's joy is unmistakable. He says nothing, but his whole demeanor lightens at the news that Ramo is free. Marcus drops the boy's arm, hating this response in his son. He expected it and wished it would not happen, but his own temptation to duck, to leave Ramo twisting in the wind, made it imperative that he act. He could not, from cowardice and spite, let injustice stand.

He starts down the steps toward the tired Bentley. The American woman and her son are getting in their car, a bright red Fiesta, obviously new. She has started to climb in the left side of the car, the American habit asserting itself. She is obviously frazzled and now she's embarrassed, because he's seen her silly mistake. When she looks at him, her chin is lifted defiantly, but her eyes are full of tears.

She is not beautiful, he thinks, appraising her from some dozen feet away. Her face is too long and its angles too sharp, her hair is thin and flyaway, and her grey eyes, inside dark circles of fatigue, are set imperfectly far apart. For a moment, he cannot move. He simply looks. Then he realizes it has been a long moment. Her son and his son and she are all watching him stand in the center of the dusty schoolyard—speechless and staring at her. Behind her on the road, a runner passes, headed west, the dark skin of his naked chest iridescent with sweat.

Marcus fumbles with the inside pocket of his suit coat and pulls out his card. The palms of his hands are damp. He crosses the yard quickly and offers the card to Lucy Langston. "In case you need to get in touch," he says. "About the boys," he adds urgently, when she does not take it, and then she accepts the card, nodding, avoiding his eyes, saying nothing.

When she reverses the Fiesta to point it at the gate, she backs over a raised knee of the banyan roots that mine the yard, briefly hanging up one rear wheel off the ground. Leaning on the Bentley's drive-side door, Marcus watches her gun the red car fiercely to free it. She succeeds, but the back bumper bangs the root hard on the way down, and she drives away with the bumper at an up-tilted angle. She could hardly have failed to feel the jolt, but she doesn't get out and check the damage. She doesn't even slow down.

Peyton is framed in the Fiesta's passenger window as she pulls into the road, his big eyes fastened on Marcus. The boy's soft face has hardened slightly from an unwelcome wash of cold truth. Marcus swallows hard. From behind him and inside his own car, Zef says, "We outta here, or what?"

7

Lucy prepares the Thanksgiving turkey, the stuffing, the baked yams and a pumpkin pie, even though on the island this day is just one more Thursday in November. The kitchen of the large house they've rented, on a cliff above Bermuda's most famous beach, Horseshoe Bay, quickly overheats—despite the steady chugging from one of the six window air conditioners Darrell ordered and TransGlobal paid for, because the oven seal leaks and the weather is still, this far into the year, sunny and humid. By late afternoon, when Lucy is harried and sweaty, worried about Peyton (who is once again closeted in his room with his newest, most grating CDs), and more anxious than ever about hiding his recent three-day suspension from Darrell, she realizes she's never before prepared the Thanksgiving meal all by herself.

Back home in Darien, her mother would have insisted even during her final years on a bright fiction of helping out, parked on a stool blocking Lucy's path from sink to refrigerator, swallowed in a flowered caftan with sleeves preventing her doing any useful work, and smoking when she was under orders not to, all the while declaiming the ways the women at the garden club and the altar guild might improve their lives if only they would just get into therapy or read the classics or somehow *work* on themselves—before tipping suddenly into misty depression and bearing herself away to commune with

Ravel via her Steinway's keys. Lucy's father, for whom Peyton was named, always pitched in, even before cancer took her mother, turning off his cell phone no matter what crisis roiled his office, rolling up the sleeves of his dress shirt and taking direction from her good-naturedly while her older sister Cyn, who would not come near a kitchen once she passed the bar and became their father's law partner, mixed the martinis and watched football with Darrell in the den. If this was a year her frantic schedule in commercial real estate permitted her to drive down from Hartford, Darrell's mother would come. She would undertake the most drudge-like task available — rubbing dried-on water spots from the crystal or scouring the roasting pan — setting a Catholic example amidst their group of laissez-faire and lapsed Episcopalians.

Lucy had never cherished Thanksgiving at home, but now, on her own in this strange place, she misses every single thing she's left behind, even the mundane and the stressful. She carries a stack of her gold-banded Lennox wedding china to the dining room table, spread with freshly ironed linen and framed in a window-wall's view of turquoise sea and cobalt sky, the island's tourist-famed South Shore. The view takes her breath, as it does each time she encounters it. So much ocean, such a tiny scrap of land at so great a distance from every other land mass — that anyone at all lives here, much less an entire small society, seems so accidental as to be implausible.

Not a drop of fresh water beyond rain has ever graced the island, and no indigenous inhabitants except a few species of lizards and birds; she has read this in the books she pored over in her struggle to build enthusiasm for the move. Early in the sixteenth century, the Spanish marked the island as a place to avoid, naming it for the explorer Juan Bermudez when they mapped its reefs as navigation hazard on their route to the New World. If not for the popular success of Shakespeare's *Tempest*, inspired by a ship wrecked on those reefs in a hurricane in 1609, English adventurers might never have laid claim to Bermuda, arriving first in search of ambergris and pearls, and then, finding only rock, scrubby trees, and an unobstructed sight line to the trade route, importing slaves and prisoners to build a navy outpost for the Empire.

She sighs and sets the table for six. Their guests for the evening are the Hepperings—Jonathan, a chartered accountant Darrell met through work, his wife Felicity and their son Thomas, who, it turns out, is in Peyton's class at school. On the island just three months so far, she and Darrell have no friends, only acquaintances, and at the time she broached with Darrell the question of whom to invite, she thought it could be fun to share the American holiday with Bermudians who might become friends. But when the Hepperings arrive, punctually at seven and just behind Darrell who has come straight from the office, she realizes that the evening ahead will likely be as much work as its preparation has been.

She senses in Darrell a short fuse. Wound up from a long day at work but eager to make a good impression on the Hepperings, he remains cross with her about the damage to the Fiesta's bumper; a replacement bracket is on order from the factory in England, at double the usual cost because of island customs' duty. When Jonathan Heppering bows over her hand as they are introduced, she's reminded uncomfortably of Headmaster Cotter with his British accent, unctuous manners, and pitiful comb-over. Felicity wears pearls with her beige linen shirtwaist, and peppers her cheery speech with emphatic statements that strike Lucy with pinpricks of judgment: "How *fortunate* you are to have found such an exceptionally *fine* house on the rental market. And air *conditioners*—do you really have them in *every* room?" Thomas does not accompany them, a fact his parents downplay. Jonathan seems not to hear Lucy's inquiry about him, and Felicity says, "Thomas so wanted to meet you, Mrs. Langston, I *know* he did." His absence is obviously a relief to Peyton. He says brusquely to Thomas's mother, who blinks in response, "I don't know him. He doesn't sit near me."

Over dinner, once the customs of the American holiday have been examined and the food praised beyond what it deserves, the conversation stumbles as the men's talk turns to the deteriorating business environment. Not only has 9/11 slammed the U.S. economy and dried up the tourist business, a major reinsurer on the island, a competitor of Darrell's firm but a client of Jonathan's, has announced relocation to the Cayman Islands because of the worsening labor troubles in Bermuda and the perception (erroneous, Jonathan says, but inevitable, given the recent debacle of pro-labor, anti-American pickets blocking the entrance to the global business development conference, for which his firm was a major sponsor) that the political climate on the island is unstable and hostile to foreign investment.

Jonathan speaks with considerable authority on these matters; he's recently been appointed to complete the term of a majority member of Parliament who resigned for health reasons, and his views on the perfidy of labor unions and especially the perfidy of the Opposition are vehement. The women smile awkwardly at each other and chew, since a second, female conversation with Jonathan seated between them is not possible. Peyton neither eats nor speaks; he stirs his food around the plate. Finally Darrell, obviously bored — how grateful Lucy suddenly feels for his habitual impatience — catches her eye and interrupts Jonathan.

"I'll tell you a local issue I'm curious about." Darrell gestures with his fork in Felicity's direction, to draw her in. "What's the story with that old black man in the wheelchair, the amputee, over in Warwick village?"

"Lemuel Trott." Jonathan's answer is immediate.

"That his name?" Darrell continues, pointedly addressing Felicity. "Lucy and I saw him the first day we came out here to look at this house and since then, every time I go over Camp Hill to gas up the car, there he is again."

"He sits out there six days a week," Felicity says. "It's a *shame*."

"He's a landmark, darling," Jonathan says, smiling at the whimsy and covering Felicity's hand with his own. "Traffic might mistrack without his signals."

"He's pitiful," Felicity insists, withdrawing her hand, and Lucy, recalling her first sight of Mr. Trott, sympathizes with Felicity's opposition to this chauvinist husband she's saddled with but disagrees with her conclusion about the wheelchair man. His situation is pitiable, but his presence, that first time and every time since, she finds oddly striking.

Parked day after day right behind the curb in a dusty lot in a poor neighborhood, he wears, no matter the heat, long-sleeved shirts of dark strong colors, often the royal purple priests wear for Lent, and an ancient straw boater that matches his beard — full, white, and tinged venerably with yellow. As the Langstons drove past him that first day, he'd raised his hand and waved at Lucy with the calm beneficence of a king or archbishop. She rode in the back seat that day to favor Peyton, and she had gotten up on her knees, turning all the way around to keep her eyes on the man. She couldn't help it; she thought she'd never seen anyone so intensely *human* — vibrant and simultaneously fragile. As the Fiesta drew slowly away, crawling in a queue of traffic toward town, she watched him waving amiably to each car and scooter that passed, drivers returning the gesture with broad motions of affection.

Peyton, from the front seat, had told her to sit down. "Don't stare at cripples, Mom," he quipped, and Darrell, who'd missed it completely, said, "What? What was that?"

She glances down the table toward Peyton, and finds his chair empty; he has gotten up without her noticing it. Jonathan, seated to her left at her dining room table, deftly severs slices from a drumstick while sharing Mr. Trott's history. "Passjohn, black chap that runs the Opposition, made his reputation on that man. Tried his civil case, filled the papers with cant about restitution for loss of the man's legs, lost the case and then, the minute he was elected MP, tried to push through a special bill for compensation."

Felicity, adding wine to her glass, remarks, "Passjohn's never changed his stripes, either. Always out to get anything he can for himself and his kind. He sides with the union, the Rastas and all the malcontents, anyone who's against law and order."

"Striped he may be," Jonathan says. "Man had a white wife."

"Actually, on Guy Fawkes night we met —" Darrell

begins.

Lucy is on her feet. "I need to check the dessert," she says, although there's nothing about a pumpkin pie, removed from the oven hours ago, that needs checking.

Felicity chimes in, "Let me help you," and Lucy, the heat receding from her face, tells her firmly, "No."

In the kitchen she stands inside the oversize pantry with the light off, picturing—in details she realizes she's been hoarding for the two weeks since their encounter at Somers Academy—Marcus Passjohn's high forehead accentuated by his close-cut hair, his hollowed cheeks and deeply expressive eyes. She cannot forget the look in them when he handed her his card. Nor the way they sought her first when he walked into Cotter's office late. She still has his card in her purse; she's not dared touch it since she put it there. She's forty-one, so it's not as if she doesn't know when a man is attracted to her, even now, even this long married. It's not as if she doesn't know when she's attracted back, either, but in this case the circumstances are so odd, so embarrassingly *inappropriate*—he's a black man with a high-profile reputation as a troublemaker, and she's a housewife coping badly with her son and her household in a foreign country—yet the pull of what this man telegraphed her in his gaze is strong. She *wants* to know who he is behind that gaze.

She takes a deep breath and blows it out her mouth. Leaving the pantry because she must, she hears more about Marcus, this time news of his former wife, in Felicity's piercing voice.

"She was a *communist,* in the days when that meant something. Passjohn himself—"

Darrell interrupts doggedly. "What happened to Lemuel Trott's legs?"

Felicity says, "*He* says the Lord took them back."

"Gangrene," says Jonathan. "From untreated diabetes."

"I don't understand." Lucy approaches the table. "I mean, I understand diabetes and gangrene, but why wasn't it treated? And how could anyone try to claim compensation from the government for that?"

"The hospital was closed. Everything was shut down. The

island was under martial law."

Lucy drops into her chair. She wants to touch Marcus Passjohn. She wants to *feel* the warmth, the kindness, the extraordinary purposefulness she sensed in him, that night at Guy Fawkes when he took her hand. Darrell, putting aside his fork, asks, "Martial law?"

"In 1977," Jonathan answers. "It was quite the mess. A pair of black fellows was hanged for the assassination of the governor and the police commissioner. Duly tried and convicted, on plenty of evidence, even a letter of confession, and legal appeals all the way to the Crown. The result was... anarchy. Riots, arson, looting. It required troops from Britain more than two weeks to restore order."

"So that's what Passjohn was referring to in his speech," Darrell says slowly.

"Just so." Jonathan's cleaned his plate. His fork rests tines up across it, his etiquette above reproach.

"The events of '77 are not talked about here, not publicly, and never with visitors," he continues. "But now that you live here," he looks Darrell in the eye, "it's important that you know what we live with. During the riots, white people and white property were targeted. A number of buildings, including a hotel, were burned and several people died. Innocent citizens were pulled from their cars and scooters, and attacked. The radical and low-life elements responsible for it, Rastafarians and their ilk, went largely unpunished, and the ones that were incarcerated have been freed, through Passjohn's efforts."

"Is Passjohn directly involved in the present unrest?" Darrell inquires. "The newspaper makes it sound like he's an instigator."

Jonathan, his lips a thin line, replies, "What do you think?" He pushes his plate away. "I'll tell you what *I* think. They stick together, that kind. Passjohn himself was in England in '77, but ever since then, every time there's race trouble, he's in the middle of it. And what he may really be up to, we can hardly know, can we? We see it in the international newspapers all the time, don't we? Terrorist connections to Islam through malcontents in London—blacks as well as Pakistanis. Some of those cells have been active for decades—"

Jonathan's pitch and color are both rising and Felicity's hand is patting his sleeve. He pauses to look at it. With a jerk he lifts his face and speaks again, stridently, to Darrell.

"Fundamentally, this is an economic issue. You'll appreciate that, Langston. The color of these chaps is not the point. I'm not one of those people who believe intelligence and ability reside in the racial genes. My point is the need for common sense on the part of people who make speeches and push legislation. Strikes and civil disorder kill the economy. The tourists don't come and business shuts down or leaves. Passjohn and his followers, they're ignorant as well as arrogant. The Premier is useless because he's spineless; he wants nothing but to stay in office. His justice minister Isaiah Barnes, because his ambition is to be premier, is someone we can work with. He's not particularly bright but he's enterprising and that makes him cooperative. And I tell you, the people who have common sense have got to take charge before order breaks down completely. We are *at risk*."

Jonathan's cheeks are flushed. His remonstrative finger stops poking the air, and he looks squarely at Lucy, who is herself flushed and agitated, and then, abruptly and apologetically, Jonathan turns to his wife. "I hadn't meant to bring bad news to dinner, darling, but since I've gone this far, I may as well tell you the rest." He pauses. "There's been a shooting. Have you heard?"

Lucy turns quickly toward Peyton's chair, still empty. She's glad he's not hearing this.

"Everyone on the island will know by tomorrow," Jonathan says, sighing. "An elderly gentleman, longtime member of Parliament, one of the Tuckers, fine old family, shot in the head right in his home last night or early this morning, by a black man."

"They caught the shooter?" Darrell says.

"No. Whoever did it took money and electronics and cleared out. But we have Horace Tucker's word on it, before he lapsed unconscious, and that's enough. No white man would have shot him point-blank like that. Now Tucker's in a coma, in hospital."

Lucy has made an involuntary noise of protest at Jonathan's smooth segue from the racial identity of one armed robber to the indictment of an entire race. Now all of them are looking at her. Her father's liberal politics lobby to seize her tongue, her mother's training in good manners and the art of hostessing clamps her mouth shut, and the result is a strange and uncomfortable grimace. From behind her, Peyton's music comes boiling up the hallway from his bedroom. She rises from her chair to find out why he left the meal earlier, and to escape the tension at the table, but Darrell's expression signals her adamantly: she is not to leave him alone with this. She is to sit down.

She does so.

Jonathan's hand and Felicity's are now clasped on the snowy damask. "They're like *children*," Felicity is saying. "When they can't have what they want, first they scream and then they destroy things. And now they have *guns*."

Darrell, his tense face lined with fatigue, says, "Surely the situation's not so acute as you think."

"It's going to be quite acute," Jonathan replies, "if we do not act decisively to stop it. But believe me, we will act."

Thanksgiving dinner has degenerated at this point so far from what Lucy imagined when she planned it that it's difficult to regain any ordinary social footing. She allows Felicity into the kitchen to help her cut the pie and brew coffee, and while fighting her distress over everything she's just heard at the table, she listens absentmindedly to Felicity, working energetically to lighten things up by listing all the colonial sights Lucy should be taking in around the island in her free time. Fort Scaur, Fort Hamilton, Fort St. Catherine, so many fine forts all over the island, and the British naval yard and the old prison there—restored now, with some excellent exhibits and quite nice shops—and did she like to walk? Nearby there's the Railway Trail, and toward the island's east end, Spanish Rock, bearing the carved date that is the earliest sign of human habitation.

"Have you seen *that*?" Felicity says. She's talking louder

and louder because Lucy's said nothing at all since they came into the kitchen. "Shall we go to Spanish Rock *together*? Let's *do*. It's been ever so long since I've been there."

With a dessert plate in each hand, Lucy blocks Felicity's path into the dining room. She stands right in front of her, and asks in pointedly rude disregard for her guest's choice of subjects a question she really wants answered: "Why didn't Thomas come tonight?"

Felicity looks like a cat seized by the tail on its way out the door. Her brightness crumbles and for a moment her eyes search Lucy's with some kind of plea. Then she says, averting her eyes, "Jonathan just wouldn't hear of it. Thomas got in trouble, a fight, after school today." Her voice is low now. "It involves a black boy who picks on him, it's happened several times before, and Thomas seems not to be holding his own. He tattles, and Jonathan is very displeased about that."

Lucy stares. This story must in some way pertain to Peyton's odd attitude about Thomas. She says, "What does Thomas say is being done to him?" Perhaps Peyton is being picked on, also.

Felicity shakes her head rapidly. "Please don't say anything to Jonathan," she says. "Don't say I told you." She touches Lucy's arm. "He can be harsh."

Lucy says, "Poor you." It's an arrogant, bitchy comment, but she cannot help herself. She's American, and she doesn't have to pussyfoot past the truth the way Felicity does; she doesn't have to know her place, with a husband or within a social hierarchy: it does not occur to her at that moment that she knows very well this assertion is not true.

When the Hepperings finally leave, Darrell says, "Well, they're not keepers," and Lucy heartily agrees. Together they eye the mess of plates and pots piled on every one of the kitchen's lengthy counters. Neither one of them has energy to tackle the cleaning tonight. "I'll do it tomorrow," Lucy says. Darrell nods with relief. "Dinner was great," he says, and she nods, knowing they both know that even the food was not what it should have been.

He pours them each a drink and they sit down together in the living room, too dispirited to remark further on the evening's disappointments. The sea on the other side of the window wall, a blank blackness now, is audible, as is the growl from Peyton's high-powered stereo—a gift Darrell bought him to assuage the departure from Connecticut. This house is big and low and wide, set into a shelf carved in the cliff face, impressive in just the ostentatious way Felicity characterized it. Darrell has rented it at great expense, subsidized by TransGlobal, because it was the nicest thing available on the rental market when they arrived, and as expatriates they cannot buy. The house is dank and, except for the magnificent view, as characterless as a barracks inside and out. Lucy's not expressed this opinion to Darrell. Now she wonders what she can tell him about Peyton that would help her with the situation at school without tipping Darrell's stress into outburst.

She should have told him about the suspension, of course, but once she'd lied to Cotter, on angry impulse, about the notes and Darrell's whereabouts, telling Darrell became complicated. She'd gone to the meeting aware that Peyton was very nervous but never imagining the seriousness of the problem; she'd been sure she could handle it, as she's always handled all childrearing and household matters while Darrell handles his job and their income, their habituated division of labor.

She begins. "Peyton..."

Darrell, bestirring himself, interrupts. "Yeah. Where is that kid? Why did he leave the table like that? He never came back, that was rude."

She takes a breath and tries again. "Darrell, lately Peyton has been..."

"I'm going to talk to him right now. He should know better than to behave like that with guests."

Her husband strides down the hall and shoves Peyton's door open without knocking. Maybe it will do some good. Maybe what Peyton needs now is a man's push. All his life he's been her child more than Darrell's, the bond between them sacred and secure because both her pregnancy and his birth had been fraught. But those eleven years of heart-to-heart closeness might just as well never have existed, the way things feel now. When he disappeared on Guy Fawkes Night she knew he'd made a conscious choice to hide from her and to hurt her, because it was the second time he'd done so. The first time had been in Connecticut, on the last day of the Langstons' lives there.

The house in Darien had been emptied, the movers working for more than twelve hours, a long rainy day late in June. At the end of that endless day, when the time came to get in the car and leave, she and Darrell could not find Peyton anywhere. She'd walked outdoors carrying a little sack of trash from their final dinner, Chinese takeout, toward the garbage can when she heard Darrell call her name agitatedly and then shout, "Where the hell is Peyt?" Together they searched the house, calling his name, the sound reverberating off the bare walls. They opened every door and checked each closet and crawl space, Darrell hurrying faster the more upset he became, Lucy dragging with dread and exhaustion.

It was almost dark when they went outside, searching the yard separately, still calling his name, but softly now, their voices uncomfortably piercing in the thick suburban silence, the soft summer rain. When they had not found him anywhere in the half-acre of wooded yard despite a quarter-hour's search, Darrell got in the rented car—both of theirs had been sold by then—slammed the door and gunned out of the driveway, lurching down the street, stomping the brakes at every house to peer through his rolled-down window into the ornamental bushes framing the yards. Lucy went inside and methodically called the homes of each of his friends and soccer teammates.

She stood on the front steps of the house she'd lived in for ten years and wrung her hands together because she did not know what else to do. What was it she had failed to do that this had befallen her family?

When Darrell pulled into the driveway, her heart rose and

then fell. Only the driver's side door opened; he'd come back alone. Hope pitching her headlong, she'd imagined herself falling on his chest and his arms closing around her. He got out of the car and slammed the roof with his fist. "I can't find Peyton," he said, his voice as pinched as his face. The near neighbors had come out of their houses by now, some gawking, most offering to help.

The search started all over again, in the house, in the yard, on the phone, with more than a dozen people involved.

Nearly two hours into the hunt, while Darrell was on the phone insisting to the police they get involved, Lucy found Peyton. In a hopeless, helpless attempt to restore the tiniest bit of order to life, she'd picked up the bag of trash she'd dropped, and entered the redwood enclosure that screened the garbage cans from the street. There, behind the bins, head pressed against the wall of the house, face soaked with rain and tears, eyes swollen nearly shut from crying, was Peyton. He cowered like a small frightened animal when she shoved the bin out of the way. She knelt in front of him. They neither one spoke. All Lucy could process was a single revelation: that he could not possibly have failed to hear them calling his name. He'd not wanted them to find him.

She tried then to kiss his cheek and he swatted at her, almost but not quite striking her face. She stood up. She told him firmly to get up, go in the house, and get his father so they could leave. He obeyed, back straight, head lowered, and fists clenched. She followed him into the house where she cleaned him up as best she could with paper towels while Darrell phoned the police back and sent the neighbors home. Afterwards, they drove away together to a room reserved at an airport hotel, seated three in a row in the boat-sized rented Lincoln—the same kind of car in which they had ridden four-and-a-half years earlier to Lucy's mother's funeral, but that day, all of them in the back seat with an anonymous undertaker's man driving, and this day with Darrell at the wheel, Lucy at the window, and Peyton between. No one said a word during the entire hour's drive from Darien across Westchester through Queens to JFK. She had told herself, holding her own hands tightly in her lap, what she wanted to tell her husband and her son, that they would live past this, they would—for people lived past worst things every day of the world.

And now, walking wearily to the kitchen to wrap the perishables and put them away, she reminds herself that is exactly what they are doing here in Bermuda: living past that last day in Connecticut, day by day. Then she notices Peyton's school shoes, discarded by the door to the garage. Picking them up, she stares at clots of pink sand adhered to the rubber soles with thick gobs of black beach tar. Angry, she drops the shoes and turns away. She will have to scrub them with solvent to dissolve the tar, as she's had to do with her own shoes after a long beach walk, but—she turns back to look with puzzlement at the shoes again—when today did Peyton go to the beach? She picked him up after school and for the rest of the afternoon he stayed shut up in his room, the damn CDs blaring while she cooked.

She hears Darrell coming out of Peyton's room, and heads down the hall to meet him, wanting to know what Peyton has told him. Darrell shrugs. "Kid's asleep," he says, "like I want to be."

When they are in bed, in the huge master suite with the drapes swept back so that the room's fourth wall is the sea, Lucy cannot fall asleep. The sound of surf breaking on the rocks keeps her awake. Outside, thirty feet below the window, the long curve of Horseshoe Bay ends in a mass of rugged rock towers. By daylight, the longtails—terns with pencil-thin, ten-inch tail plumes, so white they seem lit from within—circle those towers in slowest slow motion, riding updrafts. By daylight the water beneath them is an utterly clear aquamarine near the shoreline, a bruised purple farther out above the reefs, and, some hundred feet beyond that, an abrupt, opaque, deepwater indigo. When Darrell, who had the key from the leasing agent, first threw open the front door to show her this house, Lucy looked down a cluttered foyer past someone else's ratty living room furniture through two sliding glass doors into that view: water and sky, blue on blue, infinite and empty. Her head swam and she laid her hand on Darrell's arm to avoid falling. He read her touch as appreciation and hugged and then kissed her.

"Spectacular, isn't it?" he said. "We're going to be happy here." He'd held her face between his hands and kissed her again, then turned her loose to stride further into the house, narrating its features, optimistically implying the efficacy of each one in sending the Langstons forward, into new lives beginning that day.

She extends her hand and strokes Darrell's back tentatively. He stirs, then turns to her drowsily. She opens her legs and pulls him atop her body. He touches her in the ways he has for sixteen years, her body begins its response, and they make love. When he enters, he kisses her mouth once, then puts his face in its habitual place against her neck. She holds onto his heaving shoulders, tight, as to a lifeline, and only when she hears by his breathing that he is about to come does she apply herself to her own habits, touching herself, shifting the angle of her pelvis so she can try—and this time she succeeds—to climax.

It's over quickly, and afterwards, she feels uneasy. Sex never seems to fix the longing that prompts her to summon it; most of the time she's more anxious after sex than she was before because something she needs desperately—and about which she feels desperately guilty—something she cannot name, but that drove her out of the house to the cabin in the Berkshires three years ago—never happens. She does not know what it is. All she knows is its absence, some intuition of what it would feel like if she found it...but it is not there. Never there. She feels for the feeling each time like a foot probing hesitantly for a stair in the dark—and draws back, each time, suspended in anxiety.

Each time she learns the same lesson: it's a mistake to try. Each time she puts herself to sleep afterwards by analyzing her mistake. She explains to herself that whatever it is she yearns for doesn't exist. She is yearning for—nothing! So she had better learn to stop yearning. And keep her thoughts moving.

And mostly she does. But sometimes she doesn't, sometimes she just can't get the mass of her misery to move.

When she sleeps, she has a new dream. A black man running.

He's loping down the South Shore Road toward town, past that colonnade of royal palms on the straightaway at Hungry Bay. He is lean, his muscles and ribs clearly defined. The mass of his dreadlocks floats behind him, weightless, a cloud.

She stands barefoot—she has lost her shoes—in sharp gravel alongside the road amid a throng of onlookers she can sense but not see. The runner streams past her without a glance. She smells his sweat. Sees it gleaming on his skin. In the dream, she has something to tell him, a secret no one in the crowd behind her can know, something so important that she sweats and strains to speak it as their anonymous breaths fall on her bare arms.

But her mouth will not open. And when she wakes, she doesn't know what she wanted to tell, nor why.

Over breakfast she finally tells Darrell that Peyton is having trouble in school. She doesn't elaborate. Peyton is in the shower, and she has to get this said before he gets out; she's told him not to tell his father about the suspension. She's certain Peyton understands that this secret serves him, but she also knows that keeping it troubles him. It certainly compromises her. She punished him—confiscating the new stereo for the three days he was suspended—for his lie to her about the notes he should have brought home from school, but now she makes him lie to Darrell, because she's lying. She scrapes and scrubs the soles of Peyton's school shoes above the trash can while she asks Darrell about the possibility of another school. "He's not adjusting well to Somers," she says. "I don't think it's the right place for him."

Darrell is rinsing his cereal bowl at the sink. His eyes sweep across the dirty dishes on the counters from last night;

she can feel his distaste for the mess and the immediate effort he has to make to repress it. He says, "You've seen the government schools here, Lucy. You know we don't want him there. Berkeley Prep's the only other private school with an academic diploma and it's a predominantly black school. I don't think they'd take an expat, especially now. So Somers Academy is pretty much it. Everyone I talk to says it's an excellent school."

They hear the door of the hall bath bang against the stop as Peyton throws it open. In a few seconds he'll be in the kitchen. Darrell picks up his briefcase and reaches for his helmet. He does not complain about riding the scooter so she and Peyton can use the one car the island's law allows each household, even though he catches soot in his ears every day and gets doused when there's a downpour. He says, "Lucy, you heard what Jonathan said last night. You can see what I'm dealing with here. Race riots and labor strikes are not what I bargained for when the company sent me here, and New York doesn't want to hear my troubles; everybody there is still reeling from 9/11. They think Bermuda is remote and I'm safe, but every time I turn around I have to get on a plane. Did I tell you I've got to go to Frankfurt in two weeks? You're going to have to work with Peyton about school — I'm at the limit of what I can handle."

He straps the helmet on, starts to leave and then turns back, hesitates, and bends to kiss her cheek — awkwardly, his lips reaching at her from inside the plastic shell on his head. She hears Peyton's sock feet, padding up behind them. Darrell, squeezing her shoulder, says, "You'll do fine, Lucy. You always do."

He hugs Peyton. Then he leaves for work. Outside the door he pulls open, the sunrise is an incendiary orange.

She drives Peyton to school, preoccupied with what she has and has not told Darrell, how angry and disappointed he'd be if she did tell him the rest. Peyton does not talk and neither does she, although she knows they should. Finally, at a stop sign, she puts her hand on his arm. He turns her way slowly, as if coming back from a distance. She says, "We've got to be honest with each other about what's happening at your school, Peyton. If I know, maybe I can help. Are the boys there picking on you?"

He looks at her for so long she has to pull away from the stop sign because someone behind her honks. When her eyes are on the road, she hears him say, very quietly, "School sucks."

"Oh, Peyton." She slows down, thinking she'll pull over and they'll talk.

"It *sucks.*" Suddenly he's shouting at her. "Did you hear me? Somers Academy sucks and there's not one fucking thing you can do about it."

She feels slapped, as much by the truth of what he says as by his uncharacteristic vulgarity. In the pull-through at the schoolyard, watching Peyton trudge up the steps, she consoles herself that at least Zef Passjohn is not inside to make things worse. She recalls her first sight of Zef, in this yard, the first week of school when she was late picking Peyton up because she'd misjudged afternoon traffic patterns. She saw no one standing in the yard, and her worried heart had just begun to pound when both boys dropped out of the banyan tree right alongside the driver's side window, making her jump. They laughed at her. Together, in meanness, they laughed: her skinny, blond son with babyish bowl-cut hair, and that other, darker boy on the other side of the divide of puberty, the evidence unmistakable in the girth of his forearms and the faintly lupine weight of his jaw. She'd observed that dichotomy before, in the Boys' Club program in Stamford where she volunteered as a literacy tutor. Zef was thirteen, not twelve, and tough rather than sheltered; that difference, surely, was all that threatened her. Still, it had been all she could do not to say, to that handsome, tawny-brown young man with unnaturally light eyes, *Go away. I don't like you,* the urge to do so as visceral as if the hair on her neck were lifting.

That feeling was a premonition, she thinks now, not the

retrograde racist moment she judged it to be then. Zef is a troubled boy who causes trouble to distract himself from his own pain; she's familiar with the type from trying to teach them. And yet Zef, this bad influence she needs her son to avoid, is Marcus Passjohn's son. And the very second she allows his name and his image into her thoughts the memory of his hand touching hers ripples through her flesh, and every cell of it responds. How is this possible? Why is this possible?

She heads west on Middle Road to the intersection with Camp Hill, where that road climbs the ridge and descends to the South Shore Road and home. She passes Mr. Trott— purple shirt, straw boater, benedictory smile—and waves at him like everybody else does. As her car labors up Camp Hill through steep switchbacks, raising a cloud of red dust, a motor scooter passes her, headed downhill, carrying two black men, a ladder and multiple buckets of paint. Scrawny chickens forage alongside the road and a cow, tied to a stake by its horns, gathers flies in the corners of its large, patient eyes. Near the top of the hill, in a working class neighborhood of tightly clustered, brightly colored houses with doorways flush with the street, she passes one no different from the rest except for its name, *Basil's Dream*, and its paint, an eye-rending chartreuse. And she wonders, as she does every time she passes it, twice in each direction every school day, about the reason or no-reason so ethereal a name got attached to so frankly squat and lurid a structure, the paradox begging to comment, she cannot stop thinking this—she has too much time for thinking—on either the dream or the dreamer.

She pulls out of a curve at the crest of the ridge to a panorama of land and water—the houses, tangerine orange, school bus yellow, crayon blue, terraced one above and against the other; the sun-drunk rocky fields below them; and the scintillating sea beyond—and feels herself thrust face-first into the damn beauty of this damn difficult place.

She pulls over. She can barely breathe. Her thoughts snag on the feeling and she labors to explain to herself why: the colors, the faces, her emotions assault her. In her earliest days in the rented house, when the prevalence of dark faces at the bus stops and in the shops reminded her constantly that her life in Connecticut had ended, the green brakes of oleander lining these roads blazed with hot pink flowers lifted resolutely to a merciless summer sun. Sometimes what she remembered when she looked at them was the equally hot pink of the cool, blowzy blossoms of the peonies she left blooming in her backyard in Darien the day she moved away. Amid the black faces staring back at her with curiosity or suspicion or righteous affront, there appeared the pale face of her neighbor Mike, his thick glasses and bald top spotted with drizzle, standing on her deck in Darien with his teenage son Lawrence, a forever-dependent child born with Down syndrome, grinning in innocent *joie de vivre* alongside his father's humble depression, shoving uncomprehendingly into Lucy's hands a framed photograph of the home she was forever leaving.

She stares sometimes into that picture, shot from across the street and at an angle in the low, yellow light of late afternoon that made the redwood façade of the house a rich ginger-brown and the leaves of the copper beech tree towering alongside it a shimmer of burgundy in the breeze lifting and turning them, and she pictures Mike, a man she befriended—cautiously, at arms' length, because he was more lonely than she was—kneeling in the garden behind her house, meticulously loosening from the soaked and clinging earth a piece of her garden, to transplant to his.

Darrell speaks into the ear of her memory, standing behind her at the sink in their Connecticut kitchen, where the white splash tiles turn back at her the same glare as did the snow banks in the Berkshires and the forged steel blades of the chef knives in the cabin those weeks she spent alone trying to breathe, trying hard not to stop trying, that lapse in her attention to her husband and her son buried and never resurrected. Darrell says, "The move will be easy. You won't have to do a thing." His hand settles on her shoulder, and from inside the untruth of his assurance, she replays the sound of her mother and her sister, from a remove of more than thirty years, laughing at her as the electric doors of the train from Darien to Manhattan part like curtains at 125th Street in Harlem, revealing to Lucy's pre-school self a carnival of new shades of face and loud clothes and interesting hats; her mother and her sister roll their eyes, and when she gets up to pass through that door, her mother's firm hand settles on her shoulder and sits her down hard. *"For heaven's sake, Lucy, we don't get off here."*

She wipes her face, surfacing. She contemplates the sea and its shore. She decides to walk the stretch of beach before her, Warwick Long Bay, before she cleans up the Thanksgiving mess from the cliff house kitchen. And then, abruptly, three pieces of this morning that didn't fit but should have snap together in her mind: Peyton, his shoes and the sand stuck to them. Yesterday he walked a beach at some point, even though he spent the whole day, ostensibly, at school or in his room. He had no sand on his feet when she picked him up at Somers. The car is new, she habitually checks his feet when he climbs in. He had to have gone to the beach while she was busy cooking. No other explanation works. And if he's lying and sneaking, Zef must be involved.

She grips the wheel as if she might fall without something solid to hold onto. She is going to have to watch him more carefully. She is going to have to confront him, make rules and enforce them, be suspicious of infractions. And she needs to tell Marcus Passjohn to tell his son to leave hers alone. He gave her his card for that reason, in case something came up about the boys. She will have to stop flirting inside herself with what it might mean if she talked to him. She will need to be firm with herself and with him. She will give him no chance to touch her nor make her look at him; she'll use the phone and be brief.

She pulls back onto the road and heads home, to the day-after-Thanksgiving dishes. Her eyes sting from crying, but... cresting the hill, she senses a mystery beginning. Her heart lifting. Rising up instead of giving up. This odd feeling has to do with Marcus, and she knows it is the wrong feeling, but she can't stop it. She doesn't try. She feels ground beneath her feet, the earth lifting smoothly to meet her next step as if she were running, not driving, down this hill.

8

Marcus arrives at his office in Parliament Building before seven a.m. one day in the first week of December, having passed through an armed checkpoint manned by the Regiment, the island's national guard, on his way from Rose Hill into town. With the gunshot white man Horace Tucker still lying in hospital in a coma, no shooter apprehended, and the veracity of his account of who shot him, and why, the topic of increasingly paranoid and contradictory speculation in the press, over dinner tables, and on the street, the race grudge Marcus is accused of resurrecting now displays robust and insidious life.

Lifting a box of files from the Bentley's passenger seat, then wrestling its maimed door latch shut, he can't keep himself from feeling a very personal anger that it's the assault of a white man rather than the dumpster deaths of two black men that gets the Regiment on the street to "protect the citizenry." Nothing tangible has happened to further challenge civil order since Tucker went on life support, but his shooting's affront to the status quo is a palpable danger to the people with the power to call out the legally sanctioned guns, and the danger *that* creates for everyone is as real as the AK-47 Marcus has just observed trembling in an eighteen-year-old conscript's pale hands.

He lets himself into his office. Turning the key, he feels the lock already disengaged, and when the door swings open, he sees far more mess—sliding from his desk to the floor, spilling from its drawers and his filing cabinets—than he left behind yesterday. The office has been ransacked, not too thoroughly but with no attempt at all to hide the trespass. He sets down the box very carefully on the seat of his desk chair, the one available clear surface, then pulls his hand across his weary eyes, gritty from last night's bout with insomnia. As if he could soothe himself. As if.

Without addressing what might have been read or taken— what difference could knowing make? whatever it is, it's already in play—he picks his way across the littered floor to the window facing Front Street. Forehead pressed to the glass, palm cupping his stomach, which aches from too much black tea too early in the day, he looks down through first gray light on the buses, cars, early pedestrians, and the empty wharf where in better days cruise ships would have been tied. His day began at five a.m. with a call from Althea Trott. He doesn't remember when she last phoned him; despite their lives' long entanglement they seldom speak socially. She prefers to record her grievances at his shortcomings—his failure to live up to his own and others' myth-making—on paper, in long, rancorous letters mailed simultaneously to the newspaper and his office. This morning, however, her phone call conveyed some very specific plans she's made for him. She apprised him of her conviction that the dead black men, her cousin Rufus and his friend Breem, were killed and dumped by Cisco Suggs, punk and snitch and, she claims she knows this for a fact, Government-paid provocateur. The police have told her the case is closed, but she means to reopen it, and to that end, she's apprehended Suggs herself. Marcus had stared at the phone, at her invisible insistent voice emanating from it, trouble he has no idea how to handle—but he agreed to meet her at noon today in her bakeshop on the ground floor of the modest building her mother bequeathed her, Basil's Dream.

Rufus and Breem's deaths have not, in fact, been overlooked by the authorities; Marcus has personal knowledge of this. Only two days ago, two detectives, with a sweating, miserable

Officer Eugene Outerbridge in tow, visited Marcus right here in Parliament House, asking a series of questions about the dead men, the reason for Marcus's interest in them on the day of their discovery, and the dovetailing of their reputation as petty criminals, as *miscreants*, with Marcus's publicly avowed commitment to violence and bloodshed. Yesterday's *Gazette* carried a front page story decrying the honorable Opposition leader's dishonorable financial transactions: it's a matter of public record now that Mr. Passjohn's in default on his mortgage; sources allege he's offered his alma mater Berkeley Prep a "donation" to reinstate his son there, and court records show he posted bail just last month for the "well-known Rastafarian black separatist and convicted terrorist, Ramo Wylie, arrested on Guy Fawkes Night in connection with the sabotage there."

The hammering on the frame being constructed around him is almost the only thing Marcus can hear this morning. Abruptly he turns away from the window and makes his way down a deserted hallway to the large, sunny corner office belonging to the justice minister. Isaiah Barnes' door is open — he is notoriously at his desk before dawn for the bracing example this provides his staff — and Marcus walks right in. He closes the door firmly behind himself and speaks.

"When you have shut me up, Isaiah, when you have removed me from the scene, do you think no one else will step forward to speak? Do you not believe that the truth will out eventually?"

Isaiah's broad backside is parked atop his desk front. He holds the morning paper in his lap, a coffee in one hand and a buttered roll in the other. The monogrammed cuffs of his white dress shirt contrast crisply with his thick dark wrists. The wingtips that gently drum the mahogany desk front are new, glossy, and expensive. "Come again?" he says, disengaging his glance from the newspaper slowly, blinking as if Marcus has disturbed deep concentration.

"Did you have my office searched?"

Isaiah chews a bite of roll thoroughly and wipes his mouth with his hand before answering. "I don't know what you're talking about, Passjohn."

Marcus steps in closer. "I see what you are doing. You, and by extension, those you serve, have done all you can to ratchet up people's oldest fears, and now you will make a scapegoat and string it up, so that Government can appear to protect the people from their fears."

Isaiah's expression suggests thoughtful appreciation but his gaze slides past Marcus. "Nice speech," he says. "And you're right, it's a nervous world we live in. Here on this island, where the gross in our Gross Domestic Product depends entirely on the one product we have to sell, our tourist-friendly, commerce-friendly image, we have got the radical black fringe preying on white folks—"

"Drop that tired race card, Isaiah." Marcus shifts to place himself once again directly in Isaiah's sight. "You and I both know the real issue is indeed GDP. Money is power. Those that have it intend to keep it, and those that can't touch it are desperate."

"You the one played the race card, Marcus, breathing fire at Guy Fawkes. I just followed the suit you led." He circles his desk and seats himself behind it in his capacious black leather chair. Marcus notices the faint sheen of moisture on the slender roll of neck flesh Isaiah's white collar squeezes toward his ears.

"So it appears," Marcus says. "That's a perception quite a few people carry now, one assisted by you, the police force you direct, and the press that toadies to the Government that pays you. But *you* know that what I said that night came in response to two bodies in a dumpster, plus the race reasons *and* the money reasons that got them there."

The knot of Isaiah's yellow club tie rides his Adam's apple up and down as he swallows. He picks up a thick paperbound book from the desk, roughly thumbs the pages, stops, and slams the book—a dictionary—back to the desktop. "Since you so fucking smart, Mr. Honorable Passjohn Sir, since you have got so much to say in Parliament and at the public podium about who should shut up and who shouldn't, who knows the right words and who doesn't, I don't know why

I got to explain this to you, but here goes: If the not-white people on this island are going to touch any of the big money, especially when it's such nervous, foreign money, we have got to make whitey feel safe. Troublemakers like you, and your Rasta friends, and your union friends, who are determined to be black first and citizens second or not at all, have got to shut up. And if you need assistance in shutting up, then so be it. It is the function of government to maintain order."

When he's finished, the tips of his fingers, poised on his desk edge, quiver like birds just short of take-off.

Marcus says, "You're desperate for some reason, aren't you? Whatever you've done, you're improvising."

Isaiah spins the chair on its ball mount, turning his back. He lifts a cigar from a humidor on the credenza behind his desk and offers it, as he rotates the chair back around, to Marcus, who waves it aside. Isaiah bites off the cigar's end and digs the nub from his mouth with his forefinger. He says, making unblinking eye contact with Marcus for the first time that day, "It's whitey's tune on the turntable, yeah, but I can remix it."

The staccato clicks of high heels on ceramic tile in the hallway announce the arrival of Isaiah's secretary. A Windows operating system wakes up with musical good cheer, and Government begins a new day.

"Whatever it is you're doing," Marcus tells Isaiah slowly, "it's all about you, isn't it? Your ambition. Your survival."

"Survival." Isaiah speaks around the unlit cigar, and Marcus watches it bobble. "I believe you've nailed the issue, Passjohn. Our government, our citizens, their jobs, and our civil order need to survive. And to that end, to answer the question you barged in here with, yes, shutting you up would help. But what's *imperative*—you like that word? it big enough for you?—is that we catch the black son of bitch that shot the good citizen Tucker, and hang him. And the blacker and the nastier the shooter, the more effective the solution for everyone." He pulls the cigar from his mouth and points it at Marcus's chest. "For that reason, any black son of a bitch with dreads will do."

Marcus takes one full step backward in reaction to so preposterous an equation. Around the cigar, Isaiah mumbles, hands busy shuffling the papers in front of him, "I'm kidding, Passjohn. Bad joke. Bad taste. I apologize. But I'm feeling testy now, on account of it's way past time for you to leave."

Some hours later, striding into the lurid green building that houses Althea's shop, Marcus loosens his tie. His anxiety is strong enough to make his breath shallow. Exactly what he fears he couldn't name if someone cared enough to ask, yet his body and his mind seem independently certain it resides inside Basil's Dream. As the screen door slaps shut behind him, he sees nothing but a clutter of cheap plastic chairs and small round tables, the glass counter case half-filled with bread and pies, and, across the room, worn wooden stairs leading to an upper floor where various relatives of Althea live from time to time, including most recently her cousin Rufus, his underage girl, and their baby. The only person in sight, seated on the bottom stair beside Althea's special pride and joy — a huge, outdated fax machine salvaged from some expatriate's moving day trash — is a teenage girl with glasses, bad skin, and a loose shift pulled over her drawn-up knees. A sullen sentinel, she points wordlessly at the door to the back room.

When Marcus pulls that open, he's shocked to see Kenrick Desmond, who should have had no way to know of this appointment, seated opposite Althea on up-ended institutional-sized tins of vegetable oil, amid heaps of flour sacks and three battered, dented filing cabinets, repositories of Althea's decades-long correspondence with Government ministries, the editor's desk of the *Gazette*, and Marcus. The air is so thick with suspended particles of flour that Marcus feels it clinging to the hairs inside his nostrils. Kenrick's sharply creased dark wool trousers and nipped-waist suit coat are frosted with it, and the light from outside, a great block of it let through a glassless window, the louvered wooded shutter shattered and hanging in shards, glows iridescent from a cloud of flour motes floating in it. Althea, a curling stripe bronzed into the brilliantined dome of her hair, a load of gold bangles ringing her fleshy forearms, bears a heavy dusting as well, as if someone has shaken a sieve over her. Between them, lying naked in a position almost fetal amid a burst-sack puddle of flour, bound at the ankles, knees and elbows with silver duct tape, is Cisco Suggs. His mouth has not been taped, however, and Suggs—a slight, bland-featured man appearing oddly unfazed by his circumstances—acknowledges Marcus's arrival with a sneer: "Here comes our stand-up man."

"Dry up, murdering dog," Althea says, driving the toe of her shoe, broad and flat, flesh spilling over the straining leather, into his thigh at an angle that makes Marcus know she means to make Cisco wish he could protect his privates. She rests that foot on the small man's hip and addresses Marcus. "I catch him for you. He the one kill my cousin and Breem." One gold tooth up front glints when she speaks.

"I see there's been a struggle," Marcus says, indicating the gaping window. A stomach spasm makes him want to bend double, and he stands uneasily in flour shoals shifting on the breeze slipping past the broken shutter. His pants legs are whitening, as is Cisco's beige, racially indistinct skin.

"We only took him down after he broke out the window heaving twenty kilos of lard through it," Kenrick says. "She's had him shut up in here since last night, but he was free to move around and keep his clothes on, until he tried to leave."

Marcus wants to say, What are *you* doing here? He cannot get his sleep-deprived brain to cogitate what it might mean to find Kenrick, his lieutenant in Parliament, here. He says, slowly, "Who stripped him? Who taped him?"

"Took them both to do it," Suggs says, sneering again. "She's big but she's clumsy. And he does exactly what she tells him to."

When Althea steps down hard on his hip, calling him a limp-dick weasel, he says, "Big ass, big mouth, how was it I ever thought I could tell a difference," and she bends to strike him in the face with her open palm. Kenrick tells her, "Ease up," and Suggs, blood welling from his lip, asks him, "Were you big enough to find the difference 'tween this bitch's mouth and her cunt?"

It takes Kenrick on one arm and Marcus on the other to pull her off the bound man. Marcus tells Althea she's just added assault to the crime of hostage-taking. He tells her sure, he understands she wants vengeance for her cousin's death and the manner of that death but that she cannot, because he will not let her, take the law into her own hands. He wants to ask her how much of this rage is for a lover who's jilted her—now he's caught onto that—and he does *not* want to ask about what he thinks he's also catching on to, that Kenrick, half her age and the son of her foster sibling, is or has been her lover. He avoids looking at Kenrick as they push Althea's bulk against the wall, and he asks her why she's so sure Suggs is the murderer.

"He write it all down." She's panting; she's heavy and often short of breath. "An' he show it to Rufus."

"Lying bitch. I never did that. Showed it to you after you plied me with that damn big ass of yours."

Suggs sings this out, as if with some recollected pleasure, and Althea, maybe only because she's winded, ignores him. She says, in spurts of breath, "He give Rufus, an' Breem, too, great big wads of cash to do ever'thing he tell them to, and ever'thing Suggs done, ever' fire he set, ever' store he make them vandalize, ever' man they beat up and drop, he write it down. Little red book. Blood-money book."

"Where's the book now?" Marcus asks Suggs.

"It's not on him," Kenrick says. "We checked."

Suggs says, "I burned it. Why'd I keep evidence like that around?"

Marcus thinks, What made you create evidence like that in the first place? But he knows why: if not for protection from the power that paid him, then for leverage against it. Which means Suggs most likely has not destroyed it.

Marcus asks Althea as she sinks to the tin Kenrick's pushed beneath her, "What is it you think I can do with him?"

She looks him in the eye and blinks. He sees from her expression she's not really thought that far. She acted on impulse, depending on Marcus to know what to do. He doesn't.

She says, "He kill his own kind. He deserve to die."

"You want me to kill him for you, Althea? Because if somebody doesn't, you might?"

Kenrick, standing by the window now, brushing flour from his suit, says, "I think it's justice she wants, Marcus. People do associate you with that concept."

Kenrick, Marcus notes, no longer respects him as he used to. Probably he never deserved the respect the younger man once gave him so freely but he doesn't understand why it's only now begun to fade.

"Take him to the police," Kenrick goes on. "Make them charge him. Make them suspect him, at least."

Marcus laughs bitterly. He squats at Suggs' feet and begins stripping off the tape. "The police don't want him. He'd cause them all kinds of pain, particularly if he produced that little blood book for them." He rips tape from around Suggs' knees, noting without much feeling of his own how the man flinches as the adhesive yanks hairs out. "The police would not believe a word I said, either." He raises a palm, admonitory, to stop Kenrick from interfering. "Isaiah Barnes recently sent a few of his minions to question me about Rufus and Breem. To treat me like a suspect-in-the-making. And this morning my office was burgled, a fact that seemed no surprise to our justice minister."

He's freed Suggs' arms. Althea, heaving herself to her feet and needing more than one try to succeed, says, "You let him go, somebody kill him, he wrong so many people." Her hand closes on Marcus's forearm, and her nails, false ones, onyx black and rhinestone-studded, dent his flesh. She wheezes when she speaks but the heavy gold loops in her earlobes swing with her vehemence. "That red book. We got to have it before he die."

Marcus hears Kenrick, behind him, locking the door. He watches Suggs, unsteady on legs that are surely numb, shift almost imperceptibly toward the window. He pretends he doesn't notice. He says to Althea, "When this little coward is desperate enough, when he sees, finally, how it serves him, that evidence will turn up in hands that can use it, and it will be nothing but trouble."

"Listen to the pot calling the kettle a coward," Suggs says.

"Aren't you a coward?" Marcus asks. He still squats, his knees and his belly hurting.

"Aren't you?" Suggs responds. There is eye contact, and he's gone. Out the window, stumbling, naked.

Kenrick exhales audibly. "You let him go. You *let* him go."

"I couldn't stand breathing his craven stink."

Althea's two palms land with force against his chest, knocking him nearly off his feet. He catches himself, his back against the door. She says, "You *doin'* nothing. Nothing come out o' you ever but *words*."

Her voice breaks and Kenrick reaches for her shoulder. She turns on him. "Don' you go condescendin' on me, little Kenrick Desmond. Wearin' Oleg Cassini and sittin' high in Parliament now but I remember you in a droopin', drippin' nappy."

The complex shame on Kenrick's face makes Marcus avert his eyes. He reaches for Althea's hand because she's crying; he can squeeze it once before she snatches it away. He recalls scrubbing her cousin's congealed blood from the back of his own hand just before she last indicted him as a man of nothing but words, minutes before his speech at Guy Fawkes.

"Words are my way, Althea," he tells her. "My sword and my Achilles' heel. Government wants to stop my words. I will not shut up. That way there's at least a chance I'll encourage someone to take my place when I fall."

"You settin' youself up as savior." Althea bites down on the last word, turning her back and sinking to her knees in the flour smearing the floor. "Same as what you claim you do for my brother when he lose his legs. Talk big about making ever'thing right and do nothin' but make a mess I carry all my life."

"I'm nobody's savior, Althea. That much is surely clear."

He leaves, slipping out the door Kenrick has unlocked

for his own exit, passing the teenage sentry now pulling a fax from the machine while she balances on her hip a bare-bottomed toddler with a dripping nose. This would likely be the baby-mama and the child Rufus left behind; Marcus hopes the bankroll Rufus also left is thick enough to carry them a good long while.

On the doorstep, flush with the street, he finds Kenrick waiting. Leaning on the Bentley, parked as close as Marcus could pull it to this ugly house with its ridiculous name. He offers Kenrick a ride to town.

He declines. "My scooter's in the alley."

Marcus peers around the corner of the building, sees it half-hidden behind a collection of battered rubbish cans, and speaks the question he thought he wouldn't ask. "What brought you here?"

"I came out here to talk to her about...a problem. You know she and my mother go way back. Then Suggs showed up." He shrugs. "One thing led to another. You know."

He does know. The terms between him and Kenrick are under revision. He intuits this has to do with Althea, in some subterranean but important way beyond any sex that may have happened. Walking round the Bentley's nose to the driver's side door, he finds the ancient car has been freshly vandalized, the words *live like us* scratched into the dull paint with the point of a key. He traces the new scar with his finger. Kenrick, from the mouth of the alley says, "Something wrong?"

He waves Kenrick on his way. Pulls his own keys from his pocket and considers obliterating the words, enlarging the scar. Just how *should* a righteous black man behave?

Leaving Althea's shop, Marcus drives the two kilometers downhill through s-curves toward the dump and the cluster of dwellings on its fringe where the tiny house she shares with her brother Lemuel stands right next to Ramo Wylie's place. Marcus will have five minutes, even as much as ten, should he get stuck behind a slow-moving vehicle, before he arrives at Ramo's door. In the interim, to still his breath and quiet the roiling in his gut, he lets his thoughts free to seek a place where problems are at bay and no consequences yet exist: his date, tomorrow, with Lucy Langston.

Of course it's *not* a date; they've each been meticulous about terming it a meeting, and a meeting, about the boys, is in fact what it is. But for reasons he does not examine, the rendezvous feels like a date, and that feels *good*.

When she called him, a week ago, he was thrilled. Shocked, but thrilled — like finding an unexpected and very large check in the mail. First he'd let her say what she needed to say — that his son was what was wrong with her son. She was right, of course, and he told her that. Clearly she hadn't expected him to agree, so a little silence arose. He thought he could hear her thinking where to go from there, and he recognized she might solve the problem by saying good-bye. So he said quickly, "We should talk some more." She didn't answer, but she didn't hang up. He heard her catch her breath. "About the boys," he reassured her — and himself. "Surely we can find ways to help them both, and we can do a better job of that if we both know something about the individual family circumstances." She didn't answer. Marcus, feeling his heart beginning to race, said, "Look. My son got your son in trouble. I feel bad. I like to fix things where I can. I realize you're offended, and you probably don't want anything more to do with me or my son, but I'd appreciate the chance to help. I really would."

His humility, fundamentally sincere, had been sufficient to embarrass her. She said, "Okay," and he chose to overlook the fact he'd just manipulated her. His own need to have some of what her presence gave him was way too imperative, as instinctive as gulping air.

"Lunch?" he said quickly, naming a day. Again she hesitated, and he found himself up against the paradox of the nondate-date problem. Where exactly could they meet? Neither privately nor secretly, as that would make it a liaison, but it was best not to be seen together in public either. Virtually no one on the island would fail to recognize him, and as a pair they would certainly stand out. He'd had to say — so he could puzzle out the logistics — that he'd get back to her. And he had, that same day, for fear she'd change her mind. "The Botanical Garden?" he asked then. "Is that all right?" Public but private, too; very few people went there. "We can walk or sit on a bench and talk a bit."

"I've never been to the Botanical Garden," Lucy said. "I hear it's beautiful."

That simply, the date was made.

Still, Marcus's spirits droop the moment he pulls into the dirt lot at Ramo's Cycle Repair. A police cruiser idles at the door and two officers, both white, speak with Ramo, their hands at their loaded belts.

Crossing the lot from his car to the shop, Marcus draws stares from the various working folks currently unemployed, sitting on chairs in the yards and on the front steps of the little cinderblock houses behind Ramo's shop. Lemuel Trott is parked in his usual place, three feet back from the curb, urging traffic along, waving gently.

"Dis not de Parliament, mon," Ramo says to Marcus. His lips lift off his teeth, strong ones, for he still has a mouth full of them after fifty years of poverty and incarceration. A foot taller than the officers, Ramo speaks over their heads, and when they see Marcus, they get in the cruiser quickly and go.

Ramo laughs at them. "Po-lice run when dey see my defender comin'," he says.

Marcus does not laugh. He asks Ramo what the officers wanted.

No warrant, just questions, Ramo explains, about arson and guns. "Dey stop here to chat. De po-lice like *I-an-I* so much."

I and I, the Rastafarian's imperial we. Always it annoys Marcus because, always, it lets Ramo sound bigger than one man. Makes him God and self and brethren, all in one breath.

He asks Ramo the question he's come armed with. "Who

shot Tucker?" Ramo drops a name Marcus doesn't know and adds affably, "He gone." On a small boat to a larger boat and back to Barbados. "Crackhead. Bad mon." The gun, Ramo is not sure about. The police have it or so they've made him think, even though Marcus has heard they don't have it. Ramo, however, they've told a different story: they have a gun and they have prints.

"They have your prints on file. You think of that, Ramo?"

"*I-an-I* do, yes," he replies.

Marcus shakes his head. "I've come to warn you. Government needs a shooter to hang. A bearded black goat like you, the kind people love to hate."

From behind Ramo, Marcus hears something metallic, the sound of a tool, perhaps, tossed against a can. He hears voices, too—young ones, in whispers.

Ramo says, "*I-an-I* got somet'ing to tell you. Night de Guy Fawkes fire, *I-an-I* hear you speakin' Jah's tongue. 'De black mon reveal de black mon to he-self,' you say. You righteous, Marcus, e'en you don' know it."

Marcus is rummaging for exactly the right words to express how little he cares what Ramo and his Jah judge him to be, given the fruitless years—sometimes it seems like his whole professional life—he's spent defending "*I-an-I*" from the law, when a dog bursts out barking. Marcus catches sight of Peyton Langston bolting down the lane from Ramo's back door past the house Lemuel shares with Althea.

Marcus sprints around the shop and through that door. Doubtless Zef was there but left first and only the white boy set off the dog. As his eyes adjust to the shop's dim light, he takes in the battered counter and an ancient till. Shelves loaded with tools, used pedals and brackets, and a few new scooter parts in dusty plastic bubble packs. Rasta mottos pinned to the walls, a pedagogy for those customers who can read:

One God, One Aim, One Destiny.

All black men are brothers.

Cowards cannot win.

He turns away, fatigue making his feet heavy. On the dirt floor, oily rags are piled amid buckets overflowing with greasy salvaged screws. The place is a firetrap. Ramo still fills the front door and Marcus asks him the one question that levels everything between them: "Where is my son?"

Ramo removes his crochet cap and wipes his face with it. Unbundled, his locks hang to his waist. He says, "Let de boy be."

"He's not going to school. He comes here instead. Nothing I want means anything to him."

Ramo steps inside. "To what end you sendin' you fine son to a white school?"

"He's not in a white school. He's in government school, now, since no other place would take him."

"Gov'ment school be white school," Ramo counters. "What they teachin'? White ways. Black mon's place."

As Marcus leaves, Ramo speaks to his back. "De problem you havin', Marcus, is that you are mix' up. Sometime you see black, sometime white. You wife, de pretty English lady, she confuse you. She confuse you boy, too. She gone, long time before. Let mix-up be gone."

Marcus's gaze drops to the metal cot in the corner, with its single dingy blanket and the night pot beside it. A slatted wooden box at the foot of the cot holds a folded pair of ragged pants, a stained shirt, a bowl, and a pipe.

"What should I make of that white boy in your shop, Ramo? I suppose he is a truant, like Zef. My boy, and now a *white* boy, cutting school to come here. There is ganja here. These boys are minors." He looks the tall man in the eye as he speaks. "Ramo. You are courting trouble. The police have all they need to arrest you any time."

"That de truth always," Ramo replies.

From opposite sides of the one-room shop, the two men regard each other. Ramo says, "Some new trouble devilin' Zef. White boy, he a sign. Zef needin' somet'ing, very bad."

Marcus draws a deep breath and expels it. "If that's so, Ramo, I have no idea what it would be. And whatever it is, it doesn't seem likely he wants it from me." Quickly he walks out the back door, forestalling the hand that wants to cradle his gut.

The full sun outside half-blinds him. He has to walk with extreme care to avoid stumbling. Women with baskets and men in dirty boots and sweat-stained shirts stare at his face and his floury suit as they cut through the lot on their way home to lunch or back to work. He goes not to his car but to the curb, his dress shoes filling with dust. He is late now for a meeting with Opposition colleagues, to draft a response to the armed checkpoints' pressure on civil liberties, but he must speak to Lemuel before he goes. It's been such a long time since he's visited with Lemuel who once visited him almost daily, when he was a small boy and the mother he barely remembers had died and he belonged to no one in particular. Young Lemuel came then in the evenings, weary from a day's work begun before dawn, his hands full of treasures: broken golf tees, lost pennies, the scarred stubs of scorecard pencils.

Here is a man who served his white masters like a dog.

With those words, his first speech before Parliament, Marcus tried to honor Lemuel.

...he caddied their clubs and fetched their drinks and cleaned their cleats at Fairylands Golf Course for seventeen years until circulation problems lamed him. And when poor circulation progressed to no circulation and gangrene chewed his flesh, the white doctors he'd waited on let him wait...

Marcus remembers raising into the air a photograph of Lemuel in his wheelchair where he'd already sat, by the day of the speech, for ten years. In the nearly deserted gallery a cub reporter sat scribbling and behind him—oh, he sees her ghost clearly—Lydia's stern face, a form of fuel he needed, and before Marcus more seats empty than filled—members gone home early, a Friday in June, so long ago and so hot, the ceiling fans treading humidity—but the few faces Marcus faced were white, and he told them clearly what he thought they needed to hear.

...while British troops blocked the roads and pointed guns and searched citizens for signs of their intention to harm white people, Lemuel Trott had to wait. But his gangrene did not wait, and when the doctors came out of hiding they took off his legs, leaving Lemuel Trott to wait again, this time for justice, denied, still, to this very

day....

The day after that speech Marcus visited Lemuel and Althea at home. Lemuel's hands held the day's *Gazette*, reporting his cause had been denied and anointing Marcus, in a black-banded editorial, a dangerous radical to be watched. Althea said, "We got nothin', but you makin' out well enough." Lemuel said, "De Lord bless you, Marcus. He make you tongue burn righteous and de men stand afraid."

Now, sixteen years later, Lemuel's stooped shoulders sway in time to the bobbing of his old white head and his yellowed hat, as he prays. "De *Lord*," he says, at intervals in a stream of what sounds to Marcus like gibberish. Lemuel's eyes are shut, his arthritic hands curled on the folds of trouser tucked under his stubs.

Marcus bends down and speaks softly into his ear. "How you keeping, Lemuel?"

The old man's attention comes up the way a window shade snaps at just the right pressure. "Oh, de Honorable Mr. Passjohn, oh, de honor all mine, sir." The claw hands open and lift. "I keeping bery well, bery well. And you, sir, how goes de gov'ment? You leading de people to de truth?"

"Don't you hear what people say, Lemuel?" Marcus squats beside the wheelchair, one hand on the handle wrapped and rewrapped in tape blackened with sweat and dirt. The chair would fall to pieces if Ramo did not repeatedly cobble it together with wire and crude welds. "Don't you know about the shooting, the searches, the strike on the docks and the layoffs, and the housing project canceled?"

Lemuel sways. His head bobs. "If dey problems in gov'ment, you fix them, Marcus. Dat job de gift de Lord give you."

Marcus presses his lips together and stands up. He wants to quit. He wants to go home and go to bed. Once he had a successful law practice, but it's flagging because he has not tended it; he tended instead the Opposition and tried in that way to tend the damn country. All his life he's pushed himself to always try harder, but now he sees that he never really accomplishes anything except to push. He gets up early and pushes all day, and the next morning when he gets up again the same stone is waiting, cold, and at the foot of the hill.

He pats Lemuel's shoulder. "God love you," he tells the old man. God had better, he tells himself.

From the cycle shop's doorway, Ramo watches. He lifts a hand — good-bye, or a benediction. Marcus nods at him curtly and leaves. He drives to his office, disregarding the speed limit. He does not permit himself to think of the softness of his pillow.

When he does sleep that night, he has a disturbing dream. He is running. His head aches from the pounding of the blood in his temples, and the dust-laden air he pulls into his lungs burns him. His whole chest, he thinks, may be on fire but if so, the fire is inside; he cannot see it. Beside him, Ramo runs, too. They are going nowhere, for there is nowhere to go, and this is sad, so sad he cannot bear the weight it — a hat made of lead or stone, squeezing his skull, the broad bill of it interfering with his vision. The people who line the road, thousands upon thousands of them shoulder to shoulder, talk and talk as he passes them but the heavy hat crushing him impedes his hearing. Ramo, dreadlocks streaming, lopes alongside him, his teeth luminous as the alabaster insides of shells. Lemuel rides Ramo's shoulders, legs intact all the way to his toes and bouncing on the tall man's chest like braids. Lemuel's face, lit with laughter, splits open, a bud bursting, a flower come into its own.

The following day at noon, Marcus sits on a concrete bench beneath the oldest and biggest flame tree on the island. Fifty feet tall, its umbrella-shaped canopy half-again that broad, the tree is a star specimen of the Botanical Garden that is nevertheless overlooked by most visitors. More vigorously persistent across a century and a half than the original arborist and subsequent construction crews were capable of imagining, the big tree grows inconveniently close to a service parking lot and a former stable now housing mowers and a tractor. All summer the tree's crown will be crimson with thousands of frothy flowers, but now, ten days into the reduced day-lengths of December, the tree is naked. The weather, courtesy of the Gulf Stream that surrounds the island, remains hot and bright. The sky is a strong, unmarred blue, and the flame tree's bare branches and long, dangling seed pods throw a thin lattice of shade on Marcus's shoulders.

He has given Lucy directions to the service lot, a simple turn off Berry Hill Road behind the hospital. Now he has nothing to do but wait, and the seconds are long. He arrived early — he couldn't help it; he's thought of nothing else for much of the morning — and he can't help being nervous either. He has no way of knowing whether she'll keep an appointment just because she's agreed to.

She is not late. At precisely twelve-fifteen the red Fiesta pulls into the lot. She stops in the middle as if she might change her mind and turn around, then pulls the car to the far side of the lot and parks, the damaged, uptilted back bumper facing Marcus.

She's taller than he has remembered. He notices this the moment she gets out of the car. She is also thinner and more angular in the face and her posture than he recalled. Less pretty, less soft, more distinctively and sharply Caucasian. His feelings, his thoughts, swirl and lurch. He tells himself this confusion is good, these realities will help him stay sensible. She is wearing a suit, narrow black trousers and a matching loose jacket over a bright red shirt, smart in an American big city way but all wrong for the island and this season. Her fine blond hair, shoulder-length, sweeps across her face on a gust of warm air and she lifts a hand to pull it away. He sees the heavy solitaire in her wedding ring glint. She is peering at the tree, rather than him, through chic, small-lensed dark glasses. He stands up, in case she has failed to notice him.

"Oh," she says, coming quickly across the lot. From her tone he is certain she's pretending to have only just noticed him. She removes the glasses and tucks them in her purse. "Have you been waiting long?" The smile she offers is tight. The expression in her unmasked eyes is wildly nervous.

"Come sit down."

Surely he must help them both get through this, since he orchestrated it. He gestures at the concrete bench. She trips on a chunk of crumbling asphalt, catches herself on the hand he extends but immediately turns loose. Still, his skin has come alive in the spots where her fingers pressed it. She looks away, her lips set in a thin line. She's wearing lipstick, which she was not on either of the two prior occasions he's seen her.

They sit down, after he's specifically assessed how much space he should leave between them, and decided on slightly less than a person-width. Then he realizes that the view from the bench is only the parking lot, a good thing when he was waiting for her but ugly and awkward now. He says, "I guess this is not such an attractive place, but it's quiet, easy to find from the road...." He hears his voice trail off. His chest burns.

He feels himself blush—warmly but invisibly behind his dark skin. She, on the other hand, cannot camouflage the color that lights her cheeks; it competes with her blouse. Several seconds pass before he notices they are each lost in the study of the other's face and eyes, and that for him both the lostness and the silence that results are a far deeper pleasure than speaking.

"It's nice to see you again," he says finally.

"Yes." She looks at her lap when she speaks. Then she clears her throat.

"I've made some changes with Peyton," she announces. "I've taken more control, and made an effort to reestablish respect between us."

She speaks as if addressing a board of directors, but she's biting those lipsticked lips. Marcus's attention dances between listening to her and staring at her while his body registers all the signs of rising desire in the presence of a woman he wants. She has confronted her son—some issue about beach sand on his shoes and how that is proof that he lies and sneaks off. He has denied this and provided an explanation just plausible enough that she can't quite dismiss it. Peyton is extremely offended by her accusation; because they've always been close and she's always trusted him, she's in a quandary. They've settled it, for now. She'll allow him to ride the public bus home from school as do most of the bigger boys at Somers, but he must come straight home — she'll note his arrival time each day — and there must not be one single instance of trouble at school or poor grades henceforth. She and Peyton have written this into a contract and they have both signed it.

Marcus smiles at her while she gazes at him and the lips he wants to kiss almost but not quite tremble with distress. What a preposterous — and American — solution she's devised. A contract, with a child! Already it's a disaster, since he's just seen Peyton, yesterday, running from Ramo's shop during the hours he should have been in school, but Marcus does not tell her this. Zef is the reason Peyton was at Ramo's, even Ramo said as much, so Zef is the one who needs dealing with. *I can fix this for her,* Marcus thinks. *It's within my power to make happen what she needs to happen.* And if he did...? ah...he imagines her melting in relief into his arms, her mouth opening, her body softening.

He asks her gently if she realizes that riding the bus home from Somers involves a trip into town to transfer lines, that buses are late and connections often missed, and that Peyton's arrival time at home will not be that certain. She says she does know, and he sees from her expression that she's dodging something. She's so easy to read, everything she feels is all over her face.

"I have to trust him," she says.

He is about to say that no, she doesn't, and she had better not, when she says, spitting it out like a bad taste, "I had to make some kind of deal with him. Darrell doesn't know about the suspension or any of the problems with school. We need him not to know."

"Why?" Now Marcus cannot quite read her, except to be sure she's miserable.

She shakes her head at an enormity he will not understand. "There is so much stress between us. When we came here, we both thought things would get better. And they did at first. It's a better job for him. A new beginning for all of us, he said. And the island, it's very beautiful. It *hurts* me, how beautiful it is."

She is looking at him, gray eyes brimming. How much emotion resides in this woman. He should know better than to court it, surely it will well out all over him...and cause so much trouble...but he wants it. He wants to soothe her, and he wants to drown in her response.

"Let's walk," he says, abruptly aware that right now he cares nothing about helping the boys, that everything he's said about that is nothing but pretext to get her to be near him. His willingness to manipulate his own thoughts, to lie to himself as well as mislead her, astonishes and scares him.

She stands up when he does, and they stroll away from the flame tree and the service lot onto a broad slope of lawn that rolls away down hill for several acres to the main gate on the South Shore Road. They step on short, dry grass that crunches lightly beneath their shoes. Once, negotiating a low spot, they bump shoulders and neither one apologizes. He smells her perfume, something he recognizes but cannot name. To say something that won't shock either of them, he tells her the name and origin of the trees they pass — each one huge and distinct, together mapping the reach of the Empire that brought the British here: the Norfolk pine from the Pacific islands, banyans from India, the kapok from the Caribbean, and more flame trees, from Africa. At the foot of the hill, royal palms colonnade the South Shore straightaway, dividing land from the notch of turquoise sea that is Hungry Bay.

She tells him she's seen the editorials in the newspaper defaming him. She uses that word, "defame," and when he remarks on that choice, it comes out that she's rather cognizant of the law and its terms, for her father is a defense attorney in the States. She mentions as well the letters to the newspaper's editor, in support of him, including an extremely vehement one in this morning's paper from someone named Althea Trott, alleging a Government scheme to subvert the efforts of black citizens to secure justice for recent unsolved murders by framing the Opposition leader for the deaths along with much of the other recent trouble on the island.

"Is it true?" she asks.

"That I'm a murderer, or that there's a plot against me?" he says, teasing darkly to see if she'll laugh.

"You know what I mean," she says earnestly.

He is touched by her concern. "It appears to be true that some people are out to get me," he tells her. "No one can prove it conclusively, yet."

"What will you do?"

"We—the Opposition—will look for proof and build alliances. In the meantime, Government plays with rumor and innuendo and I stand up to it as best I can. That's how it's done here."

A fine sweat shines on her face; her black suit is too warm in this sun. He tells her she is an intelligent and perceptive woman, and he asks her, given that, why she feels responsible for every problem within her family. Why doesn't her husband help her?

She looks away across the broad lawn, to the white mansion that is the Premier's ceremonial home. "Darrell is very busy," she says. She speaks quietly; it seems to cost her to say her husband's name. "He works so hard. And now, with things in the world as they are, all the traveling he must do is arduous. He's exhausted. He's busy. I can't ask him to do things for me."

It's pain, Marcus suddenly understands, that softens this woman, that unbends her angles and undercuts her smart suit. Her voice, and her eyes when she again turns them his way, overflow with longing.

To comply gives him great joy. He bends and kisses her. Her lips resist only momentarily, then give in and cling. Her palms rest softly on his chest. He feels how sad she is and, perversely, that makes him happy. She needs him! He pulls her firmly into his arms and holds her, and for the moment the embrace lasts, he believes he can give her what she needs when her husband cannot.

"I have to go," she says.

"Of course."

He watches her hurry across the dry lawn and pick her way through the pot holes in the parking lot to her car. What else could she do but leave? They could not lie down in the grass and love each other. They cannot go to his home or hers. No hotel or hideaway exists on this tiny island where they'd not be remarked upon instantly. No doors are open to them, no refuge exists, except that contrived one inside his mind and outside of time.

She looks back at him, once and piercingly, before she gets in the Fiesta. Then she drives away. This is when he tries to see who might have noticed him kiss a lovely, married white woman in the middle of a broad and sunny public lawn. He spies no one and takes some ridiculous reassurance from that.

He's getting in his own car when he recognizes they've resolved absolutely nothing about the boys. There'll be reason to call her again, and soon. And although he knows better, this problem feels like a gift. It feels like salvation. That stone he's pushed so long rolls away down the hill behind him. When it reaches the bottom and grows still and heavy, waiting on him, he won't be there. He doesn't know how he knows this is true, he simply feels it.

9

Lucy needs sanctuary—not from Marcus but from her feelings. She opens the door and drops into the driver's seat, sinking right down into the kiss. Her whole body hums with its enfolding inerasable presence; she hears it like air in her lungs, like blood in her arteries. It came from nowhere, she could have run before it befell her, but it will not now be left behind. It is essential. Several weeks will pass before she fully understands this; only gradually will she realize she's living two lives at once, one with desperation and one with determination and that—kiss-driven—she will often not be sure which is which.

For now, she turns the key, shoves the Fiesta in gear and drives toward home. But along the way she stops to buy a pack of American cigarettes at absurdly inflated island prices. She begins, thereafter, to smoke again, at first only now and again and secretly, two or three times a week when Darrell is at work and Peyton at school and her time is her own. She has quite a bit of time. Shopping and cleaning can be made time-consuming, as the house is large and the drive to the store interminable at the legal limit of 20 mph, but she has nothing else to do—no friends, and no commitments beyond the house, her husband and her son.

Those lacks are things she should be working on, and she does try, sometimes. She allows Felicity Heppering to introduce her at a series of teas to the society matrons who would need to accept her, in every sense of the term, for membership in the island's equivalent of the Junior League, the only civic organization open to women except the Anglican cathedral's Ladies' Auxiliary (Felicity belongs to both). Lucy attends services at the cathedral, once, and tries the Presbyterian church in Paget Parish, recommended to her by Felicity as less formal and perhaps more palatable to Americans, also once. Mostly, however, what she does is walk, for hours every day, increasingly long distances, along the roads and beaches of the South Shore.

Barefoot in the chilly scrim of receding surf, she strolls the tide line and peruses the sea's offerings, tossed up on the un-raked but still pink winter beach: shoes of every style (always singletons), spent condoms and pens, scissors, knives, bottles and cans and Styrofoam cups, splintered wood and segments of twisted, rusted wire cable, all of it tangled in slimy seaweed, fishing line or miles of unspooled magnetic tape and everything, everywhere, coated with pulverized plastic and clotted with chunks of black tar. She wonders if the island's tourists, before they stopped coming post-9/11, had any idea what they swam with, in that gorgeous turquoise sea.

When Peyton's home and she can't walk, she smokes. This indulgence gradually becomes more frequent and less secret. Darrell is so often away, to the States or Europe, that he doesn't notice, and over time she stops caring that Peyton does. There are, after all, quite a few things about him that she notices and does not approve of. Sometimes she can see herself take a childish, passive-aggressive satisfaction from disappointing her son's expectations of her, since he seems so damnably determined to disappoint her. He wants nothing to do with her. He mostly follows her rules. But he closes his door and locks it, and cranks up his stereo to the maximum level she will tolerate without complaining, using it to keep her at bay—for she does hesitate to brave that wall of noise to attempt a one-sided conversation with him, especially knowing he'll likely be either sleeping or mind-melded to his computer or PlayStation, gaming his life away.

And she has — to her shame she recognizes this truth — her own form of gaming. Marcus — on a chaise lounge like the one on her balcony. His eyes closed, the lids slack, his shoulders loose. Unaware of her, simply there.

She studies his lips. Not pink like the white men's lips she's kissed all her life until now. Mauve. A color she admires as belonging to the evening sky, a color with which she is entirely unfamiliar as flesh. She does not touch them. They are parted, slightly, on an inward smile, some private pleasure she will respect by allowing it to continue undisturbed. She examines the planes of his face and the texture of his brown-black skin, the color of rich cake, pebbled with flat pores across the bridge of his broad nose, thick and smooth like new buttery leather across the arch of his cheekbones and the softened hollows beneath them, then coarsening and darkening, becoming distinctly black, underneath the shadow of his beard.

This is her favorite fantasy of him, her favorite self-indulgent game. She looks at him from within the safety of his not looking back. A more frightening, more compulsive fantasy arises unbidden when in her daydream he opens his eyes and she glimpses through them his longing and his loneliness and feels it pull her nearer and deeper, the mystery of the palpable, inexplicable pain in him snaring her through her memory — a vivid one — of his sometimes flatly appraising male stare and her own gut-grip response to what is promised her on the pillow of his once-tasted lower lip.

Oh, sex. She understands clearly the very moment this fantasy rears up that allowing it to unfold is stupid, wrong and dangerous. She is giving in to pure hormonal panting, like a teenager. Sometimes she shuts it right down and stands up to work or walk or smoke, angrily. Other times, with the perverse illogic that leads her to light up right in front of Peyton as if that act would spite *him*, she pursues the sexual fantasy as if by doing so — driving herself to it and through it — she can resolve it. Exhaust it. The urge for sex, she tells herself, is relatively simple to satisfy. She can take care of it, herself, in this daydream. She removes Marcus from the chaise lounge, and places herself with him in or on or near a bed. She removes clothes. Sometimes her own, sometimes his, sometimes a tandem process. Quick. Slow. Top to bottom. Bottom to top.

She has some trouble with detail in this part of the fantasy. Imagining the two of them without clothes is challenging, as she insists on honesty about her body, which is no longer young. Her thighs are chicken-traced with broken capillaries. Her breasts tired and flat. Marcus is thin, but still he is a middle-aged man, soft in his middle. Picturing him (her?) removing his underwear (boxers? Jockey shorts?) often proves not possible. To gaze upon an erection there, graphic in her imagination, shocks her but to envision anything else is absurd. She abandons this tack, and fast-forwards events to a naked embrace. Under the covers, on top of the covers, uncovered right on the floor. No matter. This, her imagination can handle. This she can pursue like a mesmerizing reward.

But there is no reward. Just guilt and confusion. The sex she conjures leaves her worse off, just like the real sex she still sometimes has with Darrell. No one can know what is inside her head, she tells herself, but when Darrell comes home she's certain he can read it all over her. Her fear of what he might ask leads her to avoid him. And when Peyton seeks her out and she should pay close attention to *his* attention, she feels her knowledge of the pictures she makes of Marcus separate her from her son, even as she reaches toward him, half-a-beat too late for having had to put aside the mental game.

This mess is horrendous. But it's all contained inside her head. If she keeps it there, they'll all be safe, won't they? Oh, what had she been thinking, meeting him, alone, to talk, instead of handling the whole thing by phone as she'd planned to from the beginning?

She resolves repeatedly to stop this, all of it. But inside her the kiss lives on. Always, everything comes back to the fact of it. To Marcus. To his shoulders at her eye level, the white dress shirt, the soft skin above his collar. His face, close, coming closer. He is not handsome. He is warm. Kind and concerned. His heart is his power. The kiss is its mark. She is marked by it.

And so, even knowing she is wading from the tide line of fantasy toward infidelity, she talks to Marcus when he phones her—about their boys, yes, but also about how lonely her life on this island makes her. She calls him back when he sends her an e-mail note, and listens sympathetically while he reveals, scrap by scrap, according to what's top-of-the-heap that day, little tastes of the personal and political and financial vulnerabilities his visibility and his history on the island cause him. And finally, a few times, with the impulsive abandon of a fistful of cigarettes lit up right in public—and an after-guilt that slams her into chain-smoking and brooding—she agrees to meet him. She walks out of the cliff house through the island's wild, bright beauty and—on a beach, in a garden, at a park made empty by off-season and a global plague of terror—straight into Marcus's company.

Middle row, third seat from the front, in a desk that will rock if he's not careful, Peyton Langston keeps his eyes on his reader and his feet, as required, flat on the floor. He knows how to keep still; he's had practice and this is lucky. In Connecticut, in the marsh blind he built with his best friend Riley and their teacher Garhett, he learned to be so quiet that only his heart and his breath were in motion. So quiet herons stiletto-stepped past him, unknowing or uncaring, and fish hovered trustingly close. Here, in the eighth form class at Somers Academy, where he is imprisoned and always on trial, stillness may—he hopes—ensure his survival.

Behind a heavy desk on a platform at the front of the room, Mr. Ratherly sits paring his nails with the same pen knife he uses to slice his lunchtime apple and sharpen his pencils to a razor point. Peyton doesn't need to lift his eyes to know what the teacher is doing—shards of fingernail skid across the desktop. On four sides of Peyton, thirty boys breathe anxiously or angrily and ooze stink, dressed identically in khaki slacks, button-down white shirts, neckties striped red and silver, and navy wool blazers bearing the Somers crest on the breast pocket. So few months ago Peyton was happy at the Darien Alternative School where in the Waldorf tradition Garhett was more his guide than his task master, and people wore exactly what pleased them and did their lessons on the floor if they wanted to. Then his parents dragged him to this island and shoved him into this school, where Ratherly runs class like a commandant getting off on the smell of fear, and this morning's assignment is memorization of five pages from the *Iliad* as "a callisthenic for the mind."

Silently Peyton slides his feet an eighth of an inch closer along the warped floor boards. The ugly brown shoes that first marked him a fool feel heavy as rocks. Everybody here wears brown shoes by rule but nobody's shoes have such thick crepe soles, such childish string laces.

The shoes are his mother's fault. He cannot rely on her anymore. She used to take his side, they used to be tight, but now they barely speak. He tells her what he's got to have, and she interrogates him—about his homework and whether he has notes from school. She checks her watch every afternoon as he walks into the house. She lets him know when dinner's ready and leaves his laundry folded in his room. Beyond that, she avoids him and he knows why. He saw the way Zef's father stared at her in the Academy parking lot on the day he got the suspension. He saw the look on her face right afterward when she sat down in the car. He is eleven but he is not stupid. When the phone rings, she gets there first, and if anyone, even the evening news, mentions the name "Marcus Passjohn," she perks up, and leaves the room. He has tested her, pointing out a newspaper story about a speech in a church. Her eyes got bright, her face went blank, and she walked into her room, shutting the door quietly behind her.

And she insists *he's* changed! When she made that bus-ride contract and made him sign it, *she* said it was because *he* tells lies. But she's told him not to tell his father the truth about Somers because, she says, "Some things are better left unsaid, for now."

Ratherly raps on his desk and thirty-one pairs of eyes snap up. Lifting his wooden ruler, Ratherly draws a bead on a boy to Peyton's right, a black boy, one of five in the class, a boy with cinnamon-colored skin and freckles who stares at the floor when he's called on because he never has the answer. His name is Deshon Bridgers, and what he's done now Peyton doesn't know. Deshon bites his lip and squeezes his chin to his chest. Ratherly replaces his ruler on the desktop and returns to his paring. He's smiling, even if his oily face won't show the crease.

Peyton's father tells him Somers is an excellent school, the best on the island. He's explained that his employer, TransGlobal Reinsurance, has paid the very steep tuition and pulled strings to have Peyton admitted. But even before classes started, on his orientation tour with his father beside him smiling and shaking hands, Peyton got in trouble, for staring at Ratherly's knees, ridiculous, hairy bumps sticking out midway between the hem of dark blue Bermuda shorts and the rolled tops of yellow knee socks held up by sagging elastic garters. When Ratherly spoke his name, snapping "Langston" as if Peyton were a dog being called to heel, he looked up and saw on the man's face a version of the same contempt he himself was feeling. He tried to hide it, but too late: Ratherly had noted it down. A few days later when his father showed up at breakfast with brand new Bermuda shorts and tall socks sandwiched between his usual wingtips and dress shirt, jacket and tie, Peyton made his face a mask. If this was how men dressed here, of course his father would buy right in. *"When in Rome, Peyt..."* he'd say if Peyton asked him why. But Peyton knew better than to ask.

A belch like a buzzer erupts from a desk behind him and to his left, nearest the open windows. Ratherly leaps up, livid. Clearly he doesn't know which boy is the culprit, but Peyton does. Thomas Heppering. Peyton keeps his eyes on his book, but strains his vision to its furthest periphery to see what will happen since Thomas, because he tattles, is as close to a pet as this teacher allows.

"Deshon Bridgers," Ratherly says thoughtfully, "how you sing! Serenade us again, won't you?"

Peyton's head swivels, in spite of the rules, at the sound of such flagrant injustice. Deshon is the least likely person in the class to have let a belch fly, and Ratherly has to know it. Something comes pounding up through Peyton, a shout or a curse, and he closes his mouth firmly to keep it down. Deshon mumbles, "No, sir, it wasn't me, sir."

"Bridgers," Ratherly says. "You have the answer. Excellent. *Excellent.*" He drops one palm and most of his weight on Deshon's desk. "Give it to me."

"Sir?" says Deshon. Peyton can see Deshon's fingers beneath the desk top, twisting the fabric of his slacks.

"The answer, young man. Who belched?"

Deshon's frightened knowledge of Thomas's guilt falls across the classroom like a shadow. Everybody except Ratherly knows. *Do it. Please do it,* Peyton thinks, knowing that Deshon will not. *Nail that jerk.*

And Thomas, reading the will of the class building against him, speaks up. "I can help him, Mr. Ratherly."

Ratherly pivots. "You have the answer, Heppering?"

Thomas has little pig eyes and curly hair shaved off on the sides and piled like suds on top. He looks the part of a stooge. "Oh, no, sir. Not the answer, sir. I meant I can serenade if Deshon cannot." He says this with plenty of what people on the island call cheek, and somebody behind Peyton is bold enough to snigger.

Ratherly looks from Thomas back to Deshon. Peyton feels something lethal stirring between them. "Bridgers," says Ratherly, "do you wish Heppering to assist you?"

"No, sir," says Deshon quickly, his eyes on his desk. Someone black in the back of the classroom utters a single hard word, lost in the general hiss of in-drawn breath.

"You wish to refuse help, do you?" Ratherly says. "Heppering is *trying* to help you."

Ratherly aims his bullying at the top of Deshon's bowed head and Peyton is sure the black boy feels the same pounding in his veins that he does. Through the thump in his ears it is hard to hear what Ratherly says next: "Carry on, Heppering." While Thomas clowns, puffing and blowing, shaking his gut and saying, "So sorry, sir. No gas on *my* stomach," peddling to himself the attention he needs to turn aside blame, Peyton thinks resentfully of his father, who made him come here, who will not listen to one single word that says this place is anything other than "opportunity."

"If you find it so difficult to perform, I can help you," Ratherly says. His voice makes it clear Thomas's antics are no longer useful.

Peyton rotates his head cautiously left, one inch, then two. He sees Ratherly, Thomas and the ruler between them, Ratherly's fist at one end of it and a fold of Thomas's fat stomach, in sweaty, smudged shirtfront, giving way to the other.

No one sniggers now, and Thomas gasps slightly as Ratherly pushes with the ruler more firmly. From the yard outside, filtering through the louvered shutters propped open on steel rods, come the sounds of the younger boys being summoned in from recess. The handbell ringing, the scuffling line forming, silence suddenly imposed.

Peyton sees Thomas strain. His face grows red. Ratherly waits with ominous patience. Peyton ventures a glance at his watch. He bites the skin alongside his thumbnail and tastes blood. Four minutes remain until their recess. If Ratherly will let them go. If Thomas can burp on command.

He does. He lets loose a long curling belch, louder than the first one, and as every head turns, the teacher says, "Ah. Well done, Heppering. A most hearty bleat. Now be so good as to trot off to the headmaster's and inform him that you have twice belched in class this morning without apology and are in need of some stiffer correction than I can offer."

The beet color drains from Thomas's face. Ratherly signals him toward the door with his ruler, then walks lightly, as if the floor has become springy, back to the platform and his desk. From there he addresses Deshon.

"Look at the trouble you have caused with your intransigence, Bridgers. Do not think that your classmates, nor I, will soon forget it."

Ratherly sits down. "Dismissed," he snaps, still two minutes ahead of the bell. Pins-and-needles shoot through Peyton's feet when he stands.

When he's with Zef, he escapes his prison. Buzzing westward that night on the back of Zef's scooter, slowing not even for the stop sign where the South Shore Road joins the Middle Road, Peyton's life, like the scooter's two-stroke engine, shifts through a rapid series of gears to jibe with Zef's momentum. To achieve this Peyton has had only to crawl out his bedroom window at five minutes before eleven, leaving his CD player on and programmed to shuffle.

"What's it like at government school?" he asks the black globe that is Zef's helmet, inches from his nose. Above the boys the moon is round, the night pale with its white light and long shadows. They've just passed the school building, which Peyton has seen before in daylight: three white rectangles of cinderblocks in a bare, sandy yard. More like a barracks than a school. Better or worse than Somers Academy? he wonders.

"I don't know," Zef says. "I don't go."

"You don't go? At all?"

"Couple times."

The words sing past Peyton's ears on stinging cold wind. Are they true? He knows by now that Zef lies easily and often. But he knows too that Zef lives free by making up his own rules.

Like Zef, Peyton wears a long, dark hoodie sweat shirt under a zippered nylon windbreaker, and wide jeans layered with deep pockets. Because it's January, night and day now equally damp and chill, he's had occasion to make his mother take him to the back of town where the shops are small and the customers black, and on the tightly packed rounders of cheap Chinese-made clothing, his hands sought out the colors and shapes that replicated Zef's things while her eyes avoided his and both of them kept their mouths tight shut.

Inside his windbreaker, nestled on his narrow chest, is a white plastic Safeway bag full of fireworks. He touches it. Over the holidays just past he's been home—except the house that was home all his life till now belongs to strangers, and Riley, his best friend since kindergarten, has a new best friend, a girl. The fireworks Riley gave him in consolation,

Peyton gives his replacement best friend Zef. He smuggled them through customs in the pockets of his oversize pants, sweaty and weak-kneed in the security line, but despite post-9/11 touchiness, no one touched him: he's a blond kid with blond, American parents.

The scooter flashes over the drawbridge at Ely's Harbour. Halfway up Wreck Hill to their left a house burns like a wreckers' beacon fire, flames rising half-again its height, dancing in the shore breeze. People dash back and forth in moonlight rosied with firelight, and a pump truck with flashing lights maneuvers into position. Zef leans hard left, heading them up the hill.

Police swarm the road ahead, so Zef, underage and unlicensed, slows and veers again, downhill along a narrow lane. Peyton's been close enough to see that the big, yellow house burns on only one side, through its upstairs windows, and close enough, too, to notice or think he's noticed Thomas Heppering amid the family dressed in nightclothes standing in the yard. Someone had an arm around some pudgy, pudding-headed boy standing stock-still and staring, a stake pounded into earth.

He tells Zef's head, Zef's black helmet that bangs his forehead when they take air over bumps, "That was Thomas Heppering's house."

"Nah, not likely." Zef takes a curve. "But if it was, man, that's sweet."

Peyton keeps still. Zef guns the scooter. They need a quiet place, a long way from cops, to set matches to their contraband.

Zef drives them to Ft. Scaur. A place they've come before, a place Peyton said would be perfect for playing army and Zef said was better for drinking beer. They've not been back to do either, and now, in the middle of the fort, nothing is left after two centuries of disuse but earthworks and the brick-and-mortar lintels at the openings of the tunnels that mine the hill, linking gun ports trained east on the Great Sound to those facing west, guarding Ely's Harbour and the open sea. They dump the contents of Peyton's Safeway bag onto a weedy patch of concrete.

Zef whistles. With the flat of his palm, he skims the three dozen firecrackers. Peyton squats beside him naming off the treasures. Screamers. Whippersnappers. Black cats. Mega flashers. Cherry bombs and smoke balls. Strings of pistol poppers. Illegal in Connecticut and all the more so on the island amid a ban on weapons and explosives of any kind. Peyton basks in Zef's pleasure, something he's not earned before. He feels older. He feels strong. He looks out across the water, where Ely's Harbour mirrors an orange smudge from the fire on the hill above, and the teak-trimmed schooners rock gently at their owners' private docks. The muted tap of halyards against masts plays like a soundtrack in a life Peyton is making up as he lives it.

"You got your lighter?" he asks Zef.

The bag in Zef's hands, Peyton leads the way into the tunnels, running them like a hound on scent, delirious with dedication, fueled on Zef's company and Zef's submission to his lead, guided first by the moonlight collected in doorways and thereafter by intuition only, in full darkness.

In a slit of light focused by a gun port, they set up. Using as torch the fat silver lighter Zef stole long ago from his father's house, they lay out the firecrackers in rows on the ground, digging the stems into the soft dirt. Their breathing echoes loud and urgent off moldy walls and sagging ceiling, as if they really are soldiers. Guerrillas. Terrorists. Patriots. Rebels. In his games with Riley and neighborhood boys Peyton played all these roles but with Zef it's no game because they've left home and the ammo's live.

The sound and shock from the first explosion loosen Peyton's knees and threatens his bowels when he runs. They run each time down the nearest tunnel, each blast reverberating like they're deep inside a massive woofer. Pain pounds Peyton's ears and adrenaline jerks his limbs and Zef flails beside him, wild-eyed and grinning. When Zef lies panting in the dark on the dirt to rest, Peyton does the same and Zef's hand settles on his shoulder, and Peyton sees his new friend's green eyes shining like an animal's in the dark, the only thing he can see, and he knows, he *knows*, he's exactly where he's supposed to be.

Zef's about to touch flame to the last string of poppers when instead he lifts it like a torch between their dirty, sweating faces. On the stem of the lighter Peyton makes out what Zef says are his father's initials, the engraved letters M and P curling around each other like vines. "You and me, bro," Zef says, pointing at the vines. "Tight."

From six inches away Peyton smiles back. "Tight," he repeats.

Zef's eyes hold his like a grip. He says, "We not the only ones getting tight." Peyton's mind downshifts.

Zef sits back on his heels. He looks away and then back, his face disappearing then re-appearing inside the little circle of flame light. "Bro," he says. "Marcus sat me down for a heart-to-heart. Told me not to mess with you. Told me to *leave you be*. I said what's it to you, and he said your mother and him have discussed us."

Zef snaps the light shut, disappearing. Inside his head Peyton feels the presence of his mother's shut mouth and blank face swelling like a bruise. He tells this feeling, Go Away.

Zef, in the dark, sing-songs: "Yo mama, so pretty, so blond, so worried 'bout her boy, her baby, you—"

"My mother does not—"

Zef cuts him off. "*My* mother is a bitch like yours, white *bitch*, drop me like trash and leave. I never see her my whole life and now she's thinking maybe she might take me back, inviting me for an interview, except I have to get there without my father because he told her, 'It's best not.' My mother says my father says I shouldn't see her because he thinks she'll fuck me up. You see how they mess with us, doing what the *fuck* they want to do, fucking us up because they the ones fucked up...."

Peyton hears Zef's voice crack, but the light is back, Zef making a circle of thumb and forefinger inside it, and the butt end of the flaming lighter going in and out. "Like this yo' mama, my daddy, *discussing*."

Peyton shuts his eyes hard. You have to hit a boy who says what Zef said about your mother but the one he wants to hit is her.

"Shut up! shut up!" His mouth is shouting this without his permission when Zef puts flame to the poppers.

They run from the explosion, tripping, careless, angry, and hear men's voices. Loud, on top of them, on a grate above their heads. Flattened hard against the oozing wall, Peyton's cheek touches stone inches from Zef's, and the smell of cave fills his head.

Zef takes him by the arm, squeezing till it hurts. "Get us out of here, fast," he hisses. "You got us in, you get us out."

Peyton's heart threatens to bang its way right up his throat but he leads Zef back the way they came, then up a crawlway through an air vent, and like rodents they wiggle up and out, scraping themselves raw, scrambling over sand spurry and the scaly roots of casuarina pines. Belly to the ground, they slink to the scooter in a stand of palmetto that spears them through their jeans as they pull it clear, slam helmets on their heads and jump astride.

The engine turning over brings the men on the run — police, the flashing blue light of their car crowns the hilltop. Zef hurls the scooter skidding down the gravel drive into the road and around a curve as the cruiser begins to roll.

Peyton grips the scooter seat with both hands, nails dug in, wind burning his face. He tells his heart he *will* get home. Zef knows the back roads and they can, if they have to, ditch the scooter and jog home through alleys and backyards. When he gets home he'll slip in through his window and insist, tomorrow, if questioned, that he's been there all the time, and if he's caught coming in, he'll lie, and he'll be in some kind of trouble. No matter what, tomorrow will come and he'll get out of bed and be re-imprisoned inside school, and no matter what he says and what he does, he'll be in some other kind of trouble there.

He lifts a hand from the seat and sets his teeth into the sore flesh at his thumbnail. Bites down, and chews the tab of skin he slices free. He's in trouble all the time, but his life's in motion. He's not in Connecticut. Stillness won't save him. His mother won't either. She's nothing but more trouble. He spits the hangnail, and bites down for another one. He's on his own now. Zef — and his mother — have shown him the road.

10

Jonathan Heppering is headed home, locking his office door behind him, when Cisco Suggs taps his shoulder. Jonathan jumps, embarrassing himself. He's further disconcerted to not immediately recognize this smooth-faced man in the dark bland clothes of a thief who is inside the offices of Frith, Stearn & Heppering, Chartered Accountants, at half-past eight in the evening. The reception area is deserted and shadowy. The entire building is quite likely empty. Jonathan's mind races ahead to the code he must punch into the phone to summon security. The recent attack on his home has unnerved him, as it would any man; and the fact that Horace Tucker finally died yesterday and his family and a mob of their supporters immediately mounted a justice vigil outside the police station has got everyone's fears on yellow alert. But Suggs introduces himself and Jonathan places him, from a glimpse some months ago, similarly unwelcome, similarly after-hours, in the hallway outside the office of Justice Minister Isaiah Barnes.

That day Jonathan stood amid a small clique of bankers, merchants, solicitors and accountants convened to discuss very privately with Barnes some plausibly deniable strategies for securing the country's civil order and maintaining its appeal to the international business upon which their individual livelihoods all depended. That day, as the group

140   Christine Hale

dispersed, Jonathan almost did not see Barnes hand Suggs a fat, wallet-sized envelope, and he comprehended—and resolved immediately to forget—Suggs's role and identity only as the man disappeared down the darkened hallway. Now Jonathan is face-to-face with this unlikely thug he knows he and his cohorts have funded, close enough to note the unblemished shape of the man's skull beneath his longshoreman's snug knit cap, and the exceptionally long and fine-boned fingers with which Suggs draws from an inside breast pocket of his pea coat a small notebook bound in smudged, abraded, vermillion kid.

So transfixed is Jonathan by the good leather and the tidily manicured nails that pinch it that Suggs succeeds in pushing the notebook into his hands before he thinks to withdraw them. The pages are filled, almost to the final one, with deeds, dates, figures and names, captured with an accountant's succinct yet comprehensive precision, and rendered in tiny, highly legible handwriting. Jonathan processes quickly while he turns the creamy moleskin pages—here is a record of services provided along with the payola, the payees, and the entire list of payors—including Jonathan's firm and his very own name. Everything anyone needs to upend the island's business elite, indict Isaiah Barnes and bring Government crashing down.

"You need this," Suggs says.

"I think not," Jonathan replies, thrusting the book back at its author.

Suggs's hands now reside deep in his pockets. He says, evenly, "You, and others, will want to know what your money paid for."

Jonathan says again, reflexively, "I think not," and Suggs laughs. The sound is quite unpleasant.

"You *think* not," he says. "What a magnificent truth. You, and your kind, you do not think. But you do need to know."

"I don't want it." Jonathan lets the book drop to his secretary's desk.

"That's a shame, because it's yours now. Bought and paid for. What you do with it is your business. If I were you, and

I thank my dead-broke alcoholic parents I'm not, I'd use it to blow the whistle on our esteemed justice minister. He's started things he can't stop. The independents are always operating, and now they're inspired. Or incensed." Suggs's hands exit his pockets and adjust his cap, pulling it down tighter over his small ears. "How do you know, for instance, who authored the fire at your place? Or why?"

In response to Jonathan's livid silence, Suggs says, "See? The burn Isaiah started for fun and profit's gone completely out of control."

He turns away, toward the door to the back stairs marked by a glowing red Exit sign. Jonathan strides after him, seizes his shoulder and spins him around. Suggs is such a diminutive man, the effort required is minimal. And Jonathan regrets it, almost at once, when he feels his arms behind him in an astonishingly strong grip and the blade of a very small knife pricking the point of his chin.

Suggs says quietly, his face very near Jonathan's, "Read the book. It's all in there. It ends on the page with the two men I killed, in order to keep my hands on your money, two men I used to call friends. I don't mind, really, if I kill one more, a coward and a leech who's nobody's friend and entirely worthless to the world except as a source of money. And dead bodies."

He presses the knife upwards slightly and Jonathan feels the flesh split. He does not feel pain and that anomaly troubles him.

"Sit down," Suggs says. With his knee he nudges Jonathan backward. "Sit down in that chair."

Jonathan obeys and Suggs releases him. He backs away and Jonathan sees that the knife is, in fact, a scalpel. Lethal, shining, quite phallic. Suggs's free hand closes on the Exit door knob. He says, "You asked Isaiah for your money back. You don't get it back. It's coming with me, because I need a way out of here. My friends, if I had any, are dead, and that means Barnes and quite a few other people need me dead. So I get a boat ride and a new life, and you get the book."

Just before the door slams shut behind him, Jonathan

hears, "Good fucking luck, prick."

In the elevator, on his way down to the street, Jonathan presses a handkerchief to the small wound under his chin, now stinging, and takes stock of his options. Suggs's red notebook is tucked inside his jacket in a clean white envelope from his secretary's desk. In his briefcase is a police report stating that the fire that gutted three rooms of his home was ignited by a crude firebomb tossed in the window—a wine bottle filled with turpentine and stuffed with a burning rag. Jonathan is a conservative member of Parliament and his accounting firm a prominent business partner of American and British corporations. Anyone who wanted to scare him or people like him for any reason at all could have struck a match and tossed that flaming cocktail, or found someone to do it whether for money or hatred or sheer meanness.

The notebook, the police report and the complex and impersonal vulnerabilities they suggest, in such proximity to his sensible, sensitive person, disturb Jonathan deeply. Government is indeed corrupt and Isaiah Barnes dangerous, and Jonathan may ultimately need this evidence of conspiracy to forestall worse evils, but in the meantime he doesn't intend to hold it.

When the elevator stops at the second floor, Darrell Langston gets on. TransGlobal's offices are downstairs from Frith, Stearn & Heppering's, and it's not unusual for the two men to pass in the elevator or the lobby. Tonight Langston looks flustered. He carries an audit-size briefcase as well as a laptop slung on one shoulder. He glances at the blood speckled handkerchief in Jonathan's hand but doesn't ask. He says, when he's asked, that he's flying out again, at dawn tomorrow, a trip he can't postpone even though the airports are still nuts from the recent shoe bomber threat in London; he has terrible connections through Atlanta to Miami to reach Grand Cayman by late afternoon if he's lucky, and Jonathan concludes, ah, yes, TransGlobal is one more foreign insurer preparing to relocate. At the lobby, Jonathan seizes the moment. He reaches inside his jacket.

"Langston, my man," he says, foisting the envelope into Darrell's hand, "this is something personal I shouldn't take home. Put it in a safe place, will you? Hold it for me in case I need it."

He hurries away into the night before Langston can refuse. He can't trust him not to open the envelope, of course, but if the man does, he'll likely not know what to make of what he sees, and if he does grasp the meaning, he'll be frightened, into silence and complicity.

Isaiah Barnes cooks alone, on a dull, wet Sunday in mid-January, his kitchen redolent with ginger, black pepper, cloves and lime. A fish chowder bubbles companionably on the stove. Fifty-two square feet of imported black granite counter top (he's recently renovated his Riddell's Bay cottage, *Hove To*) evidence the scale of his culinary effort: multiple pots and ladles, dripping whisks, a hand mixer, graters, sieves, and chef's knives of all sizes, droplets of gravy, smears of grease, and errant small chunks of raw fish and meat.

He's made cassava pie, the island's signature dish. Chicken thighs, drumsticks and cubed pork loin in a custard of sixteen eggs and two pounds of butter, seasoned with grated nutmeg and plenty of sugar—colonialist largesse bound with the grainy starch of the West Indian cassava root brought to this island by slaves. Slices of this pie are just excellent fried in butter. Traditionally it's Christmas food, but Isaiah wants it now.

Without pausing to clean, he's begun a rum chiffon pie. Yolks, black rum and strong coffee heat in a double-boiler. He's beating the egg whites stiff when the telephone rings. *Damn the timing.* He cannot afford to break stride with so many pots on to boil. While he balances the receiver on his shoulder, he continues whisking, and listens to a minion from his office, assigned to monitor the weekend Internet news feed, report that a Canadian insurance company is leaving the island "for expanded opportunity" in the Caribbean. The number of foreign deserters totals five now since September when the world got the shakes and commerce turned even more fickle than it was before.

Isaiah sighs. He folds whipped cream into the peaked egg whites, quick, quick, before everything falls.

He reaches for words, and finds some: His career can be likened to a soufflé. It rose so smoothly. His linebacker's instinct for opening holes served him well on the field of justice. The lily-white police commissioner hates his big black balls but the street cops love his lead and Suggs did his bidding, at first, for a dime on the dollar. Passjohn— self-righteous egghead— seemed easy to finish off. Stir some old trouble to a new boil, drop a few matches in the right or random places, and blame the scorched pots on the old Marxist firebrand.

When Isaiah was little, like most island children, he watched a lot of Disney on video. He remembers *The Sorcerer's Apprentice*. It's not quite funny to find himself feeling like one now.

Arsons and enforcements he never asked for spark from ones he did, and Suggs—where *is* that union turncoat that set the union yapping and snapping at Isaiah's heels? With his name on Immigration's stop list, the weasel can't have left the island. But he's vanished.

Horace Tucker's family is howling for justice; they called on Isaiah right here in his *home* (minus the peaked white hoods he thought he could sense them yearning to wear). His boss the Premier, who once gave him free rein, showed up here, too, on crutches from his gout and even more bug-eyed with rage than when he insisted some months back Isaiah could damn well shut down the union and shut up the Opposition with one fat arm shoved up his fat black arse. This time he shouted, "Armed checkpoints? Isaiah? You cuing up '77 all over again? I'll feed you to the mob in pieces before anybody comes after me."

The racist asshole's got a point: now the union members, mostly black and always touchy, are walking out wildcat all over the place, in support of their dead brothers Rufus and Breem, in solidarity with their stand-up front man Marcus

Passjohn, in protest of Government's repression of their civil right to mouth off. The dockworkers struck ages ago when Isaiah first sent Suggs in to unveil their kickbacks and their thievery, but now it's sanitation and the buses shutting down on issues no one can spin, and the hospital orderlies threatening to join. If the nurses go, the hospital closes, and if baggage handlers and maintenance shut the airport, everything—next summer's tourists, should there be any, and all commerce, foreign or not—will stop.

Everything but the bubbling and the boiling in people's blood.

Gently Isaiah sets his chiffon pie on the fridge shelf to chill. He stirs the chowder, inhales its rich aroma, spoons himself a bowl. Food is his solace. Suggs was his mistake. He can see that now. He'll have to rise above it. From Tucker's death and the threats it's breeding, he'll just cook himself up some additional opportunity.

He pictures Passjohn's prissy hectoring about truth, lies and scapegoats in his office not many weeks ago. He pictures the very hot black body of the woman he had in bed here last night who told him—naked and astride his chest—her fantasy: to fuck that skinny Passjohn because he's so fucking smart and such a stickler for probity. He'd not known that last word till he looked it up when she left, and in the meantime he'd fucked her harder than she wanted to be fucked because he also remembers how Passjohn put him down on the floor of Parliament in front of the full house laughing at a word he'd mispronounced.

Isaiah flings his empty soup bowl into the sink. Good thick British crockery, it doesn't break. He retrieves it and refills it with chowder. If some blackassed Rasta bastard were to swing, for the sake of security, for the sake of peace, for the sake of quieting his boss, what little would be lost, and what greater good gained? Any one of that kind that didn't commit this crime has committed, or incited, or will incite or will commit some crime. Permanently angry people. Permanently dangerous.

The American administration has got it right: pre-emptive

security *is* the only counter to insidious, invisible threat. Good people deserve to feel safe. They expect to feel safe.

Isaiah pulls the pie from the fridge even though it's not gelled, grabs a spoon, snaps on CNN and sits down. Depression sits nearby. The brand new rims he just installed at great expense on his SUV, twenty-two inch spinners, haven't done a thing to correct his mood, so here he cooks and he eats, a serious vice for a man his size with his cholesterol numbers.

You push on, he tells himself, heaving a mighty sigh. Power's a burden, and the righteous can never set it down. Passjohn's new woman may be opportunity, although embarrassing the expatriate community at this point might carry a too-high cost. Isaiah opens wide and spoons in pie. He tells himself: more pictures. There's always ammo, if you've balls enough to use it. You stop believing that, you're dead meat.

He falls asleep halfway through the chiffon pie. The cassava pie in the oven will burn to a sooty crisp before he wakes. But in his dream, he pulls the oven door down and bastes his beautiful meat pie, pouring soup stock through a hole in the crust. He scrubs sweat from his face with his sleeve and rubs his eyes, and inside this dream he remembers another dream. He rode men's shoulders, moving fast through a boisterous crowd. That accountant Heppering, snake in a suit, rode an escalator, his hands full of paper. Somewhere there's fire; Isaiah smells smoke. Flesh on fire. But under everyone's feet are ripe yellow loquats, crushed to a slippery pulp. There's not but one thing in the whole weird dream that doesn't scare hell out of Isaiah: and that's old Mr. Trott, smiling and waving in his wheelchair beside the road. Like Jesus, like Santa Claus, like the sorcerer with the right word to stop the flood — so comfortingly sane and familiar.

11

Marcus's desk, like his life, is a mess. This morning he avoids both. The patch of sky framed by his office window has the color and weight of pewter, and now and again rain leaks from the clouds, further bedraggling the red and green plastic Christmas garlands still strung lamp post to lamp post, even though that season is four weeks past. The absence of sunlight depresses him, as it always does during the island's brief, drippy winter. How on earth did he survive his years in England where it always rained?

In those days, Lydia was his light. They met in October, when the leaves, the slanting sun and her hair shared the same tint: pale gold. He thought then, he thinks now, of the flesh of ripe apples. Her mouth, her sex, their juicy, rampant love: what flared between them was that sweet. Here on this island, autumn does not exist except for a slight gradation in light, from clear to a thicker gold that he has never since failed to recognize and to rue, because when he was twenty-one and entirely alone in England he discovered autumn and Lydia and love at the same time, on an unplanned weekend in Kent.

He turns away from the window's dismal view and Lydia's ghost within it. For his second meeting with Lucy, just before Christmas, he chose Stonehole Bay on the South Shore. A honeymooners' picture-perfect destination. He toyed endlessly in private with the irony and the significance of asking her to meet him there, close to her house, technically public, but completely deserted in winter.

They arrived separately and walked the short beach several times, discussing the boys' respective situations. She urged him to try listening to what Zef did not say as well as what little he said, and he found her concern—given the trouble Zef had caused her, given her own intractable difficulties with Peyton—remarkably generous and insightful. He said, before he knew the words were coming, "You give me exactly what I need." She looked away, looked back straight into his eyes and said, her face reddening, "No, it's you who give me what I need." After that they could not speak but took hands to help each other over the slick, barnacled rocks. In the lee of the sandblasted monolith with its single round eye that gives the bay its name, they held each other.

The sun had sunk very low. The standing stone threw a long shadow. The wind, picking up for evening, made Lucy shiver. She said she had to leave to get home before her son did. She dipped her head to hide eyes Marcus knew were filled with longing, and he reached for her. She came quickly into his embrace and while he pressed her flush against him he felt proud and unashamed. He kissed her deeply and she kissed back, and as self-consciously as if he stood on a podium before a crowd of thousands he vowed silently he would protect her from his lust and her need. What was between them would be only what it was in that moment: circumscribed passion. A pure flame.

By the time he shut his car door and watched her walk away, he was already asking himself whom he was kidding with such bullshit chivalry. They are riding a bullet train of desire headed in one direction only; he wants to sleep with her and thinks about it often, in detail. He wants more: the completion, the conjugal comfort, of holding her and feeling his instinct to guard her rise. Their most recent meeting, under the pines in the Anglican churchyard at St. Anne's, felt tense and unsatisfying. She'd just come back from family holidays in the States; he'd missed her and been lonely as he always was during the holidays; and she, although eager to set the date and name the meeting place, arrived late and seemed equally eager to be on her way. They had trouble keeping a conversation going and they did not touch. The dead in their whitewashed vaults seemed oppressively present and Lucy's openness tainted, partially reclaimed by contact with the way her life used to be, a life in which he would mean nothing, or nothing but disaster. They parted, ten days ago now, without making plans, and since then he's wondered obsessively if she will agree to see him again.

He sits down with a resolution to work but ends up tilted back in his chair, staring at the paddles of the ceiling fan rotating, dreaming of making love to a white woman, as if that would save him, or help anyone on this beleaguered island.

The phone rings and his hand closes obediently on the receiver. He answers and is stung, in return, by Althea's voice, tense and demanding.

"Marcus, you got to do something. Cisco Suggs makin' to leave de island, people talk how he buyin' false passport." Chesley Bridger's house, she tells him, burned to the ground last night, this social worker's modest home destroyed in retribution for his role in distributing inside Government offices the broadsides she churns out demanding truth, justice, and new elections, immediately. "My house, Marcus, my shop be next."

He does not suggest to her the obvious, cowardly response: she could protect herself by doing less. By doing as close to nothing as possible. She could leave Suggs' fate to others. She could just let her cousin be dead, since he already is. He doesn't suggest this because he knows it's not valid. Even cowardice wouldn't necessarily protect her from *her* fate. She's a woman, a black woman, a woman with limited resources and large pride, and all those truths of her condition make her vulnerable to destruction.

"What is it, exactly, you think *I* can do, Althea?"

"You make them listen. We askin' justice for Rufus and Breem. Same thing white people demandin' for Tucker. White people avenge dey own. Black people got to stand up, too."

He tells her he has stood up. He tells her what the outcome was.

He learned yesterday from his loyal old friend Eugene Outerbridge of talk at the police station that a warrant for Ramo's arrest as Horace Tucker's murderer will soon be issued. Marcus went immediately to the chief judge to say there had better be substantive evidence. The judge, a Tucker himself, was on his way from chambers to courtroom, dressed in his black robe and white wig. He put on his poker face to listen, and then said nothing. Not a word.

"You see, Althea, I have no power. I have in the past deluded myself that I do, but I don't."

"Then you got to get the means to have it. You got to get Cisco's notebook before he gone."

He tells her she's right. He doesn't tell her he has no plans to do so. And then Kenrick walks in to suggest lunch, and he's able to ring off with the excuse of a visitor with urgent business.

Outdoors, sun stabs through the clouds but a fine rain falls at the same time, typical winter weather, one squall after another. They do not speak, which suits Marcus, but he notes that Kenrick seems broody.

In the sandwich shop, Marcus shares with him his experience with the judge and what Althea's just told him, and Kenrick says, "She's right. It's her leafleting and the retribution it's raised that you need to respond to. That's where your leverage with the public will be because it cuts across color lines. Most people don't want other people's houses getting torched, since their own might be next."

"You're suggesting I throw Ramo to the wolves," Marcus says, chewing egg salad.

"I'm pointing out that the wolves already have him if they want him. I'm suggesting that your choice be pragmatic."

Kenrick has bought a chef salad and seems not to be enjoying it. Marcus carefully folds wax paper around the half of the sandwich he can't stomach. He can explain to no one the complicated obligation he feels to Ramo, a matter of impersonal legal principle he cannot separate from a deeply personal resentment of Zef's preference for the Rastafarian over him as father—and the resultant compensating imperative to not allow the personal to subvert the political. To Kenrick he says only, "The right choices are often not practical. Didn't you tell me not long ago you and I are two fools too foolish to abandon our principles?"

Kenrick winces and Marcus recognizes in the expression that briefly freezes, then flees the man's features a shadow of the shame that shifted the ground between them that day they confronted Suggs inside Basil's Dream, the same day Marcus first stumbled into knowledge of Kenrick's hidden ties to that place and its proprietor. He says now, unaware the words are coming until they are out, "I'm not going to ask you any embarrassing personal questions."

Kenrick surprises him with a level stare of several seconds' duration. Then he says, "I do need to ask you a personal question."

Marcus's heart jumps. He says nothing.

Kenrick says, "How do things stand between you and Zef?"

He's never before voluntarily broached the topic of Zef. Marcus has long had the impression, carefully unexamined, that Kenrick dislikes his son, and he knows why. Zef's the incontrovertible evidence of Marcus's most significant and lasting failure of blackness: the white wife. Plus—he knows this, too—Zef is a pain in Kenrick's ass because of the constant political trouble he causes Marcus.

Of late he's taken steps to get Zef under control because of what his delinquency with her son is doing to Lucy. Kenrick knows, because it makes Marcus late to the office, that he's driving Zef to government school in the mornings now. He's ordered him to stay there. He's told Zef there will be serious consequences if he's found again at Ramo's or with Peyton Langston. "I will put a stop to this, whatever I have to do," he shouted, striking the kitchen table, and only when Zef said, "Tell me another joke, Marcus," did he wonder exactly what it was he threatened.

What power, exactly, does he have over Zef?

He explains none of this to Kenrick, saying only that he's being strict with Zef about going to school.

Kenrick looks as if sudden indigestion pains him. He says, "Zef hasn't shared with you, has he, what's making him act out so? Has he said why he did what he did that got him expelled? Do you have any idea what's bothering him?"

"Do you?" Marcus asks. Kenrick looks away, which Marcus finds very odd.

"Of course not," he replies. "I have concerns, because he's your son, I care. That's all."

Marcus is about to pursue that remark when justice minister Isaiah Barnes pulls up a chair to join them as if he's an accustomed lunchtime companion. They are startled into silence.

"I got something for you, Passjohn," Isaiah says without preamble. His signature yellow suspenders are bright broad stripes on his white shirt that strains at the line of buttons crossing his belly. He seems to have put on some pounds since Christmas. "Something tangible," he says, "to help our people. Something your party and mine can support."

Isaiah pauses to take in half his sandwich, pastrami on rye oozing melted cheese, in two bites. He chews forcefully. Kenrick repeats, "*Our* people?"

"I thought you had a point the other day about people's fears," Isaiah says, speaking to Marcus and ignoring Kenrick. "I reflected on it." He leans in close. "Couple days ago, driving home from the office, it came to me like a dream. Your old friend, Marcus, Lemuel Trott. You know, I've passed that fellow for years, like everybody else, but it's like I just *saw* him for the first time that day. I was coming off a bad day, a real bad day, and there he was, smiling and waving. Waving and smiling, at *me*! Made *me* feel damn good, and that's when it hit me. It's a picture. *He's* a picture. A message everybody could use — perseverance and a smile, in the face of adversity."

Isaiah's hand lifts from the table to demonstrate Lemuel's gesture. "Some kind of theme poster is what I'm thinking," he says. "It'd show that old guy some respect, be a real honor for him."

Marcus gazes at Isaiah's hand where it now rests on the table not far from his. The skin black and plump, glistening with youth and oily good health.

Kenrick says, "A poster. A piece of paper. You think that's tangible."

"Well, hell, yeah. A poster is something everybody can see. Like a flag."

Kenrick jumps up. He says, "Fuck you, Isaiah."

Marcus continues to stare at the place on the table where Isaiah's hand had lain. Isaiah ignores Kenrick again but, pushing his chair back to stand, he says to Marcus with an undertone of miffed disappointment, "Well, think about it, okay?" and then, abruptly jovial, he adds, "Hey, Passjohn," and Marcus finally looks up.

Isaiah winks theatrically. "Keep that fly zipped, man."

Kenrick says, "What the fuck?" and Marcus, counting only three rendezvous—but a dozen or more emails stored on his burgled hard drive and several phone calls, on lines that likely are not secure—says nothing. Not a word.

Driving fast into Warwick, heading for Ramo's to tell him about the impending warrant, Marcus nearly clips a man walking on the verge. Speeding, passing a truck, Marcus has pulled carelessly too far to the right, and in the startled second he straightens the wheel and regains the road, he sees the man's face. Sunken, lined, the whites of his eyes yellowed, the white wool on his head yellowed, too. In the single moment their eyes hook, the forbearance of the wrinkled face gives way to fear and then immediately to rage as it registers the nearness of the miss. The man raises his cane and shakes it at Marcus, thrown long past him now by the speed of the car, but in the rearview the man's shape lingers and shifts, becoming in Marcus's mind Lemuel Trott who is also old and white-haired, and who should be angry at Marcus but never is.

By the time he reaches Ramo's shop, another squall has

blown through, causing brief rain and drawing in its wake a stiff, steady wind. Grit and paper trash swirl through the lot as he pulls in, and a sudden fierce gust threatens to rip the Bentley's door off when he opens it. Ramo is pushing Lemuel's chair into the wind toward the shelter of Althea's unlit house. The old man's hands cover his face and Ramo is hunched and squinting.

"Gale comin'," Ramo calls out to Marcus, who's shielding his own eyes from the blowing sand. He is about to approach Ramo, to deliver his message and help him with the chair, when he sees his son and Peyton Langston coming out the front door of Ramo's shop.

"Goddamn," he shouts at them and Ramo, but the words tear away on the wind. Two plastic garbage cans from someone's yard skid down the road, losing their lids and bouncing like paper cups at a breezy picnic. Marcus hustles through the blow to the doorway, grabs both boys by the arms and drives them before him to the Bentley. He shoves Zef into the backseat and gestures at Peyton to get in the front.

Dropping into the driver's seat, wrestling the door shut against the wind, he says to Peyton, "I'm taking you home. Tell me where you live."

Peyton, in a small voice, does so, and Marcus pulls out of the lot. In his rearview, he sees Ramo struggling to heft Lemuel's chair up Althea's porch step. Why, he wonders, has no one built a ramp? Or has it blown away or broken apart? Ramo sets his shoulder to the chair's frame and lifts. So be it, let him stoop and strain, Marcus thinks, pressing the accelerator. So be it, as well, that he does not after all give Ramo the warning he came here to deliver. It is Lemuel who needs protection, from the cheap use to which Isaiah wants to put his maimed life. And from his sister, whose machinations in the world leave her brother home alone, and vulnerable.

Ascending the ridge on their way to the South Shore, no one talks. Peyton stares out the passenger side window, and Zef slouches sullenly in the back seat. Marcus glances at Basil's Dream as they pass it, shuttered against the storm, but lights blazing in the shop downstairs. No doubt Althea's in there, running her mouth, maybe typing broadsides and sending out faxes, while her brother huddles in their damp home by himself in the dark. Why is Lemuel not inside the warm, bright shop beside his sister? He knows the practical reason: Althea has no car and no way to move her brother anywhere his wheelchair won't take him, but—really—why the separation? Why so many short human distances so unbridgeable; why, so often, a single step and yet no ramp?

Negotiating the s-curves on the downhill side of the ridge, he recognizes the complicated gap he's bridging—driving for the very first time to Lucy's house while bringing her, for the second time, her son who has run away with his son. He says to Peyton what he should have said, for her sake, long ago. "Zef is no good for you. Stay away from him, you hear?"

From the backseat comes the response he knows he deserves for betraying his son for hers: "Fuck you, too, Marcus."

Peyton stares out the window as if no one's said a word. His teeth are set into the reddened flesh alongside the nail of his thumb.

On the South Shore cliff where the Langstons live, the wind blows at least forty miles an hour, with far stronger gusts embedded, but in the driveway, between the house and the rock face behind it, there is some shelter. Lucy opens the front door before he can knock. She jerks Peyton into the house behind her, barely looking at him, and stares up at Marcus. She has to hold the door against the wind with both hands. Her face is tense and very pale; her hair twisted into a knot so tight he can see the hairs strain the skin at the nape of her neck. She is nakedly glad to see him even though she is also obviously distraught. Briefly, from the doorstep, he tries to explain the circumstances that bring him here. The wind punches at him. The sea on the other side of the house smashes like a wrecking ball against the rocks. And behind him in the Bentley, Zef watches; Marcus can feel his interested gaze. Behind Lucy, in the dim foyer, Peyton stands listening.

"There's a gale coming," Marcus says. "Close your shutters, and open the windows on the lee side to equalize the air pressure inside and out."

She looks nervously at the nearest window, where the shutters are open and the sash closed.

"Call Darrell," Marcus shouts over a rising howl in the wind. "Get him to come home and help you."

"He's off the island," she shouts back, and through all the noise, he hears her fear. But there's nothing, not a thing, he can do. He wants to touch her. He wants to secure her damn windows for her, but he can't, because the boys are watching. He smiles at her, a pathetic attempt at encouragement, and gets back in his car.

On the way home he lets Zef have it. Has he been in school at all today, why in hell does he persist in courting the Langston boy's fascination, creating pain and trauma for that family? Just where does he think that kind of meanness and his endless truancy and his complete disrespect for all forms of authority will land him? In prison, maybe. Like Ramo. Is that his goal?

For a long time Zef says nothing. Then, abruptly, he says, "Why the hell you care? Since I'm so damn 'no good,' why you care?"

"Of course I care, you idiot. You're my son, I have to."

"You do not. You don't give a shit. Why don't you give me to my mother, you want so bad to throw me away."

"Your mother? What's she got to do with any of this?"

"You lie to me about my mother."

"I do not."

"You do. You lie, you lie, you lie—"

"Shut up, Zef."

"You shut up."

"I will not. I am the adult. You close your fucking mouth."

Zef does not. He barks Shut-Up-Shut-Up-Shut-Up louder and louder, whatever Marcus yells back. Marcus fights with the steering wheel. Rain and salt water blow across the road in sheets, the wind repeatedly shoving the car onto the shoulder.

When they reach Rose Hill, he takes hold of Zef the moment

they step inside. He means to make the boy look him in the eye. He means to rip apart the knot of rage that strangles them both. What happens, somehow, is that Zef's back smacks against the actual wall and Marcus's hands clamp both his shoulders, pinning him. That there is something wrong with this boy, no love in him, no goodness, only meanness, that he's been nothing but trouble from the day he was born, this is what Marcus feels. Some of it he says; he can't keep his mouth closed. He hears shouting: "Why are you *so fucking difficult?* What is it you want? What is it you think I can do that I haven't done?"

What he sees while he yells is Lydia with a sallow face and exhausted eyes, and Zef, the accidental baby they were never sure they wanted to have, slung over her shoulder at two in the morning. Zef screaming with colic, Lydia stinking of sour milk he's spit on her, and Marcus with a case to argue in the morning. No one can sleep. No one has slept since this baby was born.

He feels Zef's fist on his jaw. A glancing blow, the boy's arm half-pinned. Before he knows he's doing it, he's struck his thirteen-year-old son with his own fist, in the chest. He hears him cry out and feels a knee rise hard into his own groin. Zef says, "You shut up, you motherfucker. You lying *fucker*. You sending back letters my mother sends me and you chasing after Peyton Langston's mother. It's got nothing to do with me, all right."

Marcus is bent double, confused and hurting, trying to pull himself clear of this—understanding nothing except the nothing that's here for him, nothing but pain—when he sees Mrs. Alvarra. She's watched everything from the kitchen doorway, a wooden spoon in her hand. Zef's bedroom door slams, and Mrs. Alvarra registers the sound with a flinch.

His hand on the wall for support, Marcus has a sudden vision of Zef at five or six, an ashy-kneed kid seated on a stool at Mrs. Alvarra's feet as the housekeeper paged and snipped the newspaper for coupons, her lips in a line, the pinch of her fingers and of her shears rhythmic and precise. Marcus passed by, coming in from eighteen hours of work or going back—a zombie, blind from pain at his powerlessness to keep Lydia from leaving him, and from the ambition and the drink that partly anesthetized the pain; so exhausted and so driven he was gasping for his breath—and he saw without really seeing that Zef was being punished for some infraction of Mrs. Alvarra's many rules, expressed in those days almost entirely in Portuguese. He recalls with great clarity Zef's narrowed nervous eyes, old beyond his years and already angry, seeking and at the same time dodging his.

It never occurred to him then that he could or should do anything to address this, and that fact strikes him, now, as extraordinary. He goes to the aid of strangers. He's expended his life trying to help his beleaguered people. But his son he did not help when he had the chance because, in truth, he did not see him. He knows he could not stand to see him, because Zef's wound too greatly resembled his own, and no one was there to heal either of them.

Mrs. Alvarra's eyes, now as then, regard Marcus with unmasked disapproval and not a shred of pity. She places the spoon on the kitchen counter, retrieves her purse from the shelf beneath it, and lets herself out. In the sink, she leaves the dishes and the dishwater standing.

Seated in his neatly vacuumed living room, Marcus listens to rain sluicing from the roof through pipes in the walls to the cistern beneath the floor. He remembers when he considered this the sound of replenishment. Today he finds menace in the deluge. The empty white couch facing him is ghostly in the gloom. He wonders, dimly, how it is Zef knows or thinks he knows about the two letters Lydia sent Marcus amid ten years of silence, both of them two years ago, both of them dropped back into the postbox marked, "Return to Sender" the same days they arrived. A mistake. And the weight of the mistakes, the failures, the disappointments he's authored for himself and for his son are all stones, piled so thick and so heavy on his chest he can barely breathe.

Then the phone rings, and it is Lucy, and he is overjoyed. He cannot believe the miracle of her voice in his ear at this moment. She tells him a window has blown out, water is coming into the house, the landlord does not answer his phone, and she doesn't know who else to call.

"Please, Marcus," she says, "I know I shouldn't ask you, but can you come?"

"Of course," he answers. He leaves the house immediately.

In the morning the sky had been dull gray-blue and the sea flat—what's come to seem an ordinary winter day on the island—and then after lunch Lucy had looked up from the novel she was reading, believing she heard someone knocking at the windows on the southeast corner of the house, knocking long and loud, with great need or very bad manners, and when she turned the corner into the kitchen she discovered that within the last hour both sea and sky had gone a bilious green, and white caps reached up toward the ropes of rain just beginning to fall from lowering clouds as the wind swept up water from both and smashed it against the house. Standing there alone in the cliff house as the power went off and unnatural midday half-dark took hold, she remembered hearing that winter gales on the island could be just as strong and destructive as hurricanes but more dangerous, since they arose without warning and moved unpredictably.

Several hours after Marcus brought Peyton to the door, a torrential rain has washed out part of the driveway and flooded the area in front of the garage door, making it impossible to leave even had she wanted to chance putting the car on the road, and the rude knocking of the wind has risen to a beating roar, like the sound of a prop plane's engine accelerating, punctuated with wall-shaking thumps when debris strikes the house, and a shrieking rip when the window is blown out and disappears, replaced instantly by an in-rush of rain. The house, she knows, is very solidly built, but roofs do come off; she knows that, too—both gales and hurricanes spawn tornados. When she finally sees Marcus making his way on foot down the steep drive, clinging to the stone balustrade in what is now a river, she must push with both hands and her shoulder to open the door into the wind and let him in. He slips inside on a blast of grit, salt spray and torn wet leaves, her bare feet slide from under her on the foyer's damp tile, and the gale slaps the door shut hard behind him.

He is drenched and haggard — and a very welcome sight. She shatters instantly into three competing responses that preclude her from doing anything except getting up from the floor — she flings her arms around him and clings only in her imagination, while her body backs up in recognition of how ratty she looks (a baggy sweatshirt reaching nearly to her knees, hair straggling and face flushed from the exertion of mopping), and her mind screams caution and indictment because Peyton is right behind her, witness to every nuance between her and this man she has no business letting in. All she can do is say to Marcus, "Thank you," emphatically but quietly. To Peyton — dressed in Scooby Doo boxers, no shirt and enormous rubber waders that Darrell once bought for a fly-fishing vacation he had to cancel — she says, "Mr. Passjohn has come to help us." Her son's face is a silent war of contradictions: clearly any possibility of rescue is welcome but her choice of rescuer is not.

Behind them, the house is humid and stuffy and dim; although the wind's force is beginning to diminish as the storm blows through, the power is still out. Marcus, touching her shoulder lightly, pressing his fingertips into her skin the moment Peyton turns away, steps ahead of her from the foyer into the central hallway, and immediately his hand goes to his ear.

"You feel that?" he asks, turning back to look at her. "The air pressure in here bending your eardrums?"

She nods and he explains. "These thick walls trap it. Have you opened any windows?"

She remembers now that he told her to do this earlier. "I forgot," she says. "Is that why the one in the kitchen blew out?"

If only she'd done what she was supposed to, some of this mess could have been avoided. All she has done for hours is mop and sweat and worry. She also phoned Darrell in Cayman, and although she reached him right away—something of a miracle given the storm, and the fact he's at the negotiating table—his response was maddeningly matter-of-fact: What did she want him to do? What did she think he *could* do, from that distance? "Nothing, I guess," she'd said, feeling stupid. "All right then," he replied. "I'll be home tomorrow. Call the damn landlord again and threaten to withhold rent, and if you still can't get him, call Heppering."

She had put down the phone and warred with herself about the rage she felt. Years ago she'd stopped expecting help from Darrell because he could never see she needed any. His work came first, and he did not comprehend her wish to not always be alone with problems even while she handled them. She knew this about him and had known it for ages, so why get mad now? Years ago, when Peyton was tiny and she handled his fevers and his asthma by herself because Darrell was working, and before that, when she handled two miscarriages and then complete bed rest by herself, because he was working, she would blow up at him and call him selfish, but it did no good, it only made the marriage colder, and so she had quit. Fighting was pointless.

"Crack open all the windows on the sea side now," Marcus is instructing Peyton. "The wind's switched to the lee."

Peyton, going nowhere, shifts weight from one foot to the other but with a question rather than resistance flickering in his eyes. He says, "The water in the toilet, it's swirling around like a tornado."

"Whirlpool," Marcus answers, laughing, and more gratitude—along with a tide of longing—floods Lucy. She and Peyton can both be stupid or wrong and Marcus is amused instead of impatient. She follows him toward the kitchen as he says, "That comes from the pressure differential, too. Low outside because of the storm, high in here—"

"Just open the windows, Peyton, like he says," she interrupts and then wonders why she's being short with her son, as if she's competing with him for Marcus's kindness.

The tile floor in the kitchen is a shallow pond. With a blanket, Lucy has made a dam at the doorway to hold the water out of the rest of the house, and she and Peyton have been trying to keep the water from rising over it by mopping with sponges into a bucket. "That's resourceful," Marcus says, pointing at her dam, then removing his shoes and rolling his pants legs. In the corner where the window used to be, rain and sea spray are gusting through the three-by-six-foot hole where the window is missing, frame and all.

She says nothing, and watches Marcus survey the situation, her arms at her sides and her hands balled into fists inside the sweatshirt's stretched-out cuffs. She feels tension leaving her back and her shoulders sinking as they relax; she'd not been aware until now they were hunched by several inches toward her ears.

"Is there a sheet of plywood or a tarp, somewhere in the house?" Marcus asks. He smiles at her. He looks happy rather than stressed, and she smiles back. She sees how he wants to reach for her and anticipates his touch but exactly at that moment they both hear the slosh of Peyton in his waders coming up behind them.

"I don't think we have anything big enough and strong enough to cover the window," she says, taking one step backward, away from Marcus, but Peyton pipes up that there is a storeroom belonging to the landlord in the basement.

"It's locked," she says.

"We'll unlock it," Marcus replies.

On their way down the stairs, he says he figures the owner of a building in this kind of location must have storm supplies on hand even if he's too lazy or careless or passive-aggressive to inform his American tenants about it. Once Marcus knocks the doorknob off with a hammer and lights up the storeroom with the flashlight Peyton fetches him, they find several sheets of plywood along with masonry nails and a hammer. Peyton, Lucy sees, is very excited by the act of breaking and entering, and he remains enthusiastic and cooperative while helping Marcus struggle through the sodden work of fastening the plywood over the window hole. Rain is beating down hard but they work from inside the house, and because the storm is moving inland and the wind speed dropping, they eventually succeed. Lucy hands them nails, and mops around their feet, and when they are done she makes coffee, heating water in a tea kettle on the propane range.

They carry the cups into the living room to get away from the disorder in the kitchen. Peyton has changed clothes and sits deep in the couch cushions. Marcus, in an armchair facing Peyton, wears over his wet clothes the dry blanket Lucy has offered him, but she, cross-legged between them on the floor, is still in her damp pants and sweatshirt. She shivers in little seizures that jerk her skull back and forth atop her spine, and her bare feet are noticeably bluish, even in the light of the candles on the coffee table. Marcus regards her with concern; he begins a suggestion that she change her clothes but then his eyes shift toward Peyton who is staring at them aggressively, and in response Marcus sits back in his chair and compliments her coffee, heavily laced with hot milk. Impulsively Lucy reaches into an enameled wooden box on the low table in front of the couch for the cigarettes and lighter she stashes there. She lights up without apology or explanation and draws deeply, hoping the nicotine will perk her up or at least stem her shivering. No one speaks, the house is silent and damp as the pendulum clock ticks and the candles burn; she tries to keep her eyes off Marcus and then his fingers are touching hers, sending the familiar electric thrill through her, as he plucks the cigarette away.

"Put this out," he tells her, holding it in the air between them, and Peyton, jumping up, says, "I'll do it." As her son bends to the table to grind the cigarette out in the ashtray she washes between each indulgence, Marcus catches her eye and shakes his head slowly. *Don't do that, it's bad for you,* his gaze tells her, and she's lost, falling into him, impassioned by this tiniest of intimacies and the boldness it takes to impose such familiarity in these circumstances. A fresh spasm of shivering wracks her and in a chaos of physical guilt and desire she recalls exactly, in her cells, what it felt like once upon a time to adore Darrell in a similar way. When they'd barely begun dating he invited her to a performance of the chamber orchestra in which he played second violin but had, on that occasion, a difficult solo, the long unaccompanied passage called *cadenza*, which he told her, his face plainly vulnerable, he lacked both the technical skill and the nerve to play well. Wouldn't she come, he pleaded quietly, and sit where he could see her eyes, and help him, steady him if he faltered? She'd agreed, of course, and in the very last plaintive and perfect tones of Albinoni's unfinished *Adagio*, he finally lifted his eyes to hers, telling her with his gaze, *It's yours, I did it for you*, and she had felt herself fall, joyfully, hard, into whatever came next, his naked love the drug that made anything possible and everything worth it.

She's not realized she's staring, too still and too steadily, at Marcus until she hears Peyton say, "My dad called right before you came." Peyton's face and tone make it clear he's ready for Marcus to go, now that the job of being hero is finished, and Lucy is so startled by Peyton's abrupt assertiveness that it takes her a beat or two to realize that he's had a conversation with Darrell she was not party to.

Marcus stands up. "Oh. What did he—"

"He's in Cayman," Lucy says quickly, and to Peyton, she adds sharply, "When did you talk to him?"

"You were mopping. I called his cell from the phone in his study, and he called me right back."

"I didn't hear it ring," she says, as if that makes any difference, and Peyton, ignoring her, speaks to Marcus. "I told him about the storm *and* the window."

She falls silent then, and Peyton doesn't continue. Because neither of them explains anything, Marcus prompts. "What did he say?"

Peyton replies, "He said he was sorry we were having trouble but there's no way he could get back any sooner than tomorrow. And then he told me that he already talked to Mom and told her to call Jonathan Heppering."

Now no one says a word, for several seconds. Then Peyton, his voice overloud, goes on: "But Mom had already called you."

Marcus's face looks gaunt and exhausted, even in the candles' gentle light, and Lucy remembers, then, that he has enormous problems of his own, at work and at home. Marcus says, to Peyton, "I'm glad I was able to help. I'm glad of your help, too, Peyton."

Another silence follows, in which Marcus drinks down the rest of his coffee, and Lucy watches him while trying to look as if she isn't. This man, necessary and impossible in her life, standing awkwardly in the drafty, graceless room of a cliff house she did not want, amid the beautiful, expensive, and very American furniture that doesn't fill it up. Her son sits in the center of the couch with his arms draped along the back, as if he were the man here and will take up as much space as possible to prove it. She plays with the elastic that had bound her hair, now stuck to her neck with sweat and rain. Marcus sets his empty cup on the table.

"I have to get home," he tells her. "Zef is alone." To Peyton — an admonishment that catches them both off guard — he says, "Be good to your mother."

After that, Marcus makes his way to the door without further speech, stepping over the waders in the hallway. Lucy is right behind him, moving almost before she's aware she's going to. She follows him outside, closes the door all the way behind them so they are hidden by it, and then, sheltering from the wind, presses her cheek wordlessly against his chest. His hand goes immediately into her hair as his other arm encircles her. Momentarily, before guilt can bite her, she clings, and mind and body release a fantasy that melts her: His head, between her hands. Her legs, wrapped around him. Their bodies arching, sweating and stretching and bursting together, his body a cup pouring her pleasure.

And already, mindful of Peyton on the other side of the door, she is letting go and he is, too. She says, "I need to see you. Alone." He answers without hesitation, "*Yes.*"

"You'll call me?" she whispers.

"Yes. Tomorrow."

She kisses the V of his throat where his top shirt button is undone, tastes his sweat, smells his flesh and steps backward, one hand on her lips and the other on the doorknob.

"I'm taking you with me tonight," Marcus tells her, his

voice hoarse, his eyes very dark. As she slips back through the doorway, she knows what he means. She feels it low in the belly. Each of them, tonight, carries the other to bed, alone.

She closes the door and walks past Peyton standing in the hall, straight to her bedroom.

Marcus climbs the flooded driveway to his car, her pale, vulnerable face a pearl glowing inside his body all the way home, through wind and rain and a gale of desire.

12

By the time Darrell gets back, he's figured out what Jonathan handed him a few days ago, and he doesn't want it. Government corruption, here of all places, does not surprise him, but that he — a non-citizen with a family to protect — should hold proof of that corruption, this is not a good thing. The vulnerable position he's in has made him crazy throughout the complex business negotiation in Cayman. He will give that notebook right back to Jonathan.

From the airport he takes a taxi to his office and drops off his bags. Then he goes straight downstairs to the offices of Frith, Stearn and Heppering, but Jonathan is not in. The receptionist, a black girl dressed up like a lady executive, in a business suit and high-necked silk blouse, with nails, hair and makeup all the epitome of professional elegance, says he has taken a half-day off.

Darrell is surprised. One of the things he likes about Jonathan is that he, like Darrell, does not operate according to the common local work ethic: in at 9, more or less, and out at 4:45, minus all possible personal days.

"Are you sure?" he asks the girl.

Not bothering to glance up from the set of charts she's collating, she ignores him until he feels his face start to color.

"Why would you imagine I might be mistaken?" she asks, finally, in the arch intonation that black business people here, especially the females, seem to take with him.

"He's at home then," Darrell says, more cautiously.

"I should think so," she answers, her focus remaining on the charts, "but about that I might be mistaken."

Having consulted the company directory the girl pushes toward him for Jonathan's home address, Darrell sets off. Already it is four o'clock. He will take an early day himself, accomplish this errand, and get home to his family before dark. Riding the scooter, he's immediately chilled; the air is damp, an extreme humidity barely short of rain. Although the temperature, at nearly 60 degrees, is balmy compared to the sleet he passed through in Atlanta, he's been way south in the Caribbean for three days before that, where the sun shone every day and the thermometer topped 80 in the afternoon. He liked it on Cayman, frankly. A lot of empty space, more Americans than Brits, a minimum of locals to contend with, and a kind of frontier feel to the financial community – the buildings all big and brand new, the attitudes rough and ready, the rules and protocols as yet unwritten. If TransGlobal does decide on a relo there, he will not mind. On the other hand, Lucy and Peyton, who were reluctant even to come here, will undoubtedly balk.

His usual route home follows the scenic curves of the South Shore Road, but this evening, in order to travel more directly to Jonathan's house, Darrell points his scooter down the island's straighter and busier Middle Road. Before long he sees he's made a mistake; homebound traffic is heavy, fortunate motorists with their windows rolled up tight and the more numerous scooter riders hunched inside yellow ponchos. The souped-up cycles of the young locals speed right up the center line, slinging oily water off the pavement as they pass, while Darrell wallows along in the stinking diesel wake of a pink bus that stops at every other intersection.

In a sudden red glow of the bus's brake lights, Darrell applies the scooter's hand brakes. Then he swerves right to pass, forgetting to check first for traffic behind him, and from the scooter that sweeps around him on the right comes an oath, too thick with island intonation for him to comprehend more than its hostility. He does catch the cool, superior gaze of the young woman seated sidesaddle on the back of the motorcycle, her slim dark legs, in stockings and high heels, nonchalantly crossed and one arm loosely round the waist of the man driving. While he's staring, a second cycle passes and the fleeting hand of the male passenger riding pillion snakes out and shoves him, tipping his scooter and nearly throwing him to the ground.

The bus belches black exhaust and pulls away; the car behind him sounds its horn. He drives more tentatively thereafter, cursing the asshole islanders and pulling onto the shoulder whenever he can't maintain a safe distance between himself and them. He's heard what happened to white motorists during earlier racial troubles. Entering Southampton Parish, not far from the turn to his own house, he passes a commandeered Docks Corp. truck, the windshield smashed, the cab graffitoed, and the sea container hooked behind it broken open for looting. He sees no one and nothing left inside, only traffic making a wide bend around it.

Problems here are going from bad to worse fast, he thinks, and things in the States are in a mess, too, people panicked about security and the economy in the gutter. He doesn't know where things are *not* a mess; it's as if there's no way to escape it. Even in sunny Cayman he felt the chill, in people's general reluctance to talk about anything happening anywhere else in the world.

Only when he reaches Jonathan's home, on Wreck Hill above Ely's Harbour, does Darrell recall that Jonathan and his family quite recently were victimized. One side of the large, dull yellow stucco house is blackened. Tarps cover the damaged timbers and broken stucco, but the thick canvas has been wrenched loose by heavy rain and wind from the gale that passed through while he was away. At the foot of Jonathan's drive, Darrell stops the scooter and puts both his feet on the ground. Jonathan's lawn, indeed all the lawns he's passed on his way out here, are layered with storm litter, leaves and twigs pulverized by the wind into a thick, unsightly mulch. Now for the first time since his plane landed, Darrell remembers that his own home has been slightly damaged in the storm; he clearly recollects Peyton's nervous chatter and Lucy's stiffness about it over the phone. He feels stupid for forgetting all these facts of other people's lives, and this conclusion feels unpleasantly typical of his always difficult interface with the world beyond business. *Insensitive.* This is a word his mother hammered him with repeatedly, and Lucy used it, too, when she was younger and hotter and used to blow up at him, which made him furious at the time but which he misses, in some ways, because now she has so little to say, and never, anymore, does he find her hot. She is passionate about nothing anymore, as far as he can tell.

He finds Jonathan in the garden behind the house; at the front door Felicity, looking untidy and stressed, a kerchief on her head and soot on her face, directed him there. Jonathan, on his knees, has his hands in a hole in the dirt. Beside him is the hairy root-ball of a plant that is only a bunch of leafless green sticks cut short. Carefully Jonathan puts the plant in the hole and spreads its roots atop a cone-shaped mound of soil. From ten feet away, Darrell observes the gentle precision of Jonathan's movements and marvels at his expression in profile, which is serene.

Darrell clears his throat. "Dear God, Langston, what is it?" Jonathan says, sounding more weary than startled.

Darrell first expresses polite regret about what's happened to Jonathan's home. Jonathan says it will mend; a contractor's been engaged. Darrell inquires about the plants. He hadn't known Jonathan was a gardener. Of course not, is the reply. "This is a private passion," Jonathan says.

He stands up, slowly, grimacing at the midpoint over some catch in his knees, and brushes dirt from his trousers. He explains that he's setting out roses, shipped FedEx from the States in the cool season, the only time they survive the trip and can get established before the summer heat. When they arrive, he plants them immediately, mixing the island's sandy soil with loam he imports from England. Two more root-balls are at his feet, and he names them all three for Darrell, as if introducing children: Peace, Fortuneteller, Lady Blush.

"But you did not come here to talk about roses," Jonathan concludes.

Darrell zips open his windbreaker and reaches into the inner pocket of his suit coat underneath. Before he can extend the envelope to give it back, Jonathan says no. His own hands clasped behind him, he says, "You should keep that. It may be you who can put it to good use."

Darrell demurs. The notebook is dangerous.

"The situation is dangerous," Jonathan corrects him. "You see what's going on around here." He indicates with his head the charred side of his house. "Government is going to fall. That notebook shows why it should. The hand that holds it may determine what new government arises."

"I've got nothing to do with the politics here," Darrell says. "The problems you people face are of your own making—"

"*You people?* You think you are separate from our problems?" Jonathan smiles bitterly. "Are you and your kind not one of our biggest problems? Without the tax-exempt companies like yours, without American money, we are nothing. All of us here dance your tune."

"What if I just burn it?" Darrell says.

Jonathan regards him with his head slightly cocked. "You might. But I don't think you should. I believe you should give it to the police. Let justice, such as it is, sort things out. I want nothing more to do with it; you can leave this island, but I cannot."

He sinks to his knees again, among his roses. "Please go home now, Langston."

When Darrell gets home, the boarded kitchen window feels like a personal affront. Neither Lucy nor Peyton says anything about it, not a word. The huge piece of plywood darkens the room and makes the whole wall ugly. To top everything off, Darrell realizes he never thanked Jonathan for the help he must have given Lucy during the storm, and that as a result he ought to call the man and apologize, when all he feels is anger about the condescending attitude Jonathan's

172   Christine Hale

just shown him.

Lucy's attitude is no good either. He figures she's upset about being on her own when the window blew out. She's like that—he knows that pretty well after all these years. She handles everything just fine but she wants him to tell her so, and to cheer her along while she does it, but he can't do more than he's doing. He's maxed out, all the time, and she, since she doesn't work, just doesn't get that.

She avoids him. Together, barely speaking, they looked at the crude plywood repair. Where the masonry nails were driven in, chunks of plaster are knocked out, damage bound to result in a charge from the landlord.

To mollify Lucy—by including her in one of his problems, because that's what she always used to tell him she needed him to do—and because it *is* a problem, a big one, he shows her the notebook listing payoffs the justice minister has made to a provocateur. He tells her what he thinks it means: proof that Government itself stirred up much of the unrest now threatening to topple the island's social order. Before he's finished talking, she lifts the little red book right from his hand. She reads it with an interest so avid it stuns him.

"Who gave you this?" she asks. Not "what will you do with it," not "ohmygod, how awful," but "who gave you this?" as if she wishes it had been given to her.

He explains about Jonathan. She says, "Are you going to keep it?"

Her color is high. She looks at him quite fiercely. No doubt she thinks he is involved in something he cannot handle.

"Yes, Lucy, I think I shall. For the time being, I'll keep it. Until TransGlobal—and we—can leave this hell hole, I think I'll keep this under wraps. When we're gone, they can tear themselves to shreds." He takes the notebook from her and locks it in a desk drawer in his study. She stands in the hall and watches him do that, but she doesn't say anything else.

Later he knocks on Peyton's door and goes in. He sits on the bed, where Peyton is sprawled amid textbooks and papers and CD cases. The stereo is turned up so loud and the so-called music is so completely unmelodiously abominable that

Christine Hale   173

Darrell finds it difficult to stay in the room.

"How's school?" he asks loudly, over the music, to break the ice.

"Fine," the boy answers, looking at the ceiling.

The music pounds Darrell. He remembers Lucy saying there was some adjustment problem at Somers, but Peyton doesn't seem concerned. "You enjoying yourself?"

Peyton's face rotates toward him. His expression doesn't change.

When he doesn't speak, Darrell gestures with an open palm at the contents of the room. His long, lanky son, in boxers and a tee shirt, looking older and more sullen than Darrell remembers him, reclining amid large pillows like a pasha. The sturdy pine furniture transplanted from Connecticut, the books, soccer balls, stereo and speakers, sports posters, television, video games, legos, model planes, computer, and rock collection, all from Peyton's room in the house in Darien. "You look pretty comfortable in here," Darrell says, raising his voice again to compete with the music.

Peyton simply looks at him.

"You're comfortable here," Darrell says, stressing the second word. "Right?"

"Everything's great, Dad." In the flat tone, Darrell hears a challenge he's not prepared to answer.

Peyton returns his gaze to the ceiling. A few seconds later Darrell leaves the room. It is impossible to talk to this boy. He can't imagine how Lucy manages; he can only hope she's better at it than he is.

13

By the middle of February, each morning's newspaper delivers a fresh dose of bad news about what the world has come to. The island now teeters on the brink of a general strike that will shut down not only transportation, sanitation and the hospital but the docks and the airport and thus all import of food, while at home in the States Enron's fraud tanks the stock market at the same time bombs fall in Afghanistan and the government warns Americans that terrorists are an omnipresent domestic threat. Lucy's focus is narrow. Some days she can barely get out of bed, she feels so debilitated by confusion about Marcus, anger at Darrell's preoccupation with business, and guilt about her sullen, troubled son.

She's seen Marcus only once since the storm, at Stonehole Bay again but this time a desperate, truncated meeting—a police cruiser pulled into the car park and left abruptly after a tall, very dark officer got out and looked at them, seated together on the sand. They both knew they should not be seen together again; but for five days afterward all she could think about was his touch and his glance, the kindness and desire and the sadness palpable in both, so she called him, at the office because she didn't want his housekeeper or Zef to pick up at his home. Their talk was cut short when someone walked into his office, but not too short for her to be certain he was pleased to hear her voice, and not before she told him what she could not make herself withhold: that she had seen exactly the proof he needed to trip up his adversaries, the red notebook that lay in her house, in the desk drawer in her husband's study.

He said he'd call her back but he did not, leaving her to stew desperately for another week in the possibility she'd disgusted him with her willingness to betray her family and her ethics. Then, last night, she finally saw him again—on the television news. Sitting beside Darrell in the living room, she watched Marcus be beaten and arrested.

First, she heard the news anchor announce that Cisco Suggs, suspected of complicity in the so-called Dumpster Deaths and the resultant unlawful protests amid the black community, had been apprehended that morning, at a checkpoint in Paget where a young black Regiment conscript, who happened to be Breem's godson, recognized him despite a disguise. Within hours, however, Suggs went free: no charges and no evidence he was trying to flee, despite the fake passport he carried, according to a police spokesperson. Althea and fifty union men and women marched on the police station bearing banners emblazoned, "Two dead black men more than *equal* one dead white man," setting off a confrontation with two dozen keepers of the vigil for Tucker; they were engaged in round-the-clock prayer for the arrest of his murderer. Before long, more sympathizers on both sides showed up to hurl words across the police lines separating them. Rocks and bottles appeared in cocked fists, and then Marcus turned up.

Lucy knew he meant to try to mediate. She saw it in his face and in the gestures of his long hands, palms turned down, patting the air at chest level as if by soothing it he could calm the angry, contorted faces he addressed. Yet the news anchor explained to the viewing public that the Opposition leader's presence had been instantly incendiary. Enflamed by Passjohn's history of vocal support for the rights of known terrorists, citizens trying to lawfully observe a justice vigil for the late Horace Tucker, a victim of hate crime, demanded that Passjohn leave. Anti-Government agitators, already in defiance of the law for protesting without a permit, reacted to police efforts to remove Passjohn, peacefully and for his own safety, by attacking both the police and the legally permitted vigil participants.

Via live footage replayed on tape, Lucy watched Marcus approach the candle-carriers in the vigil line, attempt to talk to the leader and get shoved. Supporters pulled him clear with the help of two police officers. Someone from the union contingent put a bullhorn in Marcus's hand, but a rock struck the officer nearest him and arguments and scuffles broke out on all sides. Marcus shouted through the bullhorn, "...not let them conquer...dividing us...," but the camera panned to union strikers piling out of vans newly arrived at the scene, shouting and stabbing the air with placards.

At that point the audio from the altercation ended, and the news anchor reported that Cisco Suggs had to be taken into protective custody because of protestors' threats. Caught squarely in the middle of two seething groups of protestors, Marcus was struck from behind, and his knees buckled. She watched him tumble face first to the pavement, boots kicking him on the ground. Her hand clapped over her mouth to keep sound or something worse from coming out. Darrell, eyes on the screen, lifted a hand to tug her back down beside him and pronounced these islanders a legion of idiots, black and white alike, who deserved the trouble they made for themselves. Peyton said, in a tone undeniably snide, "Sit down, Mom."

The TV coverage shifted to a different point in the story— oh, yes, it was taped, she recalled that. She saw Marcus on his feet, a bleeding cut beneath his eye. Then, while a heavyset black woman raised Marcus's fist into the air for the cameras, white police officers closed in on them both.

Lucy left the room at that point; she had to. She shut herself into the bathroom to calm her breathing and stop her tears before they started.

This morning's paper continues the story: Marcus and Althea Trott were arrested at the scene and then released at Government's behest with no charges filed "because of national security and the volatility of the situation in the streets." Police had trouble quelling the disturbance, which developed into a near-riot. Store windows on Front Street were smashed, according to a brief report in the paper; some looting occurred, and a police car was rolled over and set afire. Had Marcus been jailed, the anti-Government factions would simply have more fuel.

When she drives Peyton to school, both of them sit bleakly silent, he chewing his cuticles as if they are his breakfast, and she feeling, in each pinch of his teeth, her shame at his judgment and her failure to relieve his suffering. She has always been certain it is a mother's job to do everything in her power to spare her child pain and distress. Confusion over what to do and what to feel—how to be *right*—paralyzes her, and she lets Peyton leave the car with only one attempt, unsuccessful, to leave a kiss on his cheek. When she returns to the house, she goes straight to Darrell's study.

She uses the spare key from the top of the bookshelf—stashed as she knows it will be beneath a heart-shaped granite paperweight (a long-ago gift from Peyton to his dad)—to open the desk. The Frith, Stearn & Heppering envelope enclosing the notebook of sums paid to Cisco Suggs by Isaiah Barnes lies tucked inside an unlabeled hanging file folder. She knows exactly where it is. More than once since the night Darrell showed it to her, she has checked; more than once she has slipped the notebook from the envelope, read it, and imagined the complicated relief Marcus might feel to hold it in his hand. But this time she resolutely pockets the envelope, replaces the key beneath the paperweight and the papers atop it at the exact angle she found them, and drives to the copy center in town, a thirty-minute trip. She makes one copy of each page of the notebook and, on second thought, a copy of the blank face of the envelope bearing Frith, Stearn & Heppering's return address. She drives, at the minimal speed limit, all the way back home to replace the book and the envelope inside the file folder, as if she had never touched it. Only then does she phone Marcus's office and discover from the receptionist that he is taking a sick day. She changes her clothes, fixes her hair, puts on some makeup, and drives back to town and out the other side, to Rose Hill. She knows exactly where the house is; she located it during the weeks he did not call and she sometimes drove past it, just to look. Now, pulling into the drive as if there were no reason not to, she is sweating. Her fresh shirt is damp beneath the arms, and her hands are slippery on the wheel.

Marcus has not been beaten since he was a young man at the Marxist demonstrations he attended with Lydia in London. He knows he's in no shape to take it now, although his hurts are not severe: numerous deep bruises, a sore kidney, some very stiff muscles. Fortunately the picketers on both sides were of truly divided loyalties. Enough of them believed in his good intentions — or at least his right to go on living — to step in front of those who wanted to kick him to death either as a representative uppity black man or a black leader who failed to lead. He consults the bathroom mirror in this white merchant's house he will one day soon give up to a white-owned bank. The cut on his face, from a boot's steel toe, follows the curve of the cheekbone beneath his right eye for three inches. The wound is swollen but neatly stitched closed from a late night in the ER where the doctors work without nurses, who are out on strike. The mirror shows Marcus a man with black skin and a pummeled face. If he were photographed now for the television audience, would his wound widen or narrow his appeal? Does the mark make him more frighteningly black and angry, or just more acceptably subjugated and therefore merely black?

He touches the face on the mirror. The skin before him is more black than brown but lacks the blue cast of the darkest men, like Ramo. He gazes at himself: one limited man; one lonely, tired and fearful man, trying to stand up but rather easily knocked down without providing to anyone the *example* he still believes it is his job to deliver. Lydia was right. What he's been able to accomplish has proved startlingly deficient, compared to the destiny he and so many others of so many shades and beliefs once trusted him to possess.

A tap at his front door startles him. He's given Mrs. Alvarra the day off after asking her to drive Zef to school this morning. The knock is too tentative to be Kenrick or the police. He throws his robe on, slightly ashamed about that as it's nearly noon. When he opens the door, he stares in amazement.

Lucy looks as if she expects him to shut the door in her face. He pulls her into his arms, forgetting the robe, lifting her off her feet. Then, smelling the sweet scent in her hair and reveling in the warmth of her chest against his, he remembers everything else—who they are and where they are and how anyone might see.

He pulls her inside. He shuts the door.

"I had to see if you were all right," she says. "I saw what happened, on television, last night."

He leads her to the living room and sits down beside her on the white leather couch. "I'm fine," he tells her. "Uglier than I used to be, but fine."

She touches the cut beneath his eye gently. Almost reverently. That stops his breath. Her tendernesses are so sudden and, always, he is stunned at the rush of emotion they release in him.

She withdraws her hand and says, "I'm sorry." Her face says she's misread his held breath as resistance. "I think I have been presumptuous with you." She goes on, in a rush. "I've brought you something. I came here to give you this."

From her purse, still slung over her shoulder, she pulls a sheaf of folded pages. He knows what this is. It's what he needs to pull the plug on Isaiah's scheming. It's what she told him on the phone she had. She holds it out to him, her face open and expectant. He has only to accept it to position himself, with Kenrick's and Althea's help, to lead a new government. He doesn't want it. He doesn't want to be the cause of what will happen to her for giving him this. Even before he knew about the notebook, even when all she offered were kisses and her own vulnerability, he hadn't wanted to be desperate enough and reckless enough—toward her, himself, his son, his people—to take it. He's tried to be, since Lydia left, a man who needs no one. That he once again needs a woman—a white woman, and the soft, trusting help she gives him—that truth is humbling.

He takes the photocopied pages and reads them quickly. It is exactly as she said.

"I didn't dare bring the original," Lucy explains. "I put it back exactly where it was, locked in his desk drawer."

"You took it from your husband's office?" He imagines, despite himself, who might have seen her take and return something surreptitiously from the executive offices at TransGlobal Reinsurance.

"No, no, his study at home."

"This information is vitally important," he says, acknowledging what she already knows. "It will make heads roll. Shift public attention from Althea, the union, Tucker, even Ramo, to the culprits in Government."

He ought to tell her he can't let her steal from her husband, not for him. But that would hurt her.

"I was careful. No one knows," she says. She yearns so openly to be loved.

He embraces her, touches his lips to hers.

This feels exactly right. Nothing like betrayal. Not the least bit like error. Her mouth opens, her arms wrap his shoulders, and, kissing her deeply, he hears something fall in the kitchen—or does he? He doesn't, surely. She is sinking back into the cushions beneath the weight of their mutual desire, he is allowing her body to lead him deeper into this moment while with his lips and his hands he pushes, too, hurrying them down the path, and he hears something else. Definitely something. The back door, closing? He sits up, hands still on Lucy and calls out sharply, "Mrs. Alvarra?" Has that woman come anyway, when he asked her not to?

They stand up and he hurries to the kitchen, Lucy following him. He sees no one. The window in the breakfast nook is open. The weather is blustery, and the louvered wooden shade on the lower sash has come unfastened and blown back against the inside wall, knocking to the floor one of the braided strings of garlic Mrs. Alvarra hangs for good health and good fortune. Behind him in the kitchen doorway, Lucy nervously smooths her rumpled hair. Outside, yellow sun alternates with cloud shadow as the wind blows spring across the island.

"It's nothing," he tells her. "A loose shutter." He smiles to reassure her.

"You're sure?" she says. "My car is outside. Anyone would know—"

"It's all right," he says. He replaces the garlic braid on its hook and closes the window. They cannot stop now. She is more beautiful and desirable than he has ever seen her. Soft with longing, torn with fear, vulnerable and in need of him. He feels in his own body what she needs. He can give her this, so easily, for it is the same thing he wants. He kisses her neck and cups her breast. Her response is quick and hot: teeth on his neck, hands low on his hips, sliding lower. He takes her hand, puts a finger to her lips, walks her with him to lock the back door and the front, then leads her to his bed.

She has been there so many times in dream and daydream that it seems natural to undress her and caress her bare skin. Easy to open his robe and watch her pale hands enjoy his skin and deplore, in the sensitivity of their touch, his bruises. How simple and natural to lay her down and spread her fine blond hair on his pillow, to taste her and touch her inside and out and then sink deeply home in her, at last. What is strange, what astonishes him, is the force of her joy. When he imagined making love to her, he could never picture her expression; now her face is living and responding beneath his lips and fingertips and tongue. Her eyes wide open and reacting to his, the tears on her cheeks trapping strands of her hair, her earlobes and the flesh inside her mouth livid with appetite. And the sounds she makes! She is feasting. And he is the perfect, necessary meal.

Afterwards he thinks about the price that will undoubtedly come due for such raw abandon. Lying with Lucy in his bed in the gloom of a golden afternoon gone dim and showery, he denies those thoughts by admitting the existence of nothing but the way her skin clings to his, and the sound of their tandem breath—slowing now. Eventually the ache in his injured muscles and the bruised organs deep inside his torso reasserts itself. The outside world drips back into his consciousness relentlessly. Tires hiss on damp asphalt at the foot of the hill. A neighbor's garage door rolls up and back down. Then the phone rings once, Lucy startles in the circle of his arms, and he strokes her long back, comforting her while he listens to the machine pick up, click and whir, and then print. A fax coming in.

He tries to ignore it, but the spell is broken. She gets up. "I have to go home," she says. Pale naked sylph, moving fast, she disappears into his bathroom. He follows and they shower together, quickly. Her face is pure fear now. He does his best to reassure her that everything is and will be all right. This is such a tremendous lie that he can find no words with which to tell it; he has to settle for holding her face between his hands and trying with his eyes to will her to trust him. Then he kisses both her breasts and takes the nipples in his mouth before she can pull away. He needs her to come back. He needs her to have more desire than fear.

Only when her bright red car has left his drive does he think about the fax. He remembers as well the photocopied pages she brought him, which he carelessly left lying on the coffee table in the living room. When he goes to retrieve them, they are not there. His heart jumps up his throat, but he finds them on the floor. He looks around, sees no source of draft, no easy explanation for why they fell. He picks up the papers and notes for the first time the final page, the copied envelope from Frith, Stearn & Heppering. He shakes his head. What those accountants are doing in this he doesn't know, but the net of trouble entangling him, and the island, is wide and complex. He goes to his desk in the corner of his bedroom and pulls the fax out of the machine.

It is from Althea. Her message concerns Ramo. This morning the police came with a warrant. They found the murder weapon, the gun used in the Tucker shooting, in his shop. While they searched—and planted what they meant to find—he jumped on a scooter and got away. He has gone to ground, Althea says, and Marcus knows what this means, and why Althea's not phoned him. She alone knows where Ramo is hiding, and she'll not have that fact prized out of her even by Marcus.

In the last lines of the fax, there is more bad news. A photographer sent by Government came today to take pictures of her brother Lemuel. She ran him off. If not for Ramo's trouble, she'd not have been home. What more does Government want from her brother? she asks. How dare they even ask? Now that Ramo will no longer be in his shop to keep watch, she can do nothing to protect Lemuel, not unless she locks him in the house all day while she's working.

What the fax doesn't say — explicitly — is, How will *you* help me? Marcus touches the cut beneath his eye. While he was with Lucy, he forgot about it, but now it throbs. He dresses and leaves for the office, to share this latest news with Kenrick and make some attempt to protect Lemuel and defend Ramo. He does not take with him the pages Lucy brought. He locks them in his own desk drawer. He cannot, not yet, not today after all else she has given him, sully her or what they feel for each other with the brute machinations of politics and pride. He also does not answer Althea's fax. Hasn't he proved to her in two failed attempts already that he cannot get for Lemuel what she thinks her brother deserves? She asks a third time at peril of more disappointment, for Marcus has never been more sure that he is just a man. Just one particular fearful and fallen, stumbling and striving man — blessed, for the moment, with love.

Arriving home, Lucy discovers Felicity Heppering on her doorstep, a basket of loquats in her arms. Felicity says the ripe fruit overloading the tree in her backyard is a *certain* sign of spring, at *last*, and she wants her American friend to have *both*. Felicity's expression is both eager and angry: eager to believe that she and her efforts matter, and upset that not even Lucy — another stranded, dispensable female who shares her plight and thus ought to share her priorities — honestly cares about how hard she tries to be who she's supposed to be.

Lucy, nervous, brittle, guilty, has never heard of loquats. She had no idea the present cold and blowy February weather could be spring, and she cannot understand why Felicity persists in regarding their underdeveloped acquaintance as a friendship. She knows she has been no friend to Felicity; she's made no effort at all, by determined preference, which shames her. Awkwardly the two women smile at each other in front of the same door where Lucy tasted sweat on Marcus's dark throat. She takes the basket of yellow fruit, resembling tiny, thin-skinned melons, thanks Felicity effusively, invites her in and is relieved and freshly shamed when she says she hasn't time to stay. As Felicity returns to her car, parked at the top of the shabbily patched drive, Lucy notices the practical brogans she wears, smashing a loquat fallen from the basket to the porch tile, and providing excellent traction up the rutted gravel incline.

The fruit basket looks pretty on the sideboard in the foyer. Lucy leaves it there because she doesn't know what else to do with it, and she thinks it may do her some good to be forced to see it each time she passes. Felicity has decorated the simple woven basket with a big, starched bow, on which she's stenciled Bermuda bluebirds in two colors—blue backs and rose-colored breasts; and that undeniable evidence of Felicity's patient effort poses Lucy a question she feels she ought to answer. Why is it she doesn't want Felicity for a friend? Why do the basket and its perky bow assure her of that, when she ought to be impressed, when, God knows, she could use a friend? A woman friend might be her salvation in the fix she finds herself. Adultery, and the theft of the notebook contents. So much deceit. She can't decide which betrayal is worst, but she knows she's become someone she did not ever imagine she could be.

Still, it's the loquats, not Felicity nor her basket, that turn up in her dream that night.

She finds herself closeted with Mr. Trott in a bus shelter of the sort found all over the island: a three-sided hut of coral blocks, shaggy with lichen. She sits on the slab bench in the back, conscious of the coldness of the stone beneath her, the dirt everywhere around her and the odors of urine and mold in the gloom. Outside it rains hard, a fourth gray wall of water.

Mr. Trott, from his wheelchair, offers her a loquat. A thumb-sized melon, yellow, translucent, so ripe its softly furred skin is stretched taut. Lucy smells the fruit, its scent faintly honeyed but sharp, too, with hidden greenness inside. She nods tentatively, and immediately Mr. Trott presses a loquat to her lips. Laughing, he mashes it against her teeth. The skin bursts. She hears it pop, and juice drips messily from her chin onto her hands folded in her lap.

She knows her hands are folded. But when she looks, they are not; they hold a stick, and the stick, stirring the leaves and trash and loose mortar mounded in a spidery corner of the shelter, unearths flowers. Great red velvet chunks of sweet william, and candy tuft, and peonies — hot pink and sweet and blowzy, like the ones in her garden in Connecticut. Sinking her bare hands into the muck, Lucy lifts out the flowers and pulls them to her lap, to keep.

14

Just before 9 p.m. that same day, Zef pushes open the door to Ramo's empty shop. Inside — as dark as the night Zef steps out of — the jumble of battered scooters and scooter parts and rags and tools and cheap crockery and oily newspapers on the dirt floor attests to the ravage of the police search that sent Ramo fleeing.

Zef picks a path through the mess and sits down in his usual place, a high stool behind the tall, old-fashioned wooden counter scavenged from a razed hardware store. He cut school today, disappearing down a side lane toward town the moment Mrs. Alvarra's car pulled away, and in the hours since he slipped out the kitchen window at Rose Hill, he's searched unstintingly for Ramo, riding his scooter till it had no more gas, then jogging and finally trudging on foot to every out-of-the way shack or shade tree or grocery bench he's ever known Ramo to frequent, asking those he passes who might know, getting suggestions but no answers, and having no luck. Tomorrow he will begin again. Maybe tomorrow Ramo, or word from Ramo, will find him. Facing the counter is the low cane-bottomed chair where Ramo would sit if he were here; Zef can just make out its shape, the wood worn pale from age and resembling old bones, a vague faint glow in the darkness.

He studies the chair's emptiness, breathes raggedly, and

slips off his sneakers—wet and stinking. He is thirsty. After several long minutes, he pulls the letter from its hiding place in a cubby beneath the counter top. The letter his mother sent him from the Netherlands, via Kenrick Desmond, who hates him, who put it in his hands saying, "Best your father doesn't know about this." Opening the letter, turning its two pale blue pages back to front, he sweeps the flat of his hand across the loose, ragged handwriting, tracking uphill. She wrote in a hurry. Or she's habitually messy. He has no idea which, of course. In the letter she calls him by the name he's never used, saying, "Stefan, you deserve a chance to decide if you want to know me." She says, "I wrote your father about contacting you, and he wouldn't let it happen." With the fat silver lighter he stole from his father he makes a tiny light and reads the words again.

She could be lying—in either statement, or both. He doesn't know. He has no way to know. That his father lies, he has no fucking doubt.

You lie to me about my mother!

I do not. I do not lie.

But he does. And then he punches.

Zef digs deep in a pants pocket and comes up with the button. A dish-shaped orange button with a beveled rim, the sole access he has to his mother. His thumb blindly circling the familiar slant of the rim builds inside him a dull pain and an incomplete picture. The shoulder of a housecoat or a nightgown polka-dotted orange and green, the curve of a woman's neck—skin soft and fair—and a button, big and orange, just out of reach of fingers he knows are his. Sometimes he sees his own baby hand reaching, but he may be imagining this part. When he was six and his mother long gone, when they moved from the old house he barely remembers to Rose Hill, he found the button on the floor in a closet Marcus never used once she left.

He balances it now rim up on the counter top and spins it. He flicks the lighter for a flame to help him watch it spin. The shop's strong smell—motor oil, ganja, boiled vegetables and the damp packed dirt of the floor—comforts him. He was eight or nine the first time he came here, with his father, who had release papers for Ramo to make his mark on—and the tall, tall man, black as a starling's glossy wing, rag-thin and jaundiced from six years in prison—sat Zef up on this stool and let him work the till, which was empty, back and forth, back and forth, until he broke the spring and all he said, when Marcus shouted about it, was, "Leave de boy be, he happy."

"Leave it be," was what he said, too, when Zef finally read him the letter he'd carried day and night in secret for two weeks. "You happy?" Ramo asked first. "You want to leave we and live at de Hague with de white lady an' white people ever'where round you?" Zef had said nothing because Ramo knew, he *knew* without being told that Zef didn't know, had no idea, and how mad it made him not to know. "Give it me," Ramo said, and slipped the letter in the cubby. And after that it stayed there. When Zef came to Ramo's sometimes he read it, and sometimes not.

Peyton Langston's mouth when Zef showed him the letter made a big round zero. He said, "She's your mother. You can't just forget her."

"She forgot *me*."

Ramo'd stepped between them. He ignored Peyton, as he did every time Zef brought him. He said, "She gone, Zef. You fadder right about she; she leave you, now let her be."

Zef spins the button. Slaps it to the counter. Closes it inside his fist. His father let his mother leave but now he's found a new white woman. He replays as he has a thousand times all afternoon Marcus's words to Peyton's mother, taking papers from her hand: *This information is so important.* It could make *even Ramo* safe from Government. Marcus dropped the papers to put the drop on the woman, but Zef has not stopped thinking about putting those papers in Ramo's hands, to make him safe and free.

He could take them from Marcus—and get punched again. Or he could take from Peyton's house the notebook his mother copied and locked in a drawer. Or, if Ramo gets locked up in prison again, he could take this letter and write his mother and see if she wants to take him. Ramo has urged him to be black like Jah made him and leave his mother be. Ramo has told him never to take anything, especially from white people. "Ever't'ing between black and white be takin'. White people takin' what dey want, black people takin' what dey given." With the flame from the silver lighter he reads what he wrote himself on the lip of Ramo's empty till: *Give only black truth to white people.*

Turning words in his head and the beveled button in his hand, Zef decides. He will make Peyton take the notebook. That way Marcus will not know, and Zef will not take. Peyton will do the taking, and Zef the giving. He will in that way give a black truth; he will make the white boy mind. And he will get for Ramo what he needs to stay free.

He returns his button and the lighter to is pocket. He pulls on his stinking shoes, slips the letter back inside its cubby, pulls the frayed door to behind him. When he jogs up the narrow alley between Ramo's shop and Althea's house, a window is open and he sees Lemuel Trott inside, wide awake and watching him. Lemuel doesn't wave like he does all day out by the road. He looks old and sick and tired and close to dead. Zef stops long enough to stick his tongue out as far as he can—so far he sees its thick pink tip extending beyond the end of his nose. Then he runs. Lemuel Trott is a truth he does not want to feel.

At Peyton Langston's house, Zef taps the bedroom window relentlessly until Peyton opens it, and then threatens to get louder and wake his parents if Peyton doesn't come out, bringing money to gas the scooter. When he does, Zef hustles him up the drive and down the road to where he's hidden the scooter behind a grocery open late and selling gas. When they ride, the wind off the ocean is strong and cold, and both of them shiver. "Somewhere good, bro, and just long enough to get the job done," he's told Peyton, who's too scared to ask more than where they're going and how long they'll be out.

Zef pilots the scooter west, into the poorer parishes, toward the island's narrow, jagged fishhook point. This far from town and the Regiment's checkpoints, the road is not quite deserted, but because of the curfew, whoever is moving does so quickly, keeping to the shadows. The scooter flashes across the short bridge to Ireland Island, the last one in the chain, whines past the tilted white slabs in the abandoned naval cemetery and the crumbling military barracks, strung now with the clotheslines of the island's most destitute blacks. At the end of the road is the old British Dockyard, where slaves and prison labor once built ships for the Empire.

They pass beneath a portcullis gate set in walls ten feet thick and three centuries old. The crenulated watchtowers of Casemates prison rise from concentric rings of chain link fence topped with coiled razor wire, and beyond the prison, balloon-shaped fuel storage tanks squat like alien space ships. At the island's very tip, the security lights of the shops, the marina and the historical exhibits built recently for tourists twinkle innocently. Zef stops the scooter on the dark side of an overflowing dumpster near the outermost prison fence. His flesh has gone numb, and Peyton, seated pillion, is silent and quivering against his back.

"Gimme your knife," Zef says, swinging himself clear of the scooter. Peyton gets off, stands wavering in the sand like he hasn't got land legs, then drags from his pants pocket the multi-bladed knife his father brought him from a recent business trip to Zurich. He offers it grudgingly; Zef knows Peyton thinks he'll keep it. He slips his hand in his own pocket for the fat silver cigarette lighter, encounters the button and sweeps its bevel once by habit, then extracts the lighter and holds it out to Peyton, as if for a trade. Peyton eyes it, and then him. Briefly the wind dies and the stink of this end of the island blankets them: rotting garbage heaped on barges not yet dumped at sea, and oily fuel fouling the salt water, from tankers that flush their holds illegally close to shore.

Zef hooks Peyton's gaze, stares into his eyes — blue-grey and round, not so different from the grey-green of his. He assesses the shape and the features of the face around those eyes. Narrow and fine-boned, very white-boy, very different from his own. Compared to Peyton, Zef is black. Compared to

Ramo, even compared to Marcus, he's close to white. He will never be the right color, because he is neither color, a fact that will never change. He spits beside himself in the sand.

He opens the knife and examines the blades, listening to Peyton's short, anxious breaths as he takes his time doing it. He settles on the broadest, strongest blade. Squatting, bracing the lighter against a rock, he works the knife hard against the soft silver, gouging out the curling monogram of Marcus's initials and in a semi-circle around the scar, carving the letters of his own name. Z, then E. At F, he hands the knife to Peyton, and tells him, "You finish the job, bro."

As he does so, Zef says, "I been wanting to do that. Been needing to make it mine. But I needed you to help me." He smiles at Peyton, whose breaths are still shallow. When Peyton folds the knife's blade and holds it out, Zef says "Put it away. It's yours." A quick crack of pleasure crosses Peyton's pinched face.

Zef sinks the scarred lighter back into his pocket, ticks the button once, and leans on the scooter seat. The only sounds are the suck and stir of the surf beyond Dockyard walls and somewhere down the road a nervous, yapping dog. Zef directs Peyton's gaze to the sheer face of the prison: salt-scoured limestone and a scattering of tiny, barred windows, not a one of them lit.

"Up there's where Ramo's gonna be," he tells Peyton, "if you don't help me."

Peyton stumbles to his feet. "I'm cold," he says. "I want to go home."

"I'm talking to you. About Ramo. You think it's warm in there?"

"Probably not," Peyton mumbles, studying the ground.

Zef kicks sand, and kicks again. "Fuck you," he says, watching fear blossom on Peyton's face. "You think it's cold out here?" He backs Peyton toward the fence. "Put *you* inside that prison. Think there's anybody in there doesn't want to go home? Doesn't want to get warm?"

Zef says, "Had me a gun, Ramo wouldn't go to prison."

"You haven't got a gun, have you?"

"Nah, no gun." Zef turns away. "But I need you to fetch me the next best thing. Some paper that works just like one."

"Let's go. I just want to go. Please."

Zef points again at Casemates, shakes his head. "Put you inside that prison, your rich daddy buys you out. Put Ramo in there, and this time they'll hang him."

He throws a leg across the scooter, sits down and fingers the key. "Listen. In your daddy's study, in a locked desk drawer, there's a red notebook with a lot of pages listing names and sums. It's inside an envelope that says Frith, Stearn & Heppering. A little, bright red notebook. Shouldn't be too hard to find. You get it, and you bring it to me. That's all you got to do."

"No." Hunched and shivering, Peyton sounds surprisingly firm.

"Bro. One thing, and exactly one thing, I need from you and you tell me 'No'?"

Peyton shakes his head. "I won't steal from my dad."

"After all the cover I gave you at Somers? You got one other friend on this island?"

Zef considers his silence. He looks up at the prison, back down at Peyton. "Okay. Bro."

His emphasis on the second word makes Peyton flinch. Zef reaches into the construction rubble beside the dumpster and selects two broken bricks, each one fist-sized. Balancing the scooter between his legs, he hefts a brick in each hand, testing for parity. He nods at Peyton, sealing an agreement they haven't made, and tucks one brick into his jacket pocket. With the other he gestures to Peyton to get on. When Peyton hesitates, he says, "Come on. A minute ago you wanted to leave." He sets the second brick in Peyton's hands. "Here's a souvenir from this evening. Keep it in your pocket."

When they are halfway back to the Langstons' house, deep in the shadows of a stand of casuarina pines tossing and groaning in the wind, Zef leans the scooter hard right and veers onto a dark residential road. The sudden tilt and downshift nearly unseat Peyton, who scrambles for balance. Zef pulls the throttle hard in response.

Bits of mica in the pavement glitter. The brick in the left-hand pocket of Zef's windbreaker rests heavy on his thigh. He eases off the gas and lets the scooter drift. They sputter slowly down the center of the unlit lane, passing sleeping houses and parked cars.

"Pick one," he instructs, pulling his brick from his pocket with his left hand, keeping the right one free for the throttle.

"No."

"Bro," says Zef, "I heard that word too many times tonight."

The scooter is almost idling; Zef has to weave to keep it upright. "Come on, do it, come on, do it," Zef hums, just above the two-stroke chortle of the engine. He feels Peyton tense and shift his weight, but nothing more.

"Fucking *do* it," he snaps, and fires the scooter straight at a dog-leg turn in the road and a car parked in it. He aims precisely at the reflectors in the car's tail lights, blinking in the white shake of the scooter's high beam.

Only at the last possible second before collision does Peyton tear the brick from his pocket and let it fly. It crosses Zef's shoulder as he leans left and the scooter clears the car's fender by millimeters. The sound of the brick's strike is lost in a spray of gravel Zef sends up, spinning the scooter one-eighty to head back the way they came. Lights pop on in houses on both sides of the road. He sees the dent Peyton's put in the hood. For one frank second he lets go both handlebars to fling his own brick at the next car. There's a satisfying crunch. Downshifting, he jerks the throttle wide open. The scooter bucks and bores forward, away from lights and agitated voices, into the thick dark and back onto the main road where he sinks quickly and righteously to the cover of the speed limit and the shadows of the pines.

Peyton neither shifts nor speaks until they reach the bushes opposite the turn into the Langstons' drive. Then he's off the scooter almost before it stops rolling.

"Hey," Zef calls after him, "you forgot something."

Peyton stops in the middle of the road, shaking visibly.

"You forgot to ask how I know about that notebook. You

don't want to know, do you?"

"No."

"But I think you got to know, bro, because I got to get you to help me."

He beckons Peyton closer, but he doesn't budge. He just stands there, shifting one foot to the other. Then he starts to cry.

"You're a baby," Zef says, and tells Peyton fast before he runs home exactly what he knows, his voice loud and harsh. "I know because I heard your mother tell my father, right after she gave him a copy and right before he fucked her."

Peyton's hands rise to his face. Zef lifts his foot and poises it on the kickstart lever.

"I didn't watch them do it. Couldn't stand to. But I do need that notebook. And I can't take the copy Marcus has, or he'd be on to me. So either *you* get it, or I'll tell your dad what I just told you."

"No," says Peyton, stiffly backing toward home.

Zef calls after him, "You will. If you don't, I'll make you wish you had."

He stomps hard on the kickstart and the motor turns over. Buzzing away, he feels bad but he tells himself he feels better than he did in Ramo's empty shop. This way, Ramo has a chance. And that helps, a little. He tells himself it does.

15

Lucy's slick shoes—the beat-up blue flats with red parrots rampant on the toes—make the climb to Spanish Rock especially treacherous. All the way up the twisting trail Marcus walks behind her, in case she slips off her feet. It's his fault she's not dressed properly for a hike; he didn't tell her what to expect when he phoned her early this mid-March Wednesday and asked her to drive out to meet him here. He hadn't himself considered what to expect—he's not been to this place in years, and he never thought hike-in-the-woods when he called her. Instead he envisioned her body and her face, and himself touching both in the privacy of the thick stand of pines he remembered at the foot of the trail. He fantasized, too, the pleasure of offering her the panoramic view from the high cliff that is the Rock. He forgot that the trail only begins with a resin-scented carpet of pine needles, and quickly becomes a bare dirt rut skirting the hillside's limestone knuckles and needle-pointed clumps of Spanish bayonet. Now Lucy hauls herself up the steepest parts of the trail, grabbing low-hanging limbs and exposed roots, and he is treated to the beauty of her determination and the lure of her hips and thighs, in jeans.

By the time they emerge at the cliff top, all he wants is to take her to bed. They have five times made love since the first time, a month ago, and each time fueled him when he was about to fail, and each time was serendipitous, a sudden leveling of a path that is mostly blind curves, steep climbs and sheer drops. To see each other, even to speak, they must play the odds. Sometimes she can't get away from home, or she's not alone when he phones. They plan to meet and then his schedule blows up, or at the end of an especially difficult day he has abruptly lost both nerve and appetite for the risk a meeting always entails. Other times it is she who turns evasive, suddenly deaf to suggestion.

But passion persists through all the whipsaw troubles, and it's a good thing, Marcus tells himself, to have one thing in life that won't quit.

The near riot that left him beaten four weeks ago subsided at first into a tense standoff between anti-Government protestors and the Tucker family's vigilantes. When Government released Suggs from protective custody, Isaiah's SUV was torched, with no one claiming responsibility. That same night anti-Government graffiti, *Justice IS blind — to the murder of Rufus and Breem,* appeared in black spray paint on the white walls of Camden House, the Premier's home. The result was an announcement by Government that the "Rastafarian compound" (Ramo's shop and the houses around it, including Althea's) would be razed as a public health hazard — Isaiah's private revenge but a public sop to the Tuckers' faction, since the destruction might well flush Ramo from hiding and allow the murder warrant finally to be served.

Within a week, Isaiah appeared in lifestyle news clips golfing at Fairylands with the Tuckers ("the Minister of Justice, formerly a star of American football, tries his hand at a new sport"), and Marcus had stepped firmly up to his plate of the island's trouble by filing as attorney of record for the fugitive Ramo Wylie, and entering motions to quash the murder warrant and block Government's condemnation of Ramo's and Althea's properties. Right away Marcus received a final notice of foreclosure on his own home, Rose Hill, from his bank, and now, this week, he finds himself the target of a parliamentary ethics investigation.

When he talks on the phone with Lucy, he tells her all this

and more. The simple act of telling soothes him and helps him think more clearly. When they find their way to bed, the grappling they do there directly addresses everything that matters. Every question, every precipice, every doubt feels met and conquered. In the aftermath, with her blond hair sweat-matted to her pale scalp and the flesh of her breasts and throat chaffed red, his own body as dripping and glossy and rank as if he'd run for his life, they gaze into each other's eyes while their breathing subsides. Too quickly, worry and guilt and danger and the need to move fast and cover their tracks overtakes them, and then words return, for the purpose of cajoling and calming, creating half-truths and promises, sweet sidesteps, the words always inadequate but all, except in bed, they can have.

For that they use his house, on Wednesdays—Mrs. Alvarra's regular day off—during the hours school is in session. Only once has he gone to her house on the cliff overlooking Horseshoe Bay, and there they made love in the shower. Darrell was away in London but Marcus could feel, in the bedroom as they stripped each other, how Lucy avoided with all her nervous might the king-size bed and her husband's intangible presence there, and that day the sex, standing up, slippery, burning then freezing as the hot water tank emptied, was more athletic and frantic than satisfying, and the best part came afterwards, in the kitchen, when she made him eggs and coffee. At two in the afternoon they sat in the breakfast nook, steaming mugs in their hands, empty plates and that morning's folded newspaper between them, the repaired window he'd once boarded for her against gale force winds now flooding them in blazing blue-white light reflected off the cobalt sea while beneath the table their knees touched gently—fifteen minutes of completely restorative, completely larcenous, domestic bliss.

That release, too, crumbled rapidly to reality when she asked him about Zef and he told her, quite truthfully, that he despaired of ever breaching the boy's thick contempt. "I told him, like a *supplicant*," he admitted to Lucy, "every detail of what I've undertaken for Ramo in the last two

198   Christine Hale

weeks—everything humanly and legally possible and all of it to my detriment—but he's unfazed. If he speaks to me at all, he's fixated on getting Ramo to come out of hiding, and keeping him out of jail when he does." Her response, a rueful, comprehending sigh, made him know—he *felt* the correspondence between them resonating in his own chest— that her next words would be about the contempt Peyton has developed for her, and Marcus turned cowardly and changed the subject. He knows his son and their affair are the catalyst for the way her son's changed.

He told her instead about a recent small success he's had which she catalyzed: the Warwick Youth Center will not close, to Althea's considerable satisfaction, but will operate two nights a week at least through the summer on a grant from the cathedral's Ladies' Auxiliary, a source Lucy suggested. Now he's looking for a similar private source for his long-delayed on-call health transport for indigent seniors like Lemuel Trott. It is only with Lucy he discusses such things, these days, not Kenrick, and it's her advice, at least as often as Kenrick's, which influences his political decisions. He avoids his workplace confidant these days because there's so much he has to not say. When he cannot talk to her, he sometimes discovers himself telling her his worries anyway, in his head, and taking comfort in what he imagines her response to be.

And when he cannot sleep all night, when he evades Kenrick, or lies to his son, or disappears from places he should be to turn up in places she's arranged to be, he asks himself: Is this relationship extraordinarily wrong or miraculously right? Is it a means that enables him to do the right, hard things? A means, pure and simple, to go on living? Or is it the end, a dead end, the lip of a cliff from which, when it collapses, as it must, all his decades of good efforts will fall to ruin?

Atop Spanish Rock, the wind comes in heady gusts from the northwest, chill despite the high, pale sun. Lucy wraps her bare arms around herself, and Marcus wraps himself around her. His chin rests in her hair just above her ear; his arms fold atop hers beneath her breasts; her bottom settles warm and tantalizing against his thighs. She leans into him, and that makes him feel solid. Fifty feet below, waves smash themselves to iridescent bits on tumbled slabs of limestone and basalt.

At first they do not speak, then Lucy tells him she's reading a biography of Marcus Garvey she had her father send her from the States. He's touched and very surprised; some time back he mentioned, just once, that his mother named him for Garvey, the Jamaican-born printer's apprentice who became in America in the 20's a black nationalist so charismatic among the poor and working class that the federal government tried him for mail fraud, imprisoned and eventually deported him. "Twenty thousand people at a time listened to him speak in Madison Square Garden," she says, "and still even the NAACP wanted nothing to do with him. What a waste."

Marcus nods, stubble at the rim of his jaw catching in her hair. "He was too dangerous. A militant *and* a populist. Malcolm X's father was killed by the Klan for following Garvey. My mother's mother admired Garvey greatly. She read his books on black history, and my mother, who did not read them, saved them for me."

"Your grandmother and mother had great plans for you," Lucy says. She has taken his hands in hers, their arms still entwined across her chest. "Maybe they foresaw where you'd stand."

He can think of no just response to her admiration, because he wants it but is sure he does not deserve it, and for a long time, again, neither of them speaks. The empty, windblown seascape before them, flooded with ever-shifting light, is stunning, and he enjoys holding her, but he can't keep his mind from puzzling over how to suggest they leave and meet again at his house. In his bed. She says quietly, "What did you do with the photocopies I gave you?"

He wishes to think he's not heard her correctly. He says, "What? No more paper, please, madam, my office is papered over already."

She repeats her question, with only the slightest smile at his lame joke.

"I have them, still, in a safe place," he answers. The

notebook pages, folded inside the copied envelope, lie in a locked drawer of his desk at home.

"You're not going to use it?"

He feels umbrage in her tone: what she has done for him is not appreciated. He moves, shifting his stance but not loosening his hold on her.

"I have it. I have it for when I really need it."

She squirms free. The wind whips her hair across his face as she turns around, strands of it stinging his lips.

"You need it now," she says. "Nothing has changed, except for the worse. Isn't that right? They—Isaiah and plenty of others—are coming after you more personally than ever. And everybody not in Isaiah's camp is after you to do something to stop him. You have a trump card. Are you not going to play it?"

"That notebook is a detonator, Lucy. It will set off more explosions than I can control."

"You're not in control," she tells him fiercely, "but you have the power to disarm people who think they are. You need to use what you have before it's too late. Before someone destroys *you*."

"The question of the source will inevitably arise," Marcus says sadly. He touches her arm, stroking the bare length of it. He hates the necessity of openly admitting between them the dirt and deception that is inseparable from the power and sweetness of their affair. He makes himself look into her eyes, wide with nervous determination. He says, "You know you'll end up as part of this mess, in some public way, and that doesn't necessarily help me. Ruining your life won't keep Ramo from being framed. It won't do a thing to protect Lemuel's dignity. And it surely won't make Zef hate me any less."

Bitterly, she says, "I'm up to my ears in mess already, Marcus. My options are not pretty, nor very numerous, either."

They're fighting, albeit quietly, for the first time. He tries to embrace her, to stop the breach, and she steps backward, dangerously close to the edge of the cliff. He seizes her shoulder, she flings his hand off, the wind gusts, and he shouts through it.

"I don't want to bring this thing down on you, Lucy. I don't want you to suffer, and more than anything else, I don't want—can't stand—for this—us—to be over."

Voicing his fear brings them both inside it. She flattens herself against his chest, and silently they hold on. He watches a squall lift off the water and ride the wind toward them, a flat-bottomed barge of thick gray cloud, moving fast.

"Have you told Kenrick you have a copy of the notebook?" Lucy says softly.

He doesn't answer her.

"Give it to him," she pleads. "He'll know what to do, and then you won't have to decide."

The squall dumps rain on a patch of sea a half-mile out; the water beneath the storm is leached of its turquoise light and goes dead gray, mirroring the inside of the cloud. She cannot guess, and he will never tell her, how important it is that Kenrick not know he is in love, again, with a white woman.

"Look." He releases her. "Look at the Rock itself. That's why people come here, and we've taken no notice of it."

Pulling her with him to the site, he kneels. He guides her hand to a shelf of stone at the extreme edge of the cliff, thrust out like a stubborn lip above breakers two stories below. He places her hand inside the bronze cast of what was carved, in 1543, into the limestone. The mark could be a handprint; it fits her hand well enough. But what cradles her palm is really the weathered, nearly obliterated shape of a crude, lopsided cross, and the round holes in which the tips of her fingers now rest were once the numerals of the date.

"Do you know the story?" he asks her.

She laughs, a small, wry sound at a joke internal to her. "A woman who had dinner at my house"—she shakes her head at the memory—"told me I simply *must* come here, with her. I haven't, on purpose, and I remember that, not what I was supposed to see here."

He tells her the date and traces the cross, with his finger, on the back of her hand. He explains what is known and conjectured about the carving's source. The survivor of a shipwreck, presumed to be a Spaniard by the early colonists who first saw the mark, hence the Rock's name, but more likely, given the date cross-referenced to shipping records, a Portuguese.

A historical mistake, he tells her, persisting across centuries, and the event itself only a faint, distorted echo of the unrecorded agony of some unknown sailor's lonely death. A human hand marked this rock, whether in faith or desperation, and nearly five centuries later it fits another hand, and that stark connection — past to present, human to human, no explanation and no mitigation of anyone's suffering — it is all the story anyone has.

He covers her white hand with his black one, and bows his head to hide evidence of the tears that suddenly threaten him, and that are not for the sailor, who was undoubtedly a gun-running, slave-trading bastard, no matter if he was Spanish or Portuguese. Lucy's other hand touches his shoulder, and she says, "Look."

Squatting side by side, dampened by the mist trailing the squall, they watch until the wind dissipates a rainbow that had burst the light into its spectrum colors, leaving only ordinary sun and shadow.

She stands up. "Marcus," she says, "don't hold back on my account. You can't keep me from facing trouble." She rips a stiff, flat leaf from a bay grape bush growing out of the cliff, pleats it and then shreds it as she speaks. "I'm going to have to tell Darrell what I haven't told him about Peyton. His most recent grade report is terrible and full of tardies. Clearly, he's lying to me, and he must be seeing Zef. Darrell is going to find out, and it had better be from me."

Marcus opens his mouth to tell her that he will put a stop to it. He's tried before, of course, but this time he'll make sure that Zef leaves Peyton alone. He will send Zef away, off the island to boarding school if he has to — he's considered this before, but knows he cannot afford it. He says it anyway.

"That's the worst thing you could do," she says. "However

impossible he is, however he hurts you, he needs you. You are all he's got."

"It's Ramo he wants. He's got no use for me except to despise me—"

"Then that's another reason to do something he can truly admire. Whatever it takes, you're the one who has to bridge what's lost between you." She touches his face, fingertips gentle on the pink scar from the stitched cut beneath his eye. "Peyton and I are the ones who are leaving, Marcus. We're going to have to move again. Darrell's been going back and forth to Cayman. He's lobbied TransGlobal to relocate the business there, and it's about to happen."

She kisses him then, quickly and hard, and that's it. The truth is out, and there's nothing more to say. He cannot allow her to leave the island, yet nothing he can do will keep her from going. If her husband goes, she can't stay, even if she wanted to: her permission from Immigration to live here is conditioned on her spouse's employment. It's not as if Marcus never thought this could happen; after all, one insurer after another is pulling up stakes to go. Rather, it is something else he has schemed with himself to overlook.

All the way back down the trail, following her again but in danger in this direction of slipping and falling on her, he thinks confusedly about what to do. Repeatedly, he bumps against nothing-he-can-do. When they reach the stand of pine trees, when the sweet-smelling needles are beneath their feet, he stops her.

"Come to my house," he says.

Her eyes go wide, this time with anxiety and pain. He sees that she wants to as desperately as he does. He sees, too, that she is going to say no this time.

He presses her with his body, his gaze, and the most urgent words he can muster. He is shameless because he *needs* this. How much more time will there be? How many more chances like this one? He pleads. No one at his house. No one waiting for her at her home either. Please. Just please.

She's about to say yes after all. He feels her yielding, he is joyous, and then they both stiffen simultaneously at the sound of boys laughing and shouting, some distance away through the trees, from the direction of the sand lot where their cars are parked.

They spring apart and move swiftly off the path, hurrying overland amid trees and underbrush toward the parking lot. Fifty or more boys come boiling up the path; they wear Somers Academy blazers. Several classes combined, a field trip. Lucy's slick leather flats have betrayed her; one has come off, caught by a root, tripping her. Marcus stands beside her, screening her with his body while she retrieves the shoe and puts it on, and the boys surge past, oblivious to two more adults who are not in their way. Behind the boys come the teachers and assorted mothers who have carpooled the boys here. Some of them are known to him by name or sight, and doggedly he faces them, daring their reaction, but not before he notices that Lucy has seen someone she knows. Her face is rigid with embarrassment, and the stout, mousey woman staring back at her is equally overwhelmed, her jaw literally hanging slack.

He sees Lucy to her car, parked beside his distinctive Bentley and flanked by the dozen vehicles driven by the school group. She is very upset; she does not want to talk; she just wants to go. Closing her car door, he says through the open window, "Call me."

She says, "Peyton was not with those boys. He wasn't, was he?" Her hands grip the steering wheel even though the car is not moving.

"He wasn't there," Marcus says immediately, even though he's not sure. The boys paid no attention to him and Lucy; he's sure of that.

As she drives away, he observes, with the odd, useless precision of shock, that the Fiesta's back bumper has finally been repaired: it looks as good as new.

They've been caught, but how serious must it be? No reasonable, exonerating explanation comes to mind for why he and Lucy would be alone together in the woods at Spanish Rock, but they were not touching when they were seen, he does not think her son saw them, and perhaps he and Lucy, when she is calmer, can come up with some believable means of repair for this. For now, all he can do is get in his own car and leave.

He presses the accelerator. He tries to make a plan. He will go and speak to Kenrick about the notebook. He will think of a way to suggest there is access to a copy of the notebook without revealing how he knows this. And he will do something about Zef. He will think of something he has not thought of before; he will find a way to give up something he's held onto for too long: the idea that nothing can change except for the worse, the stultifying fear that the disparate forces of his life are going to tear him apart.

Lucy has given him the image of himself as bridge. She has reminded him of the power of his namesake's chosen position: Marcus Garvey precariously positioned between the powerless and the power brokers, and, even in falling to ignominy, linking his cause to the hearts of those who rose up to follow him.

Marcus smiles inside his dark presentiment of defeat. Whatever he can do to turn the tide of chaos in his country will help Lucy stay. Anything he offers Zef will be more than he's risked so far. All repairs are the same repair; he will believe this. It is hope.

Felicity saw them clearly and recognized them both. Lucy is certain of it, and the shock makes her almost sick. She drives very rapidly, without regard for the island's absurd 35 kph speed limit and without the slightest idea of where she's going. What *has* she been thinking, all this time—that no one would *ever* know what she was doing? Did she believe she and Marcus were *invisible*? She hurries along the straightaway near Brighton Hill, headed west toward Hungry Bay. Invisibility must be what she's relied upon. She has worried endlessly about right and wrong, she's felt guilty and exhilarated by momentous turns, she's judged herself a bad mother, a deceitful wife and a morally weak person capable of acts she never in her life thought she would be, but she has never thought realistically about getting caught red-handed.

And she's denied to herself the real cost her behavior has created for Peyton. The rules she made for him in December and the contract she made him sign, the wall of shame and silence she's built between them to hide her infractions of their bond; in her mind she's not only made the affair invisible to everyone else, she's hidden its full reality from herself. But no amount of contrivance and deception on her part can mitigate the cost to Peyton. His latest term report and the headmaster's accompanying letter inform her in black and white that her son—always, all his life, an excellent student—will now have to repeat this grade if his final term is not a complete turnaround. And only now when she knows she has to stop hiding does someone else possess the power to unmask her. She is caught, no matter what.

What Felicity will do about what she saw, Lucy has no idea. She also doesn't know what *she* will do if it turns out that Peyton was among that group of boys that went galloping by. Maybe he was not, like Marcus said. If Peyton had been there, she would have known. After all, she is his mother. But she might have missed it, she really might have, because her son was certainly not what she was thinking about right then. Which should she hope for, there or not there? If he wasn't with his class on this field trip, where is he? He could be anywhere. He does as he pleases, and she's not stopped him. She forces her attention to these facts she had best face right this minute: she has no idea where her son is, but she does know where her husband of sixteen years is. In his office in town, working hard, making plans to move the company and his family to what he thinks is a safer place, completely unaware that his family is hardly his family anymore.

Distracted, she speeds right past the cop parked in the bushes, radar pointed straight at her. Her foot finds the brake at the same moment her eyes find, in the rearview mirror, a second cop on a motorcycle, pulling into pursuit behind her. She presses the brake firmly and pulls to the side of the road. Why, she wants to ask the officer when he approaches her rolled-down window, are policemen trapping speeders when there are arsonists and unauthorized strikers and corrupt politicians and even murderers moving freely about the island?

The officer, white and so young his face is barely whiskered, is very polite. He seems actually to feel sorry for her, for being such stupid, easy prey. He examines her island driving license and the car's registration. "Your husband?" he inquires, pointing at Darrell's name on the yellow slip of paper. Lucy feels her face color, although there is no reason to, yet.

The policeman hands her a copy of the speeding ticket. "The date you're to appear in magistrate's court is here," he says helpfully, indicating with his finger. "There'll be a fine— maybe $400. And you're going to be off the road," he adds.

"What?"

"Maybe a year, more likely only six months, for the first offense. Got you clocked," he says, apologetic. "Over eighty kilometers, they lift the license. It's mandatory."

She thanks the officer—an absurdity—and watches him return to his motorcycle and his hiding place. As she drives away, slowly, the ticket flutters at her from the sun visor where she's tucked it. Off the road, for driving fifty miles an hour. Darrell will be furious at her for her carelessness and the inconvenience and expense it will cause. And without a license, she won't be able to keep tabs on Peyton by driving him where he needs to go...and she won't be able to drive anywhere to meet Marcus.

She drives past the turn to home. She drives and drives, at exactly the ridiculous, snail's-pace speed limit. She passes mounds of uncollected garbage, some of it heaped in black plastic sacks and some of it simply heaped. She passes a house that has been burned and abandoned. She passes black people walking because there are no buses, and standing about in groups because, with the strike spreading and no tourists arriving, they have no jobs. They stare at her, or her bright red car, and she keeps on driving, ashamed at her relief at leaving them behind.

She drives all the way to Dockyard at the island's western tip and turns around in the shadow of the prison, because at that point there is nowhere else to go. On Middle Road in Warwick, heading east now, she sees Ramo's shop. If he were there instead of hiding, would she go in? Would she dare ask the tall, intimidating Rastafarian where Peyton is, since he would surely know Zef's whereabouts and the boys are likely together? In the lot outside the shop, there's an unmarked white van with a wheelchair lift, and on the lift, as she passes, Lucy recognizes Mr. Trott. As the wheelchair rises, she slows down. The lift jerks when it stops, and Mr. Trott's eyes go saucer-wide, but he's smiling into the empty air around him. He seems both lost and unafraid, and in that way unworldly.

Lifting a heavy hand from the wheel, she waves at him. From mid-air, he waves back. Marcus told her how long Mr. Trott has been in that chair. Twenty-four years. She hears the words exactly as Marcus spoke them; the echo of the remorse they carried reverberates now in her chest.

She is passing Somers Academy when she realizes where she is headed. Approaching the school, she imagined herself pulling into the drive and walking up the front steps, disheveled and nauseous and probably unable to speak without stuttering, to ask if Peyton is there, to contend with Headmaster Cotter's contempt that she does not know and has to ask. She is not going in there, not today. She is going to Marcus's house. She remembers his tenderness, his urgency. His *please*.

She does not know if he will be home, and when she pulls into his drive she sees that he is not. She parks there anyway, because it is his house — for now. It has not yet been taken from him. She stands on his veranda, gazing down on the Great Sound, the little brushy islands that dot it, and the sailboats in their slips at the Royal Yacht Club. In this neighborhood, garbage is piled up, but there are no burned-out houses, and no unemployed workers walking the streets. The people who live here do not need buses, but they do need the hospital, and food, and failing that, a functioning airport in order to fly away. She does not know what the answer for this island will be; Marcus does not have it, but neither do his white neighbors, who would prefer not to be asked.

She is writing him a note, having not decided where she can safely leave it, when the Bentley pulls into the drive. His face breaks into joy when he sees her, and she goes happily into his embrace. In the second their bodies meet, nothing is wrong anywhere in the world. He kisses her and she kisses back, hungry, hungry.

"Come inside," he says, and then, very kindly, "Is something wrong?"

His simple kindness. That he sees, that he reads her face, that he cares about what troubles her, it breaks her. "I got a speeding ticket," she says, and tears come. This smallest problem among all the problems that beset them both leaves her crying like a child.

"I can take care of it," Marcus says. "It's not a big deal. Give it to me; I'll fix it."

She gets the ticket from the car and puts it in his hand. Then they go inside, he locks the doors, and she flings herself into his open arms. She pulls him down with her into bed, into love. Blinders off, she is living. She feels this truth. This — Marcus — is what she needs.

The strong pale light of spring pours across the bedroom carpet strewn with their clothing, flooding the walls, soaking the flung bedcovers and inundating the bed where their perspiring, striving bodies take refuge.

And in the next room, the phone rings, the fax machine whirs. What spews forth is news from Althea: Government took this afternoon what it needed from Lemuel, then returned him to his place in the dirt. Her friend who's a typist on the editor's desk passes on this story that will run with a large photo in tomorrow's *Gazette*:

> Mr. Lemuel Trott, who is wheelchair bound, is one of the first beneficiaries of Government's new Medi-Mate Service, riding in style to Health Service Facilities in Court Street. With temporary funding from a consortium of international companies, Medi-Mate offers seniors and the disadvantaged disabled free, on-

call, door-to-door shuttle service for hospital and doctor visits, using a vehicle leased by Justice Minister Isaiah Barnes at his own expense. Elders and others without automobiles who cannot comfortably use the island's bus service can now travel to their healthcare appointments in an air-conditioned Isuzu van, and, as Mr. Barnes points out, this service is all the more useful during the current unsettled conditions adversely affecting public transportation.

16

When Peyton enters his father's study, the room is dark. All the rooms on the cliff side of the house are dim even in the middle of the day. He snaps on the overhead light. There's no need for stealth. His father has gone into the office in town — only for an hour or two, he said, because it's Saturday. His mother has gone grocery shopping. That's where she claimed she went, and it could be the truth. With the docks shut down now by anti-Government pickets, food comes in on planes, and appears in the stores a few crates at a time, here and there. He is sick to death of boxed macaroni and cheese, something she recently brought home in quantity.

He envisions a bowl of it now, microwaved semi-warm, tasting like cheese-flavored school paste, eaten with a spoon in front of the television. He is not hungry, but even that vile orange pasta is more appealing than stealing from his father's desk.

When he was a small boy, to sit alone at his dad's desk in the house in Darien or at the office in Stamford was nearly as pleasing as sitting in his father's lap — a mark of privilege, a childish comfort. He doodled the blotter. Punched numbers into the calculator so it spelled words when turned upside down. Played solitaire on the computer. His father did not mind. He never told Peyton to stay out of the desk drawers or leave papers where he found them. Everyone, especially

Peyton, understood that his father's work stuff was important and belonged only to him and no one else touched it.

Yesterday at this hour, Peyton lay hidden inside the one safe place he knows: the giant banyan tree in Somers schoolyard, the trunk thirty feet around, air roots the size of saplings buttressing each limb, the single tree vast as a small forest, the smell of packed dirt under it solid and secret as a cave. Recess was underway, the yard beyond the tree a churning mass of boys looking for something to pick on. He'd wrapped himself round a limb hanging low across the wall into the Middle Road, cheek flush against the smooth gray bark, eyes squeezed shut, teeth set in hangnail flesh, chewing. He'd thought himself subject to nothing but his own anxiety, and then a hand shut on his forearm. Zef, feet on the wall, chin on the limb inches from his face. Eyes shining and teeth bared. And in his hand a fold of paper with Peyton's father's phone numbers, home and office, written on it.

"You know I'll do it," Zef told him. Fear was the taste in his mouth, like the metal drain pipe in the restroom he'd been made to lick by some boys the very first day Zef, his protection, got expelled.

Now fear weights his legs and numbs his lips; were his father to catch him, he'd not be able to run nor even make up a lie. Fear inhabits him like the cigarette smoke that trails his mother; her hair and even the chair she sits in stink.

Resolutely, he sets one leaden foot on the bottom shelf of the bookcase and hoists himself high enough to reach the heart-shaped granite paperweight on the top shelf where the key to the desk drawer always resided in Connecticut. He was in second grade when he bought the paperweight for his father on a class trip to a quarry, and his father, receiving it, exclaimed, "A stone heart?" leaving Peyton unsure if the gift had been funny or stupid. The key lies beneath it still, and Peyton retrieves it to unlock the file drawer. He searches, item by item, through all the hanging folders. He finds the envelope labeled Frith, Stearn & Heppering, and inside it is a small red leather notebook, exactly as Zef described it.

He pockets it, buries the envelope deep in the trash, closes the drawer and relocks it, replaces the key, turns off the light. Finished, he stands in the doorway of the darkened study. No one is home. He could do anything he wants, in here or anywhere else.

For almost a full minute, he stands in the door, running through a list of just what all those things might be. He tries to make the list exhaustive. Then he goes into his room, which is dark because it, too, is shadowed by the cliff. He loads the tray of his CD player, and presses *Play*. After that, he lies down on his bed and pulls his old red blanket over his head.

Althea Trott's icing the hot cross buns she's baked for Easter, ten days away and coincident this year with April Fools' Day, when she thinks she sees a white boy at the shop's screen door. She sets down the pastry bag filled with confectioner's glaze amid the newspapers and black-edged political broadsides competing for counter space with yesterday's bread (seven-grain, sour dough and rye), and tonguing the sticky sweetness off her palms and from between her fingers, she ambles toward the door, tread heavy, haunches rolling. The boy's tender looks — eleven maybe twelve years old, tow-headed and pie-eyed — surprise her as much as his color in this neighborhood at this time of day, school-hours on a Monday.

But her shop's doorstep, like the narrow street beyond it, is empty. Lemuel, behind her, calls out, "Sister, my ride comin'?" She shakes her head, disdaining to answer a question she hears a dozen if not two dozen times every day. She wanted him here, to protect him — the Government people who kidnapped him, when they brought him home, excused the whole event with: "He never told us not to. He seemed happy to go" — but he cannot stay here. She cannot bear it.

Kenrick brought him, because she told him to, borrowing Marcus's beat-up Bentley for transport and enlisting the neighbors' help down at her house to load him. And in front of this self-same door she looks through now, wiping her hands dry on her apron bib, they attempted together to heft him out of it, but Kenrick — the little dandy, the brainy so-randy brat her foster-sister Louise foisted on her, whom she'd fostered in turn, on impulse, into his manhood — because he asked and she saw no reason to deny herself the pleasure nor him the experience — little Kenrick Desmond, M.P., ended up on his designer-pants knees in the dirt in front of Basil's Dream. He gasped beneath the potato sack deadweight that is Lemuel's top-heavy body, fastening her with a look somewhere between offended and aroused when she shoved him aside, with a thigh that once pillowed his, and took up her brother's bulk on her own broad shoulders.

From his wheelchair beneath the stairs beside her fax machine, Lemuel insists. "Sister, why you lockin' me up? I missin' de sky!"

Ignoring him, she turns from the door. A bright rectangle of sun interrupted by her shadow paints the worn linoleum floor, speckled with flour she should sweep away. She makes her way back to the counter, takes up the pastry bag again, and resumes marking neat sugar X's atop each bun, disappointingly dry and tasteless this year since no currants and no candied fruit peel made it past the constriction on the docks. She fed a bun from the first batch this morning to her brother who pronounced it "pleasin' to de Lord," but she'd eaten two already herself by then, on top of several half-fists of dough she'd chewed during the kneading, and she pronounced the whole mess, silently, bitterly, not at all pleasin' to Althea.

She opens her mouth and lets a hymn come out. "My Lord, Thou art a rock to me." When she bakes she always sings. And for more than thirty years she's offered piercing contralto in the Emmanuel Zion A.M.E. church choir. But Lemuel dislikes her voice; her whole life this has been so. He frowns in his wheelchair, eyes half-shut, fingers picking irritably at the pinned folds of his pants legs. Thirteen years her senior, simple from the day he was born, what wits he had went when his legs did. He's a burden, but he's *her* burden. She never denies it.

Every evening now he's here in the shop she washes him down with a hose in the sink in the back room when she changes his nappy, and then scours his shit from the sink, locks him in and leaves. She goes home by bus or on foot or by way of a ride with a man to the house her brother longs to sleep in and sleeps there alone, or with the man if she's a mind to. And some mornings when she trudges back up the hill to Basil's Dream she finds Ramo already inside, having tricked the lock and risked himself to the eyes of whatever neighborhood spies may be watching to carry Lemuel up the stairs—for breakfast in the lukewarm company of Rufus's sullen widowed girlfriend and his cranky child—and down again afterwards to his chair by the fax to smile wan greeting first to Althea and then her customers. But other mornings, like this one, Ramo has not come and she finds her brother on the floor, hitching himself toward her on his forearms, cursing her with words she'd not have known he knew, everything within his reach pulled to the floor—today a whole tray of crockery, the last of what she owned unchipped, smashed to sharp-edged bits.

Her brother calls out now, "Sister!" and presses his hands to his ears. She stops her song and her work and flicks crumbs from his shirt front. With the tip of her littlest finger, the nail long and sharp, she tweaks sugar icing from the corners of his lips. The flesh in the nail's path reddens. She tells him sternly, "God in He mercy give you this cross."

And that's when Zef Passjohn walks in. The screen slaps shut behind him, Lemuel jumps, and Zef announces, "I got to know where Ras Ramo is. I got something real important to give him."

No need to speak o' de devil, Althea thinks, *he walk right in unbidden.* "Where you get off, talkin' like that to me?" she says. She's rounding the counter, hurrying and limping and silently cursing the bad knee the Lord's seen fit to give her along with the robust hips and bosom that power her contralto and draw men's attentions but overtax her joints, and then—again—the skinny blond white boy is framed in the door.

"Who you friend?" Her question comes out in three stalled huffs; she's breathless as well as wary. Zef looks disturbed, maybe on something, sweat beads freestanding on his forehead, biceps twitching, one hand shoved deep in his pocket, fiddling with something small.

His answer is to grab the white boy by his shirt and jerk him inside where he spits out his own introduction when Zef twists his collar. "Peyton. I'm Peyton Langston."

She puts one and one and one together — the name, his American accent and the platinum hair — with a few things she knows from other sources. That expatriate white woman Marcus is seeing. The talk from all quarters about what the hell he thinks he's doing. *What* the hell he's doing, she can pretty well imagine. Her question is *why*. With everything that's going wrong for all his people, why's that man that eluded her hot crush at twelve and twenty and thirty-five pursuing again — again! — what best will damn him and the rest of them? She smiles at Zef unkindly, baring her gold tooth up front.

"The devil in you got the uppermost hand," she says. She advances on him now without hesitation. "What you up to wid this white boy? What trouble you pullin' down on you fadder? On the rest o' us?" Her hand shuts on his arm and she hisses close to his face, softly, with venom, "Why you not *leave*, little devil? Ever' time I see you I see de devil looking out you green eyes, why you not let that woman take you?"

Zef explodes like she's ignited him, kicking her shins, fingers jabbing and tearing the bronze-streaked dome of her hair. "You know where Ramo's at. All kind of people see him coming in and out of here all the time. Black bitch, fat bitch, you tell me where he stays."

She slaps him. Knocks him right off his feet. Peyton wiggles clear, runs, trips, and falls. She pins Zef in a chair with a fist in his gut like a ball of dough she's about to knead and lunges with her other hand for Peyton. She catches movement on the stairs behind her brother. Ramo. She freezes.

Like breath on a windowpane. Not there, then right there. Might have been upstairs all along, might have slipped in the back just now.

Zef heaves in her grasp. From a deep pocket in his pants leg he pulls a small book bound in red kid and lifts it toward the stairs. "Ramo! If you have this, they can't arrest you. You won't have to hide. I heard Marcus say it."

He shakes the notebook open, and flings it. Althea exults: Suggs's damn little Government-damning notebook, risen from the dead.

Ramo scoops it from the floor before she can shift her weight to reach it. He says, "You take dat from you fadder?" but he doesn't open it. He turns and picks up Lemuel's hand instead and squats beside him, holding the hand.

Zef writhes in the chair like an up-turned turtle and Althea turns him loose. She points at Peyton, cowering beneath a table, face pinched up just short of crying, "*He* de one doin' the takin', from he fadder, I wager you that."

Ramo's eyes brush them each briefly. He examines the notebook's pages, holding one after another to the light, looking through instead of at the words and numbers. He does not read because he has never learned how. He asks Zef, still in the chair, "Why you bring de white boy here?"

Peyton's shifting toward the door. Althea launches herself at Ramo, at the notebook that will change her dead cousin from garbage to Government's downfall as Peyton blurts, "Zef made me do it."

The notebook rises beyond her reach, Ramo taller than she by more than a foot. Looking into her eyes, he rips a handful of neatly figured pages from their binding, and holds them between thumb and forefinger as if the paper were decomposing shreds of flesh. "Why Zef do this t'ing?" he asks her. "Who makin' he hurt so deep he have to hurt back? Who passin' paper that belong nowhere but in de fire from a little man's hand to a boy's littler hand? An' who make he mother leave, in de first place, wid a lie?"

His eyes, jaundiced, bloodshot, make her think of entrails—a butchered goat, a gutted fish. He says, "Althea Trott, you appetite for men and meanness make you de devil's handmaid, sometime."

He lifts the notebook still higher. Tears more pages from the binding. Zef's glance jerks from the pages to Ramo's face and back.

"Dis shit," Ramo says, crumpling the paper and dropping it on the boy's head and lap and the floury floor around his feet. "*I-an-I* tellin' you, stealin' be shit. Covetin' white ways, white t'ings, is shit." He gestures at Peyton, flattened to the doorframe. "He got no-t'ing you need."

Ramo bends and presses the notebook back into Zef's hands. "Where dat lighter you take from you fadder?"

A submissiveness Althea has never seen there before floods Zef's face. Slow seconds pass, then he extracts from inside his windbreaker a fat silver cigarette lighter and places it on Ramo's open palm. He strikes the flint. Althea shouts, "Don't!" at the same moment flame licks paper, greedily. Zef's face closes down, even with paper burning and red kid smoldering in the cup of his two pale-palmed hands.

Althea whips the apron over her head to bat the burning coal to the floor. The lighter strikes her foot and skids. Lemuel's voice hooks past her, "Lord help us. We got fire! Fire!" and then she hears the screen door slap. She's on her knees painfully, smothering fire with her apron, and when she levers herself up awkwardly with ashes on her hands, she finds three white men in her shop—that photographer she ran off from her house, and two bodyguards, in police blue.

There's a scuffle when Ramo bolts. A tabletop bangs the floor. Lemuel's chair blocks the back door, and Ramo's tackled as he skirts it. Two on one, the officers have him. A nightstick in the kidneys, another one on his skull, and he's face down at Lemuel's feet, getting cuffed as the officers smirk.

The photographer, slight and balding, dressed in a suit, says, "Excuse me," as he steps over the prisoner politely. Lemuel's mouth gapes wide and his hands paw air helplessly. The photographer addresses him as if they met by introduction: "Here's a release, sir, for you to sign, for Government's exclusive use of your photos. If you can't write your name, just make your mark here—"

Althea pounds the man's back with her fists. "No pictures!"

He ducks, scrambling closer to his blue-suited protection. "Already taken, ma'am," he says without looking at her, "the day he rode the van."

Ramo, as they jerk him to his knees, says, "They take he legs already. Now they takin' he dignity too."

She can't watch Ras Ramo shuffle out, hands manacled to his feet. Breathing hard, joints screaming, she waits for the door to close and the cruiser's idling engine to rev and pull away. When she does turn around, her shop's empty. Both boys have vanished. It's just her and her simple brother inside Basil's Dream, with chairs and a table upended, and sunlight pouring across the floor. Another crossed bun's been torn from the tray, and — a single bite missing — it lies upside down on the linoleum alongside her singed apron with the charred pages of Suggs's blood book rolled up tight inside.

Peyton jogs the dusty, bending road downhill toward South Shore and home. His head's empty except for regret and odd bits of picture, still-frames archived from the seconds he lost inside the panic that played out in the shop. One frame shows Mr. Trott's face, all tongue and pink lips, a baby's scream with the sound turned off. Another frame is hot buns and sugar icing, their smell like a pleasure cloud above them, and yet another shot is his dirty hand in the tray stealing one. The last frame is the tarnished silver lighter rolling in a patch of sun. He remembers swapping the bitten bun for the abandoned lighter. Once it belonged to Marcus, who has stolen his mother; then it belonged to Zef, who made him do bad things; and once, for exactly the one moment they defaced it, it belonged to him and Zef together; and now it's his alone.

He doesn't know why he has it. He doesn't know why he wants it.

Sunk deep in a pants pocket, the lighter bangs heavy on his thigh as he runs.

17

When Darrell lands in Bermuda on Easter Monday, he carries his own bags off the tarmac. He's lucky his flight from JFK could land: the airport's barely open, operated by management and Canadian scabs. On his way from the terminal to the street, where Jonathan Heppering is meeting him, he crosses picket lines, mostly black people, who curse and jostle him despite the presence of quite a few members of the armed Regiment, most of them black as well.

Darrell has spent the holiday weekend visiting his mother, hospitalized in Hartford for gall bladder surgery. For the two business days before that, he lobbied TransGlobal's home office in midtown Manhattan to expedite the Bermuda company's move to Grand Cayman, or, failing that, to authorize him to move his family either ahead to Cayman or back to the States. He invoked, in a meeting with the human resources vice president, his contractual access, as expatriate employee, to TransGlobal's emergency evac provider. The man stared at Darrell as if he'd threatened to drop his trousers. "That policy's for wars and earthquakes, *disasters*, Langston," the v.p. said, his face turning reflexively to his south-facing window and Ground Zero in the distance, "not one more round of race trouble on a two-bit Caribbean island."

Darrell did not explain to this company officer, a resident of Short Hills, New Jersey, that Bermuda is not in the Caribbean, that the trouble was less about race than power and money and who wields them, and that enough trouble of any kind in such a small place was not much different than a war, at least for the people living there. "We'd like to get out before disaster happens," Darrell said. The man pursed his lips at Darrell's continued impingement on his valuable time, and referred the request down the chain to the relocation committee, for review.

Now, at the airport curb, Jonathan awaits him in his tired green Toyota hatchback, doors locked and a cudgel across his lap. When he phoned Darrell over the weekend in Connecticut, having tracked him down through Lucy, he reported the near closing of the airport and explained that taxis were not meeting flights, as even non-union drivers prefer their tires unslashed. Darrell is grateful for that heads-up and the ride but feels certain Jonathan is here only because he wants something, for ever since the day he visited Jonathan in his rose garden with the notebook in his breast pocket, the man's avoided him quite handily. Sure enough, as soon as they've pulled clear of the fractious congestion at the airport exit, Jonathan announces that it's time Darrell returns to him the envelope he's been holding.

"Look at this mess," Jonathan says, his face tight with distaste. He hooks his thumb back over his shoulder toward the airport, then renews his grip on the club in his lap. "Government's lost control. No one's in charge. Malcontents everywhere, one side shouting and marching, the other ones camped on the courthouse steps clutching candles and singing hymns. Hair-triggers on everybody's hostility, and in the midst of this, that idiot football player Isaiah Barnes means to hang a black man for a murder. If he succeeds in executing this Rasta—and he's trying to expedite the trial, to have it over before elections in the fall—he'll get '77 all over again: the riots, the anarchy, a stigma that will damn the economy for years—and by God, that incompetent fool Horace Tucker is not worth it!" Jonathan gestures at the graffitioed slogan, *Will three dead black men cancel one dead Tucker* spray-painted on the concrete balustrade of the bridge they are crossing.

"No man of any color is worth this hell."

They are driving on the causeway over Castle Harbour, the road a two-lane ribbon of white concrete, the water jewel-blue on either side and barely a shade darker than the sky. Darrell notes with irony what Jonathan overlooks: just five months back, over Thanksgiving turkey, Jonathan's hair-trigger didn't need a jury to verbally convict a black fella and recommend his hanging for the death of one white backbencher, but now, at Easter, with his own hide as well as his livelihood threatened, he's trying on a more liberal view.

"I need that notebook," Jonathan insists, "and you had best get it to me before someone worse comes for it. People—the chap that gave it to me, and worse—have been coming round to ask for it. They're liable to stop asking and simply take it by other means; these types are not pleasant to deal with, let me tell you."

Darrell's body goes cold with knowledge of that notebook's proximity to his son and his wife. He tells Jonathan, "I don't know if I kept it or not." He's not wanted to remember that he did, so much so that only when he was seated opposite the HR veep in New York did it strike him that he could have used the notebook right then to substantiate his case for the extent of the threat facing his family. It's quite a dangerous bit of paper, and on the flight home, he determined that since it's in *his* possession, *he'll* be the one to make use of it.

He takes some pleasure in Jonathan's flabbergasted expression. Clearly the man's torn between disbelieving that Darrell could be stupid enough to discard the notebook, and doubting that he's got the balls to use it to his own purposes. With the windows down and the balmy air of spring-turning-summer rolling across them, Darrell details the dispirited populace and depressing business conditions in New York City through the rest of the ride into town, employing a cool and desultory politeness he feels must surely be the effect of his complete familiarization with British mores. They are stopped three times at Regiment checkpoints, but each time they are waved through without a search while armed soldiers remove the seats from cars with darker drivers. Periodically

Jonathan reiterates that he must have that notebook, and each time Darrell hoists him higher on his own petard, replying with bland reassurances that he will certainly look for it the moment he reaches home this evening.

He parts from Jonathan in the elevator on his way up to his office. Then, leaving his bags there, he goes immediately back to the basement parking garage. His scooter awaits him, and he rides it straight home, arriving shortly after two in the afternoon.

Lucy is out; the garage is empty. In his study he unlocks the desk drawer and lifts out the file where he put the notebook. Rapidly he flips through the file's contents. After a second, more thorough pass, he yanks open other drawers, paws through files and then shoves aside the hanging folders to search beneath them. Cursing out loud, he is dumping the contents of the overflowing wastepaper basket onto the carpet when Peyton appears in the doorway.

Darrell almost cannot speak, he is so tightly focused on his search for the notebook that has somehow, impossibly, gone missing at exactly the moment he needs it. Then, glancing again at Peyton's blanched face, he realizes two things that punch him in the gut: first, he's not seen his son in days; but wait-a-second, the boy is not in school at a time when he surely should be.

"Are you sick?" he says, moving toward Peyton to embrace him.

His son ducks, shakes his head, and backs out the door. Very strange behavior, and one more aggravation to Darrell, barely holding his head above the tide of inner agitation threatening to swamp his ability to think clearly and behave properly.

"Why aren't you in school? Is today another damn holiday here?"

Peyton shakes his head again. "I told Mom I was sick," he says.

He is standing in the hall in boxers, bare feet, and a tee shirt that is not clean. A wad of cut and knotted rubber bands circles one wrist like a bracelet and a chain of safety pins hangs around his neck. He looks depressed, not sick. Hair hangs in his eyes, his expression is furtive, and he has the hunched, tense posture of someone who's not slept well in several days.

Darrell says, "You told your mother you're sick, but you're not sick?"

Peyton's eyes say he's terrified.

"Where is your mother?"

"Out." Peyton's voice breaks, mangling the word.

"Where is she?" Darrell repeats. He feels his pent-up frustration hooking to Lucy's absence, and he doesn't understand why, except that more and more even the most ordinary interaction with her can spark this frantic feeling of fury.

"She said she was going out to look for groceries," Peyton says, and Darrell, to calm them both, replies, "Okay. I'm sure we need food. I know it's hard to find."

He reaches for his son's shoulder. Peyton looks even more unhappy when Darrell touches him. "What's wrong?" Darrell says. "Why are you so nervous?"

They are almost eye-to-eye; Peyton has gotten very tall, very fast, this year. He says, "Dad, I didn't want to go to school because—" He jerks his gaze away, and blurts, "I hate it there, and I'm failing out."

Darrell feels the world tilt. "What?" he says. "Failing? How can you be failing? You're not failing."

His voice gets louder with each statement, backing Peyton down the hall. "Ask Mom," Peyton says. "She knows."

"What is going on here?" Lucy's voice cuts across Peyton's. She is standing in the foyer at the top of the hall. In each hand she carries several small plastic sacks of groceries, different colors from different stores.

The accusation in her voice, and the temerity of her accusing him of anything makes Darrell blow.

"You tell *me* what's going on," he shouts at her. "Peyton has just told me he's failing out of Somers Academy, and that you know it."

She sets the groceries on the floor. She starts down the

hall toward them, her keys in one hand, jangling together as she walks. Darrell cannot stop shouting at her. A tide of rage surges through him and he cannot make himself listen to her words. Her mouth opens and closes, her face works in anger and upset and eventually tears, and he shouts and shouts at her, and backs her up the hall. Everything has gone wrong today, he tells her. He has lost an important paper. A very important paper. And in the middle of looking for it—he has turned the study upside down, he cannot find it, there will be dreadful consequences—he discovers that Peyton is telling her lies in order to stay home from school, and that she's lying, too—how long has she been doing this?—by saying nothing to him, not a word. Not saying what needs to be said: that's lying. Doesn't she know that?

"Everyone's lying!" he yells. "Except me!"

His wife and his son: their two frightened faces are the same face. Round grey eyes floating in tears; pale, ravaged faces with hot flags of color in the cheeks and wet blond hair straggling into the eyes.

"I will not have this," Darrell says, steadying himself. Forcing his head above the flood of his anger and back into clear, forceful thinking. "I will not allow you to lie to me anymore. You will do what I tell you to do. You," he points at Peyton, "are leaving this island the moment I can secure transportation. You're going back to the States, to a decent school. A quality boarding school where you can stay until we figure out where it is we're going to live. And you," he turns to Lucy, whose mouth is pinched shut, "you are going to come in here and help me find this document, and you're going to tell me every single step by which Peyton, and you, have gotten him into this fix."

He wants to slap her. He has never struck her, he's wanted to but he's always known he'd never do it, and he understands that something is very wrong now because he no longer feels that sense of utter impossibility. Also he feels an erection rising. He is able to imagine very clearly knocking Lucy down and going at her as hard as he can, hurting her as hard as he can, in as many ways as he can, all at once. Anything to break open her closed face, which is like a fist in his own face. Anything to breach the back she turns to him like a wall morning and night, and the clamped-shut pussy she protects with drawn-up knees when he reaches for her under the sheets.

She says nothing at all, even though he's stopped shouting, even though her tears still drip. Peyton, big boy that he is, is sobbing, and she reaches past Darrell to comfort him. Peyton flings himself away from both of them and slams the door of his room so hard the latch breaks and the door flies open again. Instantly his music starts up, growling and grinding and screaming, reverberating in the stone walls of the house. Lucy follows Darrell meekly into his study, where he watches her stare at the mess on the floor with an expression he cannot read. When he finds amid the crumpled papers the empty envelope marked Frith, Stearn & Heppering, and asks her how on earth this got in the trash, she turns her hands palm up.

"I have no idea," she tells him. "That's the truth, Darrell."

He wants with all his battering heart to believe her. But he doesn't.

18

The next morning Lucy feels numb. Things between her and Darrell are irreparably broken, it's only a matter of time until the end arrives, but she cannot feel anything. She cannot even think. With Darrell at the office and Peyton at school, she stands on the balcony, smoking the last cigarette from the last pack she owns, staring down into surf swarming over the rocks. Winter is long gone and spring, very brief on the island, is finished, too; summer's heat has begun, in April, to build. Only halfway to its zenith, the sun stings the exposed skin at the base of her neck. Sweat beads at her hairline and slides down inside her shirt between her breasts. In the water below, trash clings to the rocks where the waves have thrown it—each successive breaker dragging some debris away but depositing more.

She flings the cigarette into the surf and goes inside. Until her eyes adjust to the dimness, she cannot see. A headache stabs her brain, and she puts her hand on the high back of a dining room chair for balance. The exquisite shaping of the fluted wood, its smooth polish beneath her palm, summon memories she's not visited in a long time. The pleasurable purposefulness of drawing a chair like this from the fine set of eight, for one dinner guest after another, during the decade she and Darrell have owned them, two-thirds of the span of their marriage; and the purchase of the chairs, in youthful, ebullient trepidation and hope when they could ill afford them, furnishing a house in the days when each mortgage payment was a stretch.

She sees again her mother, frail and bony in one of these chairs at some family gathering when her father announced, because her mother made him be the one to say what everyone could see, that the cancer was back. She recalls the strained expression of her neighbor Mike in contrast to the soft, fat face of his son Lawrence, a toddler then, seated side by side in these chairs, opposite her and Darrell, she holding Peyton, a babe-in-arms, on the single occasion Mike came to dinner, alone with his child on Saturday night because his investment banker wife was working on a deal she couldn't leave. She listens again to Darrell's terse remark thereafter that she'd best be very careful, as neither that desperately friendless man, nor his venal wife, nor the nosy neighbors across the street would know what to think if she continued to befriend him. She feels all over again in her chest her decision taken in that moment to invite Mike carefully only as far as the kitchen but to offer herself freely as his friend and Lawrence's friend, just in the afternoons and the evenings and on the Saturdays when Darrell was working, tending deals he could not leave, because Mike and Lawrence were indeed desperate—and so was she.

She slumps against a wall. Beyond the morning's numbness lurks fear, and the pain these memories spill is an acid eating rapidly through the last bricks of the wall that contains it. She drifts through the house, trailing fingertips along walls and across door knobs, peering into rooms where today the familiar furniture and decor seem as much someone else's as this barrack-like house does every day. The door to the study is shut, and she does not open it. Probably the mess is still on the floor. She doesn't know what Darrell will do about the missing notebook. That is as far as she can get, pushing her thoughts, forcing them to move.

When she drove Peyton to school this morning, he asked her, "Did Dad find what he was looking for?" An obvious question, to which she answered no, yet in his breathless phrasing of it, she thought she sensed a difference in him. Less crispness in his separation from her? An opening she could enlarge? Peyton surely knew things were breaking, the family cracking right over his head. In the car with the question barely off Peyton's lips, she thought maybe they were both reaching toward the way things used to be between them. She thought maybe they'd found a door. She stopped the car, put it in park, and held out her arms, heart poised to leap up when they shut around him. But he did not move. A complicated series of feelings registered on his fine features, and then he turned face forward. "Mom," he said, "if you don't drive, I'm going to be late for school, and I'm in enough trouble there already."

His voice was cold, and she distinctly saw him square his narrow shoulders.

She should have told him right then that she would never allow his father to send him away. She should have made clear that no matter what she will not lose *him*. But she was too numbed in that moment by her desperate wish not to know how much he knew about her.

She leaves the house. She walks not to the beaches where she's so often met Marcus but north and inland instead, climbing the ridge through the s-curves of Camp Hill, retracing the road she drove this morning taking Peyton to school. The simple act of putting one foot in front of the other is mildly comforting, and the colors and smells of the island flood her senses, giving her something to feel besides fear.

Tall oleanders bearing the first white and hot pink blossoms line both sides of the narrow, bending road. Tangles of bay laurel and elephant-eared philodendron cling to coral cuts in the shade. Chicken coops, sleeping dogs, wash on the line, televisions flickering through open doors testify to ordinary life in ordinary houses, the daily business of living on the island, despite crisis on all sides. As she climbs the ridge, heat beats her and sweat rivers down her legs. Her muscles work and her shoes fill with dust. Compost heaps and backyard gardens, a yellow horse so close to the fence she smells his animal skin, heavy birds with mustard-colored breasts weighing down branches above her head, shouting *kis-ke-DEE!* Her footfalls send lizards skittering, and the oleanders when she brushes them release a shower of white petals and a medicinal smell.

At the top of the ridge, she smells yeast bread baking and her stomach growls in response. Her breakfast this morning was that last cigarette. Across the street—a crumbling asphalt track barely wide enough for two cars to pass—is the ugly green building with the improbably lovely name she passes each weekday on her way to Peyton's school. Basil's Dream. Standing in the doorway is a heavyset black woman with a broad gold stripe spiraling the oiled tower of her hair. That this woman is Althea Trott, Lucy knows, from Marcus.

Crossing the street, she asks, "You have fresh bread today?"

Althea's dark eyes slip all over her. With a shrug of infinite weariness, she turns her back and steps inside her shop. Lucy is drawing deep breath to bridge the snub when she realizes Althea is holding the screen door wide for her to walk through, and she recalls suddenly the exasperation of the old black man who sold her and Peyton ice cream from his wheeled cart on Front Street in their first weeks on the island. She gets now what she could not catch then, that most black people on the island are both patient and worn out with the self-absorption of the white people their livelihood requires them to serve.

Inside the shop, she takes in the faces of Althea's dozen or so customers, all black. She notices cheap white plastic chairs and tables, Mr. Trott in his battered, duct-taped wheelchair by the stairs—chin on chest and dozing, the empty bakery case and the shelves behind it, also empty, and on a rack on the counter, six steaming loaves of whole wheat bread.

Some people have their loaves already, in clear plastic sacks in their hands or beside their coffee mugs on the tables. A few stand chatting by the counter, waiting for this batch of bread to be dispensed. Every single one of them has turned to stare at her. She smiles, feeling extremely white.

Althea says brusquely, "You come in here for bread?"

If she buys a loaf, someone here will not get one. If she

says no, then what has she come in for? The reason for the refusal, and the condescension inherent in it, will be obvious.

"Do you slice the bread?" she asks. "Might I have half a loaf, or a slice?"

"I cut de loaf, who want de rest? The part you don' want." Althea stares at her, and her tone is insolent, but amusement plays in the small muscles around her mouth.

"Serve the others," Lucy answers. "They were here first. I can take what's left."

She crosses the room—her knees shaking as she pushes through her urge to flee—and speaks to Mr. Trott, who's raised his head at the sound of his sister's voice. She's never talked to Lemuel, just waved at him like every other passerby. She's never seen him except from the car. Close up, he has the eerie translucence of an old sick person with one foot in the world beyond; she remembers that quality in her mother in the last months before she died. He smells very slightly of urine, but he's dapper in his shirt of faded Lenten purple, offset with the Easter white of his bushy beard. As she grasps his hand to shake it, the yellow stains radiating from his lips into the hair around his mouth remind her of the loquat he once pressed to her lips. Its ample juice staining her own chin, the sharp taste—she gasps. She hears the sound she's made. She *dreamed* that loquat. And the dream ended with flowers in her lap. To cover her consternation at confusing what is real with what can't be, she pulls up an empty chair and sits down facing Mr. Trott. Althea, handling customers, watches her.

"Lemuel?" Lucy says. His expression changes, but he's listening, not looking. His eyes have pale blue clouds of cataract at the centers. She holds his hand—thin and chilly, the fingers curled stiffly, the nails ridged and split. How fragile and imperfect his connection to this life. How insubstantial. Just flesh, she thinks, and breath, and some notions about what's required to keep the two together.

Althea bumps her elbow with a plate bearing a thick slice of warm bread. Lucy thanks her and eats, while Althea slides a chair close and wedges her broad hips into it, facing Lemuel, her back to the people at the tables behind them, her muscled forearms, sheathed in a chain-mail of narrow bangles, resting on her thighs.

"How is Lemuel doing?" Lucy asks politely when Althea does not speak.

"Poorly. He wastin' here, indoors."

She wheezes quietly between phrases. Perhaps she's not as strong as she looks, Lucy thinks. She is heavy; maybe she, like her brother, is diabetic.

"Next week he goin' back to he place by de road. He got to live, while he can." Althea's eyes follow Lucy's fingers, tearing the bread, lifting it to her mouth. "Marcus 'elp us" — she gestures, sweeping over the heads in the shop to include unseen neighbors outside — "stop Government, in de court, from knocking down my house, so Lemuel goin' back. When Marcus free Ramo, Lemuel be safe there, again. In de meantime, the neighbors got to watch him. I have to mind de shop here. I cannot sit wid he down there."

Lucy's nodded before she thinks about what her knowledge might signal Althea. Yesterday Marcus told her of his surprise at the success of his request for an injunction — to protect the buildings — amid the news they shared when she stopped at his house for a moment between grocery stores. Mrs. Alvarra was inside, but he kissed her anyway, on the veranda. Another memory swells inside her unbidden: his lower lip between hers, mauve and full, soft and sweet like ripe fruit.

Althea says, "You de one."

Lucy squeezes the empty plate in both hands and feels how brightly she blushes. Althea's statement is loud and confident. Did everyone hear? Conversation in the shop seems suddenly to have paused.

"Love," Althea says just as ringingly, "it a fine thing." She shifts in the chair, spreading her lap wider, addressing the room. "It keep my bones loose. Keep my age down." When she grins, the gold tooth shines, and her audience plays back at her, grinning in turn, one or two adding, quietly, amen. "Love got a price, too," Althea says. "Ever'body know it."

Upstairs, a baby squalls, and the voice of a young woman rises impatiently, shushing the child.

Althea leans in close, and the strong scent of her hair oil fills Lucy's head.

"Marcus got so much work to do," she whispers. "You see de fix we in. No food getting' in." She gestures with her head toward the empty counter and shelves behind her. "Strike shuttin' ever'thing down. No jobs. No money. Ever'body angry, carrying guns, looking for guns, setting fire. And Government want to knock down houses, and kill another black man. My cousin Rufus stay up there with he girl and they baby, before he die an' turn up trash in de dumpster."

Pointing, she directs Lucy's attention to broadsides taped to the wall behind Lemuel and the fax machine. A large, poor-quality black and white photo of a graying Rasta man with long, matted dreads. Two smaller ones, equally fuzzy, of younger, close-cropped men. Several paragraphs of dense and grainy small print beneath each one.

Althea closes her eyes and hums a phrase that sets someone behind them singing a call on the Lord's mercy. She stops abruptly, and loosens the empty plate from Lucy's hand. "Marcus doin' better, girl, since you come along." She sighs, starts to say more, falls silent. Then, speaking briskly, she says, "You raise he up, and that a good thing. But...de price! He don' belong to you."

Her hand, warm and wide, encircles Lucy's wrist. The black-on-white contrast spills Marcus into Lucy's feelings and heat lifts through her as she raises her eyes cautiously to Althea's, only inches away.

"Mrs. Lucy Langston," Althea says, "I tell you a truth I tellin' nobody else, ever. When Marcus bound up, sufferin' in love, wid he wife Lydia, I tell her he lovin' me. Comin' to my bed one time, two time a month. A lie. It give me pleasure to hurt she so. And him. I got mean spite in me, as well as de Lord's light, and some amount of love. I tell Lydia a lie, and I tellin' you de truth. For de same reason: he don' belong to you, white lady. He got work to do."

She heaves herself up and starts back toward the counter, walking heavily and wheezing lightly.

"You son, you think he don' see? The truth painted all over

him."

Lucy feels her back pressed hard to a wall: Peyton's squared shoulders. She built that wall between them with the lies she told and made him tell. He's reinforced it with fury at what she's done and will not admit. She could tear it down with a word, or no words; all she need do is admit what her sweet, short spring has cost. All she has to do is end it.

She gets up slowly, in pain. Says good-bye to Mr. Trott. On the way to the door, she keeps her eyes on the scuffed and torn linoleum. Althea is there before her, holding the screen open, offering a clear plastic bag containing the thick heel of a loaf of bread.

"I owe you," Lucy says, "for the slice." She pats her pants pocket, hoping to feel coins but she has nothing.

Althea shoves the bread into her hands. "Nobody want it," she says. "You take it."

Stepping into the hot, dusty road, squinting in the glaring sunlight, she says, "Althea, I want to ask you one thing. I want to know about Basil's Dream." She points at the wooden placard besides the door that names the building.

"What you wan' to know?" Althea says, her eyes and tone weary but some liveliness playing around her mouth.

"Is anyone here named Basil?" Lucy asks. "Did Basil name this place? Is there any reason for the name?" The building is squat and ugly, painted a green as bilious and unappealing as the platter-sized toads that swell and split in the puddles after every heavy rain. Whose dream could be so squalid and bear so lyric a name?

"No Basil," Althea says. The bangles on her arms sing as they shift against one another. "Don' need Basil to know ever'body havin' some kind of dream, and it mean what they think it mean. What they thinkin' change sometime and then de dream change, too."

When the screen slaps shut behind Althea, Lucy walks away so disoriented she might well have been inside someone else's dream. Heading downhill fast, the bread heel in its clear bag swinging from her fist, she worries Althea's answer the way she chewed the bread.

We all tell ourselves stories about our lives, she thinks, and the telling, so we think, makes them true. Our dreams are another story, and we call them lies. But dreams happen and life happens, both true stories while we're inside them. More than one truth at the same time is paradox, and paradox, inhabited, transforms us. Always at all times there are as many truths as there are people living lives, as many dreams as dreamers.

Lucy cries now because she knows what to do and knows, too, that she will do it. She hurts in every cell, but her stride lengthens. She feels everything, the whole complicated truth in all its contradictions. It hurts, and she is free.

19

Mrs. Alvarra meets Marcus on the doorstep with resolve set hard into every feature of her lined and leathery old lady face. Zef, she says, has been in his room all day. *All* day. She has been all day at the house, also, so with authority she speaks that he did not once come out. She believes he did not leave his room also on Monday, and she asks herself has he spent as well the weekend of Easter in his room. She demands of Marcus to know — arms akimbo with ten years of history on his tendency to be absentee parent — when *he* last saw his son.

Marcus questions himself and cannot remember. He is exhausted — for the past seventy-two hours he has hardly slept, whether working or lying awake worrying. Over the holiday weekend, Lemuel Trott was forcibly returned by Isaiah Barnes' Medi-mate van to his place by the curb in front of Ramo's shop because the Justice Minister, pre-empting Althea's plan to have Kenrick move her brother home anyway in the coming week, secured an injunction to uphold the rights of Lemuel Trott to live where he pleases, handily creating a human rights issue in the media at the same time Lemuel's picture sprouts iconic all over the island on Government's *Perseverance, and a Smile!* posters. Ramo's arraignment in Tucker's murder has just been docketed for the coming week, and the Tucker faction has upped the ante by re-locating their justice vigils from the front steps of the courthouse to the entrance of the marble-vaulted cemetery at historic Old Devonshire Church where Tucker now lies buried amid generations of the island's founding families.

In response, Marcus pointed out to the press that a corresponding vigil for Rufus and Breem might well be held at the dumpster in the parking lot beside the courthouse back door where their bodies were found—except that refuse container has been reassigned by the provider after that particular location was revealed by a consultant's utilization study to be unprofitable. This morning the *Gazette's* editor responded to Marcus's sally by plucking a line from his "incendiary" Guy Fawkes Night speech, *"we have got some problems and they are getting worse,"* recycling it as headline for an editorial calling for Marcus's indictment as accessory to Rufus and Breem's murders—since "the preponderance of the evidence available to the public suggests" that Mr. Passjohn either paid or was involved in a scheme to pay Cisco Suggs to arrange the hits. The editor wrote that on the basis of Mr. Passjohn's undisputed record of associating with lowlife figures and championing the criminal element, and his recent documented financial improprieties, he be immediately censured by the ethics committee investigating him in Parliament, so that voters might finalize their choices for this fall's elections.

Yesterday's mail brought Marcus a notice from the bank that foreclosure on Rose Hill was complete, the property to be offered at public auction in thirty days. Tomorrow's agenda features a meeting Marcus absolutely does not want to have: Althea has insisted she must talk with him face to face; and Kenrick, in an about-face from weeks of barely speaking to Marcus, strenuously insists that Althea is right, they must "get the facts on the table." And—most painful of all—yesterday evening and again this morning at the office Lucy tried to reach him by phone and he has not returned her call, because a clear bad feeling plagues him about what kind of news she needs so urgently to give him.

"I think Zef's probably all right," Marcus bluffs Mrs.

Alvarra, while attempting to assess—through the thrumming of the headache that never leaves him now and another plume of stomach acid searing his esophagus—if there's *any* possibility this could be true. "He's been going to school as he's supposed to," he hears himself say. "I think that's why he's home more in the afternoons."

Even to himself he sounds reprehensibly vague and defensive. In the ten days since Ramo was arrested, Zef's shifted from oppositional to genuinely withdrawn: sweaty, dead quiet, and home in his room with the door shut, more often than not. Marcus *has* noticed this, despite his preoccupation and a fervent wish not to.

"You go in there now," Mrs. Alvarra orders him. "The door is locked, there are smells, I hear nothing for hours—"

Her chin is lifted and her face set in its familiar mask of righteous umbrage, but Marcus sees a shine in her eyes that is either tears or the anxiety that will soon produce them.

"Are you going to let me in the house, so I can?" he asks her gently, because in her insistence that he listen, she is blocking the door.

Zef's door, when Marcus reaches it, is indeed locked, and when he presses his shoulder and his cheek against the louvered white wood, preparing to lean into it hard and shout, he detects a smell. Not death, but the stench of unwashed body and ganja. He rattles the door and yells and rattles it harder and precisely at the moment he forces it, the lock clicks on the inside, the door swings open, and Zef stands before him looking like a vagrant. Or a Rasta-in-training. Shirtless, ragged drawers barely clinging to his hips, he is filthy and his hair rubbed and twisted into the nubs of dreadlocks.

His appearance is as defiantly offensive as a thirteen-year-old can manage, but his eyes are vacant, and Marcus gets it in the gut, finally—Lucy's admonition. He hears it in her voice: *You are all he's got.*

He steps past Zef into the room, completely unlit, blankets blacking out the windows, the floor obliterated with strewn clothes and shoes, hip hop magazines from the States, scrawled school papers, broken-backed books and an overlay of candy wrappers and spent soda cans. Zef, without a word, sinks down with his naked back against the footboard of his bed, head in hands, elbows hanging from his knees. Marcus stands in the midst of this mess and its stink, looking at his son—an intelligent boy. A kid with potential. He feels fear with an intensity he's not known for many years. He feels helpless, a sensation he's not inhabited since his own lonely childhood. Who knows how to deal with something like what is before him now? Who tells you, when you become a parent, Things can get so bad, so beyond your ken and your control, you will have no idea how to live your way from this moment into the next.

The silence in the room grows protracted, and the airless stench stifling. Zef does not lift his head from his hands.

Marcus asks, "Can I open a window?"

"Knock yourself out," Zef mumbles.

Marcus jerks the coverings off the windows and wrestles with the sash and then with the slatted wooden storm shutter on each window, cranking them out on metal poles and letting in a rush of light and outdoor smells. What a relief to grapple physically with anything; he can assure himself he is doing *something*. When he turns around, he finds Zef curled fetal with knees to his nose and a dirty undershirt hiding his face. One hand holds his ear and the other is beneath the shirt but... is Zef's thumb in his mouth? Marcus yanks the shirt away and seizes his son's wrist. He pulls, and fingers emerge wet with saliva and clutching ... an orange button.

Before he's comprehended more than that, Zef is on his feet and swinging at him. Marcus ducks and Zef explodes, flinging himself around the room, ricocheting from floor to wall to dresser top, kicking everything his feet encounter, hurtling across the bed to the bookshelf and throwing anything he touches, tearing posters off the wall, sending lamps and the bedside table crashing to the floor. Marcus cannot move and cannot speak, so stunned is he about what this might mean to both of their futures. Flattened to the wall like a trapped witness to a grisly crime, he watches until it stops.

When it does, the room is wrecked, holes in the drywall

and furniture splintered, and Zef crouches panting on the peak of the mattress he's upended from the bed. "You said you'd keep Ramo out of Casemates. You didn't," he shouts. "You blew him off. You let them take him."

"Zef." Warily Marcus moves toward his son. Carefully he rights the fallen nightstand. "Zef, I can't get him out right now. It's a capital charge. Bail is beyond my means. Beyond the means of anyone willing to help him. I've petitioned to reduce bail, I've filed as his attorney of record, *gratis*, and I'll be there at every step of the court proceedings, just like I have been since before you were born."

He sits down and pats the floor beside him gingerly, as if the mess there rather than the one inside his son threatened all order in their lives. "Come here, Zef. Come down here."

He doesn't move.

"Ramo does matter to me. You know that. We have our differences but this is a matter of principle. He's been framed. It may take years, it did last time, but I'll get him out, eventually —"

A ceramic lamp smacks to pieces on the floor at Marcus's feet. Shards wing his knee and sting his bare forearm.

"One time you told me my mother was coming back, too," Zef shouts. "You remember that?"

Marcus blinks. *My mother.* How seldom, almost never, those words cross Zef's lips.

"You said she'd figure out what it was she'd left, and then she'd come back."

Marcus struggles to remember if he ever said that. The floor beneath his fingertips slicks with his own nervous sweat. He might have said it. In some long-ago desperate moment precursor to this one, he might have. But if he did, he lied. He'd known from the day he found her gone — she'd precisely halved the checking account, left her wedding ring on his bedside stand, and taken with her every last possession, even the ashtray she brought into the relationship — that she would never be back.

"Zef. I couldn't stop her. I couldn't make her stay. She left me, too." This last is something he's never said aloud, and it makes him gasp, like a punch in the solar plexus. The force shoots bitterness, a pellet caught in his craw, right out of him. And in its wake loss rises like a tide to singe the backs of his eyes. He is about to cry, in front of his son.

"Why?" Zef screams it. "Why'd she go? What did you do to her? She left for *some reason.*"

Marcus lifts a hand, uncertain if he's reaching for Zef or his own suddenly spinning head. "Zef, truly, I'm not responsible for everything. I do what I can. Sometimes I say what comes out because it seems at the time it will help. And sometimes I don't know what to say. Or do."

Zef says, "You're a liar. My mother wants me back, but you wouldn't tell me. You don't give a shit what happens to me."

Marcus's hand has drifted back to the floor, where his fingers now test the warped grain of the antique cedar planking in a patch cleared of trash and shards of broken lamp by his nervous fumbling. He doesn't know what Zef's talking about although it registers in his thoughts at some level that Lydia did send him two letters he returned to sender and that Zef seems somehow to know that. He does know what he wants, or rather, what he needs. He needs his son to absolve him, for the way his stoic silence about Lydia has wounded them both. And separated them. And driven Zef to Ramo, in search of what Marcus never gave him. He looks up mutely at Zef, perched atop the mattress like a miserable bedraggled raven.

"I should have done a lot of things differently, Zef. But it's not my fault your mother left." Tears balance on the rims of his eyelids and despite his shame he does not brush them away. His voice breaks when he says, "I swear I'm not responsible for that."

"I guess not," Zef says, slipping down the sagging mattress to sit on the floor. He is close enough now to touch, but Marcus feels ashamed to reach for his son for comfort, and Zef, turning bloodshot, exhausted, drug-burned eyes his way, does not offer any. He says, "I guess you're not responsible for much, Marcus."

Less than twenty-four hours later, operating on a few hours' fitful sleep and more cups of coffee than he can remember, Marcus pilots the Bentley along the Middle Road toward town, Kenrick stiff and brooding beside him, through a landscape pervaded with suffering and confusion.

Uncollected garbage is piled higher than the car at intervals along the road. Manor houses stand shuttered, their wealthy owners hiding inside or departed for the States or Europe, while in the working class and poorer neighborhoods, people cluster in parking lots and on the stoops, unemployed and waiting on news or rumor to move them. In town, the sidewalks are vacant, and storefronts, some vandalized and others closed for lack of business, boarded up. Traffic is sparse, as gasoline runs out because the labor shutdown—now a general strike affecting all workers—means nothing is off-loaded on the docks; when present stocks of fuel oil are depleted, the power company's turbines will stop turning and electricity all over the island will go out. The hospital has already shut down, lacking supplies as well as labor, and this morning, a last straw, the airport closed, stranding even those with the money to leave, and ending air cargo as means of importing food.

All this is for Marcus only a backdrop. Zef's face—bitter, desperate, as closed to hope as a death-row inmate's—is what he sees no matter what is in front of his eyes. He tries to speak of this to Kenrick, without knowing why. With no expectation of relief. He simply says, "My son is in a dreadful state."

In response, Kenrick looks at him. Looks into him, Marcus thinks. For an awkward moment, Marcus driving, Kenrick twisting in his seat as if it's painful to move, they lock eyes. Almost immediately, Kenrick turns away and Marcus has to blink, tilting himself back swiftly from the brink of tears.

Kenrick says, "I'm sorry to hear that. I've hoped for something different."

Marcus nods. He does not believe Kenrick, and that hurts.

They're returning from a tense and inconclusive parley with Althea and, to Marcus's considerable surprise, Cisco Suggs. The four of them crammed into the tiny front room of Althea's home so that Lemuel, on the curb in his chair, remained in his sister's view through the open door. Also visible through that door were two unmanned but heavily guarded bulldozers—sprouted up overnight like mushrooms in wet weather and signifying Government's intention to defy the injunction Marcus won to halt demolition of the little cinderblock houses belonging to Althea, Ramo and their neighbors. While Althea described to Marcus the marches, the bricks and the bottles her supporters are prepared to launch in response, he observed the Regiment conscripts, armed with automatic rifles, young black men from neighborhoods like the one they menace, as were the rank and file of a convoyed garrison the Bentley passed on the way out from town, its officers, however, white and British and hardened to human carnage in Ulster and Kosovo.

Marcus had ceased listening to Althea, his thoughts spiraling through desperate scenarios of the island's future and his son's fate, when Suggs—thin, pale, chain-smoking—announced quietly that the notebook in which they all had taken such interest back in December, he had given, in January, to Jonathan Heppering, front man for the money that funded the activities its pages detail. Then Althea, looking flatly at Marcus, explained in painstaking detail the circumstances of the notebook's destruction in her shop—how it arrived there in Zef's hands, the purpose for which Zef apparently intended it, and, most curiously, the means by which he'd acquired it, from a white boy, an American named Peyton Langston. Althea said that name with great clarity, and Marcus, avoiding her eyes, noted that Kenrick showed no surprise about any of this. That caused him to take into himself like a great dry wad of bread forced down his constricted throat the conclusion that the meeting was a kind of set-up, an underhanded confrontation engineered by Kenrick as much as Althea over just how much Marcus knew, and why, about that notebook and the hands it had passed through.

Now Kenrick's fingertips aggressively drum the Bentley's window sill. To make conversation, Marcus says that Suggs appeared far less unhappy naked and duct-taped a few months back than he did clothed and ambulatory today.

"The little bastard's made himself toast," Kenrick replies.

"You think he deserves whatever happens to him?" Marcus asks.

At first Kenrick does not respond. Then, as if Marcus has criticized him, he says vehemently, "I think we're all accountable for our actions. I do. Our actions and our *in*actions. It matters to me that we live that way. *I* try to live that way."

Marcus steers carefully through a curve on a roadway with no shoulder, no margin for error. Approaching town, he's threading a winding route through back roads and lanes, avoiding roadblocks. "Okay," he says, "I know that. I know how much self-discipline matters to you."

"I think you have no idea. How much it matters. When I am operating on false premises I am miserable."

"All right," says Marcus, confused, but conscious they approach dangerous ground.

"It's not all right," Kenrick says firmly. He sits face-forward, as rigid as if on the witness stand. "I want you to know I am partly responsible for Zef's difficult state. I passed to him a letter from his mother, that she directed to me to circumvent you. I am accountable for that."

Marcus takes a deep breath and expels it slowly. He tries to process what this extraordinary admission means. The Bentley is climbing the curves of Pitts Bay Road above the Great Sound, the final approach to Rose Hill. But the familiar world he views through the windshield seems to tilt now a few degrees off upright.

Kenrick, still not looking at him, says, "I need to know, Marcus, in what way you are accountable. How did Zef get that notebook? Why did he say you said it would assist Ramo's defense?"

On both sides of the road, the flame trees' broad canopies have leafed out. Soft green feathers. Lush. In only a week or so, as the temperature continues to rise, these trees will blossom, throwing crimson splashes of passion against blue sky, bluer sea, and the crenellated white rooftops of the spacious homes beneath them.

Marcus speaks slowly. His eyes seek Kenrick's. "I don't know by exactly what path the notebook moved from Heppering's hands to Zef's. I do have some idea. More importantly, I have a copy of the whole notebook, and yes, I will need to make it public now to bring Isaiah down."

Kenrick stiffens visibly. This is, Marcus sees, more revelation than he expected.

He hurries his words. "I've been reluctant to use this evidence before it was absolutely necessary because of...the interests of the party who provided it to me." He hears what he sounds like. Like Government. Like he is grabbing for plausible deniability.

"The woman," Kenrick spits. "The white woman."

Marcus sighs. "The woman, yes." He has to glance out the side window to hide his expression. He is amazed at how warmly the feeling of Lucy floods him, even as he damns himself by confessing her.

"The married expatriate white woman for whom you recently fixed a traffic ticket." Kenrick's voice is acidly contemptuous.

"You knew that?"

"Your friend on the force Eugene Outerbridge told me. Quite a few people know that and quite a bit more, Marcus. We're not stupid. We're not blind." Kenrick again beats his fingers against the cracked leather of the Bentley's sill. "What I did not know was that you have had the means to counter Isaiah and chose not to, to protect her."

"I didn't make that choice. I hadn't decided what to do, not until today. What's happened in the last few days—"

"How long, exactly, have you sat on this?" Kenrick is shouting. "How can you justify such selfishness? What you should have done for Lemuel, for Althea, for goddamn Ramo—for Zef, for God's sake—you've *not* done, for her sake."

"It's not that simple. What's she's done for me—"

"Fucking spare me what she's done for you."

Marcus does. Kenrick would not get it. He would not get anything about a white woman, especially not love and renewal.

"I'll do what has to be done now. We'll take the copy public today. But it won't necessarily help anyone. It may just fuel the fire. Create more chaos."

"Government will fall," Kenrick snaps. "Elections are five months away and now they'll happen sooner. You will stand and you will win."

"Or there will be anarchy and martial law, all over again, or worse. What happens if there's no confidence among the people in either party, if we have meaningless elections and some lame coalition at the helm?"

"Is this a situation out of control or an opportunity for significant change? For a damn revolution. A coup?"

"You tell me, Kenrick. You're the seer. You're the one fueled with such hot confidence in what I can do."

"I think I lost that," Kenrick says. "Your lies, your deception—and my own, about Zef, my stupid self-serving response to your depression and your indecisiveness—together we two fools have cost me that clarity. That balance."

Both men stare silently out their respective windows. On the pink stucco wall that encircles Rose Hill, someone pasted a poster of Lemuel Trott weeks ago. *Perseverance, and Hope!* it chirps. Since this morning someone has defaced it, the slogan and the wall a mess of illegible black spray paint epithets that nevertheless leave Lemuel's beatific face in view.

Marcus pulls the wheel hard right and swings the Bentley into Rose Hill's drive. Lemuel's life, and Lemuel's suffering, cannot be wasted. "By God," he tells Kenrick, "I will do what it takes—"

"The hell you will," Kenrick interrupts him, his voice venomous. "Because here's your bitch, ready to receive you."

Pulled well into Marcus's yard, screened but not hidden by the luxuriant overgrowth of blooming hibiscus flanking the veranda, is Lucy's red Fiesta. He sees her sitting inside, the back of her head, her pale flyaway hair, just visible on either side of the narrow peak of the contoured seat back. He's failed to answer her message, so she has come to his home to deliver it.

Kenrick leaves the car while it's still rolling. He slams the Bentley's dented, misaligned door with extravagant force, flings Marcus a look that names him not just traitor but coward, and walks away fast, down hill, toward town.

Marcus knows she's come to tell him their relationship has to end; he reads it on her face, and he doesn't argue.

Instead he rests his head on her breast and lets her heart drum the truth into his ear. They have seated themselves on the white leather couch in the living room, facing the wide-open french doors and the veranda, the frothy hibiscus and photogenic lawns spilling down the hill to the Sound with its bristle of sailboats. Zef is out. Mrs. Alvarra is not there either. They do not speak, but sit curled together, facing one another on the couch, his knees drawn up next to her hips and her thigh flush with his, both his arms around her, her hands cupping the nape of his neck, his face at her throat. She smells the way he knows she will smell—faint familiar perfume plus a tang of sweat from the long day's heat, overlaying the weak, sharp scent of her skin—and all together this closeness is a comfort, still, despite the fact that it's ending.

Eventually she speaks. Tells him she's been inside Basil's Dream, talked to Althea, spoken to Lemuel. She's seen how much depends on him, and how much she's got to face. When she left the cliff house this morning, Darrell was on the phone to New York, to TransGlobal's headquarters, demanding that his son and wife be evacuated immediately. Peyton would have been sent away already were it not for the closed airport.

"What happened today in Warwick was nicely timed to bolster his argument," Marcus says, describing for her the bulldozers and the Regiment on the move. He can picture Darrell Langston's distress, and it causes him a pang. That man is doing what he believes is best for his son.

"Peyton has to be my choice now," Lucy says quietly. "I have waited too long to make it." She strokes Marcus's back, as if he were the son, and he is grateful for the caress. Soon she will have to get up and leave. And he will stand up and do necessary things that trigger inevitable consequences.

"You will use Suggs's notebook now?" she asks.

"I will," he answers. "I have to." Briefly their foreheads touch. She has been a respite. She was never a place he could stay.

"You must go on being what you've always been," she says, her palm over his heart.

He shakes his head. "Maybe my mother did name my destiny," he says, touching Lucy's cheekbones.

How she believes in him. He kisses her, her mouth opens for his, and they go on sitting on the couch, wrapped in each other's arms and silence, with no impulse toward bed. Sex seems beside the point; they are surely as close now as they will ever be. For twenty minutes, for half an hour, they are still because when they move, their affair will end.

Finally she stirs. She kisses his eyelids and the corners of his mouth, studies his face, runs her hands up the length of his arms, then down his back, over his hips to his thighs, to memorize his body that way. She cries without making a sound. When he follows her to the door, he is crying, too.

"I'll see you again," he says.

She says, "We don't know that."

After a moment, he nods.

He sees her out, holds her face in his hands at the car door, and calls after her as she reverses in the drive—as if she'd be returning in time for dinner: "Be careful. I love you."

Back inside Rose Hill, gathering his keys, checking messages, preparing to find Zef and deliver copies of the notebook to Althea, the press, the police and the judiciary, he feels much as he did in the aftermath of his public beating in January—sore and disoriented—but this time at a far deeper level than in the body. Then he was mired in a depressive rut from trying for so long in the same ways to make people see what they wanted to forget. Then, the mirror showed him a weary, uncertain black man with a pummeled face. Now, his heart is lacerated but the face he'll show his people is who he really is, a vulnerable, newly hopeful man who feels twice born.

20

The following day, just before one o'clock, Darrell is summoned away from contentious negotiations with New York on TransGlobal's evacuation policy by a phone call from Jonathan Heppering. They must meet for lunch. A matter of importance they must discuss at once. No, absolutely it cannot wait; does Darrell not know that all hell is breaking loose in Parliament, in the press, in the streets of the western parishes? "Government's called out the Regiment," Jonathan adds before he rings off, "so do keep your wits about you. Those of us with common sense have lost a battle, and we may well lose the war."

Fuming at the man's highhanded manner, Darrell strides through the oddly empty downtown streets toward the restaurant Jonathan named, a pricey power lunch place. The rank piles of garbage on the curb and the sullen faces of the few people he passes along the way disgust Darrell. This country does not work because these people who so adamantly call it *their* island keep on shutting it down with their lethal pissing matches about who owns what and who used to own whom and what there is never enough of for any of them now, which is money. Other people's money! These islanders—especially the political leaders and more especially the black ones and most especially Marcus Passjohn—they talk the talk of economic self-determination constantly, but with neither the capital nor any resources other than salt and sand, they cannot walk it. These people need American business, but they cannot be nice about it. Even the intelligent and educated ones like Jonathan Heppering bite the hand that feeds them.

His pulse pounds in time with his footsteps, which are accelerating. The distance to the restaurant is short, less than four blocks, but the day is oppressively hot and the humidity rising. Sweat from Darrell's forehead runs down his neck to soak his stiff white collar.

The people at TransGlobal in New York are no brighter than the people he has to deal with here. Decision makers there are clueless about the way the local situation threatens not only his family but the survival of the insurance subsidiary they've charged him with managing. His family can hardly find food and they cannot even fly out of this hell hole now, and all the home office people can tell him about is their own internecine politics, this quarter's inadequate bottom line, and a post-9/11 forecast of indefinite recession, gloom and war. They were willing enough last month to ship him to Cayman to try his and the company's fortunes in a new office there, but whatever disasters may befall him, his wife and son — even the business once he gets there — that will all be his problem, whether or not he has any control over the circumstances.

When he gets to the restaurant, at one-fifteen, no customers are visible inside and no help is in sight. Tapping loudly on the glass front door, which is locked, Darrell manages to summon a waiter from the kitchen who lets him in but appears very nervous. He twists the linen napkin that should have been draped smartly over the arm of his dinner jacket, and his long upper lip trembles, making his callow face even less attractive. He's an Aussie by his accent; no doubt he wishes he'd stayed down under. Briskly, Darrell ascertains that he *can* have lunch — the door was locked "for security" — but that the single entree is swordfish, which has been frozen.

"Fine," Darrell tells him acidly. "We'll be two for the swordfish, only do thaw it out."

The waiter does not laugh, and Darrell finds he cannot

help taking that personally. He is doing the best he can under ridiculously stressful circumstances, and even if the joke was at his expense, the man could spare a laugh.

He downs a weak gin and tonic, although he ordinarily never drinks at lunch, while he waits for Jonathan and the fish. Incredibly, given his insistence on the meeting, Jonathan is late. Twenty minutes after arriving, Darrell has nearly finished his entree and is angrily studying his surroundings: the vacant banquettes curling around a dozen tables glittering with crystal stemware and ornate silver cutlery, on linens so thick and white and stiff with starch, they bring to mind the arc of a well-trimmed sail against the island's typically cloudless sky.

Cutlery and crystal ring together as Jonathan bumps Darrell's table, angling himself into the banquette. He's flushed and the thin strands of hair normally slicked tightly across his bald pate are disheveled.

Before Darrell can ask why the hell he is just now getting here, the fretful waiter who's relocked the door behind Jonathan repeats for him his doleful information about the available entree and the unfortunate fact of its having been frozen.

"We try always to serve only *fresh* fish and produce," he says, tweaking the napkin on his arm, "but under the present difficulties we've had to adjust."

"There's quite the premium on adjustment, these days," Jonathan replies curtly. The waiter turns on his heel and Jonathan, ignoring him, says, "Next we'll be boiling shoe leather."

"What's happened?"

"You do need to know," Jonathan replies. He pauses, then plunges on briskly. "I was delayed because there have been new developments, and because I needed confirmation on some information coming from the Premier's office. You do not need to know why I am privy to such information, but within the next hour the Governor and the Premier will likely impose martial law."

Darrell cannot immediately grasp what he should worry

about first. He swallows, with difficulty, a small dry bite of fish.

Jonathan continues. "The reason for this egregious situation, which will no doubt complete the exodus of foreign companies like yours, is a certain notebook listing a certain set of payoffs. Yes. The contents of that notebook with which you were once familiar are being read right now at the *Royal Gazette*, as well as at the television station, and on the floor in Parliament, distributed in photocopy form yesterday evening by our socially irresponsible Opposition leader Mr. Passjohn. The newspaper will not publish it, of course, and martial law will make that doubly certain. But the information is circulating anyway. Every troublemaker on the island apparently has a copy, as well, and they're making more copies, by the damn dozens."

The waiter appears, bearing Jonathan's plate and its cloud of complex aroma—grilled fish, pepper, and roasted, garlicky potatoes. Darrell feels nauseous. While Jonathan sets to his meal, cutting, spearing, and eating, Darrell places a bite of potato in his mouth, tries to chew, and gives up. He washes the lump down his throat with a swig of lukewarm water.

"*They* will bring down the government instead of us," Jonathan says. "That will be the result of what you have allowed to happen."

"Me?" Darrell hears himself sputter. The waiter hovers nearby, vindictively attentive.

"Do you still have the original notebook in your possession?"

"Yes." Darrell lies for the sake of argument.

"Well, then," Jonathan replies, cocking his head as if amused, "I do wonder how a copy of a document you are holding made its way to *their* hands."

"I have no idea."

"Well, then, let me tell you something else you need to know, Langston." Jonathan's hands lie idle on either side of his plate, palms flat, thick fingers flexed. "Your wife, like your son, has made some unusual choices in terms of *friends*."

Briefly Darrell shuts his eyes. The stiff linen of the tablecloth beneath his fingertips feels as institutionally thick as hospital sheets.

"Felicity has confided in me," Jonathan goes on, "that she came upon Lucy, several weeks ago, in the woods, at Spanish Rock, in the sole company of Marcus Passjohn."

From the kitchen Darrell hears the sound of dropped glass breaking and a stifled curse. He hears as well the sound of his own blood, coursing through the arteries in his throat.

Jonathan looks at him quite steadily. Darrell flinches from the absence of pity in the man's gaze. "The sooner you both leave," Jonathan states, "the better. Better for you, and better for the island."

The waiter zooms in close to ask if everything is satisfactory. Darrell draws breath, and Jonathan answers in the affirmative. He also asks for the check.

Slowly, Darrell pushes his chair back from the table. He considers withdrawing to the men's room, his brain sluggishly weighing the benefits of retreat against the cost of the additional humiliation. Jonathan, getting up, spares him the decision.

"I must run on," he says. "Many matters press me." He places his business card on the table, a sign to the waiter to charge the bill to his firm. The gesture runs Darrell right through. Jonathan is the epitome of British probity; neither Darrell nor his employer will be expected to pay for this informative lunch.

He stands up himself then, realizing he'll likely not see Jonathan again, and wondering what on earth is the proper form of close under the circumstances.

"Good-bye," Jonathan says. Without meeting Darrell's eyes again he adds, "News like this is political news and the responses to it are political too, some of them predictable, none of them easily contained. Look to your own, Langston, and look sharp."

Darrell waits for the door to shut behind Jonathan, then makes his own way toward it, determined not to stumble. The waiter rushes ahead of him, holds the door wide with a smile, and wishes him a G'day.

Blinking, Darrell stands alone on the slate sidewalk beneath a scorching white sun, flanked by hanging baskets of fuchsia. The suit he swelters in feels like a skin that should not be his. He wants to know what has happened, what *exactly* has happened—to him, his wife, his family—because he does not get it. All his life he has worked hard to do what he thought he was supposed to do. In five-star restaurants like the one behind him, in penthouse boardrooms and the wide seats of first-class transatlantic flights, he has always felt like a warrior. But now, swiping sweat from his face by the handful, he understands he's a grunt, and always has been.

Lucy's trip to and from Somers Academy to pick up Peyton requires almost three hours. She has to take a slow and circuitous route because both the Regiment and groups of protestors block the roads, and twice the car is searched at armed checkpoints. Neither the car radio nor the soldiers who stop her explain why all this is happening, but she knows: Marcus has kept his promise to act. And Peyton, the moment he climbs in the car, tells her what he knows, what everyone says at school: Government is falling. After delivering this news, he sits silently, staring straight ahead, occasionally nipping at his bloody cuticles, while she concentrates on the road, equally silent and tense. When they finally reach the relative safety of the cliff house, she feels lightheaded and jittery, pushing the key into the lock.

In the living room, the chintz-covered couch and wing chairs from the house in Connecticut—where life was orderly, where she knew, always, what was expected in every situation, at least until the last hours of the last day, when Peyton disappeared—that old furniture from the old house that is no longer theirs stands stiff and mute and misplaced in front of a window wall of hot empty sky and blank blue sea. The door latch clicks shut behind her, Peyton steps past her toward his room, and Darrell comes charging into the foyer from his study. She is surprised to find him home early from the office, and she is more surprised by the plain fact of hatred gleaming in his eyes and focused on her.

A sound comes out of him, a hiss of contempt, or misery. He is ruddy and perspiring. Lucy knows he knows something about what she's done; the question is what, and from whom, and what he'll do in response. She stops, to let happen what will happen, and she's surprised all over again when Peyton stops, too, standing between her and Darrell. She knows her boy will not take her hand, like he always used to, in fear and in joy in their kingdom *à deux* that sometimes excluded Darrell and more often made up for his absences.

Seizing his son by the arm and bodily removing him from his path, Darrell says, "Peyton is not leaving this house again, not until he leaves the island. And you" — shaking a finger in Lucy's face — "don't you even think about helping him do anything else. Leave him alone. You've done enough."

Peyton's eyes, when hers seek them, turn her back like two shiny stones. They tell her she is indeed useless to him, and he to her. Darrell's hand clamps shut on her arm, hurting her.

"Darrell, Darrell," she says, because what she thinks, what she feels, cannot be said. Too much to be funneled through thin words.

He bursts out, "You *stole* from me."

She struggles to know what to say.

"Don't lie," he demands. "Don't lie anymore."

His face is livid, his grip predatory, and she comprehends he genuinely wants to tear her apart. And that he might do it. Ducking, twisting, she tries to get away. She means to save them both from his rage, but he blocks her. He seizes her by both shoulders and shakes. "*You* stole that notebook from my desk. You gave it to Marcus Passjohn. You gave him that, and a hell of a lot more."

Her head snaps back and forth. "I took it," she hears Peyton cry out.

"You're lying, too," he shouts, shoving Lucy hard against the wall. "The both of you are full of lies. Jonathan Heppering told me what's going on. Heppering explained to me what everybody seems to know already about my wife and that black man."

"Shut up, shut up," Peyton yells. He is between them, his skinny arms in front of Lucy's face, his hands on Darrell's chest, shoving.

"You shut up," Darrell shouts back, louder.

With a hand on each of them and all the force she possesses, Lucy pushes them apart, and Darrell's open palm smacks the side of her skull. She hits the floor. The skin of her cheek and scalp burns, her ear rings, and she's banged elbow and hip on the floor so hard they're numb, but she is far more stunned than injured. They all are.

Slowly Lucy gets to her knees. Her marriage is destroyed. Her husband hates her. Her son will never be what he would have been had all this not happened. In Darrell's view all of this is her fault and he must be right, because she *has* done the things he says she has done. Of course she should not have done such things. She was supposed to be loyal to her husband. She should never have made Peyton tell lies to hide her mistakes, nor lied to him in pursuit of her own dreams. And then like a warm place in an icy lake, she feels Marcus. She feels in her cells what his love is like: his kind attention, their fiercely joyous sex, and the long talks that were not just heart-to-heart but mind-to-mind, that made her feel alive and lively instead of frightened and alone—and she sinks back down to sit on the cold tile floor. Everything in front of her from now on will be different from anything she's known before—another kind of move, another long, bending road. She will live past this day. She will. But she cannot imagine how.

She slumps on the tiles in the foyer, her head against the wall. Darrell quietly orders Peyton to his room. She listens to her husband lock the doors and drive nails into the window sashes from outside the house—to keep Peyton in, she presumes, as well as trouble out. Then she watches Darrell sit down in the living room, alone in a chintz-covered wing chair, cracking his knuckles like a guard.

So few days ago she thought she knew what she needed to do to make things come out right, and yesterday she did it. She thought she had in that way reclaimed the responsibility she'd shirked while she stole for herself what she needed to live. She thought that with a hard decision and a difficult act she could stop more mess from happening.

Now she sees it's more ambiguous than that. Problems don't get finished up; mistakes can't be closed out. One thing turns into another relentlessly, waves advancing, breaking and withdrawing, one giving way to the next, washing some things away but always, always, bringing more.

21

Peyton sits cross-legged in the middle of his bedroom floor, alone with the lights turned off, striking over and over again the lighter that used to be Zef's. The heavy silver cylinder bearing Zef's initials scratched over Marcus's fits snugly in his palm. Beneath his sore, determined thumb, the metal wheel spins and the flame responds. Each effort produces a predictable result, and that pleases him.

It's late, well after midnight. His parents have fallen asleep, his father stretched out on the living room couch, wearing his clothes, even his shoes, and his mother by herself in their bed.

Each small flare of butane stands out red against the blackness of his unlit room. Each flame, a wavering bright hood above a tight blue heart. The rasp of wheel on flint sounds loud inside the silence of this house, an emptiness that feels thick and hot.

Peyton thinks only about exactly what is before his eyes: his scuffed and filthy sneakers. Their untied, flopping laces. His bony shins and narrow calves, a lacework of old pale scars and new scratches beneath a fine, almost invisible net of newly sprouted blond hairs. The hairs make him think about turning thirteen in three months and seven days, and where he might be by then, but resolutely he returns his thoughts to the things precisely in front of him. He stares at things and then at the thoughts of the things until they blend with each other and fuse with his feelings. Gradually as the minutes pass he reduces everything he sees and thinks and feels to the pinpoint of flame he can produce at will.

He stands up. He sinks the lighter in his pocket and for twenty minutes works on the window glass with masking tape from his desk drawer. When he has it completely covered, he spreads a bath towel against the glass to muffle the sound, then breaks it with a hammer, retrieved from the kitchen, the same one his father used to drive in the nail Peyton levers out once he's removed enough taped glass to allow him to reach it. He lifts the sash, climbs out the window and leaves it open. He sees no reason to close it; he's not planning to be back. He scrambles up the hillside to the road and then jogs.

He takes the South Shore Road, loping along the crumbling asphalt that tracks the curves high above rocky coves and pale pink beaches, winding his way toward town under strong moonlight. The familiar route is long and strange traversed by foot; he sees no one for so long a time he becomes his footfalls and his pouring sweat. The night is humid, the air almost too thick to pull through his nostrils into his lungs. When he cannot run any more, he stops in the middle of the road, panting, hands on thighs, wishing for water. His sneakers are red with the island's dust, and somewhere he has run through flowers, fallen white petals of oleander that cling to the laces. He rests, walks, and runs again. Nearly an hour later he reaches town, and his progress slows. Turning off the main road to skirt the checkpoints, easily visible from a distance, he discovers that anyone else moving in the long shadows tossed down by the high white moon avoids him well before it's necessary for him to avoid them.

He gets lost for a while in the back of town, trotting down unlit streets past small dirty houses, some of them with goats and chickens and their nasty smells in the front yards. His legs shake, from exhaustion, dehydration, and indecision. He left his parents' house decisively—disappearing from their lives and taking charge of his own—but now the question of what next looms too large to ponder clearly.

He runs again, flinging himself from uncertainty into imagination. He is a rebel, a guerrilla, a freedom fighter. He is his own game, armed and dangerous inside the video of his mind. He sprints not across vacant dirt lots and the empty streets fringing the island's picturesque downtown and the green lawns of prosperous houses abutting it, but down tangled alleys in an embattled Afghan border town. He presses cheat codes that drop both Riley and Zef into the game with him, and all of them cradle Kalashnikovs in their arms. Dodging sniper fire and returning it, leaping craters from a long night's shelling, the three of them duck cursing and lucky into the shallow cover of a limestone bus shelter.

In this way he reaches Rose Hill, two hours and ten kilometers from his parents' house. He gives wide berth to the veranda, where lights are burning and Marcus is visible — sprawled asleep in a canvas slingback chair, papers in his lap, chin on chest. He is snoring. Keeping to the shadow of the oleander hedge, Peyton moves quickly around the house to the other side, pushes through stiff hibiscus and arrives at the sill of the room he knows is Zef's. The louvered shutter hangs low above the window like a barely lifted eyelid but the sash beneath it is open. Peyton heaves himself to the sill and speaks Zef's name.

He gets no response. The room is dark but as his eyes adjust, he sees Zef sitting on the floor, knees drawn up, eyes wide open. He returns Peyton's stare with recognition but no greeting and no sign of surprise. Because he is very thirsty, Peyton climbs in through the window and asks Zef for water. With no change in his expression, Zef shoves toward him, with his bare foot, a quart bottle of Aquafina, half full, lying on the floor beside him. His head lolls back against the mattress. Peyton empties the container, then takes in his surroundings. The room has been trashed and marginally tidied. Furniture stands upright and the floor is mostly clear, but two holes gape in the wall, clothes and toiletries and broken knick-knacks lie in heaps, and nothing remains on the walls but empty hooks and shreds of poster clinging to squares of double-stick tape.

"What happened?"

"Fight," Zef replies flatly.

"Who won?"

"Nobody."

Peyton tosses the empty bottle to the bed and sits down on the floor facing Zef. "You hurt?" he asks.

Zef shakes his head, still expressionless. He doesn't ask Peyton why he's shown up here tonight — even though they've not seen each other in the nearly two weeks since Zef ran from Ramo's arrest. Peyton doesn't explain. He's not sure what answer he would give, anyway. Zef looks raggedy. He looks bad, actually ill, and this troubles Peyton but it also makes him angry. He needs a friend and Zef is the only candidate.

"Come on, let's take a ride," he says. He nudges Zef's foot with his foot. "You need to move. You look like a zombie."

Zef makes eye contact. "You think?" he says. "I look undead?" He snorts and looks away.

Between thumb and forefinger he rubs something rapidly. Peyton cranes to see, and Zef snaps his fist closed around an orange button and returns his gaze to the ceiling. His fist goes in his pocket. "It's martial law," he says. "You know that? Anybody goes anywhere, they get arrested."

"I got here just fine. Nobody stopped me."

Zef shrugs.

Seconds pass. Peyton tries Ramo as bait. "Let's ride to Casemates."

Zef shrugs again. "What's the point? I can't see him. They're nailing him for murder."

Peyton stands up. "Ramo didn't kill anybody."

Zef looks up, meets his eyes with no hedging, and Peyton gets a strange sensation. The angle of their looking has always gone the other way. Zef says, "That's the truth, but the truth makes no fucking difference. Ramo's fucked. People lied and he's fucked."

"Everybody lies, if it gets them what they want. You're the one told me that. Remember? You told me to grow up and learn to lie, like everybody else. You remember?"

"Fucking Ramo." Zef addresses himself. "He fucking gave himself to the cops."

"You wanted to see him. You're the reason he came downstairs and that's why they got him."

Zef's head sinks into his hands. His shoulders convulse.

Jittery, hands unsteady, Peyton digs in his pocket. He pulls out the silver lighter and flicks it for Zef. A little flame stands between them like it did the night they carved Zef's name over his father's. He pushes it closer and closer to Zef's face until the heat of it makes his eyes open. When he reaches for it, Peyton backs away.

"Come on," he says. "We got to move, while we can."

Zef shifts, like he might get up. "Ramo's shop. They're gonna knock it down."

"That's right," Peyton says. He backs away another step. "And the letter from your mother. You want it, don't you, before they plow it under?"

Their eyes lock. Zef on the floor. Peyton standing over him.

Zef curses. He scrambles up and rummages for shoes and ties them on. He roots in the nightstand's drawer for the key to the scooter. When he has it, they shimmy out the window and roll the scooter down the hill out of earshot of Rose Hill where Zef kick-starts it and Peyton gets on behind.

To avoid the Regiment's barricades at the entrance to town, Peyton sends Zef along the Serpentine Road through the back of town, and afterwards they slip eastward into green and rolling Devonshire, using country lanes bound with flowering hedgerows to deliver them by roundabout route to the main road south of town. Everywhere the houses are darkened and the streets empty, as if martial law is a spell that puts good people to bed. But descending Crow Lane, where the s-curves are as narrow and more tightly kinked than a real hairpin, they almost smash into the rear of a boxy and dented Toyota van running downhill with its lights off.

Zef veers and they do not collide but in the second the scooter hangs beside the van, Peyton dimly sees white faces on the other side of a large dusty square of tinted glass, and the expression he sees most clearly is a quizzical stare on a boy's pudgy face between a sudsy pile of curls and a thick neck straining the collar of a dark sweatshirt. Thinking no more than the name "Thomas," Peyton forms the word "Quack" on his lips and bubbles it at the boy who may or may not be his schoolyard tormentor just as the van's driver accelerates, cuts off the scooter in the middle of a curve and speeds away, bearing west, while Zef jumps the curb—and only because it is low and broken in exactly that spot, succeeds in not crashing.

They careen to a stop in dirt and put their feet on the ground. "Assholes," Zef breathes, wiping his hands on his jeans while Peyton, touching a bump on his forehead where it banged Zef's skull, says, "Yeah. Fuck 'em." He feels loose inside.

From there they take the Harbour Road slowly, the narrow pavement exposed to any eyes that may be watching from the harbor or the elegant houses facing it. Gazing out across the sheltered black water, thick with buoys, boats and private piers, Peyton sees orange flames across the harbor on the docks alongside town and two more patches of fire in the distant western parishes toward which they are headed. Fear floods his jumpy insides. Briefly and intensely he feels exactly twelve years old, the boy he was when he first came to the island, before he started learning to unhook what happens now from what happens next. He squeezes the lighter in his pocket, and returns his mind to the games of his own making.

When they get there, the massive yellow bulldozers sit unguarded, Althea's house is shut up tight and dark, except for a square of light falling into the narrow alley dividing it from Ramo's, but the shop—also dark—has been torn open, the shutters and frayed door ripped off, and its contents— Ramo's ratty possessions and his customers' broken scooters and appliances pulled out willy nilly into the dirt and tossed amid the burst garbage bags, oily newspapers and wet garbage dumped from the trash bins, and tires from the salvage pile in the alley. Over it all hangs the fresh reek of gasoline, stinging Peyton's nose, and causing his eyes to tear.

Zef cuts the scooter's engine and coasts it wobbling into the alley alongside the shop. A white face laced in a dark hoodie appears briefly at Ramo's window only inches from their faces and immediately more hooded figures dash out the door. One lags behind, laden with a gasoline can, large and orange and obviously heavy. He drops it to speed his escape and Peyton leaps off the scooter. The can's handle is warm in his hand when he looks up and sees the vandals' destination just beyond the bulldozers—that dusty Toyota van.

Maybe it's because of the remnants of the game in Peyton's head. Or maybe it's his suspicion that one of the people inside the dark hoods is Thomas Heppering. As he hoists the can above his head, he hates Thomas for tormenting him and that black boy Deshon Bridgers, whose house got gasolined and gutted. Thomas's house got firebombed too but Peyton skids past that fact. What he knows in this moment is his strength. It's superhuman. He feels nothing but the power of his rage. Lurching beneath the can's weight he runs after the last man escaping. "Quack," he yells. *Quack, quack, quack.* Inside his game there's a huge quacking explosion and the van blows up and disappears.

But the Toyota spins its tires and peels out fast. He trips and the can slams the ground and gurgles. He gets up and finds Zef staring. He staggers toward him, upending the can now and letting the stinking gas come glugging out over the dozers' half-tracks and the ground and his feet and the trash and scooter parts and appliances he stumbles over. When the can's empty, he lets it drop. He feels empty now. He tells Zef, "I'm gonna blow this shit up."

"Blow yourself up," Zef says. "Gas all over you."

Peyton looks down at his wet shoes and his wet shorts. Lights pop on inside the houses behind them and people talk loud. A chained dog jumps up and down in a barking frenzy. There isn't much time.

He pulls out the lighter that used to be Zef's and offers to returns it. "You do it," he says. "For Ramo, you do it. Blow this shit to hell."

He slaps the lighter into Zef's palm.

Zef says, "Get the letter. Go get it for me."

And he does. Scrambling over debris, scraping his bare knees and banging his shins, running with sweat that won't dry, he gropes in the dark for the counter and then the till and pulls from the cubby beneath it the letter he saw Zef hide there. He tucks it inside his pants and stumbles out into the alley toward the open window spilling its light, throwing a rainbow slick across a puddle of gasoline, and finds the old man watching. Mr. Trott in his chair so close to the sill, his chest, snowy-haired in an open-throated nightshirt. His hat has dropped out the window. Peyton picks it up, brushes it off, smells gasoline but drops it back on Mr. Trott's head anyway. It fits like a lid.

The old man's eyes jerk wide open. He's looking past Peyton, who spins and feels heat paint him at the same moment a boom shakes him and flame comes running over the gasolined dirt across the dozers into the shop, racing for Peyton's feet like a greedy grasping tongue.

Zef passes him, running. Peyton sees the lighter drop. The angry dog rattles heaven. Doors open and people scream.

"Fire!" Peyton yells at Mr. Trott. "Get away from the window!" And then he runs. He becomes his feet.

He runs faster than he ever has in his life and pulls even with Zef. There's more light than there should be on Zef's face, the fire behind them but Zef's skin washed pale in glaring light. A police car blocks their path, pinning them in its headlights' sweep. Two officers, one tall and black, one wide and white, get out. The white one lifts his radio to his mouth. He says, "Fire." The black one says, "Halt," and they do. Time halts, too. It cranks down so slow Peyton sees every motion of the officers' approach. Two men float toward him weightless and heavy at the same time, astronauts in a moonwalk, their faces shrinking and expanding on the heartbeat of his glassy fear.

He is caught. He prepares to die. He will tell them he didn't mean to do it. He will tell them he didn't do it. After all, Zef struck the spark. Falling to his knees, Peyton looks at Zef. He has to look up.

"Eugene," Zef says, breathless. "*Officer* Outerbridge." He speaks with a deference in his voice Peyton has never heard and cannot believe him capable of.

With one hand Zef scrubs at his baby dreadlocks as if he could erase them. The other hand he extends palm-up, a plea. For an impossibly stretched-out moment nothing happens. Then the tall and skinny black cop steps squarely in front of the white one, shoves Zef clear of the headlights toward the road and speaks brusquely to Peyton. "Explain to me exactly what you've been doing here, son."

Peyton opens his mouth. No sound comes out. His heart nearly does. Fear has flung it that far up his throat. He hears people shouting and cursing and the sound of water hitting fire and shovels striking dirt. He hears sirens far away and getting closer. But all he can see is Zef's back, disappearing into the cover of thick, pink-flowered oleander bushes. The capacity to generate speech has deserted Peyton and he can explain nothing to his captors. Yet his vision remains sharp. For the longest seconds in the world, while the cops berate him and then shove him, a thick hand pressing his skull, into the backseat of the cruiser, Peyton sees Zef running, leaving him behind.

Althea Trott, in bed with a beau in Sandy's Parish, dreams of her brother inside a blue heart of flame.

Lemuel calls, *Sister? Sister!*

Her breathing grows harsh. Her lungs heavy and wet. She tosses and groans, flings the sheets aside and disturbs her beau, who sits up and shakes her.

Lemuel lets go. A runner passes, lithe and glistening with sweat. Loquats ripen on all the trees. "De Lord!" Lemuel calls. "I goin' right in!"

Flowers burst into bloom in moldy corners all over the island. Althea sits up, and blinks.

22

Lemuel Trott's funeral is a state occasion. On a brilliantly sunny, relentlessly hot and humid day early in May, the Anglican Cathedral of the Most Holy Trinity in downtown Hamilton is packed with hundreds of the people whom Lemuel waved through more than two decades of morning and evening commutes, with Government footing the bill for his mahogany casket ordered from New York, a thick blanket of resurrection lilies flown in from Atlanta, and silk bunting on his bier bearing the motto from the island's flag: *Quo Fata Ferunt.* Whither fate leads.

Althea's house still stands, but Ramo's Cycle Repair, barely ten feet away and thoroughly soaked in arsonists' gasoline, is a heap of cinders now. Lemuel died from smoke inhalation, his lungs—already pleurisied from his long years of confinement to his chair—overwhelmed by the fumes from discarded motor oil and scooter tires piled for salvage inside and outside the shop.

The hospital reopened the night of the fire to receive him, workers returning voluntarily to their shifts as word reached them. Five days later, when he died, the airport opened because the flowers and the casket had to land, somehow. In the days in-between, both the general strike that paralyzed the island and the civil disorder that terrorized it quieted. The sanitation workers, the bus drivers, and the stevedores went back to work because food and medicine had to be located and delivered — to the hospital, first, and then to everyone else — and to do that the mess in the streets had to be picked up and the gridlock on the docks unwound. The most militant members of the union turned to shooing or shaming the looters and the hooligans home. The Tuckers' vigilantes lay low, embarrassed by reports that a Toyota van seen speeding away from the fire scene — and traced to one of their members — had filled gas cans at a black-owned station in the back of town earlier that night. The British governor went on television to proclaim a national day of mourning and rescind martial law, the roadblocks stood unmanned, and the streets became safer as well as cleaner.

Such a number of good outcomes from so terrible an event, Marcus tells himself as his middle-aged knees sink stiffly into a kneeler armored in the needlepoint of the cathedral's Ladies' Auxiliary. Still, the fact that Lemuel Trott receives a white man's funeral in a colonialist church disturbs him. Lemuel, perhaps the only genuinely religious man Marcus has ever known, would surely have preferred the open air and rough turf of the National Stadium, the only other venue large enough for this crowd, and Althea, lifelong pillar of the Emmanuel Zion A.M.E. Church, must be, at some level, offended. He observes, several pews ahead of him, Althea's broad shoulders and the absence of gold hoops in her ears and the plain black turban on her head. Had she even been asked by Government what she wanted for the funeral of the brother she's tended for thirty years?

Marcus rises wearily to his feet for the Collect and the Old Testament lesson, traditional verses from *Lamentations*. The eerie peace bestowed on so much of the island by Lemuel's death has not extended to his household. Three days ago, the commissioner of police — white, Ulster Irish, obviously deeply regretting the blemished record of command his assignment to this black place has earned him — called on Marcus in the very early morning. "Is your son home?" the commissioner inquired in response to Marcus's startled greeting. "Of course," he replied, pulling at the tie of his bathrobe and glancing for confirmation at Zef's closed door and the discarded Nikes in the hallway suggesting he was indeed behind it.

The commissioner ushered himself past Marcus into the living room and pulled from his jacket pocket a plastic baggy, the kind that could hold either lunch or evidence, and Marcus saw inside it the heavy silver cigarette lighter that disappeared some time ago from his coffee table, that bore his own initials in curling monogram and now, overtop those, some crude scratching that caused him to snatch the bag from the commissioner's red-haired hand, examine it closely, and lift to the man's florid face an expression he knew was nakedly stricken.

By the time the commissioner left Rose Hill, after ten minutes of careful and very nervous negotiation by indirection, they had agreed that Zef would not be charged for the time being, nor would he be questioned. Yet. Until he is, he's to stay at home, with a plainclothes officer watching him to ensure it. This arrangement is to continue until after the funeral. Until "certain other parties" — Marcus knows this means Peyton Langston — file a statement, or choose not to. Things are to be left to drift until some "better" moment when the unnatural quiet magically conferred by the shock of Lemuel's loss will have grown somehow more entrenched and not more fragile, an improbable moment when the distraction of the funeral still holds but before public attention rivets on new questions and old angers and a fresh round of politically destabilizing uncertainty about the real cause of this death.

Every citizen has seen or heard by now something about the evidence in that notebook, hotly denied by those it impugns, that Government had a hand — financed by its local business partners — in sparking many of the island's troubles over the past year. Protestors from both ends of the political spectrum have barely cleared the streets. Horace Tucker's murder remains unresolved, while the dumpster ghosts of Rufus and Breem still aspire to black martyr status and may achieve it, if Ramo is convicted and joins them. Already the economy lies in shambles. To those prepared to seize on and twist the threads of this tangle — the old, persistent grudge — what would it mean if Marcus Passjohn's son is named responsible for this latest and most costly loss?

Marcus can throw up his hands at the politics swirling around this funeral, but he can't stop touching his own sore feelings of responsibility and loss. The lighter from the scene of the fire is a fact Zef won't explain. The night of the blaze Zef came home on foot at four in the morning, waking Marcus when he stumbled crossing the veranda to let himself in. He stopped Zef from going into his room. He sat his drawn and shaking son down on the white leather couch in the living room where only hours earlier he'd laid his head on Lucy's chest. He drew from him the barest synopsis of what had happened—Peyton's insistence that they ride, the van, the gas, the fire, and Eugene, who'd let him go. At that point they didn't know Lemuel had been affected. He asked Zef, his voice low and level, "Which one of you started the fire?"

Zef meticulously shredded the frayed margins of a rip in the thigh of his jeans into a finer and finer fringe. Finally he raised his face and said, "You'll have to ask Peyton. Or her."

Marcus is aware now, through Eugene, that Peyton, because of his age and his expatriate status, has been remanded to his parents' custody. His questioning, too, has been delayed, pending a possible statement, but no matter what Peyton admits or denies, his case will likely be resolved by Immigration, which will deport him like all troublemaking expats, along with his parents. The shaky, one-plank bridge he and Zef built between them when Zef spoke and he listened is the good work of Lucy, Marcus tells himself, standing shoulder to shoulder with hundreds of mourners as the Gospel is read. The innocent good of her belief in his value to his people and to his son, and the carnal good of her loving body that warmed him even after she drove away. Yet that intangible, possessed-only-by-him goodness ripped away like the wall of his abdomen, guts attached and dangling, when Zef invoked "Peyton, *or her*." Hearing that, he *knew* Zef had been the one to touch flame to fuel, but that he holds Peyton—and through Peyton, *her*—responsible. And that means *he*—Marcus—is the one really responsible. All this loss is the result of his cowardice, his failure to act.

Lucy and Peyton are here at the funeral, behind Marcus by several rows and across the aisle but within view each time he turns his head. At first he hardly recognized her, in a hat and a black dress with long sleeves. Straitened, serious clothes. She looks English in that hat that hides her face and matronly in the dress, too big for her fine-boned frame.

Her husband is not with them. Peyton, beside her, blond and gawky, choke-chained in an unaccustomed tie, kneels and rises along with her, turning prayer book pages in fractionally-delayed tandem, she instructing him in an unfamiliar practice while he listens and follows. He's a child. But he is not innocent. What has he done? Does he know what he's done? Does she?

The rector begins his homily. Fox-faced and flaxen-haired, he's completely English. In the round raised pulpit, sweating in the green yoke of his chasuble, he's a weak bulb in an exposed socket.

Marcus came today intending to eulogize Lemuel if Althea would allow him. Now he walks to her pew, taps her shoulder and asks. She opens her mouth to speak, then closes it, and signs him, Yes, go ahead. He has never known her to be speechless, no matter the occasion. It strikes him that her volume, the very force of her nature, has been turned down.

The rector gives way when Marcus approaches; he stops speaking in mid-sentence and yields the pulpit, but Marcus takes the lectern. He doesn't want the pulpit's sanctifying height. Facing the crowd of Lemuel's mourners — the sincere and the insincere, the genuinely broken, the curious, and the opportunistic — Marcus says the things he should have said to Lemuel's face. That Lemuel was a simple man but never, and perhaps especially not in these last years, a simpleton. That Lemuel always loved deeply and spontaneously and well, and that his love had been a floor and a force in Marcus's life from his earliest orphaned years when that love was delivered on two strong legs in the form of odd small treasures placed into small hands, to his current middle years, when Lemuel's capacious forgiveness has served as both absolution and goad, the first of which Marcus did not deserve and the second of which he sorely needs and will forever miss.

"Lemuel Trott was a good man, and I am a bad man. He labored to make me better, and I failed him. I failed to become the brave and accountable man he considered me to already be. Between us we made perhaps a whole man, neither wholly good nor wholly bad, but with Lemuel gone, I have lost my compass and my ballast."

Some of these people in the ornate pews do not want his too-personal words to fall on them. They shut their eyes, turn away, look up, or down. The ceiling or their shoes or the creases of their trousers become important. All of them are perspiring in the building heat of the lengthening morning. Althea, her eyes heavy, looks so steadily into his that he knows she has something to tell him. Eugene Outerbridge, rigid in a stiff-starched dress uniform, keeps his gaze fixed unblinkingly on Marcus's face. The Premier and the Governor, black and white, sit side-by-side between bodyguards in the front pew, conferring in whispers. Isaiah Barnes, from whom they distanced themselves the moment his schemes on their behalf became public, sits by himself in the back, plump hands gripping the pew in front of him. Grizzled Harry Pitkin from Tourism, six weeks from early retirement since there are no more tourists to minister, sits with his face in his hands but flanked by his family of six children and their children. Kenrick—with whom Marcus has not spoken since they parted in anger at the foot of his driveway more than a week ago—leans against a column in shadow, arms folded on his chest, studying Lucy like a map. Her eyes Marcus cannot see. The brim of her hat obscures her expression. Peyton's eyes are frantic, clawing the air between Marcus and himself, and Marcus avoids looking at them.

When he steps down, others, one by one, make their way to the lectern. The rector closes his missal and sits down in the nave, and the funeral assumes the air of a subdued revival with testimonials and confessions.

Seated, Marcus steals another look at Lucy. She's turned away, speaking to Peyton. Tired and over-warm, Marcus slumps into unhappy thoughts of Zef—at home, silent, frightened nearly catatonic although he will not admit it— and the man in an ill-fitting suit and ugly tie who watches him, and Mrs. Alvarra, stern and sternly loyal, watching them both. Finally, when no more eulogists step forward, someone begins the formal prayers, the Lord's Prayer and the people's prayers, the well-worn words a drone as bells chime the noon hour. Then the rector reclaims his place to announce with lilting finality the commendation of the body, and Marcus and the others who are to be pallbearers rise to make their way toward the casket. He's hardly left his pew when Isaiah lunges up the aisle to seize him by the elbow.

The man's jowly face is a puzzle, all the pieces of his expression trying to work themselves together into a coherent message but failing to fit. He says, *sotto voce* and urgent, "This morning Ramo Wylie confessed to Horace Tucker's killing."

Marcus blinks. Not until this moment has he considered how Ramo might react to Lemuel's loss. "Someone's told him about Lemuel?" Marcus asks. He glances toward the casket and sees Althea stolidly making her way down the aisle toward him, bucking a current of mourners who attempt to detain her, repeatedly, with handclasps or embraces.

Isaiah's thick fingers curl in the cloth of Marcus's jacket sleeve. "I don't know what that son of a bitch knows, or thinks. But he dictated this to the jailer."

He thrusts at Marcus a letter, handwritten on cheap notebook paper in block capitals, unpunctuated and littered with misspellings. It is indeed a confession, and it ends with a phrase that glazes Marcus with ice. *Each man must take he some responsibility.*

He's seen and heard words of this ilk before; they are Rasta cant. He remembers thinking, irritably and not that long ago, that such words or the idea they carry would one day get Ramo hanged. He's not ever thought that gambling that outcome might be Ramo's choice. Erskine Burrows, when he confessed nearly thirty years ago to the shooting he may not have committed, claimed he did so for his people's own good. To bring them together. To reveal them to themselves.

When Burrows was hanged, Marcus lived faraway in England, stuffing his skull with white man's law, but Ramo, a hot-headed youth at the time, knew Burrows. Probably he admired him.

Dizzily, Marcus imagines what might happen. The uncertain facts of the Tucker case, the suspect evidence in Ramo's indictment, the perception amid some parts of the public that a sudden and surprising confession is bogus or coerced—this could seize history, and write a full reprise of '77 with unknowable outcome. Marcus observes on Isaiah's perplexed face a simpler version of this same conclusion; he has apparently not forgotten he once told Marcus the solution to the Tucker case was a hanging and that any black SOB with dreads would do. And now Ramo has volunteered for the job—co-opting the frame-up to his own purpose. Or Jah's.

Althea wedges herself between Marcus and Isaiah. She embraces Marcus tightly, which is shocking. He doesn't know what to do with his own arms; they hang by his side. Her face crushed against his chest, says breathlessly, "Marcus, forgive me. Lemuel love you. But I wrong you, Marcus. And I wrong Lemuel, so many time."

She is shorter, smaller than she used to be, and now he realizes why. The goldened dome of her hair is gone; an ordinary head, tied up neatly in a length of plain black cloth, presses his sternum. He lifts an arm and lets it rest atop her crown, shielding himself and her from Isaiah's eyes that way. "What are you talking about?" he asks softly.

She burrows harder into him. "Lemuel," is all she says.

Isaiah reaches around her to tug again at Marcus's sleeve. He says, "What shall we do?"

Marcus laughs out loud at the irony of Isaiah's claiming him as compatriot. Passersby stare at their odd conference. "We?" he says. "You take care of it, Isaiah. Call off your prosecuting dogs, and let me do my job."

"I'm done for." Isaiah shakes his head. "My job's gone. As of nine this morning, the Honorable Jonathan Heppering is Acting Justice Minister."

Rapidly, Marcus looks around. Heppering, a suspendered

Christine Hale   275

accountant and fledgling legislator, is not here, one VIP who didn't find time to put in an appearance today.

"Let de bastard swing," Althea says, her composure regained. "I meanin' you, Isaiah." Briefly and coldly she smiles, and the gold tooth winks.

"Marcus," Isaiah says, "listen to me, it's not over." He jostles Althea who plants her feet and does not move. "Heppering and his crew have got the Premier's ear. Peddling a new plan for international business, paper headquarters on the island for American corporations. Book their profits here, avoid taxes at home, and make no investment on the island. All the big accounting firms in the States will push it. But it hinges on stability—"

"Yes," Marcus interrupts. "I understand. Your old job, Heppering's job now, the maintenance of order—helping people shut up—will be more important than ever."

He takes Althea's arm to escort her to the nave, but Isaiah hangs on to his sleeve. "I could use some help, Marcus. I'm a regular human being. And you owe me, in fact. I knew about your—" he gestures in the direction of the pew in which Lucy is seated—"your *woman*, and I didn't out it. I could have—"

Marcus turns his back. Althea, as they plow their way up the aisle, says only three words. "She all right." She squeezes his hand, then drops it and takes her place in what has become a viewing line snaking past the casket. While the rector flaps his hands at Anglican protocol profoundly breached, one person after another approaches the bier as if it is a shrine, placing flowers or ribbons and photographs and pins among the waxy lilies atop the casket lid. Marcus stands with the other pallbearers, shaking hands and nodding and saying the necessary things while he waits, aching and not even denying it to himself, to see and touch Lucy.

She will come. Won't she? Won't she want to touch him? She'll come to the front for Lemuel if not him—she's told him how she once dreamed of Lemuel in the strangest way. Loquats! But Peyton. Her son will stop her. He will be desperate to take his guilt outside, or she will be unwilling to bring him forward to Marcus's eyes. She will protect her son, and turn her back on the man she's loved.

But she does come. Suddenly she's right in front of him. He feels many eyes fix on him as he takes her hands. He recalls the innuendo in the newspapers and TV news — mixed in with the paeans for Lemuel — the swipes at the sexual peccadilloes of certain supposedly idealistic politicians. "This time it's the Opposition in bed with expatriate interests," one editorial snickered when the fixed ticket and the source of the notebook came to light. In a particularly strident op ed letter published by the *Gazette,* Felicity Heppering poured out her grief at the betrayal she and every citizen of the island sustain when leaders wreak havoc not just in the streets but inside *homes.* "Surely there are *some* boundaries, some *loyalties,* which must not be breached by a man entrusted with the public's trust."

Marcus embraces Lucy. He holds her for what seems a long time, five seconds in which everything in the world dissolves. When he releases her and she steps back, her eyes, shadowed by the ugly hat, darkened with fatigue and sadness, look squarely into his. He says without lowering his voice, "We must talk." She replies with a decisive yes. Then she moves on as the line insists, and Peyton is standing in front of him. The boy's eyes, the same color as hers, are storms. Zef's eyes, this morning when Marcus woke him up to say good-bye, were dull with fear.

"Zef told me," Marcus says. "Please help us." He only mouths the words, but Peyton hears. He nods, stares, then pulls from the inside pocket of his blazer a dirty and dog-eared folded paper, a letter in a handwriting Marcus recognizes, with a heart-lurch, as Lydia's. Peyton shoves it into his hand saying, "It's Zef's. Give it to him." Then he reaches for his mother's hand trailing along the bunting-draped bier, startling her, causing her to turn so that Marcus almost sees her face again but cannot quite, because her son takes her arm and pulls her out of line, up the sanctuary aisle to the wide-open doorway and out into the blaze of summer light that pours through it.

When Marcus and five others carry the casket outside and

down the cathedral steps to the waiting hearse, he has the easy end of the load, the upstairs end, where his job is only to save the men in front from being pushed down the steps. His responsibility feels ridiculously too light, and to distract himself from that embarrassment and from the fact of tears rolling unchecked down his face, he looks up. Tropical sun at its boiling zenith. Cerulean sky. Whitewashed roof lines razored into its expansive indifference. And in the park across the way, the scarlet tops of flame trees lift fists of beauty toward heaven's face.

Someone clasps his hand, where it grips the brass handle of Lemuel's casket. The touch is firm and warm and male. He struggles to return his focus to the near distance of the man's face and finds Kenrick. Good old Kenrick. Immediately Kenrick lets go of his hand and averts his gaze from Marcus's leaking face, but his presence is as good as a longer touch.

He says, "I'm on it. You on it, Marcus?" The sweep of his sharp, expressive chin takes in Lemuel in his box, the polished hearse, the crowd, the cordons of police, the knot of Government figures and the tangle of media cameras and microphones surrounding them.

Marcus draws a deep and grateful breath. Between them there has just passed some simple exchange of air, mercy on both sides.

Placing his foot carefully on the next stair down as the pallbearers advance the casket, Marcus says quietly, "I heard about Heppering. New business, but business as usual."

Kenrick, keeping pace as they descend another step, answers equally softly. "They'll have to dispose of this confession from Ramo as quickly as possible."

Marcus nods. "Plead it out, since he's made it hard for them to drop the case."

"He needs you to make it harder still," Kenrick says. "I'm with you, Marcus. Can you do it? Are you ready?"

The procession has halted unevenly, leaving Marcus standing awkwardly on the bottom stair, tugging up on the back of the casket while the rest of the pallbearers, on the sidewalk, redistribute their load, and someone from the funeral home belatedly wrestles the hearse door open. Eugene Outerbridge, standing at attention in the line of blue that demarks the path to the hearse, turns his narrow, dark face their way. He's not missed a word, it turns out. "This dead man will not be thrown away," he says bluntly to Marcus.

It's not a question, but Marcus answers it.

He raises his own chin. "That's right," he says. He envisions Lemuel smiling down on them all from some place lofty where legs do not matter and his wheelchair no longer defines him. "This man shall not be wasted," Marcus declares. "This man matters."

23

Peyton pulls his mother through the streets. Her hand in his feels like a bird, a heart and feathers trembling against his fingers. He holds it tenderly, and runs. From the cathedral steps he races along Church Street, away from the hearse, dodging pedestrians and cars. She flies up behind him like a kite. When she seems about to fall, he tugs to send her higher. He rushes down Queen Street and back along Reid Street to lose fear in the heavy foot traffic of the noon hour. In Chancery Lane where the buildings lean their heads together and his arms can span the shallow stone stairs, he hears fear clattering down behind him wearing iron shoes. He pulls his mother higher still and she cries out. Is she hurt? He can't afford to look. He tears along Front Street past the wharf and the ferry terminus and the Visitors Center with its boarded windows plastered with posters that make fear go faster, so that when he runs into the park at Albouy's Point – passing the ship's bell with its tongue tied in concrete and the dark canons pointing hollow fingers at the sky and park benches loaded with lovers, black and white, kissing, who loosen their faces from each other and make eyes at the boy who can make his mother fly – when he finally reaches the Point, fear is there first. "I'm not afraid of you," Peyton shouts. "I'll tell!"

"Peyton. Peyton," Lucy says. His face between her hands is hot. She sits beside him on his bed, light from the hallway a bright bar across the carpet.

"You screamed," she says.

"It was you." He thrashes on the pillow. "*You* screamed."

"I missed the door." She laughs softly. Her face is marked red down one side from brow to jaw. "When I heard you call out, I jumped up out of bed so fast, I ran right into the wall." She lays her hand against the sore side of her face, testing it.

"I was dreaming," he says. "In my dream I was scared, because you screamed."

"No, *you* screamed," she chides him gently. "You interrupted *my* dream."

"Maybe we both screamed."

"Maybe so."

He leans his cheek against her chest, and she holds it there, hand cupping his skull. His eyelashes, long and lush and blond at the tips, brush the white tucks of her nightgown, rising and falling lightly with her breath.

The house is completely quiet. Darrell's absence is like a hole engulfing them. He's in Cayman once again, overseeing the start-up of TransGlobal's systems, preparatory to moving himself and the subsidiary there. She and Peyton will be gone, to her father in Connecticut, before he returns.

"Marcus said they'll definitely let me leave?" Peyton asks. His words pop the silence.

"Yes."

She feels an extraordinary calm. The dead calm that sometimes, mercifully, anesthetizes the immediate moment when new reality bites down. She experienced it for the first time the day her mother told her the cancer diagnosis. It befell her again on the day she left Darrell and Peyton and drove to the cabin in the Berkshires, and on the day she returned. So she recognized the sensation when it dropped on her as Peyton finally explained, on a street corner two blocks from the cathedral, exactly how the fire at Ramo's began, finally telling what he'd withheld in sullen or stunned silence from her, from Darrell, from the police and the psychologist they took him to. She felt no surprise. She felt instead a thud like a fist striking flesh, the sound of all illusion cracking. Afterwards, she and Marcus and Peyton and Zef met, at the cliff house, and talked together about how to proceed.

She strokes Peyton's face, her fingers tacky with his sweat. She repeats what Marcus promised him over the phone yesterday afternoon after negotiating with the police commissioner, something she's already repeated for Peyton more than once since then. "If you were charged by the police, it would end with our permission to live here revoked. The immigration authorities would deport us, and so we'll just go, before that happens, and save everyone the trouble."

"Leave fast," Peyton says. "Tomorrow."

"Or the day after. As soon as we can."

"After I help Zef."

"Zef will be cleared, yes, when your statement goes to the police."

"I'll tell them I had the lighter, not Zef, ever since the day Ramo was arrested. And I'll explain how the fire started because of the lighter I had, but that the gasoline was everywhere, already, before I poured any at all. Before we got there."

"Yes. Stating things that way protects Zef, who must stay here, and saying them will not harm you, because you are able to leave."

She hears strain in her voice. She cannot deny her discomfort for the ambiguous position this act will create for her son and those who will judge him — and her — in narrow, moralistic, eye-for-an-eye terms. But it is Peyton himself who has decided. When he told her on the street corner, holding her hand as if he were her small son again, he said, "I think I did do it. I think it's my fault." More of that came out later when Zef came to the house: "I made him come with me to Ramo's. I put the lighter in his hand. I told him to do it." When Marcus asked Peyton what he wanted to do, Peyton said, "I don't want to blame Zef. I want to help you. And I want to go home."

Now Lucy says what Marcus said when he left the house, shaking Peyton's hand. "This way everyone will know what happened but people will be less likely to hurt others because of it. When you go, you will take some of the blame with you, leaving less of it to cause trouble here."

Peyton asks, "Will they say I ran away? Will people say I'm a criminal?"

She sighs and shifts. He sits up.

She touches his face. "I don't think anyone really wants to charge you with a crime. Althea does not, and she is the one who has the most right to want to. The police, and Government, they do not want an incident involving an expatriate, especially now. They need the tourists and American businesses to return. Some people who are angry for all kinds of reasons will look for someone to punish, and you may be that for some of them, but if you're gone, nothing can happen to you."

"Marcus wants me safe," Peyton says.

"Of course," she replies. And he will take heat for that, she thinks. Anyone who wants to can blame him when we are gone.

"What about Dad?"

"I've told him."

"You did?"

"I called him in Cayman earlier tonight. And I reached him. First try." This strikes her as ironic. Darrell has traveled so often for business, and over the years, she's grown accustomed to difficulty contacting him in emergencies. This time he left in such a state, with management at TransGlobal in New York demanding he go the minute the airport reopened, but his consternation over Peyton's—and the family's—unresolved predicament rendering him nearly dysfunctional with rage and fear.

"He said to tell you, Peyton, that Cayman is a much better island than this one. Fewer people, more space, lots of big American cars, and close to South America. He says he'll take you to Brazil on vacation when this is over—"

"Before he left he told me he had no right to be so mad at me that last day in Connecticut when I hid. But now he'll be really angry again. I know he will."

"He's not angry at you, Peyton. I know he isn't." She touches her cheek at the base of the red mark. Peyton's admission surprises and pains her. It's an opening in Darrell, one that will never include her.

"I told him everything that's been decided here since he left," she tells Peyton.

She hears again the dispassionate finality of tone with which Darrell met and fed back each bitter conclusion she pronounced into the phone, the connection, via satellite, echoing and tinny, every phrase shadowed by its double. Peyton's confession, Marcus's negotiations on his behalf, the resulting necessity that she and Peyton leave the island immediately, and the corollary around which every sentence tacitly stepped — that they were, de facto, leaving Darrell now, too. After each statement she made, he tightened the screw she'd set with a firm and workman-like twist of his own, as if in this final decision of their marriage they were at last fully sharing the power.

"All the details are arranged," she'd said.

"I see you've been ably assisted, at the highest levels, in making your plans," he replied.

"Yes."

"It's a done deal, then."

"Yes.

"Sixteen years, Lucy."

"Yes."

Peyton's voice makes her jump. "Dad's not coming, is he? He's not coming to Connecticut to live with us."

She cannot quite look at him. "I don't think so," she says slowly. "He is disgusted with me."

"He's disgusted with me, too."

"Oh, no, Peyton. He is not. He loves you. He believes everything that's gone wrong is my fault." She lifts her chin, and tears drip from it. "It *is* my fault. I am to blame."

They are quiet again, seated side by side on his bed in murky pre-dawn light. Their breathing, in the silence that cups it, is like snow falling in deep winter. Piling up. Hiding things and revealing new shapes at the same time.

Yesterday the Bentley went streaming through the green gardens and banana groves of Paget. Marcus drove, and it was possible to simply see him — a black man, a foreigner, and the only force in her life that remains familiar and trustworthy. He wore a light-colored cotton shirt, short-sleeved and open at the throat. The fingers of his right hand held the wheel loosely; the fingers of his left curled around the gear shift knob. His skin, its many gradations of brown blending darker to black in the creases of his knuckles and the soft folds at his elbow, was everywhere glazed with a thin iridescence of sweat.

They drove together going nowhere for the opportunity to talk privately. They conferred on the terms Marcus finalized by phone with the authorities and that each of them separately explained to Peyton later. Marcus reassured her that this strategy would likely leave Zef in the clear and that whatever landed on him, he could handle. She asked him if Darrell would be stopped by Immigration when he tried to return from Cayman next week, and Marcus said he doubted deportation paperwork could happen that quickly, but that if there was trouble for Darrell he would take care of that, too. She thought, *Please, let that particular necessity not arise.* When Marcus said he would drive her and Peyton to the airport when the time came, she told him no. He said, his hand coming to rest high on her thigh, as if he were her husband, "What difference does it make now?" And immediately, that simply, she gave way to what she felt, and changed her mind.

The road they drove on was a ribbon drawing them through time and place but subjecting them, for as long as they rode it, to nothing but this time and this place. The heat washing over them through the open windows was the physical force of the island — the too-bright colors, their too-close juxtaposition. The soaring fantastic tropical trees, the cascades of flowers and ropey vines, the fecund damp smell of the island's red dirt that she would never fail to recognize, except that she would never smell it again.

"Maybe I will visit you in Connecticut," Marcus said.

She looked at him.

She pictured her name and her son's on the stop list at the immigration desk, alphabetized with the convicted felons and the suspected drug couriers. She tried to picture a place where she would live, an apartment in some Connecticut town, three or four rooms that would be home at the end of a day's work at some job she would get, and all she could see was a white leather couch and the veranda it faced, framed in scarlet hibiscus and overlooking rose gardens, white roof tops and a blue harbor with a bristle of masts. Where could she live—what town, what neighborhood, what space in the world she had ever known—where this black man and his brown son would ever fit inside a life she could have?

When so much time has passed in silence that she thinks this night must be over, Peyton asks one more question.

"Did I do murder?"

"No."

She studies his face. His eyes are deep and opaque. The snow of their breath eddies between them for several seconds. Then she says, "I don't think so."

She moves to sit as close beside him as she can, links her arm through his and takes his hand.

"Mr. Trott died from smoke from the fire, and what you did caused the fire to start burning, but you didn't light the fire, and other people had poured the gasoline and pulled out the trash that fed the fire and made it spread. So many other people have done things for so many years that led to other people wanting that fire to burn and that caused Mr. Trott to be crippled and weak and immobilized in that chair. You are responsible for some of it, but not all of it, and I think Mr. Trott would know that and forgive you. He was a man close to God who loved people and thought the best of them. He accepted the tragedies that happened in his life."

She strokes her son's hand, observing and skirting the sore, ruined cuticles. "I don't know, Peyton. There are people who will blame you, and all your life you'll wonder, but I don't think his death is your fault, or Zef's. The fault is larger and more complicated than that."

She takes him by the shoulders, pulls him toward her and hugs him.

He throws off her hug. "You said just a little while ago

you were to blame for everything that happened with you and Dad and me. But now when it comes to me and the fire, I'm not to blame because other people were part of it. That's a contradiction."

He is standing up. He's angry.

"It *is* a contradiction," she says, looking up at him, "but both things are true. At the same time. It's a paradox."

"I don't understand that."

"I don't either. I just know it's the truth."

Her palm curves over the wounded side of her face. The room is silent, the night waning. She says, "I was glad when you woke me. In my dream, I was all alone. When I heard you calling out, I thought, I'm dreaming. I can wake up."

Peyton, standing over her, reaches down and covers her hand with his.

24

In Casemates Prison, Marcus sits at a small wooden table in one of the two straight-backed wooden chairs that bracket it. The tabletop is gouged and stained. The chair loose in all its joints. A dank that never dries and has never been discouraged by bleach or cross ventilation pervades the room. The single window, barred but unglazed, set high in the thick wall, lets in a little light and much humidity. Marcus, his hands folded on the table in front of him, his feet flat on the rotting linoleum floor, waits quietly for Ramo to be brought up from his cell. Sometimes the air shifting in and out the window smells of the sea, and other times the heat-softened asphalt of the prison yard.

Downstairs Zef waits in a hard chair at the security desk, which is, as Marcus told him to expect, as close to Ramo as he'll be allowed to come, probably for many months. In Marcus's breast pocket resides an orange button—dish-shaped, the beveled rim chipped—that Zef, offering it in cupped palm, has asked him to give to Ramo. Marcus restrained himself from asking why; Zef has twice spoken with his mother by phone now but has shared nothing about what was said. In Marcus's briefcase amid a welter of court papers and scribbled research is an envelope, minus the address Marcus has not admitted he does not possess, directed to Peyton Langston and containing—Zef gave precisely this much explanation—"a letter." In Zef's lap—Marcus looked back twice from the stairs, he couldn't help trying to see who his son might be becoming—are two fat file folders, one the history of Marcus's relationship to Ramo in legal briefs and motions, and the other the future, as Zef sees it and Marcus tries to: materials they downloaded together from Amnesty International, a campaign in-the-making to reframe Ramo, this time as prisoner of conscience.

A key grates in the lock, the steel-banded door swings open and Ramo shuffles in, followed by a white jailer. Even in bright orange prison coveralls, even shackled hand to foot, Ramo is formidable. The jailer barely reaches his shoulder. Ramo takes the chair opposite Marcus, facing the door, hands in his lap because his chains do not permit them to reach the table while his feet are on the floor. His dreads and his beard have been shorn. He is thinner than he was a month ago, and more gray. He looks far older than his fifty-three years and his jaundice, and likely the gall bladder condition that produces it, has worsened. Still, he appears cheerful. He smiles at Marcus.

"Another round, mon," he says. "Worl' change up, but stay de same."

The jailer takes his sweet time leaving, fussing over his keys, assuring Marcus he's only three steps away should his presence be required. When the privacy a prisoner and his attorney are entitled to is finally established, Ramo says, "You cannot kill a problem. It beggar your solution."

Marcus recognizes the words; they appear, a quote, in a brief in that history file Zef clutches. "Some problems take new life from attempts to kill them," he says, wearily.

Ramo nods.

"A Jamaican Rasta, Sam Brown, spoke those words in the 60s."

"Maybe," Ramo says, "Jah tell I so, in a dream."

"Ramo," Marcus says sharply. He sinks his head into his hands. Downstairs, Zef is vibrant with hope that Ramo will rebuild his shop one day. Somewhere in Connecticut, a location Marcus can barely picture on a map, a woman with flyaway blond hair and a transparent heart believes as Zef does that Marcus can champion this man's way to freedom. He whispered to her, inhaling her dear, faint, complicated scent at the foot of the jet way when they parted — while their sons and strangers looked on; no privacy for their love, no mercy at all — another Rasta aphorism. *Cowards cannot win.* He meant only to encourage her, but she, her hand on his chest and her eyes on his, said, "Then you will prevail."

He knows she is wrong on the first count and for that reason most likely wrong on the second. He *is* a coward. He does only what circumstances force him to, as Ramo is forcing him now.

Ramo has gone on speaking, patiently, as if Marcus is simple or deaf. "*I-an-I* say, each mon have he road. Each mon fin' he own way to freedom."

Awkwardly, Ramo lifts his feet to the chair rung, in order to raise his hands. With his chained fists, he gestures first toward Marcus, and then himself. "Marcus Passjohn. Ramo Wylie. Two breath in one breath, an' all breath the same breath."

In less than two weeks Marcus must vacate Rose Hill and find somewhere else for him and Zef to live. This morning he received notice of censure in Parliament for two improprieties, one true and one false: the ticket he fixed for Lucy, and the appropriation of his clients' escrow funds for payments he never made to a variety of criminal accomplices, including Cisco Suggs (now formally charged with the murders of Rufus and Breem) but which the bank's records, supplied by Marcus's aggrieved mortgage holder Murcheson, seem to substantiate. The censure, he is sure, presages an attempt to suspend him from the bar so that he cannot legally act as counsel to Ramo. What he can do, what he can hope to accomplish, is so limited.

He tells Ramo, "You can pursue this path of false confession, but you may *not* die. You might end up in this prison for life, and people will forget you. People are distractible. There's always something new to turn their heads. The very ones you want to inspire may leave you here to rot."

Once again Ramo raises his shackled fists from his lap. He thumps the center of his chest. "Each mon's wisdom in he heart, put there by Jah."

"Ramo!" Marcus is out of his chair, pitched halfway across the table, their two heads nearly touching. "People do not understand your talk about Jah. They don't get it. In fact, every mention of Jah puts most of them off."

"But you, Marcus, you understandin' I," Ramo exults. "Jah's tongue speakin' to you in deep fire."

Marcus sits down. He scrubs his high forehead with the back of one hand. He leans back in his chair and feels its loose joints stretch and nearly give way. When he hitches at his pants legs, he sees the ragged repair he made himself on Guy Fawkes night, which Mrs. Alvarra has never bettered for him. Ramo beams at him across the table with sunny confidence. Fiery expectation.

He laughs, hopelessly, at where he finds himself. As he does so, Lydia's nay-saying ghost rises through him. Some trace of the way she once loved and fueled him connects through the light of Ramo's zeal to the way Lucy's love restored and still affirms him. Lydia was his fire before she turned to ice, and she left him the son he's still got to raise.

"Ramo," he says, "We don't read from the same page and we never have, but it seems I'm damn well scripted to serve you, in order to serve at all."

Ramo's bound fists thump the scarred table. "Deal, mon," his voice booms. "No more taking. We do some givin'. I-an-I set the black mon free."

The jailer's key rattles in the heavy lock and his nervous face appears at the door's grill, responding to the sound of a dangerous Rastafarian, riled up.

"You all right?" he questions Marcus.

Marcus glances round the damp, dirty room. He considers his son waiting downstairs with a lapful of history and hope, and the long odds on every task ahead. He returns his gaze to Ramo's yellowed eyes, which remind him, only because they trust him, of Lucy's.

"Sure," he calls across his shoulder to the jailer. "We ...
I and I ... we're doing fine." With his fist he taps Ramo's
knuckles. "Jah's tongue," he tells the jailer. "That's what you
heard, if you listened."

Author's Acknowledgements

I am infinitely indebted to the Warren Wilson College MFA Program for Writers, and its dedicated, talented, past and present faculty, including Kevin McIlvoy, Richard Russo, Andrea Barrett, Robert Boswell, Joan Silber, and Margot Livesey, each of whom came through for me and for this book at exactly the right moments with precisely the necessary push. Adrianne Harun always believed in this book, and me, even when I didn't. Marian Szczepanski, Karen Whalley, Barbara Klein Moss, Ellen Slezak, Ann Scott Knight, Laurel Graham, Carolyn Reed, Joan Frank, Michael Pagani, and Lisa Tucker wouldn't let me quit. My friend Margaret Bonham photocopied, collated, and proofread under time pressure, joined in the final round by Judy Fore.

This book could never have been written without the support of D.H. Amis and Edith Darter Hale, and many hours of childcare provided by Elizabeth Hoye Amis, Sara Hale Henry, and a legion of other generous women friends.

Antonia Fraser's *Faith and Treason: The Story of the Gunpowder Plot* (New York: Doubleday, 1996) helped me understand the cultural and political context of Guy Fawkes' execution. *The Rastafarians* by Leonard E. Barrett, Sr. (Boston: Beacon Press, 1997) and *Rastafari: Roots and Ideology* by Barry Chevannes (Syracuse: Syracuse University Press, 1994) were invaluable in teaching me about Rastafarian practices and view, as was Gerald Hausman's *The Kebra Nagast: The Lost Bible of Rastafarian Wisdom and Faith from Ethiopia and Jamaica* (New York: St. Martin's, 1997).

I am deeply grateful to the MacDowell Colony, Ucross Foundation, Hedgebrook, the Hambidge Center, and the Virginia Center for the Arts, for residencies at which large sections of this novel were written or revised.

Special thanks to Margie Gordyk, Cephas Gilbert, Bryant Welch, Maria Massie, Edward P. Jones, and Nancy Sample. No words will ever be adequate to thank Mc.

Lastly, I salute and celebrate Joe Taylor of Livingston Press, a fighter of the good fight, for listening to me, reading my book, and believing it worthy of his cause.

Basil's Dream (Livingston Press 2009) is Christine Hale's first novel. Her short fiction and creative nonfiction have appeared in *North Dakota Quarterly, Arts & Letters, Apalachee Review, Rivendell, Natural Bridge,* and *The Sun.* A native of Bristol, Virginia, Ms. Hale has an MBA from University of North Carolina at Chapel Hill and an MFA from Warren Wilson College. In the early 80s, she worked in investment banking in New York City; later, as the mother of small children, she lived in Bermuda. Ms. Hale currently teaches in the Murray State University Low-Residency MFA Program in Murray, Kentucky, and lives in Asheville, North Carolina. She is writing a new novel, and a spiritual memoir.